FATAL
ATTRACTION

Also by the Author

BLOOD SECRETS

FATAL ATTRACTION

CRAIG JONES

CROWN PUBLISHERS, INC.
NEW YORK

This is a work of fiction. The characters, incidents, places, and dialogues are products of the author's imagination and are not to be construed as real. The author's use of names of actual persons, living or dead, is incidental to the purposes of the plot and is not intended to change the entirely fictional character of the work.

Grateful acknowledgement is given to Macmillan Publishing Co., Inc. for permission to reprint a selection from COLLECTED POEMS by Marianne Moore, copyright 1944, © renewed 1972 by Marianne Moore.

Published by Crown Publishers, Inc.,
One Park Avenue, New York, New York, 10016
Manufactured in the United States of America

Library of Congress Cataloging in Publication Data
Jones, Craig.
Fatal attraction.
I. Title.
PS3560.0466F37   1983   813'.54   82-23451
ISBN 0-517-54926-3

ISBN: 0-517-549263
Designed by Camilla Filancia
10 9 8 7 6 5 4 3 2 1
First edition

For Brenda and Bruce

The weak overcomes its menace,
The strong overcomes itself.

—MARIANNE MOORE
from *Nevertheless*

FATAL
ATTRACTION

PROLOGUE

Because he could not follow her as closely and frequently as he would have liked, he counted himself lucky when he discovered the one place she went alone. After five weeks of sporadic watching he learned that she did her laundry on Tuesday nights, at a laundromat across the highway from the Kingston Shopping Mall. When she finished she would put the two baskets of clothing into the back seat of her car and drive over to the drugstore in the mall to buy a carton of cigarettes and toiletries. The previous Tuesday he had been fully prepared to make his move, but in the drugstore she ran into a woman she knew who walked her to her car.

Now, he sat in the parking lot slouched behind the wheel, his eyes trained on the plate-glass window of the laundromat and only swerving now and then in the direction of her car. It, as much as she, refired his rage and hardened his purpose, for what he had witnessed inside it was the reason she was chosen.

Five weeks ago he had been stopped at a red light when her maroon Mercury slammed to a halt in the lane next to him. When he looked over at it she was already in action: twisted around, she was slapping two children in the back seat, sending them in retreat to opposite corners. She continued to slap the little boy closest to her until he slid onto the floor, out of her reach. He watched her shake her finger at both of them, her mouth drawn in an ugly snarl, before she turned to the rear-view mirror and patted her hair back into place. Then her eyes met his, boldly returned his stare, and when he refused to yield she gave him the finger. The light switched to green and she roared off to the left, into Locust Hollow Estates. He took the next left and circled back through the development until he spotted the Mercury in the driveway of a brand new house that did not yet have any grass around it. From a distance he watched her get out of the car and attempt to open the rear door. But the little boy had locked it, and when she tried the other side she found that the girl had locked hers too. She tried to unlock the front door with her key but the boy leaned forward and held the button in place. She stormed toward the house and on the way picked up a tricycle and pitched it across the yard.

He sat there and wondered how long the children could hold out with the windows rolled up in the stifling heat. Finally, he put the car in gear and cruised by. Parked in the side yard was a motorcycle and a camper that had two bumper stickers: LEGAL-IZE LOVE and I BRAKE FOR BIKINIS. These and the children in the car and the house itself—a pathetic imitation Tudor that could have been built in three days—struck the very center of his revulsion; but that revulsion spawned excitement as he considered what he would and must do.

Having driven past the house at different times he learned that she was married to a beer-bellied man whose friends showed up on motorcycles that they parked on the dirt where a front yard should be. Once, through the yet-to-be curtained kitchen window, he saw them congregated, she the only woman among them, laughing while she did something at the sink; the children were in the front, squirting each other with the hose and throwing the mud the water made.

The night he came by and saw her pulling out of the driveway he followed her to the laundromat. This small detail added weight to his case against her: she would go through life slapping her children, giving people the finger, preferring motorcycles and campers with bumper stickers to a lawn and a washing machine . . . .

Now, he watched her get up from the sitting area and take her clothes out of the dryer. What intrigued him most was that she was dressed well, moved with a natural and easy gracefulness, even appeared soft and incapable of a public snarl or a raised middle finger to a stranger. She did not look like what she was, and he thought of another woman who presented one face to the world but had shown him her real one.

He picked up the mask from the seat and tucked it inside his jacket, then got out, locked the car, and crossed the highway to the mall. The drugstore was at the very end of the line of stores, and if she repeated her action of the previous week she would park at the side of it with her car pointed to the rear side-road exit.

He stood in front of the window of the shoe store, at an angle from which he could view the end of the walk. Soon, her car appeared, then disappeared on the other side of the drugstore. She rounded the corner and went in.

He ambled past the window and saw her in one of the aisles. As he moved on he hoped she had left the passenger side unlocked.

She had, but the car was parked so close to the building that he would never be able to open the door and squeeze in when the moment came. He looked about him. The mall was not crowded tonight and so there were only a few cars in this far end of the lot area; there were none at all between here and the side-road exit. He walked to the front of the Mercury, looked around again, then crouched in wait. Already, his excitement was funneling its way downward to the lowest pit of his stomach.

He heard her shoes approaching on the concrete and he slipped the mask over his head, deftly bringing the eye and mouth holes into exact position with a single gesture. She got in and he sprang up and forward, arriving at the door in time to seize it before she had a chance to close it.

Her eyes widened and her lips parted but he clicked open the knife in front of her face. "If you scream you'll be sorry. You won't get hurt if you do exactly what I say. I'm only warning you once. You're going to drive where I tell you to."

She nodded dumbly, like a child. He climbed into the back seat and squatted on the floor. "Take a right at the exit, then a left onto Eberhard. Get on the expressway going south."

The car lurched forward.

"And drive carefully," he growled. "If you honk your horn or run into anything, you're dead."

She followed the directions exactly.

Below the rippling surface of his anticipation lay a deep well of calm: he had had plenty of time to plan, select, rehearse the appropriate words he would say to her. The act itself was incomplete, almost nothing, without the words.

The car climbed the ramp onto the elevated highway that would take them out of the city and into the countryside. He stroked the foil packet tucked in his shirt; it, like the mask, was his protection.

After they had traveled a mile or so he heard her begin to gasp, and finally she spoke. "Please don't do what you did to those others! Don't leave me out here! Please, I'll give you money, I have a ring—"

He did not answer but gently pressed the tip of the knife blade against the back of her neck. She said nothing more. Except for his directions and the squeaking of the laundry baskets against the vinyl seat there was silence until they reached their destination.

1

From the pillow where his shoulder cushioned her head he watched her naked thigh cover his and slowly move downward until her toes found his ankle. She dug at it with her nails.

"Say you'll marry me and I'll stop."

He lay still and silent, determined to stay off the subject no matter how casually she approached it.

"You'd rather lose this foot than walk down the aisle, wouldn't you?" She sighed playfully. "You'd be a wonderful prisoner of war, Matt. Or one of those monks who wears a hair shirt. There's not a torture you couldn't bear when it comes to preserving your shell." Her nails dug deeper, as if going for the bone. "Is there?"

"I'm just temperate."

"Well, we sure have different definitions for the word."

He could have told her why they did, but they had already covered this territory too many times. "We have to start moving. You shower first."

The room had dimmed during their hour of lovemaking; the orange October light was retreating from the window like a satisfied voyeur. She walked to the chair in the corner and picked up her robe. Before getting into it she stretched her arms and arched her back, her tanned skin turning copper in the shadows. His gaze traced the line from her elbow to her neck, then down her spine and over the curve of her buttocks: he thought of a sleek, beautiful fish that rises with a twist from the water to flaunt its elusiveness. As the robe covered her he murmured to himself, "So young, *too* young."

She returned to the bedside, lit a cigarette, then bent over and slowly exhaled the smoke in his face. He breathed it in deeply. When she pulled back he caught her wrist and said, "One more." She repeated the ritual.

"Pleasure by proxy," she taunted.

"Go."

The smell of smoke remained as he listened to the shower run in the adjacent bathroom. She had left the door ajar; on the other side of it she began to croon "September Song" for his benefit, he was certain.

> *"When the autumn weather turns the leaves to flame*
> *One hasn't got time for the waiting game . . . "*

She took inordinately long showers; she would be in there at least ten minutes. Unlike his ex-wife, she was not concerned about drying out her skin. It would be years before she had to think about preservation. Her minor indulgences—the shower, the cigarettes, the two martinis before dinner, the countless cups of coffee at work—underscored the plainly observable difference in their ages and the less observable difference in their general optimism. Indulgence without the expectation of penalty was the privilege of the young and she, at thirty-two, could still afford that privilege. But he knew and had paid the penalty.

Still, despite her youth, she was in some ways an anachronism—one who recalled that period of his life when he was full of the kind of determination that allows no self-doubt. He watched her emerge from the bathroom and sit at her vanity with the three-sided mirror, a vanity similar to the one his mother had had when he was a child. She brushed her hair with long luxurious strokes the way his grandmother used to before going to bed. Lipstick was the only make-up she used and this she applied here, not in the bathroom as his ex-wife did nor leaning over a pink portable contraption framed with blinding lights as his daughter did. She did not own a hair dryer or one of those fashionable curling irons that resemble cattle prods. She

6

never wore earrings, and the only pieces of jewelry she possessed were her grandmother's string of genuine pearls and amber
stick-pin and her great-grandmother's opal ring. Her car was a
sixteen-year-old Pontiac convertible in mint condition. Clearly,
she was in love with antiques, and he sometimes viewed himself
as the breathing antique among the inanimate ones.

Finished with her brushing she picked up the tube of lipstick
and caught his eye in the mirror. "I thought we were supposed
to hurry."

"One more minute." He yawned. "God, I'm tired."

"Call Claudia and tell her."

"I can't. I promised."

"I'm sure she'd understand." She paused significantly. "But
then, maybe *Joanne* wouldn't."

He did not reply. The subject of his daughter was a large
portion of the terrain on which they battled.

She blotted her lips and then came toward him with her
determined yet effortless stride. Everything she did looked
effortless. Sitting on the bed she rested her hand on his chest. "*I*
have to leave soon." In addition to running her own agency she
taught a Wednesday night class in real estate at the community
college. Effortlessly.

He lowered his eyelids so she would not suspect how closely
he was studying her. There was not a single crease in that oval
face, not a line under the large, light brown eyes, and her
forehead looked like sculpted cream with no evidence of mortal
bone beneath it. What saved her from bland perfection were a
larger than necessary nose—softly sloping like a doe's—and
mischief at the mouth: the ripe lips seemed always to be parted,
ready to grin or laugh, exposing the tips of her teeth, straight
white teeth that magically repelled the nicotine that assaulted
them. Her brown hair, naturally wavy and shoulder-length,
displayed uncatalogued highlights between gold and cinna-
mon. Daily, and without success, he looked for the intrusion of
one gray strand.

"Want me to make you a quick drink?"

"Better not. I'll need one at Claudia's."

"Sustenance for the storm. And what does *she* use?"

"Nothing. White wine."

7

"If these evenings are as uncomfortable as you say, why does she keep inviting you?"

"Habit, I guess."

"Funny how she suddenly wanted to be friendly again *after* you met me."

"It's not that. She's a little desperate, Adele. After all, she's nearing fifty."

"Here we go with your senior-citizen routine."

"Be glib. But you don't really understand what she's been through."

"Ah yes." She reared back, crossed her legs, and folded her arms. "That familiar tune—implying I don't really understand what *you've* been through. All right, maybe you and Claudia have had more than your share of misfortune and maybe I've had more than my share of good luck. But I'm capable of imagining how you feel over your losses. Don't dismiss me just because I haven't experienced them."

"I don't dismiss you."

"You do. Because you idealize my life. One broken engagement—that's easier than divorce. Being an only child with parents who don't approve of *you* because they think I'm running after a father figure—that's hardly tragic. But don't write me off as an emotional midget just because I haven't been hit as hard as you. That's the worst kind of vanity and smugness." Her voice softened and was laced with regret. "I wish I knew a way to wear you down."

Unable to meet the eyes that matched her words, he rolled away and got out of bed. He closed the bathroom door and stood before the mirror. Even in the brutal, probing glare of fluorescent light nothing in his face or body reflected the emotional exhaustion, the spent spirit within. By heredity and through no rigorous effort of his own he was lean and hard as an everyday swimmer. Nowhere were there any signs of sagging: the strong and chiseled jawline was still intact, the flesh of his face, chest, and arms undappled and taut, his waistline the same thirty-two inches it had been since he was fifteen. The dramatic salt-and-pepper hair had undergone no recession, he had all his teeth, and Adele was as enamored of his legs as his ex-wife Claudia had been. And considering the amount of liquor he used to consume, the staggering number of cigarettes he had smoked before having given them up, the hue of his complexion was remarkably healthier than it should have been. He had always turned the heads of women, and in the past his vanity was flattered by the fact. Until three years ago, until the death of his son. Now, admiring glances only rekindled the unwanted memory of Terry; covetous eyes, tunnel-visioned by desires of their own, were incapable of seeing the brutishness he hid—a brutishness that his son had found, exposed, and punished. And that his daughter continued to punish. Of course, he had learned to control it, so well that even after two years Adele still regarded him as a model of gentleness. Because of this she stolidly refused to believe him when he told her, again and again, that he could never be a father again. Having a family, at least one child, was her solitary but exacting condition for marriage.

He showered quickly, wishing he could stay but anxious to be gone and get the evening over with. In the bedroom, he found her sitting on the foot of the bed and staring intently at the television. As he dressed, he watched the anchorman wrap up the newscast and thought of his own duties at the station in the morning. The weather report came on, and Adele turned on him, her expression lodged somewhere between disgust and outrage.

"There was another ski-mask rape last night."

"I heard."

"He abducted this one from the Kingston Mall," she said.

"That makes number four."

"Speaking of, I have a meeting tomorrow with two representatives from the Women's Self-Protection Group. Ever hear of it?"

"Yes. Rape prevention and victim counseling. There was a spread on it in the Sunday paper a few weeks ago. Why are they coming to see you?"

"They want a half-hour spot and Lyle doesn't want to give it to them."

"Naturally. His only worthy cause is himself."

"They've made a none-too-veiled threat. They know we've been on probation with the FCC and I'm sure they're going to use that as a handle."

"More power to them. Let Old Moneybags give up one unsponsored half-hour. Maybe it would help in catching this ski-mask creep."

He sat and put his arm around her. "I want you to be extra careful. Like tonight, when you're coming home alone from your class."

"I've got eyes in the back of my head."

"Don't forget to use the ones in front too. This guy is always described as coming out of nowhere."

In the kitchen he stood at the back door and looked out at his Cadillac and her old convertible while she rinsed out her martini glass. He had always been afraid of the covertible, imagining it overturned on a highway with her smashed to pieces under it. Now, he glanced at the cloth top and thought of how easily it could be slashed and entered by an attacker.

She came to the door and put her arms around his neck.

"What are you going to do about dinner?" he asked.

"I'll grab something in the cafeteria." Her eyes searched his and she whispered, "But tell me, Mr. Sessions, what am I going to do about *you*?"

"And vice versa."

"Time's running out, you know."

Instead of answering he kissed her. Then they got into their cars and drove off in their separate directions.

"Hello, Matt."

"Hello, Claudia."

Why, he asked himself, did they always have to say each other's name when they met?—and sounding as if they had fists in their throats.

"Oh," she said, "you parked in the driveway."

"Shouldn't I?"

"Joanne and Bud have my car tonight. His is in the shop."

"I'll move it to the street then."

"Don't bother. She can put mine in the garage later if she gets home before you leave."

The "if" struck like a slap. He had not dared to hope his daughter would have dinner with them, but he had fully expected her presence before or after. "Did she know I was coming?"

"Yes, but she had work to do at the library. A drink?"

"A light scotch and soda." He followed her into the kitchen. "So Bud went with her?"

"Yes."

"You know, there was another rape last night."

"He seems to prefer middle-aged women, doesn't he?"

"Really? Hey, whoa!" He grabbed the neck of the bottle she was pouring from.

Her mouth curled in an ambiguous smile. "You really *are* cutting down." Her eyes, not her lips, referred to Adele before she turned to the ice cubes. For herself she filled a wineglass to the rim.

He could not help assessing her as he followed her back into the living room. She had grown far too thin, excruciatingly thin. The roundness of her hips was the only remnant of the bounce and buoyant spirit that had been extinguished. He watched her turn and sit and cross her legs, revealing one bony knee; immediately, he wished he could hide from and spare her his own untampered good looks. Her blond hair that she had begun to tint at the first sign of gray was a new color, an artificial-looking beige. Although her features were fine and delicate, her face in youth and early middle age had been a horizontal one with a broad smile that revealed nearly all her teeth. Now, the face ran severely to the vertical, the less frequent smile narrow and pinched. Those meeting her for the first time might classify her as gauntly regal but Matt, with regret, found her manner stiffened by a new reserve and half-completed gestures, a manner like that of a deeply insecure schoolgirl. Both of them had lost their capacity for spontaneity, and even though he had no faith in the return of it he wished that he could somehow teach her to cover the loss more adeptly.

"How's the volunteer work?"

"All right. Reading to the old and the blind keeps you humble. But I've been toying with the idea of getting a real job."

"Doing what?" He saw his error before her face registered it: the question was too quick and incredulous.

"Well you might ask. Maybe a clothing store. I've heard they sometimes hire the inexperienced."

"You're not inexperienced. You worked at Sears twice during the Christmas rush."

"A hundred years ago. Besides, I was thinking of something a little better than Sears."

"Do you need more money?"

"Of course not. You're more than generous, Matt. You always have been."

He did not have to look far to see the accusation behind the compliment. Since morning he had been wondering what her mood might be, with their son's birthday only two days away.

"Ready to eat?" she said.

She had prepared one of his favorites, lamb croquettes. The dish itself allowed them a few minutes of impersonal conversation about how none of their friends ever served lamb. "By the way," she said, "Bud's mother has invited us to dinner two weeks from tonight. Can you make it?"

"Of course."

"Bud says her arthritis is much worse. It's hard to believe— she's such an attractive and young-looking woman."

He had met Bud's mother only once and briefly, at the engagement party Claudia gave for the couple. The woman was indeed a beauty but seemingly so unaware of it, so painfully shy and withdrawn that he had had difficulty conversing with her.

"At least she's lucky to have Bud at home," she continued. "If he'd gone somewhere else to college she'd be having a tough time of it. He's always running errands and doing things around the house. And still he manages to get all A's every term." She spoke of him with pride, and once again Matt plainly saw that Bud was coming into her life not as a mere in-law but rather as a second son.

When he got up to help her clear the table she insisted he go into the living room while she prepared the Sanka.

Purposely, he avoided what had once been "his" chair and

sat down on the sofa. With no additions or deletions, all the furniture was arranged in exactly the same way as when he left three years ago. It was a comfortable room, a sturdy well-built house with walnut moldings, a corner fireplace, and stained-glass windows on the staircase landing and in the upstairs bathroom. Claudia remarked constantly how expensive it was becoming to heat. One night last winter she broke through her veneer of politeness and gave him a withering look when he suggested closing off the heating ducts to Terry's room.

He glanced at the mantelpiece where she kept the family pictures prominently displayed, and he thought of his own apartment. It was thoroughly modern and uninspired, with cut-out doorways and white hard angles where wall met wall. After three years he still had not gotten around to furnishing it properly, never mind decorating it.

"My, we look deep in thought." She set the cup on the end table next to him. "I talked to Margaret today. She says she and Ted haven't seen you in ages."

"I wouldn't say it's been 'ages.' " It had been roughly a month and a half, and considering how often he used to see them they probably viewed this as an eternity. The Brainards were their best friends; quite naturally, Margaret and Adele were not fond of one another. The Brainard marriage had been a rocky one for the past six years, and lately their banter had assumed a sharper edge, an unrelenting intensity. His own quest for peace and quiet and serenity included steering clear of the couple as much as possible.

"Things are rougher than usual between them," she said, then paused. "She thinks he might be . . . having an affair."

"Come on. Ted's not the type."

"You never know."

"Look, she told you herself why he doesn't sleep with her. He hasn't been interested in sex since that cancer operation. I think it's that chemotherapy that does it. In any case, he wouldn't be starting up with someone else."

She looked into her cup. "You could have a talk with him."

"No way. I'm not getting involved."

"They're our friends."

"For me, they'll stay that way as long as they leave me out of their problems." He changed the subject, hoping his search for information was not too obvious. "I understand you've had a couple of dates with Dr. Zimmerman."

"Six."

"Six! You must be getting along very well."

A pinched smile appeared. "Don't be in such a hurry to hook me up. The fact is, our dates are numbered. He has very modern ideas."

"You mean about sex?"

"Yes. And I know he's getting impatient with me."

"Well, of course, you wouldn't want to be used . . . ."

"It's not that at all. He's not a user and he's genuinely fond of me. I'm fond of him. But fondness isn't enough." She hesitated and looked away. "I tried sleeping with him. It just didn't work."

His mouth began to dry up. "Maybe he's just not the one for you—*that* way."

"I doubt that anyone is."

"I wouldn't say that."

"What *would* you say?" She covered instantly with a laugh. "I wish I were the type to have escapades, but I'm not one for substitutes. The real thing or nothing."

He spoke cautiously. "Aren't you idealizing 'the real thing' a bit?"

"Maybe. You tend to when it's gone and can't be gotten back. Pride and righteous indignation sure cost more than they're worth. I'm just another case history in the old, old story."

"You don't have to be," he said, aching to close the subject although answering her would only keep it open. "There's no use in dwelling on it. We can't go back and change things."

"You . . . want to change things with Joanne badly enough."

"Do you begrudge me that?"

"No. I've given it a good try but I can't." She drank from her cup. "I'm sorry, I didn't mean to whine."

"You weren't whining."

Before they had to cast about for another topic a car pulled up to the curb in front. Doors slammed and voices approached the house.

They both came in with smiles, Bud's wide and winning,

Joanne's a dutiful stretch of the mouth that failed to counter the heedfulness in her eyes. Matt saw her look first to Claudia and, apparently satisfied that he had not marred her mother's evening, she turned to him, said hello, and bent down to accept a kiss on the cheek.

"I was hoping we'd get back before you left," said Bud, shaking Matt's hand and squeezing his shoulder.

"Would you like a beer?" asked Claudia, leaning forward on the sofa.

"Sit still, I'll get it." He and Joanne went to the kitchen, dropping their books onto the dining-room table on the way. Matt took in the young man's slightly bow-legged, jaunty gait. Along with good-naturedness and intelligence Bud exuded an appealing vitality—spontaneous but never reckless, fully masculine and yet graceful. Despite a husky assemblage of thick arms, legs, neck, and broad sloping shoulders, he carried himself as though he weighed half of his one hundred seventy pounds. The huskiness was accentuated by his medium height and contrasted by a narrow Grecian face, the large eyes deep and dark as inkwells. His black hair and smooth, slightly olive complexion resembled those of an Oriental. All of these qualities made for an odd and striking handsomeness, more so when he was with Joanne who was all willowy blondness.

Claudia caught him staring after the couple. She smiled and said: "You know, he's practically your public-relations man with Joanne. You'd almost be embarrassed to hear the praises he sings about you."

"Maybe he's overselling me," he answered and thought: Anyone else's father would look good to Bud in comparison to his own. "I can't say I see much progress in her regard for me."

"Give it time, Matt," she said softly.

"Three years is a pretty long time."

"I know, but I think once they're married—" She stopped as they approached the living room. With his beer Bud sat down in Matt's former chair. Joanne sat in the other and studied her glass of soda.

"How's your mother?" Matt asked.

"Back and forth. Some days are worse than others and some days she doesn't seem to be sick at all."

"She had to quit working, didn't she?"

"Yes, a few months ago."

"Is that going to create financial problems for her?"

"Oh, no. She's saved quite a bit and my grandmother left her something when she died."

Matt wondered if the father had ever helped the family he abandoned, but he did not dare ask. What he did know from Joanne was that Bud, after the age of twelve, could not have been much of a financial burden to his mother. He had begun working with two paper routes, morning and afternoon, and went on to being a stock boy in a supermarket; for the past three summers he had a strenuous but high-paying job with the highway department. Beginning in high school he bought all his own clothes, later bought his second-hand car, and paid his tuition his first two years at the university. Now, one of the top four students in the school of landscape and architecture, he had a full scholarship and would most likely be given another for graduate school. With a keen edge of resentment Matt recalled how Claudia had balked when he suggested that Terry get a part time job. "Not everyone needs to hide in a job the way you do," she had said. "Work may be the answer to *your* problems but I don't think it's the answer to his." The unsubtle irony was that she loved and fully admired this son-to-be who had been raised in a fashion alien to her own methods of child-rearing.

The two men talked first about Matt's work, then about Bud's classes, and finished in agreement that the new county office building was probably one of the ugliest in the state. "Maybe," said Matt, "you'll be an influence someday in changing these building trends."

"Not in public facilities," replied Bud. "I'll stick to houses, apartment complexes, maybe a nursing home or two. I want to build things that people *live* in." Finished with the beer, he took the can to the kitchen, picked up his books in the dining room, and came to the end of the sofa where Claudia sat. "Listen, Duchess, you'd better start eating right. You're beginning to look like a strong wind could blow you away."

She chuckled. "You're so complimentary."

"Ten or twelve pounds wouldn't hurt you. When you come to my house for dinner I want to see you pack it away. And," he added, scissoring a lock of her hair in his fingers, "Tell your hairdresser this color is for the birds."

Playfully, she slapped his arm. "Get out of here before I strangle you."

On his way past Joanne he ran his hand across her shoulders. "See you in the morning."

She stood up. "I'll drive you home."

He shook his head. "I can walk ten blocks. Goodnight, Matt. I'll look forward to seeing you at my house next time."

He left, and Matt watched Joanne go off to the kitchen. Once again he reassured himself: her limp was scarcely noticeable and *if* noticed could easily be interpreted as a mannerism.

Claudia whispered, "You stay for a while and talk to her. I'm going to bed to read." She walked to the doorway of the kitchen, mumbled something to Joanne, then climbed the stairs.

He sat alone, listening to his daughter open and close the refrigerator and cupboard doors and run the water in the sink— in short, stalling her return to being alone with him. Once, impulsively, he started up from the sofa but immediately sat back down. His going to her would be a breach of the truce. At last she came back, looking into her refilled glass. She took the chair farthest from the sofa. Don't jump in, he told himself, let *her* speak first.

"How were the croquettes?" she said.

"Perfect, as usual."

"She was worried they'd be greasy."

He watched her lean back into the chair and cross her legs in exactly the same way Claudia crossed hers. Except for his contribution of the strong jaw and squared chin, everything else came from her mother, including the honey-colored hair and gray eyes.

"Do you and Bud have the same class schedule?"

"No. I start at nine every day. He starts at ten three days a week and at eleven the other two."

"That's inconvenient for him, isn't it? If you had a car of your own—"

"We've worked it out. We each go to the library when we're not in class."

"If you'd let me buy you a car you could—"

"I don't want a car."

Of course not: he had bought Terry the car he died in.

"Have you chosen a definite wedding date?"

"No. Sometime next fall."

"Have you thought about where you're going to live?"

"Not really."

Another silence. He felt foolish and defeated, grabbing these topics out of the air. "Bud's right about your mother—she's awfully thin. Maybe you could persuade her to eat better."

"She's not interested in food. She's only interested in cooking it."

"She ought to give Dr. Zimmerman a sample."

"She's not lonely for Dr. Zimmerman. She's lonely for you."

"And are you . . . at all lonely for me?"

Her eyes refused to meet his, and her voice faltered in its attempted firmness. "I'm lonelier for Terry."

As much as he dreaded going out onto the proverbial limb he found the danger of it preferable to evasion and sterile courtesy. "I see. Only the dead get a full pardon."

"No. But he had problems and . . . reasons for what he did."

"Reasons for demanding understanding without giving it in return?"

"How much understanding did he get? You proved to him that day that your job was more important than he was." Immediately, she pulled back into her chair, as if realizing she had been lured beyond an acceptable boundary.

"It may have appeared that way," he answered. "But let's not forget what he did to *me*."

"He wasn't as strong as you are," she murmured. "You knew that."

"So, to get any credit or sympathy from you, someone has to be a pill-popper and smash up a car with his sister in it"—he nodded in the direction of her foot—"whose life and welfare doesn't matter to him."

The color was now leaving her face. "He wasn't thinking after what you said to him."

"I lost my temper—how many times did he lose his?"

Her expression now went from condemning to incredulous.

18

"You told him he was *worthless*." She breathed deeply. "He fought you because he loved you too much. I won't. . . . "

"Won't what?" No answer. "Won't what?"

"I won't be like him or Mom. It's not worth it."

"Meaning *I'm* not worth it."

"I live with her! All she thinks about is your next phone call or your next visit and the next meal she can cook for you. She's wasting herself and Terry's dead!"

"And I planned it that way? I never did a damned thing for any of you? I never loved you?" He leaned forward and rasped: "I did not walk out on you and your mother, if you'll remember correctly. My clothes and belongings were thrown down the stairs like I was some tenant who couldn't pay the rent. But you weren't here to see that little scene—you were in the hospital where your brother put you, you were too busy telling the doctor and the nurses to keep me away from you. Would you like to know the kind of looks they gave me those two times I tried to see you? Would you like a full account of how your mother behaved at the funeral?—I had to keep a distance of two feet. But of course," he said jeeringly, "I had no feelings about what happened. No, only you and your mother had the privilege of emotions and you played them—"

She began to cry, the strong jaw struggling to remain rigid as she covered her mouth with her hand; in her widened eyes he saw the reaction to that indomitable beast, his temper. "Joanne, I'm sorry. Please don't." She nodded emphatically to indicate she was trying to stop; finally, she did stop, but her trembling only lessened in degree.

"I—I've got some studying to do," she said.

"I'm sorry, I got carried away, I didn't mean—"

"Don't apologize. Please. I said too much. Let's just forget about it."

He knew he could say no more, but he wanted to shout "It's been three years of just forgetting about it which isn't forgetting at all." "Will you have dinner with me next week?" he asked. "I promise it won't be like this."

"Can Bud come with us?"

"Is that a condition?"

"No."

"Yes, he can come."

He drove away from the house more slowly than usual, swamped in regret and wishing that Bud could make more rapid progress in his behalf.

He took the expressway three miles across town and parked in his assigned spot under the long carport. Inside his second-floor apartment he walked around in the dark. The place was so spottily furnished—"Siberia," Adele called it—that there was no danger of bumping into things. He fixed a nightcap and sipped on it as he undressed in the bedroom.

He adjusted both pillows against the headboard of the bed, turned on the television but did not look at it. He lay staring at a thumbnail of moonlight caught in the mirror over the dresser and thought of his daughter. She did her best to hide it but her inherent softness was still there. He still had a chance to be her father again; her tears tonight were proof of that. He hoped that Claudia was right: "I think once they're married."

He was jolted from these thoughts by the news-opening announcement of last night's rape. Instantly, instinctively, he reached for the phone. She answered on the fourth ring.

"H'lo" was partly muffled by her pillow.

"Did I wake you?"

"Mmmm. I was having such a nice dream."

"I wanted to make sure you got home all right."

"Safe and sound." She yawned. "I was dreaming I had white hair and a cane and you were finally saying 'I do.' "

"If you had white hair, that puts me in my grave."

"At least you said it before I whisked you off to the embalmer's."

"A happy ending. Go back to sleep."

"Goodnight, darling. Wish you were here. And good luck with those ladies coming to plague you in the morning."

2

The two women opened the heavy wood-and-glass-paned door of WGRS's "Colonial House" and went to the receptionist's booth.

"Mrs. Richardson and Mrs. Bewick to see Matt Sessions," said one.

"*Ms.* Bewick," corrected the other.

Mrs. Richardson gave her ungainly younger companion a pronounced look of warning, then returned her attention to the bland face of the receptionist. "We have an appointment," she said.

"If you'll take a seat in our living room, I'll ring him."

The women moved off across the flagstone lobby to the waiting area which was indeed an enormous living room done in Early American: a fieldstone fireplace, a low beamed ceiling, pine planking on the floor. Six braided rugs were strategically placed where most of the foot traffic occurred. Although the wood of the furniture—seven sofas and sixteen chairs—was rough-hewn for pioneer authenticity, it was all equipped with soft cushions that were even more comfortable than they looked, as Mrs. Richardson discovered when she sat down. Ms. Bewick did not sit but instead made a tour of inspection with hands on hips and mouth puckered. She paused at one of the four windows in the rear wall and looked out at the three acres of velvety lawn bejeweled now by autumn leaves from maples, oaks, and poplars. Surrounding the entire property and separating it from a dense woods was a five-foot-high stone fence. Ms. Bewick absorbed and turned away from this view much more quickly than other first-comers did. But then, the thrust of her jaw plainly indicated her determination to remain unimpressed.

Hands still on hips, she did a reappraisal of the interior as she crossed the large expanse between the windows and the sofa where Mrs. Richardson sat smoking a cigarette.

"Quite a little empire Sloane's got here."

"It's charming," returned Mrs. Richardson. "I'm sure his employees must enjoy it."

Lacking a retort for this, Ms. Bewick scowled and said, "How can you keep smoking those filthy things after you've had a heart attack!"

"I ration them," she answered evenly and took a long drag.

With a snort, the gangly woman fell into the chair that was at a right angle to the sofa. "Be prepared for trouble with this Sessions character. He's divorced and goes around with a glamour puss half his age—Adele Densmore, she owns Densmore Realty. He's bound to be trouble. Middle-aged sexists are the worst."

"Just remember, I'm the one presenting our case. I'll be firm if firmness is needed. But there will be no shouting match."

"Firmness *is* needed. They've been giving us the runaround."

"As I said, no shouting."

They turned toward the footsteps approaching them on the lobby's flagstone.

"Good morning," said Matt.

They stood. "Hello. I'm Jane Richardson. This is "—she hesitated slightly—"Hippolyta Bewick."

After shaking hands he led them back through the lobby and down a carpeted corridor to his office. Moving in behind his desk, he gestured at the two chairs facing it.

"Would you care for some coffee?"

"That would be nice," said Mrs. Richardson.

He dialed the house phone. "Karen, would you bring a pot of coffee to my office, and three cups, please?" This summons sharpened Ms. Bewick's already disapproving eyes. He met them straight-on and said with a professional smile, "Hippolyta's an unusual name. Queen of the Amazons, wasn't she?"

"That's right," she answered crisply. "I changed my name six years ago. From Sue Ann. I don't identify with 'Sue Ann.' "

No, he thought, and if the Sue Anns of the world knew this they would undoubtedly be relieved. Ms. Bewick seemed to be of that breed that prides itself in homeliness; rather than make the conventional attempt to lessen it she set out instead to enhance it. Her face looked as long as a thigh, and she made it look even longer by having pulled her hair as tightly as possible into a knob at the back of her head. Her tight mouth clearly signaled a lack of humor; the chapped and peeling lips remained unmoistened by lipstick or even her tongue. Her clothing could not have been less flattering to the tall sharp-cornered body. A loose-fitting "peasant dress" hung down to mid-shin, well over the tops of her cowboy boots. The macramé belt was now hidden under her unfettered breasts that had descended to rest in her lap as soon as she sat down. Everything about her simultaneously drew and repelled the eye, and the onlooker was torn between pity and amusement. Matt knew that during this meeting he was going to have to keep his attention wrenched away from her.

"Your waiting room is very impressive," said Mrs. Richardson.

"Thank you. We're all very spoiled by it. It serves for meetings and parties and just plain lounging."

"And the grounds are so beautiful."

"When Mr. Sloane had the station built he wanted to make it as uninstitutional as possible."

"I'd say he succeeded."

"Let's get down to business," Ms. Bewick announced loudly, as if addressing a crowd.

At this moment, however, Karen appeared with the coffee. Matt introduced her, and Mrs. Richardson returned Karen's sunny smile. Ms. Bewick did not smile, only nodded curtly. Matt watched her scrutinize the girl with an expression of contemptuous fascination. Karen was twenty, studying to be a model; this morning she had on a silky, clinging salmon-colored outfit that resembled lounging pajamas and, in a trail, her frosted hair flowed out of the knot of a matching salmon scarf. Matt saw the homicidal glint in Ms. Bewick's eyes as they passed over the girl. That glint—as Karen poured the coffee—turned to flame and spread quickly to her cheeks. Karen departed with another smile, and when the door closed behind her Ms. Bewick looked heavenward and gasped: "How some women *embrace* their slavery!"

Mrs. Richardson's lips tightened, then parted in what Matt interpreted as a smile of apology. He liked her already. She appeared to be around his own age—a good fifteen years older than Ms. Bewick—and her fine-boned face was emboldened by engaging brown eyes, eyes that he suspected took in much more than they let on. Her choice of a navy-blue tailored dress for this meeting seemed a guarantee that the proceedings would remain civilized.

"Now," he began, addressing her alone, "perhaps you could review the structure of your organization and what you hope to accomplish by going on the air."

"What we *will* accomplish," affirmed Ms. Bewick.

"I thought," Mrs. Richardson said softly, "that everything was clear in the request we sent you six weeks ago."

"Well, we do get so many requests." This was true. It was also true that Lyle Sloane, the station's pugnacious owner, read the first paragraph of the letter, scanned the rest, then tore it up with instructions to "tell those women to take this matter to the police where it belongs." Emphatically, he declared that there would be no discussion of rape broadcasted from *his* station. Being the general manager, Matt was the smokescreen between Sloane and everyone who had dealings with WGRS; guiltily, he had composed and sent a letter designed to stall the women, hoping that in the meantime this ski-mask rapist would be caught. The rapist had not been caught, and the reply Matt received last Friday from the women's group indicated they had been made aware of the weapon at their disposal to prevent any further stalling.

"I think," said Mrs. Richardson, "we had better be candid with each other. It seems to us, being put off the way we have been, that there is no real desire on WGRS's part to fulfill our request or to take this matter seriously."

"That's for sure," quipped Ms. Bewick.

"Consideration takes time," said Matt. "You're asking for half an hour, not a sixty- or ninety-second spot."

"I realize that, but time is exactly what we don't have," said Mrs. Richardson. "In the past year, seventy-two rapes were reported to the police. In a community of a hundred and sixty thousand that number is considerable, especially in the light of how many rapes go *un*reported. And the reported number does not include those that occur at the university and are handled by the campus police."

"The university—!" he said with alarm. "We haven't had any news of that here."

"Of course not," she answered with a nod that implied he had made her point for her. "The university takes every measure available to conceal these crimes from the media. Exposing them would not be good advertising for their already decreasing enrollment. Besides that, too many girls and women are frightened and ashamed to report their attacks. Our group was formed specifically to help such women, to steer them into professional counseling and to encourage them to work with the police. For instance, your newscasts at six and eleven yesterday said this ski-mask rapist has struck four times. He has struck more than that: we have two women in our group who have been raped by him and will not report it. Imagine how many others there might be. And this man is a malevolently clever type."

"In what way?"

Her voice became grave. "I've dealt with women whose attackers were vicious and beat them but I've rarely seen any who are as devastated as this man's victims. He beats them with *words*—and those words are carefully chosen. I'm convinced he selects his victims well in advance, then stalks them. He's intelligent enough to see their weaknesses and insecurities from a distance, and then during the act he actually chants the woman's 'faults' to her. You have no idea the kind of damage this does when the victim realizes how closely she has been watched and how much she unknowingly revealed, and then to be 'punished' for it."

25

His skin prickled. "Can't you get these two women in your group to go to the police?"

"We're trying, Mr. Sessions. And that's precisely the reason we want to go on the air. To encourage all victims to contact the police and to inform women in the community of the safety measures they should be taking. And, of course, I want to promote the group and solicit membership. We are not hysterical but we are very concerned. All this was outlined in the request we sent. Frankly, we don't see any vagueness whatsoever in our presentation. It is WGRS's reaction that remains vague."

With all the air-time requests the station received, he had had to encounter scores of morons and lunatics; it was a pleasure to deal with a person like this one. Her genuine concern and controlled indignation increased his shame over the evasion. "Suppose," he offered, "we set a deadline for the format decision. Say, next Tuesday?"

"Hah!" barked Ms. Bewick. "Another stall."

He turned and spoke to her slowly, as he might to a dim child. "It is not a stall. Mr. Sloane is out of town. When he returns I will have to confer with him. We will need time for thorough discussion and planning." "Persuasion" was more to the point, but this he could not reveal to them.

"Tuesday will be fine," said Mrs. Richardson.

Ms. Bewick slid forward in her chair. "You tell Mr. Sloane we've been in touch with the A.C.L.U. and they're just waiting to hand over a complaint to the Media Access Group if we're turned down." This was the weapon hinted at in their letter.

"Hippolyta—"

"We happen to know," she went on, "that Sloane was in trouble with the FCC three years ago for time-gouging. That's fraud, and you can bet the FCC will be plenty anxious to investigate any complaint against WGRS."

"I imagine they would be." Although his temper was sparked, he would fight her with coolness.

"Well, here's something you *can't* imagine—what it's like to be raped. No man can!"

"Men can be forcibly sodomized. It happens in prisons every day."

"Women can be raped *and* sodomized!" she said triumphantly.

She stood and stabbed the desk top with her forefinger. "I was raped when I was fifteen—you don't know what a violation it is!"

"Maybe I don't, but I know *I* didn't do it."

She drew herself up and flounced from the room, upsetting the wastebasket on her way. He looked at the other woman who was doing her best to stifle a smile. "Your group," he said, "seems to have a very diverse membership."

"Not that diverse. Hippolyta is . . . exceptional."

He walked her down the corridor to the lobby. "There's one thing I want to make clear," she told him. "She won't appear on any program we might present."

"Somehow, I was hoping you'd say that."

As the two women walked to the car Ms. Bewick grumbled: "You're a lousy feminist. You catered to him."

"I was polite."

"You were compliant "

"Hippolyta, has it ever occurred to you that you can be a feminist and a lady at the same time?"

"'Lady'!" she snorted. "That's a chauvinist term. If *you'd* ever been raped—"

"Oh, do shut up about that. I'm beginning to think if it never happened you'd have nothing to talk about."

He had lunch in the Colonial House dining room, followed by a forty-five-minute meeting with the advertising salesmen, and then a conference with Judy Kent, the hostess of WGRS's "Country Kitchen" and "Personality Parade." Judy had been with the station as long as he had, twenty-six years, but she had aged no more than ten. Still pert, blond, and kewpie-doll-faced, she was self-pampered and showed in neither looks nor manner any evidence of ever having had a worry or a serious thought *outside* her work. A clothes horse who smiled incessantly and talked in clichés, she was thoroughly devoted to Sloane, and because of this many assumed the two of them were having or had once had an affair. Matt knew better. Sloane did not want a mistress for himself but rather a faithful wife to WGRS. And faithful she was: she had given up two husbands to prove it. She seemed to have no private life beyond the doors of the Colonial

House. Well aware of this fact, Claudia used to use it in her most heated arguments with Matt. "You and Judy are a pair. You'd both die outside that station. You're both so full of your indispensability . . . "

Matt told Judy of the request—and the threat—put forth by the two women. "I think 'Personality Parade' would be a good spot for it," he said.

"Oh, I don't knooowww." She frowned doubtfully. "The show focuses on people, not issues. I mean, if this Mrs. Richman was—"

"Richardson."

"—was well-*known* then we'd be justified in doing a profile on her. But what she wants to do doesn't fit our format."

"Well, creating a special spot for her will take a lot of time, and they're going to be breathing down our necks until the whole thing is over. My own feeling is, the sooner the better. You have to be the moderator anyway, special or no special."

"Why, Matt," she said with a girlish gasp and fanned her fingers on her chest. "What do *I* know about rape?"

"You don't have to know anything about it. We simply go over the information they want to cover and we make up your questions from that."

She nodded but looked apprehensive. "What does Lyle think?"

"He doesn't know about it yet. But he's going to have to be made to realize he *has* to grant this request." Emphatically, he reiterated Hippolyta Bewick's threat, reminded her of Sloane's negative status with the mayor and city council, and affirmed that a refusal would put the station's licensing renewal in extreme jeopardy. "You saw the last Community Leaders' Survey to the FCC. Three quarters of them described us as 'grudgingly cooperative.'"

"They're all so jealous of Lyle for owning the most lucrative station in the Midwest," she said. "There isn't one of them who wouldn't trade places with him if he had the chance."

"That's neither here nor there. The cold fact is if we give this group a denial we're headed for big trouble. Besides, it's a reasonable request. That's why I'm depending on you to convince Lyle."

"Meee!" Her head dipped down and back to form a tiny double chin, and her round turquoise eyes grew rounder. This was part of the ritual. Whenever Sloane needed thorough convincing, Matt called upon Judy for the task; she always responded with mock surprise. "Well, I'll do what I *can*," she replied patriotically.

"Good. I'll get to him first thing Monday morning and then you talk to him before lunch. I must give Mrs. Richardson a definite plan by Tuesday."

Minutes after Judy left, his telephone rang. It was Adele.

"Have you looked outside?" she said.

He swiveled in his chair and glanced at the window. "Yes. It's nice."

"Nice? It's spectacular! Can you get out of there early? Around four-thirty?"

"I guess."

"I'll take you for a ride in the country with the top down. And we'll have dinner at Pierre's. I'll make a reservation."

At four-ten he left his office in the administration wing, crossed the thirty-foot lobby past the living room, and entered the corridor of the production wing. He talked to the weather girl, who had been out two days with the flu. She assured him she had completely recovered, and he turned and went back to the other wing.

Judy's office was the first one off the lobby. She was not in it, but the door was open, and his eye was arrested by a new arrangement of the contents. Ordinarily he avoided her office at all costs: it had once been his, and precisely where he now stood, Terry had appeared the afternoon of the day he died. Afterward, Judy had not understood his plea to change offices with him; this one was so much larger and had two windows instead of one. He did not explain, only insisted, and she, with a tragic look of concern over his and Claudia's loss, mutely consented. "Three years," he murmured to himself and saw the room as it used to be: the sofa on the south wall, the desk in front of the windows facing the door. On a winter afternoon, he had sat at the desk listening to the FCC officials smugly define the station's violation, and he prayed that Sloane, who sat smoldering in the corner, would keep his mouth shut. The storm he had waited for was breaking and he was weak with relief; he had no idea of the other and greater storm that was approaching.

For months he had glanced over the station's logs with increasing dread and tried unsuccessfully to convince Sloane that juggling them to cover up time-gouging was a dangerous and pointless game. This time-gouging consisted of picking up a late-night network show "in progress," twenty minutes late, and thereby picking up network advertising money. Those twenty minutes were filled with a spillover of the local news; the spillover profits from local advertisers went into Sloane's already bulging pockets—although Sloane committed the fraud less for money than for the simple pleasure of cheating a network he held in contempt. Actually, the threat of detection by the FCC would have been remote had a man of a softer nature owned WGRS. But Sloane, with a blanket contempt for all politicians and a fierce dedication to doing exactly as he pleased, had alienated so many influential figures in the community that Matt figured it was only a matter of time before one of them discovered the opportunity for taking revenge. As it turned out, the complaint that reached the FCC came from an old woman who shared a four-room house with twenty-one cats and who was furious at having her favorite program delayed night after night. Before this eccentric let fall the ax, Matt's concern had turned to near-terror that increased his insomnia, his chain-smoking, and his dependence upon coffee, aspirin, and alcohol to make his body work. And the arguments with Claudia went from heated to bitter to brutal. She maintained that over the years he had become a slave to the station, more so since Sloane had given him and Judy each one-seventh interest in it. He pointed out to Claudia that she and the children did not mind spending the money that this interest added to his income. What other line of work, he asked, did she suggest he go into at his age? She didn't know. Well then, if he *could* find a different job it would surely be at half his present salary—could they manage? Did she want to give up the summer house on which they had just made a down payment? Was she willing to forego the trip to Europe, their first, that they were planning? Could Joanne do without the orthodontist and live with her overbite? Would Claudia like to be the one to tell Terry he would not get the car *she* had promised him? To all these questions she gave one answer: any trouble the station got into was not his fault, he was too involved with his job, and if he maintained the pace he was going at she would probably be a widow in five years. The truth remained that he loved his job and would lose it if Sloane ever lost his license. There was no other work he wanted or imagined he *could* do. And Sloane had not always been what he was now; twenty years ago, his arrogance was mild, even seductive, not distended by paranoia and bitterness. He could find no way to make Claudia see that two decades at a job, one you happened to like, created in you a sense of personal responsibility and allegiance. She replied that she didn't believe in any allegiance that produced ulcers and invited a heart attack. And, she added heavily, once he changed his own condition, Terry's condition would change too. But then, there was more to Terry's condition than either of them imagined . . . .

He leaned against the doorjamb and stared at the dozen or so pictures Judy had framed on the walls. They included local and national celebrities, members of the staff, herself and Sloane. No children. Neither of her marriages had produced any. Since that afternoon three years ago he often wondered if *he* should have had children. To that question Terry had answered no—with the gas pedal of a car he had owned less than three weeks.

Matt did not know at what exact point he admitted to himself that he had never loved or would love his son as he did his daughter. Perhaps it was when Terry fully realized it himself, when he declared war against his father and succeeded in acquiring a school guidance counselor as a wholehearted ally and Claudia as a vascillating one.

Fourteen months younger than Joanne, the boy, from infancy, was as different from his sister as it was possible to be. Whereas she came into the world quietly and with an inclination toward order, he entered it howling and demanding satisfaction—despite the fact that right up to the last year of his life he never knew precisely what *would* satisfy him. He gave Matt a seventeen-year lesson in powerlessness and at the end left him questioning his entire basis for love, wondering if he could love only those he could control. Terry was most definitely beyond his control and had proven it by the age of five. The boy was impervious to punishment and shrugged off spankings and confinement to the house. He was, however, a beautiful child and exceptionally bright; whether or not his popularity with his peers and with Claudia and Joanne compounded his willfulness Matt could not be sure. But then Matt could not be sure of his own motives in wanting to bring the boy to heel. The motive could have been his own upbringing which touted humility, obedience, industriousness; it could have been envy at seeing his son gain so much by doing so little; it might have been the glint of challenge in Terry's eyes that seemed to be directed solely at him; it might have been all of these. One summer day when he was eleven Terry was caught shoplifting in a drugstore. The manager called Matt at work and when he arrived at the store he learned that Terry had attemped to steal a pair of sunglasses, the price of which was one third of what he had in his pocket. The manager said the boy was not to come into the store again; Matt assured him that he would not but his thoughts were running along another line. "Why did you have him call me instead of your mother?" he demanded when they reached the car. "He said he wanted to see my father." Matt told him he could have insisted upon having his mother called. "He wouldn't know your mother from Adam but now he knows where I work and who I work for." His right hand shot away from the steering wheel and struck the boy's mouth a second after he heard "So what." At the next red light he had to hold on to Terry's collar to keep him from scrambling out of the car. At home, he recounted the entire episode to Claudia. "You told him *that*?" she said. He answered that if she had ever had a job, one with responsibility and authority, she would know what he was talking about. "Besides," he added, "he's a clever boy. *Too* clever to get caught doing what he did." And he left the room so she could ponder this. The friction between him and Terry increased; in direct proportion he found solace in Joanne even though she refused to take sides. He basked in the praise all her teachers sang about her and was pleased by her wise choice of friends—those, like her, who were too involved in studying and school activities to have time for sneering rebelliousness. She, of course, never knew to what degree she kept his intolerance of Terry in check: whenever he felt himself ready to explode at the boy he would turn his thoughts to her and tell himself that one failure out of two children was probably normal. At fifteen, Terry and his own group of friends discovered amphetamines and, for Matt, they compounded this offense by selling them as well. Pleading and punishment got him and Claudia nowhere. That year Terry failed four subjects and, although Claudia and the school counselor argued otherwise, Matt could not help feeling that the failures were intentional. The counselor got Terry into a lunch-hour group for students with drug problems, and after a few months he summoned Matt and Claudia to his office for a conference. Matt was astounded and felt betrayed by how much his son had told this man and the whole group. According to Terry, his father was more interested in his job than in his family; he had never shown any real understanding; he was self-centered and conceited. In this report Matt heard the echoes of his arguments with Claudia, and he pictured the boy lurking at doorways, gathering material for his own case. The counselor maintained that Terry was living in his father's shadow. Grudgingly, Matt asked what should be done. When the young counselor closed his eyes and announced profoundly, "Shorten your shadow," Matt had the urge to shorten the man's life. It did not escape his notice that this self-appointed authority on family dynamics wore no wedding ring.

And so, the bargaining began. Terry would give up pills, marijuana, and beer, and Matt would spend one night a week and every other Saturday with him. But this self-conscious scheduling only widened the rift, particularly when Matt saw the activities Terry preferred. The boy dismissed his suggestion of sailing as boring, fishing and hunting as "macho"; bowling was strictly for rednecks, and bridge and golf were too middle class. He told Matt they should just "rap about life": this meant music and sex. With the bedroom door closed, Terry would lie on the floor with his hands behind his head, Matt would sit in the chair, and they would listen to and then discuss this music the boy was so fond of. While the records played, Matt's skin would creep and his mouth would fill up with saliva, for he detested nearly everything he heard. The music fell into three distinct categories: the maudlin-sentimental; the explicitly vulgar; the self-congratulatory. Afterward, whole phrases would cling to him like foul odors, phrases like "Get it up, baby, and let's get it on," a near-sobbing "The world paid no mind to leaving me behind," a blasting and atonal "Can't nobody tell me what to do when I'm flying way above the human zoo." When he saw Terry's face beaming, unmistakably savoring these sentiments, he wanted to bolt from the room and sever all identification with him. There was no escape in looking at the walls, either. They were covered with centerfold nudes (which the counselor assured Claudia would do no harm) and with posters of rock stars who sported tattoos, ear and nose studs, blue and green and pink hair, and mean mouths. The music, however, was preferable to conversation. Terry asked him about his teenaged sex life, and when Matt stonily talked in generalities the boy persevered for details with the argument that his father was not being open and honest, not willing to talk man-to-man. Terry himself volunteered the specifics of his own encounters with two girls in the crowd he ran with. During these accounts Matt felt that his insides were retreating from his body and exiting out the door. He was not so graphic as Terry when he relayed to Claudia the extent of these sexual activities. Almost whispering, she replied: "Maybe we've waited too long to try to reach him." He knew that the "we" was a veil for "you." Nonetheless, he was firm in his belief that their son needed a different group of friends; as was to be expected, Terry answered that he had no intention of parting from his friends. The punishment was handed down and shrugged off with the help of liquor and pills. Claudia pleaded and wept, and Matt seethed and threatened anew.

But there did come a change, and Joanne was the catalyst. For his birthday she bought her brother a set of drums, and when he accepted her encouragement to show a serious interest in them Matt arranged for lessons. Faithfully, Terry practiced in the basement every day. At the end of six months he was good enough to join a band. The pills were put aside; Matt and Claudia now dared to hope they were home free.

A father of one of the band members was active in the Masonic Temple, and at Christmastime he hired the boys to play at the Temple's charity benefit. It was held in the afternoon; Matt was to meet Claudia and Joanne there at three o'clock. At two-thirty, the FCC officials appeared at the Colonial House to look at the station's logs. At twenty to five, the two men and Matt and Sloane were drinking coffee in Matt's office. Elliptically, Sloane had offered a bribe, and Matt was doing his best to convince the officials that no such offer was made. Sloane, he said, was under a strain from working so hard. The officials let it pass. Just as Matt was sagging with relief he looked up to find Terry in the doorway, his eyes glazed and glowering. Matt was well acquainted with the different effects that his son's various indulgences produced; instantly, he recognized the result of marijuana or liquor or both. Terry looked at Sloane, sneered, then looked back at Matt. "Wouldn't he let you go?" he said. Matt rose from behind his desk as Terry advanced into the room. He told his son he was interrupting an important meeting. "Yeah, it's the fuckin' U.N." Matt saw one official raise his brow and the other lower his eyes. Terry now spoke to Sloane: "We all know you own him, but couldn't you give him one afternoon off? One fuckin' afternoon!" Matt told him that was enough and moved in on him; Terry dodged to the side of one official. "And who are these fat cats? What big deals are you talking about?" Matt seized his arm and steered him to the door, but Terry managed to call out over his shoulder. "Whatever you're talking about, it's bullshit, that's all it is!" Whisking the boy across the lobby, Matt told the receptionist to call a taxi. Outside, they waited ten minutes. "You don't think about anyone but yourself—one lousy hour you could've taken off. No, you got to sit around and make deals all the time, big important deals. This station's a joke—that dumb Judy Kent with her dumb programs, it's all—"

Matt spoke through a wall of teeth: "Shut-your-mouth." His murderous tone silenced the boy until the taxi arrived. The officials departed a few minutes later. Putting aside his usual self-preoccupation, Sloane asked Matt what was wrong with Terry. Matt replied that he had no time to explain and went home. He stormed past Claudia and Joanne in the living room and took the stairs two at a time. The boy lay on the bed, his hands behind his head, a cigarette angled sullenly at the corner of his mouth. He glanced once at his father and then back at the ceiling. Without a word Matt crossed the room and slapped him hard across the mouth, first with the palm and then the back of his hand. The sharp cry that escaped brought Claudia and Joanne up the stairs. "There aren't even words to describe you," he said in a low, burning voice. "Maybe just one—worthless."

Claudia cried out his name but did not move from the door. Joanne, however, rushed to him and pulled at his arm. "Dad, don't! Don't say anything now."

For the first time in his life he thrust her away from him. He snatched up the cigarette that had fallen from Terry's mouth and was burning a hole in the sheet. "If you ever come to the station again I'll break you in half. You're going to write a letter of apology to Lyle and after that you are never going to mention his name or Judy's—if you want to keep your teeth. I am through with you. You're not getting another cent as long as you live in this house, so you'd better think about getting a job. If you can't afford gas for that car, then it can sit and rot in the driveway."

The doorbell rang and Claudia went down to admit the band's guitarist who was dropping off Terry's drums. Matt took a deep breath for his departing word: "Worthless." On his way out he saw the devastation in Joanne's face, but he did not let it halt him. In the vestibule he punctured the drums with his foot.

"Dad, stop him!" Joanne said Terry was upstairs, packing and crying. Matt said good, let him go to one of his friend's and find out how long his behavior would be tolerated there. The boy came barreling down the stairs and when he saw the damaged drums he kicked them against the wall and rushed out. Joanne stood still, her eyes pleading with Matt. When he turned away she ran out to the street and scrambled into the car just as Terry was shifting from reverse to drive. Claudia sat at the kitchen table with eyes closed, her knuckles in her mouth. Matt mixed a martini and took it into the bathroom where he filled the tub with near-scalding water. Ruefully, he reflected upon justice, the lack of it: if there were any, Terry should have been Sloane's son and not his own. He was dabbing his face with after-shave when the phone rang and Claudia let go a yelp. "The hospital!" she said, gripping the doorjamb with both hands as if to prevent herself from flying through the wall. "They've had an accident."

Two policemen were there in the lobby, talking matter-of-factly to the doctor. When Claudia screamed that she wanted to see her children the doctor gripped her by the shoulders and told her she could see neither. Terry was dead; he had gone through the windshield and died instantly. Joanne was on her way into surgery to have three mangled toes amputated. The doctor pulled Matt aside and whispered that the entire foot was smashed but that they had hopes of saving it. Before he left them, he asked who "Bud" was. In shock, Joanne had called out for him repeatedly.

The two parents spent the night in the lobby. Claudia, in a stupor, refused coffee and food and conversation. Matt dozed off twice and each time he awakened he was positive that everything around him was a dream. When Joanne emerged from the anesthesia she asked for her mother only and then for Bud. When the young man entered the lobby he came directly to Matt and asked to be taken to Joanne's room. The nurse at the desk evaded Matt's eyes and called for the doctor. The doctor appeared and told Bud the room number but asked Matt to remain. He explained, as diplomatically as he could, that Joanne was still traumatized and that it would be best to honor her request that her father not come up. Half an hour later Claudia came down, stone-faced, and asked him to take her home. They rode in silence all the way. When they entered the front door she stopped dead at the sight of the broken drums. After a moment, she turned and said in a cold, hollow voice: "Don't come up these stairs."

He sat in the living room and listened to the furious activity overhead. There was a crash on the staircase, and then another. Next to the drums lay two suitcases. "Stand aside," she commanded, and the next thing he saw was the long case flying through the air, the golf clubs scattering like so many matchsticks. He stood there mute as she hurled his suits, his shoes, his starched and still-packaged shirts. Finished with the removal of the bulk of his belongings, she pulled off her diamond and wedding band and tossed them down; the diamond struck his shoulder before hitting the floor. "Donate them to WGRS," she said with tears, at last, filling her eyes. "They belong to it anyway."

Tiny-voiced, he called her name, but she only answered that he should leave. She would take care of the funeral arrangements and let him know when and where.

Twice, once before and once after the funeral, he tried to see Joanne, and both times the doctor explained that for the sake of improving her condition they should respect her wish not to see him. The second time he was there Bud came down from his visit, put his arm around Matt's shoulder, and invited him out for coffee. He assured Matt he was doing his best to reason with her but would probably accomplish more after she left the hospital.

Bud did not go to the funeral. He spent the hour and a half with Joanne. Matt left the motel he was staying at and picked Claudia up so they would be seen arriving and leaving together. She would not speak and although they *looked* like a couple she kept her distance. Once, during the service, his elbow accidentally grazed her arm, and she pulled it away as if she had been stung.

Three and a half weeks later, Bud and Claudia brought Joanne home from the hospital, and within the month Claudia filed for divorce . . . .

"Boo."

He felt a finger in his ribs and spun around to find Adele eying him quizzically.

"You were a million miles away." She thrust her head around the doorjamb and scanned Judy's office. "What's so interesting?"

"I was . . . just noticing how Judy's rearranged the furniture again."

"Gee, how fascinating. You look like *you've* been rearranged." His thick eyebrows were snarled from rubbing them, his loosened tie hung at an angle toward one hip.

"Come on down to my office. I have to get my jacket and coat."

As he reknotted his tie and brushed down his shirt she sat and lit a cigarette. "So how did it go with the ladies?"

"Not bad. One of them is very nice, the other's a real bulldozer. Her name's *Hippolyta* Bewick."

"God help us. Does she have her own tribe of Amazons?"

"I hope not. She wasn't overly fond of me."

They were crossing the lobby to the front door when Judy

38

Kent's voice rang out behind them. "Adellle! What a gorgeous ouuutfit!"

Adele rolled her eyes knowingly at Matt, then swung her face around like a lighted lantern. "Why, thank you, Judy."

"Where did you get it?"

"I made it."

"You didn't! It's just adorable."

"I'll make you one too if you can get Lyle to give me some free advertising."

"Tsk, tsk, tsk," came from Judy's pursed lips as she shook her finger in a naughty-naughty gesture.

As soon as they were outside Adele said to Matt: "A few words from Miss Never-Never-Land always makes my day. You want to drive or shall I?"

"You. It's been one of those days."

"Poor baby. I think you should spend more time around Judy. She'd convince you not to take life so 'seeerrriously.' "

She nosed the convertible down the sloping driveway to the road. "I have to stop at the cleaners and then we'll be on our way."

She took her business to a small independent outfit located in a decaying neighborhood because the couple that owned it were longtime friends of her parents. She drove now to a main drag running west, and they passed two blocks of pornographic bookstores and theaters, bars that catered to prostitutes and transvestites. When Adele stopped for a light, Matt saw a tall black prostitute standing outside the entrance of the Brass Horse Tavern. Her red fish-scale pants and blouse made her look like a bespangled clarinet. She and a middle-aged man loitering at the corner were eying each other. The prostitute flexed the fingers of one hand four times to signal that the price was twenty. Matt closed his eyes and did not open them again until they reached the cleaners.

"Be right back," Adele said and left the motor running.

An amorphous depression settled over him like a light dust. All this sex, he thought. The prostitute and her prospective client; a vicious rapist whose words shattered women's lives; Claudia's "failure" with the doctor and her suggestion that Ted

Brainard was having an affair; Ms. Bewick's sex-based rancor: all of these recalled to him the wish that had begun after the divorce, his wish that he could become asexual. He still had a lingering envy for people who were, for those who found obsessive hobbies or "causes," who lost themselves in some*thing* instead of some*one*. He considered the possibility that by now he might have disciplined himself into asexuality had Adele not come along.

She returned, holding the hangers over her shoulder, the plastic sheaths mingling with her skirt in the breeze. Oh, that long-legged definite stride, performed by legs that had never once doubted where they were going.

Within minutes, they were on an expressway heading out of town. He laid his head back on the seat to look at the moist-blue sky. The air was brisk, but although the sun was nearing retirement it was still intense enough to warm his face.

She turned onto a road with trees whose branches knitted a scarlet and amber coverlet overhead. As they drove through this patchwork tunnel he recalled the admonishment she was forever giving him: "Loosen up and relax, Matt. Sometimes it's safe to just enjoy the moment."

Watching the branches skid by he let the day go with them. And for nearly five minutes Terry—even Joanne—disappeared into the back seat of his thoughts.

There were no autumn colors in Locust Hollow Estates because there were no mature trees; the developers had cleared away every one of them.

At six o'clock a car entered the subdivision, and its driver gave the painted sign a smirking look of contempt. "Locust" and "Estates" he judged as pretentious misnomers, although "Hollow," by itself, was perfectly appropriate. The glorious evening sun was no less critical, for its rich orange light accentuated the cheap materials and poverty of imagination that had gone into the construction of these houses.

The car proceeded just under the speed limit, the driver aware that going too slowly might attract attention and arouse suspicion. Two nights before, when he abandoned the woman and drove her maroon Mercury back to town, he had made a bet with himself she was the type that would not report the incident and perhaps tell no one at all. He had been more than a little surprised when WGRS opened its newscast with "The ski-mask rapist has struck again."

He was always more fulfilled when he could witness results and see in their eyes the mark he had left, the change he had effected. In this case, however, he knew that the odds were against his getting the final reward. If the woman had had a job it would be a simple matter of watching the place where she worked as she came or went. But she did not have a job, and he could not risk passing by her house more than once or twice.

The Mercury was parked in the dirt yard with several of the children's toys scattered about it, but the van with the bumper stickers was nowhere around. When the house windows revealed no activity behind them, he resigned himself to the probability of never seeing her again.

Then, a spasm of excitement shot from his stomach to his chest: on the concrete slab patio at the other side of the house she was sitting in a lawn chair. Dressed in an ankle-length robe she had her feet tucked up under her, the hands hidden in her underarms, her entire body huddled into a ball while she stared blankly at the ground.

He allowed himself only a brief glimpse and drove on, well satisfied by the sight and savoring his bit of good fortune.

3

Matt knew there was only one avenue of approach in presenting Mrs. Richardson's request to Lyle Sloane. He must mention but not dwell upon how such a program would benefit the community, for the only community Sloane had any regard for was within the confines of the Colonial House. To convince Sloane, Matt had to maximize and then underscore the benefit to WGRS, that benefit being a show of goodwill that could be used later should there be any further trouble with the FCC.

At seventy-one, Sloane was rail lean and still maintained a ramrod posture and a hawkish gleam in the eyes that had never required glasses. He stood at his office window and squinted at the landscape until Matt finished presenting his case and then, in his customary tone of disgruntlement, said he would think it over. When Matt opened the door to leave he found Judy waiting in the corridor, ready to do her part. Her face was uncharacteristically, comically earnest; she winked gravely at Matt as she slid past him and on into the office.

"Why, Lyle, what a beauuuutiful tie!" Her voice spilled forth like a battery of chimes. "Is that *new?*" she asked with great interest as she closed the door behind her.

The following afternoon, after he phoned a confirmation to Mrs. Richardson, Matt left the station early, and before going to Adele's he stopped at Claudia's for a drink. She had called him that morning to say that Joanne had been withdrawn and pensive since last Wednesday night; perhaps he could "just drop by" and she would arrange for him to be alone with the girl.

"She's upstairs studying," Claudia told him when he arrived. "We'll have a drink first and then I'll make myself scarce in the basement. I have some laundry to do anyway."

Matt's suspicion was aroused, and then his guilt over the suspicion: Was her magnanimity born from a scheme to win him back through Joanne? He chided himself and thought of how suspiciousness had advanced from a secondary to a primary characteristic in him since Terry's death. He knew he had to fight it: the last person in the world he wanted to be like was Sloane.

When they sat down with their drinks she immediately got around to Ted and Margaret Brainard and enumerated the most recent causes for Margaret's speculation about an affair. "He daydreams, he forgets things," she said. "You know that's not like Ted, not with his legal mind."

"That's hardly evidence of an affair."

"Well, *this* is: they've been planning a cruise in the Caribbean and now he doesn't want to go. Ted's ambitious, but he's always liked his vacations."

He sighed and said nothing. His ear was trained on the stairway; he wondered if Joanne would be appearing soon.

"I know things haven't been smooth between them since that operation of his," she continued, "but in many ways they *are* good for each other. I know she'd forgive and forget a 'fling,' but if he's involved in something serious—"

"Claudia, do we have to discuss it? Whatever problem they're having, there is nothing you or I can possibly do about it."

"Maybe, maybe not."

"If you're suggesting again I have a heart-to-heart with Ted, forget it. I'm not going to pump him for information to turn over to Margaret. They'll take care of it without us."

She swallowed the last of her wine and went to the bottom of the stairs. "Joanne, your father's here. I'm doing the laundry. Do you need anything washed?"

"No," came from the upper level.

Claudia left, and he waited a full five minutes for his daughter. He stared into the vestibule, at the spot where he had destroyed the drums.

"Hi." She came in but did not sit down. Her smile flickered, faded, flickered again like a fire that can't quite get started. She looked off into the dining room and kitchen, obviously to confirm her mother's absence. "Bud's going to be here in a minute to put up new shutters in my room. I'll walk out with you."

She went ahead of him, her damaged foot coming down hard and flat as it always did when she tried to walk too fast. When they arrived at his car in the driveway she turned and said, "I've been thinking about what you said to me last week."

"Oh?" He held his breath, as though the sound of it might interrupt her.

"I don't want to be unfair to you. I know you think I am but . . . it's very hard to forget."

"I don't expect you to forget," he almost whispered.

"You have to realize one thing," she said tremulously. "I'm afraid of you."

"Afraid?—of what?"

Her eyes left his, dropping to the knot of his tie. "People who love you never seem to get enough back. Terry's gone, Mom's alone, the Brainards and all your friends constantly complain they don't see enough of you. I don't want to be like them. I don't want to love somebody and then be *desperate* for him." Quickly, she added: "I don't know if it's because of the way you are or the way they are. But I won't be like Mom or Terry. I can't be."

"Trust me." He took hold of her shoulder, softly, cautiously. Except for a kiss on the cheek of hello or goodbye, this was the first touch she had allowed him since the accident. "Trust me." His arms encircled her lightly, without pressure, and he let his chin rest on the top of her head. "I would never hurt you, I'd do anything to make you happy. But you have to trust me before I can prove it."

Her body remained rigid, but her hands found the lapels of his coat. "I want to, I want to be fair, but . . . please don't rush me."

"I won't. I promise."

Her hands slipped away, and he felt her spine tighten. As much as he wanted to prolong the moment he knew that for her it had passed. He closed his eyes and released her; when he opened them he saw Bud standing a few feet behind her. The young face was awash with tenderness and satisfaction, and his smile spread beatifically.

Arm in arm, the couple stood in the driveway and watched him back his car out. The euphoria he felt from that momentary embrace lasted him all the way to Adele's.

He spooned peas from the bowl to his plate, then cut into his pork chop. He was too distracted to notice Adele's probing glances.

"You look pleased as punch tonight," she said finally. "What kind of drink did Claudia make for you?"

He knew what any discussion of his daughter would lead to and so refrained from initiating it. "I'm just glad that the Richardson business is settled. She's willing to appear on 'Personality Parade' instead of haggling for a special time slot."

"You mean Judy's going to interview her?"

"Yes."

"Oh, brother. The Betty Boop rape forum."

"It'll work out."

She waited, then: "I went past Ackerman Travel today. They have some terrific January-in-the-sun packages to Bermuda, Rio, and the Riviera. Any one of them would be a perfect spot for a honeymoon."

"Please, not tonight."

"No, January."

"You know what I mean."

"We've got to talk about it, Matt. For the hundredth time. I want a baby before I'm thirty-five. And as old-fashioned as it may seem, I'd like to be married at least nine months before I have it. You know how fast the last two years have gone." She sipped her wine and looked at him over the glass. "I wish Joanne were getting married tomorrow."

"What for?"

"Because she won't be your little girl once she's married. You know, the past is always going to be with you and it'll always intrude on the present. But to let it prevent *us* from having a future is crazy."

Later, in bed, he turned off the light and rolled over with his back to her. For a long while, long after she had gone to sleep, he lay awake, mulling over what she had said. "Future": a golden abstraction that was continually being tarnished by Experience. Yet, *she* was golden, glittering, and invaluable, offering herself for the taking. He loved her far more helplessly than he had loved anyone, but she could not be expected to settle for the cocoon of peace and childless quiet he required for the remainder of his life.

The procrastinating had to end. And he realized with dread that that responsibility was his.

The taping of the program went smoothly. Having agreed to it grudgingly, Sloane elected to stay out of sight and would not even consent to meeting Jane Richardson. Ms. Bewick was present for the rehearsal, and during it she paced the studio, scowling at everyone as though she were some messianic intelligence come to burn away rampant idiocy. When the rehearsal ended she critiqued Judy Kent's performance as moderator. Judy slunk past her, and Bewick followed, announcing in a booming voice that Judy had no credibility as a liberated woman and was conducting the whole interview like a coffee klatch. Mrs. Richardson pulled her out of the studio, sent her home with a scalding reprimand, then apologized profusely to Judy, Matt, and the program director.

The focus of the interview was on Mrs. Richardson, but also present were a psychologist from the university and one of the victims of the ski-mask rapist. The psychologist provided a thumbnail sketch of rapists' primary disturbances and motivations and kept emphasizing the term "sex as a weapon." The victim, rendered anonymous by a shadowed, gauzelike screen, gave an account of her abduction from the parking lot of a bowling alley. Like all the other victims of the ski-mask rapist, she had been forced, at knifepoint, to drive out into the country where she was raped and then abandoned. The details were grim enough, but what made them even more chilling to Matt was having to listen to them being delivered by a faceless voice.

The voice stayed with him all through the night and into the next morning—until, with a jolt, he looked up from behind his desk and saw the two silent figures in the doorway of his office. For a few seconds he could not speak and he heard nothing but the thumping of blood in his ears.

"Can we come in?" said Bud, smiling shyly.

"Of course—come, sit down."

They took the two chairs that faced the desk, and Joanne's eyes prowled the room. Matt thought she might have forgotten that this was *not* the office Terry had come into that afternoon three years ago.

Bud hoisted a thick ankle onto his knee. "No one was at the receptionist's desk to announce us, so we came right in. We thought we'd have lunch with you—if you've got the time."

"Sure I do. And the food here is very good."

As Matt led them out of the office and down the hall, Bud explained: "We have to postpone dinner on Wednesday. My mother's been a little more under the weather than usual, so I think it's best to wait awhile."

"Is it really serious?"

"I don't think so," said Bud. "She has a setback every now and then, but she always recovers."

In the carpeted dining room they stood before the steam table, deciding between roast chicken and stuffed peppers. They carried their trays to a just-vacated table at the floor-to-ceiling window that overlooked the rear grounds. Bud sat down slowly, already mesmerized by what lay on the other side of the glass. "This is really *something*," he said. "Mr. Sloane planned all of it himself?"

"More or less."

"He can't be all *that* crazy then," Bud said to Joanne, who responded with a shrug.

Matt's stomach seemed to float, even as the food went into it. He was still numbed by surprise and joy, by Bud's powerful influence in getting Joanne to come here.

Bud ate mechanically, and his continued absorption in the outside surroundings amused Joanne. She looked at her father and said, "I can't take him anywhere. If he's not inspecting the structure and materials of a room he's checking out the landscape."

"Well, that is going to be his work."

"I should have picked an accounting major."

The pause in the conversation was barely underway when a fourth voice ended it. "Jo-aaannne!" shot from the other side of the room, and the three of them looked up to find Judy Kent rustling toward them, the blond hair and huge white smile rendering her face a veritable sunburst.

"My God," Joanne whispered, "she hasn't changed a bit." She turned her face to the approaching woman and said, "Hello, Judy."

Bud stood, and Matt followed suit.

"Jooo-anne!" Judy bent over to hug her cheek to cheek. "It's been so looong! How wonderful to see you! Oh, Matt, sit down, for heaven's sake."

"This is my fiancé, Bud Hanes."

The two shook hands, Bud sat, and Judy turned back to Joanne. "You know, I was thinking of you just the other day. Do you watch 'Destiny's Daughters'?" It was a network soap opera carried by WGRS.

"No."

"Well, there's this girl on it who could be your twin. The resemblance is just unbelievable except you're much prettier and she's such a mean little thing." She glanced surreptitiously at Joanne's foot by the table leg, then covered with a sigh and a shake of the head. "I don't know how it's possible but you're even lovelier than the last time I saw you." She looked down at Bud and shook a warning finger. "Young man, I hope you realize what an absolute gem you're getting."

"I do."

"You're very, very lucky, so treat her well." She turned back to Joanne. "Now let's see you around here more often—that's an order. You'll always be a member of our little family here." She started off, then called over her shoulder. "Nice to have met you, Bob."

"That woman drives me nuts," said Joanne. "I don't know how you work with her."

"When you get past the chatter, she's good-hearted."

"Both times she came to see me when I was in the hospital I thought I'd jump out the window—she never shuts up. And everything she says always comes back to herself. She's the most self-centered woman I've ever met."

Bud grinned. "The way she said 'our little family here,' it sounded like she's married to the place."

"You've got it," said Joanne.

"Doesn't she have a husband?"

"She had two. No kids. *This* is her true love."

Matt heard Claudia's voice in Joanne's evaluation—and in the unspoken comparison of himself and Judy—and he resented it. But he said nothing.

After coffee he walked them to the lobby where Joanne excused herself to use the ladies' room. As soon as she was out of earshot Matt said, "I want to thank you for coming here today."

"*We* thank *you* for lunch."

"You know what I mean." His hushed tone and direct gaze made the young man redden and lower his eyes. "I appreciate everything you're doing in my behalf."

"You deserve it," he replied quietly. "Pretty soon we'll all be family and—I think all the hatchets should be buried, don't you?"

"Yes, I do. I certainly do."

Outside, he said goodbye to them both and watched Bud's car turn out of the drive onto the highway. He walked back toward the front entrance, springing gingerly on the balls of his feet. He felt renewed, ready to tackle the afternoon without the fortification of his customary nap.

That evening, he and Adele lay on the floor in front of her fireplace, playing chess. When his bishop threatened her queen, she took five minutes to contemplate her next move; during this pause he studied both her and the room. In his mind, she and the house were inseparable. Since they had begun seeing each other this had been his home. He looked at one wall of shelves with their uneven—and, here and there, collapsed—rows of books. There was an unused bedroom that could have served as a library but she maintained that a *living* room should be just that, especially when it had a fireplace. The furniture was a potpourri of her grandmother's bequest and those things she had picked up at auctions and flea markets. Once he had driven forty miles with her to an auction only to arrive and have her discover there was nothing she wanted. He had considered this a staggering waste of time; she had merely smiled and said she wanted to teach him the luxury of wasting time. Well, he thought now, for two years he had been wasting *her* time. . . .

His eyes moved on to the jungle of plants at the two rear windows that she, never he, always remembered to water and prune, and then to the kerosene lamp that she occasionally lit during cocktails or when they made love in front of the fireplace as the fire died out for the night. Finally, he looked at her, lying on her stomach, braced on her elbows as she studied the chessboard. Right now, he wanted to kiss that smooth, porcelaneous brow—the first of many kisses of farewell.

No, he would wait until after the holidays to make his announcement to her. He rationalized that waiting until then would not only allow him time for adequate rehearsal but would also spare her a dreary and empty Christmas.

At last, she moved her queen. He looked at her hair that the firelight was now changing from gold-and-cinnamon into a reddish chestnut. On many nights, he had seen it turn this color, and he would never forget the subtle yet glorious transformation.

Silently, he said goodbye to each glowing strand.

On Wednesday, a week later, he stayed late at the Colonial House reviewing the figures from his meeting with the advertising salesmen. It was Adele's teaching night and he had nothing special to do, nowhere to go until he met her at nine-thirty for a late supper.

"Burning the midnight oil?" Hanging on to the doorjamb, Judy leaned one shoulder into the office. She was her usual picture of freshness, looking as if she were arriving for work instead of leaving it.

"I've got an hour and a half before I meet Adele," he answered. "What are you still doing here?"

"I have been raaacking my brain for ideas about the Garret commercial. Mr. Garret wants to display a sectional that has the teeniest, busiest print in it. I've told him and Hal's told him it's going to look just awful, he should use something bold like a large floral or a stripe, but he won't listen. I don't know what kind of props I can possibly use to make it look halfway decent."

"Don't worry about it. It's his furniture and his money."

"But, Matt, it's *our* commercial. Ah well, I'm going home to soak in a hot tub and think about it." She pursed her lips and frowned. "Why don't you turn on one of those big lamps? You're going to ruuuin your eyes with that tiny desk light."

"I will. Goodnight."

She gave him a sidelong glance, then marched into the room and switched on a large lamp. "Give my love to Adele," she said.

She got into her car, started it, and immediately, ritualistically turned on WGRS-FM. She smiled through the windshield at the broadcasting tower.

During her four-mile drive she hummed to Henry Mancini, Nelson Riddle, and the Ray Charles Singers, and wished she could find a way to convince Mr. Garret how much more effective a striped sectional would be—banked by two floral arrangements.

She turned the last corner and reached up to press the control gadget on the sun visor. The garage door gave a jolt, then started upward, spilling light onto the driveway. She pulled in, thrust the gearshift into park, withdrew the key from the ignition, and reached across the seat for her purse.

Then, for a split second, she thought she saw a shadow whisk across the wall in front of her. She twisted around in the seat, looked out into the driveway, then at the two empty corners next to the open door. She hoped it wasn't another one of those pesky birds that got in and was going to take her two days to find.

She got out, pressed the button on the wall that brought the door down, and then inserted the key into the back hall door.

The figure rose up from behind the rear of the car and, as it approached, all she could see, in her freezing disbelief, was the masked conelike head and the knife in one hand, a square piece of paper in the other. The paper was then held up just inches from her face. She read the large block letters:

IF YOU SCREAM OR STRUGGLE I'LL USE THE KNIFE.
IF YOU ARE QUIET AND COOPERATE YOU WON'T BE HURT.
I MEAN WHAT I SAY.

The masked head nodded at the key in her hand, indicating that she should proceed with opening the door. The automatically timed garage light went out, and in the first few seconds of darkness she was aware only of the empty space where her heart and stomach should be.

He seized her wrist and helped her turn the key in the lock. In the kitchen he steered her along the counter, paused, and reached for a dish towel hanging from the rack over the sink.

As he tied it around her head to cover her eyes, a voice inside of her kept repeating "This is ridiculous, this is ridiculous." And when he began to ease her forward she could not feel her legs at all: it seemed that he was doing the walking for both of them and that by some insane mistake she had opened the door to the wrong house—his instead of hers.

The next morning, she telephoned Matt to say she would not be in. Immediately, he was disturbed by the hollowness in her voice. She sounded like an overplayed worn-out recording.

"A virus," she said. "It came on suddenly before I went to bed. Tell Hal to suggest brown-and-beige stripes to Mr. Garret. And tell everyone I don't want any calls. I'm going to sleep all day. If I don't feel better tomorrow I'll call you. Otherwise, I plan to be in."

Matt spread the word and got the astonished, concerned reactions he expected. In all her years at the station, Judy had been absent only six days due to illness. In fact, she had irritated a number of the employees with her Spartan dedication, coming in when she did have severe colds and contagious flu. By lunchtime, the general consensus was that if she felt no better tomorrow she should see a doctor.

After speaking to Matt, she removed both telephones from their jacks and thrust them onto a shelf in the linen closet. The entire morning she sat in a chair in the living room, glancing now and then at the sofa she knew she would have to sleep on that night. If she slept. She could not bring herself to return to the bedroom, had not returned to it since she had worked

52

herself free of the cloth shackles the night before. She had come out and sat in front of the television until WGRS went off the air. Then she had turned on the radio. Even now, it was still playing. All night, it had not occurred to her to call anyone. After a long scalding shower she had simply sat in the chair, naming the criminal, muttering the single word over and over: *Rapist.* When the word began to sound like a species of insect she stopped saying it.

His first thrusts into her had made her think he was indeed using the knife instead of himself. During it all, his hands remained securely around her throat, exerting pressure whenever she attempted to move in any way. Then came the worst. His heavy breathing turned to snorting, a snorting that deepened until it sounded like retching. And the retching spewed out the horrible words in elongated syllables until the voice was a monstrous mockery of her own. It had sounded as if she were condemning herself but using someone else's voice. Then the words had spiraled in an orgasm of judgment and contempt so firmly irrefutable that she thought she would scream. But she had had no breath to scream. Instead she began to twist and buck. His one hand tightened on her neck, the other slapped her repeatedly, but she went on because the slaps were more merciful than his mocking voice. For the few seconds that his grip closed off her windpipe, the prospect of death was more endurable than his message. Then, in one swift movement he was out of her, off her, on his feet, standing still and listening to her sob behind the handkerchief he had stuffed into her mouth. Her hands were already bound and before he left he bound her feet as well. She struggled for more than an hour to free her hands, wanting more than anything to get the dish-towel— blindfold off. And while her fingers stretched and clawed at the knot that secured her wrists she thought that his echoing words would die away if she could just get the lights on. . . .

His growling, retching voice stayed with her all day, often driving her to the mirror to study her face. But the more she glowered in attempted regal defiance, the deeper his message soaked in.

As dusk gathered she knew she could not sleep on the sofa or even stay in the house. She threw on her coat, picked up her purse, then stopped, tore off the coat, and returned to the bathroom to wash her face and comb her hair.

In front of the mirror again, she reminded herself that she was a woman famous in the community, her name practically a household word. Then, she recalled Hippolyta Bewick's accusation at the program rehearsal: "You have no credibility as a liberated woman, you're running this thing like a coffee klatch."

Suddenly, she wondered how many hundreds, perhaps thousands, of viewers snorted her name, laughed at her image on the screen. How many might actually *think* what her attacker had *said*?

Squinting ferociously at the imagined number of her detractors, she resolved never to give anyone the satisfaction of knowing what had been done to her.

Most of the staff at WGRS believed that she was truly ill and trying to hide the fact; some speculated she was going through change of life and could not manage the strain. She had returned to work after a two-day absence and during the weeks that followed, her behavior was described with numerous adjectives, some of them kindly clinical, others outrightly hostile. She grew cautious, reserved, distracted. Her famous efficiency became eroded by forgetfulness: sometimes she stood in the middle of her office, fists clenched, trying to remember where she had put a letter, a memorandum, her peppermints. When strangers arrived at the station she hung back and looked them over rather than advancing with her customary flourish of welcome. On the air she managed to look like her old self, but in her voice the girlish lilt, the ever-arcing bubble of enthusiasm, had dissolved, and her words too often emerged without the shape of inflection. She received nine letters from viewers who expressed concern, from mild to grave, and she found each letter more infuriating and depressing than the one before it. A blind girl wrote that Judy's voice was her favorite on television and that she could now hear a problem in it and hoped that soon everything would be all right. The last letter to arrive came from a man who said he had always "liked her style" and thought she was "damned cute" and figured that maybe she was at that age where she finally needed a *real* man capable of giving her both "good hot sex and understanding." He included a post office box number and guaranteed his discretion. After reading this last, she gathered together the bunch and carried them to the ladies' room where she tore them to bits and flushed them down the toilet, cursing each writer as an idiot.

After this, her behavior took still another turn: innocent statements were snapped and sneered at. Customarily, she took charge of decorating the Colonial House for Christmas, and one afternoon while she and two of the staff were trimming the tree in the living room Karen stepped in and said, "Oh, we're having all red bulbs this year?" to which Judy replied, "Yes, we are. Is there anything wrong with that?" Karen said she didn't mean anything was wrong. Judy asked what exactly *did* she mean. Karen answered that she didn't mean anything. "Then why bother to comment?" demanded Judy. Karen slunk away. Judy turned to the two astonished and disapproving faces of her helpers, felt a sudden weight in her throat, then went to her office to cry. Before the tears subsided she resolved to harden her shell.

She began to keep her office door closed at all times, now locking it whenever she left it.

She told Sloane to stop badgering her with his incessant questions as to what was "wrong" with her.

She put her house up for sale, listing it with Adele's agency.

Sloane conferred frequently with Matt. With uncharacteristic despondency, Sloane lamented the diminishing state of intimacy between himself and Judy. Confessing that he could not get through to her, that she would reveal nothing, he asked Matt to try his hand at prying the problem out of her.

Matt searched for a tactic and finally decided upon one that he knew was a long shot. He sat with her at lunch one day and opened the conversation with a lengthy sigh. "Well, this is the day of reckoning."

"Reckoning?"

"My yearly physical." It was a lie. He would never think of having his physical at this time and opening himself to the possibility of bad news right before Christmas.

"You look healthy enough to me," she said dully, and he felt a pang of regret at the complete absence of life in her voice.

"You never know. A friend of mine has a physical every six months. It once saved his life."

No answer.

"Do you have a physical each year?" he ventured.

Hard suspicion gathered at her eyes and mouth. "Why?"

"I just wondered."

"What made you wonder?"

"I—always wonder about other people when I'm going for my own." He paused. "When it's over and done with you feel a certain peace of mind."

"If you *have* a mind." When she spoke again she attempted humor. This, more than anything else in her changed behavior, made people cringe. "Maybe the doctor wouldn't find anything inside me. Maybe the x rays would come out blank." The laugh that followed was shrill and false.

He was too stunned to reply. By the time he gathered his wits and found his voice, she was excusing herself and rising from her chair.

The conversation—rather, the lack of it—haunted him for the next two days. He felt both pity and anger, wanting at the same time to stroke her and shake some sense into her.

And just when he was getting it out of his mind, Adele jumped squarely onto the subject. They were having Irish coffee in front of the fire, and after her first sip she said: "I want to talk to you about Judy."

"What about her?"

"I had to go look at her house when I listed it. It's lovely. Well built, beautifully laid out. She's anxious for a quick sale. Too anxious. I had to twist her arm to let me list it at a hundred and five. She wanted to start out at ninety." She sipped and swallowed slowly. "Matt, she's not living there."

"What?"

"And yet she's pretending to. I had made the appointment for eight-thirty so she could get to work on time. When I was running late I called her and couldn't get an answer and when I got there she said she must have been in the shower. She waited in the kitchen while I went through the house. I found both phones sitting on a shelf in the linen closet. Well, I was too astounded to say anything. She lied about the phone and she lied about the shower—the tub was bone dry. In the bathroom and the lavatory there's no make-up, no cosmetics whatsoever, not even a comb and brush—I checked the drawers."

"Are you a broker or a detective? She obviously spent the night somewhere else."

"But why should she bother to lie? Another thing, and more important. She wants to let her bedroom suite go with the house. I can tell you it's worth a few thousand but she's willing literally to give it away."

"Adele—"

"Let me finish. When I looked in the refrigerator the fruit and vegetables were all withered and she didn't even offer to perk coffee for us. And she adamantly refused to leave that kitchen and go into any other room with me."

"What are you getting at?"

"She's afraid of that house. It sticks out all over her. I think . . . something has happened to her in there. Something recently."

"You're assuming quite a lot on just a few hunches."

"Maybe so, but it's all very spooky to me. Don't tell me you haven't noticed the change in her."

He told her what had been going on at the station and then about his effort over lunch.

"She's been traumatized, and I think you and I should get to the bottom of it. The Colonial House dining room is not the place. I want to invite her for dinner. If we give her the right atmosphere she might open up."

"Do you really think it's up to us?"

"Who *is* it up to?"

He had no answer.

"You may not be close friends," she said, "but you've worked with the woman for over twenty-five years. You must have some regard for her."

"I do," he muttered.

She went to the fireplace and stoked the log so that it sparked and began to glow again. Returning to him, she said: "I'll invite her for the night after Christmas."

4

Matt left Adele's three hours before he was to pick up Claudia and proceed on to the Brainards' party. The falling snow—and Adele's complete understanding of why he must escort Claudia instead of her—inspired in him a bit of the Christmas spirit that helped to dispel some of his anxiety over the evening ahead.

This spirit was diminished, however, the moment he opened the door to his near-barren living room. Unlike the carefully chosen contents in Adele's house, his own few pieces of furniture had been purchased cheaply and hastily at the only store in the city that could promise next-day delivery. He had not even bargained with the management of the apartment complex to replace the stained and faded gold carpeting and limp green draperies. But he did not entertain here and scarcely anyone saw the place. Those who had seen it were the four or five women he had picked up in bars between the divorce and the time he met Adele.

The telephone rang as he was putting on the kettle for instant coffee. It was Bud.

"Hi, Matt. I've been trying to get you all day."

"Oh? I was—out doing errands." He did not like anyone to know exactly how much time he spent at Adele's. "Is something wrong?"

"Not at all. It's just that Joanne and I have a little pre-Christmas gift for you and we wanted to come by with it. We won't be here tonight when you come to pick up Claudia. Would half an hour be all right?"

"Sure." He gave Bud the address and directions.

It would be his daughter's first visit to the apartment, but his excitement quickly turned to embarrassment and then to shame. She was certain to notice the meagerness of effort put into the place as well as the meagerness in the refrigerator: he had no soft drink to offer her, no beer for Bud.

They were punctual almost to the minute. He buzzed to release the downstairs door, then stepped out into the hall. As they came up the stairs Joanne's smile was the least tentative it had been in three years. He wanted to reach out for her, thought better of it, and simply accepted her kiss on his cheek. Bud gave him the usual welcoming squeeze on the shoulder. He was carrying a large rectangular parcel wrapped in plain brown paper.

Matt took their coats and as he hung them up he kept his eye on Joanne, who was looking the room over. Her face registered nothing and she said nothing. He wished he could offer an excuse like "The place is such a mess" but there were not enough contents to *create* a mess.

"It's a nice-size room," Joanne offered at last.

"I've got to start doing something to it," he said bluntly. "I've put it off for too long."

"Got anything particular in mind?" said Bud as he inspected a hairline crack that ran from the corner of the kitchen doorway up to the ceiling.

"Not yet."

Joanne smiled and shook her head. "Give Bud ten minutes and he'll come up with something."

"Mind if I look around?" Bud asked.

"Go ahead, but there's not much to see."

As soon as he disappeared down the hallway Joanne said, "Wait until you see what he did to his mother's house. It's beautiful."

"I'd like to see it. When are we going to get that dinner we were promised?"

"Right after New Year's. His mother's down in Orion visiting his sister."

"Then I take it she's feeling better."

"Yes." She took two steps closer to him and lowered her voice. "I have to warn you about something. Sometimes she's very distant—you know, remote. But she's not cold, just very shy. So if you find she doesn't talk to you much, don't think it's your fault."

This warning of hers might appear small and insignificant to anyone else, but for him it signaled an increase in natural intimacy.

"Hey!" she called in the direction of the hallway. "Can we halt the structural inspection so he can open the package?"

When he and Bud were seated, Joanne put the parcel in his lap. "It's not your Christmas present," she said. "It just happened to be ready at this time."

He cringed with shame. The only drinks he could offer them—coffee or scotch—they had declined, and so here they all sat empty-handed for the unwrapping.

He tore the brown paper at the outer edge and saw the gilt frame; the first large strip he pulled away revealed Bud's face, the second strip Joanne's. Despite his natural prejudice, he thought it the most beautiful photograph he had ever seen. Bud's soft inkwell eyes and Joanne's startling gray ones were dramatically contrasting yet equally commanding. Both of them had worn dark colors so there was nothing to detract attention from the rich hues of their young skin and the gentle smiles that exposed only the tips of their teeth. There was such a hushed quality to the picture that any reaction louder than a murmur seemed inappropriate. "Beautiful . . . beautiful."

"Now," said Joanne, "where to hang it. In here or in your bedroom?"

"Well, I don't know . . . "

"Why don't you wait a while." A sly smile appeared on Bud's face. "Until I get this place fixed up for you."

"What?"

"We'll consider it a Christmas present," said Bud. "Although it'll be a little late. You just pay for the materials. I've got dozens of magazines we can look through for ideas."

"I couldn't possibly let you—"

"Yes, you can. Don't forget, I get something out of it too.

Practice. But I can promise it'll be a first-rate job."

"Then I insist on paying you."

"No way. Listen, Matt, I'm one of those lucky people whose work is also their recreation." He looked about the room. "You don't have to live like this."

The statement would have been audacious, even snotty, coming from someone else. But Bud spoke in an objective tone and he spoke the truth—as when he had told Claudia she was too thin and her hair coloring all wrong.

Bud said he would get the magazines to Matt and even make some sketches of his own, but when he began to suggest color schemes Joanne stood up. "Don't start—we'll be here all night. We've got fifteen minutes to make that movie."

After they had gone Matt propped the frame in a temporary position on the chest of drawers in this bedroom, then stood back near the doorway and stared at it. The longer he looked the more he assured himself that no matter how painful it would be giving up Adele there would be other things in his life.

Abruptly, he turned out of the doorway and walked to the smaller second bedroom. In it were a desk and a convertible sofa and a tiny chest of drawers. Smiling to himself he considered how the space and its contents were already appropriate for a visiting grandchild.

Bud drove with one hand on the wheel and with the other one stroking the back of Joanne's neck. "I think he really liked it," he said.

"Yes, he did." She paused. "God, what a depressing place! I had no idea . . . "

"No idea what?"

"That he of all people would live that way. At home he was always very particular about the way things looked. I remember Mom was perfectly satisfied with the kitchen but *he* was the one who insisted on having it done over and modernized."

"Sometimes when people live alone they tend to let things go."

"I guess." Then: "Maybe he *should* marry Adele."

Bud turned a corner and she stiffened. "This isn't the way to the theater."

"I know." He grinned at her. "But we can make the late show."

"I see. And what brought on this sudden change of plans?"

"Just that I feel very happy. And when I'm happy I love to make love to you."

"And when you're unhappy?"

"I'm never unhappy."

"I know. Very strange, Mr. Hanes."

He laughed and tousled her hair.

When they arrived at his mother's empty, darkened house he switched on no lights except the one to the upstairs hall. At the foot of the stairs he picked her up in his arms.

"Bud!" Her chuckle lacked mirth and her spine went rigid.

"Does this embarrass you?" he whispered.

"I'm—afraid you'll hurt your back."

"You know better." He kissed her deeply; afterward, she acquiesced and let her head rest on his shoulder as he carried her up.

Beside his bed they undressed in the muted light from the hall and then lay down on top of the quilt. After a few minutes of fondling and kissing, he pulled back, sat on his haunches and opened her thighs. "The wedding will make it all official but for me you've been Mrs. Hanes for a long time."

She knew it sounded like something out of a romantic melodrama, but as he entered her she knew the truth of it as well. Besides being perfectly suited for her emotionally, he was her sexual dream fully realized—if indeed she had ever dreamed in that vein before they met. Without being mechanical he was the master manipulator of her body, striking all the right chords to produce chills, gasps, ecstatic wincing, and that final sensation where she felt all her flesh racing downhill.

When it was over he nestled his head into the crook of her arm and softly placed his lips against the side of her breast.

After a moment she said: "It's very nice what you're going to do for Dad."

"It'll be fun for me. Besides, he deserves it."

"Yes, he does." She reached down and covered his hand which was resting on her belly. "I know the past few months you've been trying harder than usual to make me understand his side of things. Maybe I've been in my mother's corner for too long. And in Terry's. Maybe I've been afraid of being back in the middle again."

"Well, don't be afraid. You've got *me* in the middle with you."

There was a short silence before she asked: "Bud, does your mother really, really like me?"

"Of course she does. More than you realize."

"And she's glad you're marrying me?"

He paused, then said with firm conviction: "I know her. Our wedding is going to be the happiest day of her life."

The Brainards' rambling ranch-style house sat on a lightly wooded two-acre lot in the most exclusive section of town. The driveway wound through the trees to arrive at an enormous blacktop surface that was a veritable parking lot. When Matt and Claudia drove up there were already more than a dozen cars.

"Margaret said it was going to be a big party. I guess it's the season." Claudia's explanation was, at bottom, an exoneration of her friend. She and Matt had often discussed how each year, since Ted's operation and the resulting celibacy, Margaret's parties grew larger and more frequent. And they had increased in both proportions since the last of their three sons went off to college.

Both Brainards answered the door, looking too eager and as if they were now welcoming the guests of honor.

"Where have you *been*?" said Margaret.

"You said eight o'clock," replied Claudia. "It's only twenty-five after."

Margaret looked at her watch, and Matt looked at the drink in her hand. There was no telling what number it was, since she customarily began at four o'clock. In typical contrast, Ted had nothing in his hands except Claudia's coat, which he was helping her out of.

The Brainards led them down to the huge recreation room where the buffet supper was set up. The party was in full swing. Cigarette smoke hovered in the air like webbing; the loud talk and laughter went unabsorbed by the acoustical ceiling. Ted was immediately pulled away by two men who were discussing a lawsuit, and Matt watched Margaret go off into the smoke and noise, like a camp director, to make sure no one was sitting alone.

He whispered to Claudia, "I don't know how in hell she can stand this kind of thing so often."

"Desperation," she answered. "Just jump in and start mixing." She walked away and Matt turned around to the buffet table. As he filled his plate he spotted Ted still talking to the two men but looking at *him* with an unmistakable urgency in his eyes. Purposely, Matt worked his way to the other side of the room and found himself at the edge of a conversation-in-progress about the ski-mask rapist.

"It's just horrible," exclaimed one woman, "the way he abandons them and leaves them with no car."

"Well, if he ever gets to me," said another, "I hope it's not in winter. Brrrr." She laughed.

A third woman shrugged. "Look, at least he doesn't murder them. These days, that's the most you can hope for."

At once, Matt recalled the deadness in Judy's voice and knew he could not remain near this discussion. But before he took a step, rescue arrived in the form of Margaret who was gripping the arm of a tall red-haired youth.

"Matt, this is Ted's nephew, Steve." The two shook hands. "Doesn't he look just like Ted did twenty years ago?"

"Yes, he does."

"You tell your girl friend," she said to Steve, "I think she has excellent taste."

The boy kissed her cheek. "And so does Uncle Ted."

Her smile could not have been more painfully grateful, and when Steve walked away her eyes trailed after him, brimming with tears. Matt cringed at the effect that this crumb of kindness had upon her. He resented her for not being in better control and resented Ted for his part in destroying that control.

She blinked, clicked on a smile, and said, "How's Adele?"

"Fine. Busy."

"Having her own agency at her age is quite an accomplishment."

"She likes her work."

"Yes, I suppose that does make life pleasanter."

He looked at the pretty face now veined and clawed by the

effects of gin. Softly, he said: "Why don't you look for a job. Claudia's thinking of it."

"Maybe . . . maybe."

A woman appeared who wanted Margaret to verify an incident at yesterday's bridge game. Matt edged toward the stairway and started up. There was a pair of boots in the car: he would put them on and, with drink in hand, tramp around the snow-covered wooded grounds. He wanted to breath real air, stare at the cold full moon, hear nothing but the wind in the branches and the crunching under his feet.

When he reached the hallway where the coat closet was, a voice from behind called out his name. He halted, feeling like a soldier tracked and cornered by the enemy.

"Can't take it, huh?" said Ted, grinning but intent.

"I was just going to get some air."

"The air's a lot better in the den. Come on in for a minute."

Resentfully, he followed. Ted took his glass and refilled it at the wet bar and then poured his usual club soda for himself. "Margaret wants to put a bar on the sunporch and in the loft of our bedroom. The woman abhors a vacuum."

What about the vacuum *you've* created for her? he said silently. He knew, of course, from his own experience, that there were two sides to every sad story, and he did not want to hear either one of them. And in a second of forced honesty he considered that perhaps tonight he was so much in Margaret's corner because, unlike Ted, she made no demands on him. Instead of sitting on one of the stools he simply rested his foot on the bar railing and hoped this would show Ted he was not in the mood for serious talk.

Ted dropped two olives into the club soda and stirred them around with his finger. "I started doing this when I gave up the booze so I could pretend I was really having a martini. Now I'm addicted to the olives."

Ted's face was as stoical as Margaret's was desperate, and he looked years younger than she. After his bout with cancer he had given up alcohol, cigarettes, and sex, replacing them with jogging and health foods, and he had switched from criminal to corporate law.

He allowed for a moment of silence, then said to Matt: "You

look like a runner at the starting line waiting for the gun to go off. You've had that look for some time now. Is it with everyone or just with me?"

"I've got things on my mind."

"I'd like to hear them."

"Not now. Not until I think them through a bit."

"I've got some things on my mind too," said Ted. "I'd like to have a night out or a long lunch with you after New Year's."

"Sure. After New Year's."

Ted smiled cynically. "And I mean *within* the year." He paused and waited until Matt looked at him. "Allow me to say that I am very happy for you. The fact that you have so little time for anyone else but Adele speaks a lot for the relationship."

Later, driving home with Claudia, Matt knew that her silence was a restrained one. Finally, she broke it and with the exact question he predicted. "What did you and Ted talk about?"

"Nothing."

"You were together a long time to talk about nothing," she observed lightly.

"Look," he answered wearily, "I want you to get something straight right now. I am not going to play detective for you and Margaret. In fact, if Ted tries true confessions with me I'm going to tell him I'm not interested in hearing them."

"Do you think that's especially kind to an old friend?"

"If there *is* anything going on the way you suspect, do you think it's kind of him to involve me in it?—particularly since there's nothing I could do about it."

"He might want your advice."

"Drop it, Claudia! The subject is closed. Permanently." There it was, his temper again. The topic had not warranted such a reaction. "I'm sorry," he muttered.

She acknowledged the apology by speaking cheerfully. "Margaret and I talked about getting jobs but we've decided to try something else first. We're going to join Mrs. Richardson's group."

"What? But you haven't been—raped."

"Don't you watch your own programs? She wants victims *and* volunteers for the counseling sessions and public relations.

66

Anyway, we thought we'd give it a try. Unless you *want* me to get a job."

"Of course not." For God's sake, do what you want and don't ask me to guide your life for you . . . .

People who love you never seem to get enough back. Joanne's words to him that day in the driveway now sprang into his head. Maybe she was right—except in *her* case. If he could eliminate all her caution, wipe away all her doubts, he would gladly give her more than she could ever give back.

He and Adele spent Christmas Eve together; the next morning she went to her parents' and he to Claudia's. Bud was there and after the gifts were exchanged he sat down with Matt and presented him with a series of sketches.

"Come on," Matt protested, "I didn't want you to go to all this trouble."

"It's no trouble. Go through them and pick out the ones you like the best, then take a few days to decide. Don't be shy about suggesting changes or if you find you don't like anything about them we can start from scratch again."

After dinner, Bud helped Claudia clean up in the kitchen, and Joanne asked her father if he wanted to go for a walk. Matt nearly leapt from his chair and had to struggle to hide his overanxiousness and gratitude.

He let her stride set their pace. There were patches of ice on the sidewalks, and now and then when he glanced at her foot he wished she would take his arm. This, he knew, was foolish overprotectiveness: she was not crippled, only somewhat impaired, and thanks to all the practice with Bud her tennis game was better than average.

For a while they exchanged comments about the outdoor Christmas decorations, then lapsed into silence. He felt slightly awkward but she apparently did not, and that was the important thing. As soon as their route turned homeward she spoke.

"Mom has the feeling you've been depressed lately."

"Oh?" Pause. "Well, maybe a little."

"What about?"

"I don't know," he said lightly. "I guess when you get to my

67

age everything is pretty routine. You get bored with it but you don't relish surprises, either."

She nodded slowly, in a way that suggested this made perfect sense. "Are you expecting some kind of surprise?"

"Just the opposite. I have to give someone a surprise and I'm not looking forward to it."

She waited. Then: "Can I ask who?"

Perhaps it was too soon to initiate intimacy on such a scale, but her lack of discomfort at being alone together encouraged him.

"Adele. I have to break it off with her. She wants a family and I can't—well, I already have a family."

"You could have another one," she said in a tone that reluctantly granted permission.

"Trying to ditch me, eh?"

She obliged him with a brief, false smile for the poor joke. "But if you really love her you could work something out."

"When it's an issue like this, I'm afraid not. Babies either exist or they don't."

"Do you think you're too old?"

"I know I am."

"You're really not." With surprising vehemence she added: "I don't want you to feel old. Or Mom, either."

"I imagine we'll both perk up when we have grandchildren. The rumor is they're supposed to keep you young."

She did not answer until the house came into view. "I felt old for a long time. After the accident. I had to get used to this foot and there were so many things I couldn't do right away. I started feeling sorry for myself; there were plenty of days I didn't want to get out of bed. Mom and Bud were always encouraging—sometimes, too encouraging, if you know what I mean. One day, there was something I didn't want to do—I can't remember what—and Bud really blew his top. He told me to wait for him outside his math class, so I did. He was the first one out and he pulled me aside until this girl came through the door. My God, it was awful. Her legs looked like two strands of spaghetti, all twisted and buckled. She had to use two canes, her books were in a knapsack strapped to her back. 'I want you to watch her,' he said and we followed behind to the stairwell. She went down, those legs moving in such a grotesque way I thought she'd kill herself. There was an elevator she could've used, but she'd told Bud she needed exercise and that the stairs had become a challenge—actual excitement—for her. Then Bud said to me, 'When you get home you look in the mirror, you look at that face and that body and those legs and then tell me what good reason you have for not going dancing or to the beach with me.' I hated him for doing that to me but it was what I needed. I went on grumbling and growling for a week or two. Then I finally gave in and let him help me brush up on my dancing." She laughed nervously and fell pensive. Abruptly, she stopped, turned, and looked him in the eye. "Maybe *you're* feeling sorry for yourself. Maybe. I don't know."

"Sorry about what?"

"About Terry. And about getting older. Yes, you were cruel to Terry but I think you've learned from it."

"That's not the only reason I don't want another family, Joanne." Not quite a lie but not the whole truth either.

"Well, you're getting another son whether you like it or not. Bud's totally taken with you." They started up the walk to the house. "And if you're feeling down about hitting your fifties, watch Lucille when we have dinner there. She's younger than you are and she's got that awful arthritis to fight."

"By the way, when are we going to have that dinner. It's been promised for weeks now."

"Soon. When she gets back from her daughter's." On the porch, she laid her hand on his arm. "I didn't offend you, did I, about that feeling sorry for yourself? I didn't mean to be presumptuous."

"You weren't. I'm sure I'm capable of self-pity like everyone else."

"Maybe I was too frank, mentioning Terry. You see, it's easier for me to sympathize with Mom than with you. But I'm trying."

"I appreciate that. But it's more than sympathy I want."

She lowered her eyes and whispered, "I know."

When they opened the door they heard Bud and Claudia laughing in the kitchen. Bud appeared before they got their coats off. "Just in time," he said, then called over his shoulder. "Duchess, bring in the snacks and I'll get the cards."

At the dining-room table they played bridge for nearly five

hours. Matt accepted a nightcap, looked over Bud's sketches, and made a decision. Bud affirmed that he could begin work on the apartment the following week.

When Matt said goodnight to Joanne he whispered: "Please don't say anything to your mother or Bud about Adele and me."

"Of course I won't."

Driving back to his apartment, he was so full of thoughts of his daughter that he totally forgot about his and Adele's task tomorrow night.

Judy followed him in her own car from the station to Adele's. His hands sweated the entire distance, the moisture of guilt dampening the fleece lining of his gloves. All day at work, Judy had given him little smiles, not unlike her "old" ones; she hadn't an inkling that she was coming to be interrogated.

The scene was set when they arrived: a large, crackling fire in the fireplace; WGRS-FM on the radio; stemmed glasses frosted for martinis; the aroma of roasting duck wafting in from the kitchen. It seemed, too, that Adele's stratagem was abetted by the weather, for a light fat-flaked snowfall had begun and was framed by the two bay windows.

By the time Judy finished the first martini and accepted a second Matt could hear a variation of the old tinkle returning to her voice and she began to smile unguardedly. He wanted to stop the plan altogether but every eye signal he gave Adele was ignored.

"I showed someone else the house today," said Adele.

"Oh? Were they interested?"

"Very. But their offer is ridiculously low. Eighty-three five."

"That's not so bad."

Adele swung her gaze to Matt and then back to Judy. "I think we can wait, can't we? You're not in any hurry."

The smile disappeared and the nervousness returned. "Actually I am. I—I've seen an apartment I'd like to take and if I don't grab it now . . . "

"Are you already living in the apartment?"

"Already living—? How could I be?" The voice quivered, and there was no mistaking the hysterical glint in her eye.

Adele leaned forward in her chair and spoke softly. "Judy,

houses are my first love *and* my business. So I have both an intuition about them and a keen eye. I know you're not living in yours. And you weren't living in it when you first showed it to me."

Judy's face froze around her bulging eyes. For the moment, Matt saw himself and Adele as two children with sticks backing a kitten into a corner.

"Where *are* you living?" Adele asked gently.

"The Holiday Inn," she murmured.

"Why?" No answer. "Something happened to you in that house, didn't it? Something to scare you out of it."

Judy turned her wild eyes to Matt in supplication. Before he could respond she closed them and lay her head on the back of the chair. There followed a long pause, filled only by "Dancing in the Dark" on the radio and by the furious crackling of the burning log. "I was raped there," she said in an eerily toneless voice.

"When?"

"Almost two months ago."

"Was it—someone you know?"

"It was him, the one with the ski mask."

"Oh, God!" Adele whispered.

"He got into the garage. He had a knife and a note." She kept her head back and her eyes closed as she recounted the message in the note and how she was led blindfolded to the bedroom. She did not tell them what went on in the bedroom.

"Have you been to the police?" asked Matt.

Her eyes shot open. "No! They'd leak my name out!"

"No, they wouldn't," he said reassuringly. "You might have a clue for them, something they could use or match up with—"

"No police! And you have to promise me you won't tell anyone. Not even Lyle. *Especially* Lyle."

"Of course we won't tell," Adele said quickly.

"No one must know, no one, I won't be made a laughing-stock!"

"A what! Judy, who in the world would laugh at something so horrible?"

With narrowed eyes she looked at the floor. Her quick breathing slowed, her lip curled into a sneer, and she spoke in a guttural imitation of her own voice: "Stuuupid emmmpty laaaughingstock." She almost said it a second time but stopped and looked at them strangely challengingly. "That's what he called me. Over and over. Over and over."

Matt saw the chill in his gut duplicated on Adele's face. She said: "Judy, the man is sick."

"Over and over," she muttered.

Adele folded her hands and meshed her fingers for control. "If you won't go to the police why not at least talk to Mrs. Richardson."

"Never," she answered firmly. "All those women . . . "

"You don't have to take part in the group," offered Matt. "She'd talk to you privately."

"If I hadn't done that program with her it might not have happened!" This, she knew, was not true at all: the attack had come before the program was aired. It was not Jane Richardson she couldn't face but rather the prospect of any contact with that witch, Hippolyta Bewick. She had had several nightmares about the attack and in one of them the mask was pulled off to reveal Bewick's face.

"Then," said Adele, "will you go to another counselor of some kind?"

"You mean a psychiatrist?"

"Yes. It would help you, it really would."

"I'll think about it." Suddenly, her body sagged, and then she jumped up. "I'm sorry, I'm going to be sick." She dashed, with Adele trailing, for the lavatory.

When they reappeared, Judy was holding a washcloth to her forehead. Adele escorted her to the sofa and brought her a glass of water.

"I'd better go."

"Absolutely not," insisted Adele. "You're going to relax for a while and then get something into your stomach, even if it's just mashed potatoes." She brought Matt a second drink, and Judy sat up with renewed panic.

"You can't say anything about this to anyone!"

"We won't," said Matt. "I promise you." He was horrified and sickened by what he had heard but beyond this he was angry at

Adele and himself, for they had pried open the door to this woman's misery and were powerless to help.

While Judy forced down a few bites of her meal Adele got her to agree to a reasonable counteroffer to the low bid on her house.

Matt wanted to drive Judy's car back to the Holiday Inn while she rode with Adele, but Judy assured them her nerves were steady enough to handle the wheel. They walked her out to the driveway where, for the third time, she extracted their promise to tell no one.

5

Immediately following her admission, she began to avoid him at work. Her means were subtle—the *only* subtlety she was capable of—so that no one but he noticed. If she found that they were heading for the dining room at the same time she would veer into the restroom and then return to her office until he was finished eating. When he wandered into the production wing while she was helping to set up a local commercial or rehearsing her show she would abruptly initiate a conference with the cameraman or program director. At these times, Matt ached to take her aside and reassure her but knew it would prove pointless, perhaps even harmful.

He thought about her constantly and his ears could not forget her grotesque rendering of the rapist's words. But when he was able to wrench his mind free of her, it settled upon something equally distressing: the impending separation from Adele. All his silent and sometimes muttered rehearsals failed to bring him to action; every moment was the wrong moment. Bud was now more than half finished with the facelift on the apartment. Matt hoped that the completion would somehow inspire the courage he needed.

Claudia called him on a Monday morning and asked if Thursday would "be convenient" for him to have dinner at Bud's.

"I know Wednesdays are best for you," she said (the translation for him being: "I know Adele teaches that night and you don't have to give her up for us"). "But this term Joanne has a three-hour night class on Wednesday."

"Why a night class?"

"Because that's when it's offered."

"Oh, that's just fine! With this rapist running loose, the university expects these girls to walk the campus at night. Especially in winter."

"Matt, there have *always* been night classes. Besides, Bud takes her—he drops her off at the door and picks her up at the door. Now, can you make it Thursday or not?"

"Yes, of course I can."

"Good. Seven o'clock. You won't have to come by for us. Joanne has a dental appointment at six so I'll be picking her up there." She gave him Bud's address.

He rang the doorbell at seven sharp, and the door was opened immediately. Lucille Hanes's smile shrank perceptibly when she looked past him and saw that he was alone. "Where are Joanne and Claudia?" she asked as she ushered him in.

He told her about the dental appointment and suggested they might be a few minutes late.

Her smile returned, smaller now, and she looked at his shoulder instead of his face when she asked for his coat and told him to sit down. He turned out of the hall and into the living room and took the first chair he came to.

"Bud says you drink scotch." She walked past him to the drop-leaf table in the far corner. On it were liquor bottles, mixers, an ice bucket, a bowl of lemon peels and slices. "Water or soda?"

"Soda, please."

She handed him the glass with a cocktail napkin under it. "Would you excuse me a minute? I have to check something in the oven."

As soon as she left he recalled Joanne's warning of how he should not be put off by this woman's distance: she had yet to meet his eyes. He wondered how such shyness and reserve had allowed her to be a waitress all those years. The fact that she was a waitress at the time Joanne started seeing Bud disturbed Claudia considerably. Claudia had thought it would be nice to socialize with Lucille, even if just occasionally. But Lucille worked eight hours a day, six days a week, and had no time for lunching or shopping, no inclination to join the country club, no interest in golf and tennis and bridge, and apparently no desire to make new friends. When Claudia became firmly attached to Bud after Terry's death she was even more disturbed by the social and personality differences that disallowed a friendship with Lucille. Because of who Bud was and what he had done for both her and Joanne in their time of need, she looked upon Lucille with a kind of reverence, one that she would never be able to express in friendship.

He had plenty of time to look the room over. Somewhat smaller than Claudia's, the house appeared similar in age, sturdiness, and structural detail. Rich golden oak made up the woodwork, the moldings, the banister on the stairway, and the same quality wood was used for the built-in bookcase which had obviously been added later. The hardwood floor appeared to have been recently refinished and it formed a glowing border around the plum-colored rug. The furniture was expensive, conservatively modern with no one piece calling singular attention to itself. The walls were painted a quiet celery green to harmonize with the vivid green, light gray, and pale yellow of the sofa and three chairs. Matt liked the room at once even though it lacked a fireplace. Carefully planned and orchestrated, it was blessedly free of the usual slickness of a decorator's touch. Suddenly increased was his eagerness to see his own place finished.

At the end of their tour his eyes lingered on the bookcase. He got up and went over to it. On the third shelf was a smaller print of the photograph Joanne and Bud had given him, and on the shelf above it three high-school graduation pictures—Bud's, his sister's, Joanne's—and a much older photograph with three figures in it: they were sitting, the shot taken from the knees up, with the bench stationed against a typically nondescript backdrop that professional photographers use. Immediately recognizable was Lucille. At her right was her daughter Gail; at the left, Bud. Lucille's face was expressionless but altogether captivating. Her blue-black hair, parted in the middle, descended in waves to a thick final fold that touched her shoulders. The large dark eyes, the high cheekbones and softly pointed chin, the complexion that suggested but was not quite olive—these were duplicated in the boy who looked to be about eight or nine. He, like his mother, stared blankly ahead, his hands on his lap. The girl, markedly fairer than these two, had been captured at one of those awkward stages in puberty. The sharp angles of a skinny body emphasized but did not compliment her already substantial breasts. In contrast to the deadpans of her mother and brother, her smile was comically, touchingly overeager. For Matt, the most prominent feature of the photograph was the absence of the father.

Lucille returned, halted in the doorway, then advanced to the sofa when he turned away from his inspection.

"The older photograph is very nice," he said as he sat down. "Gail resembles her father?"

"Yes, he was—he's dark blond." She was perched at the edge of the cushion, giving Matt the impression that her presence in the room was only temporary.

"Will he be coming to the wedding?"

She shook her head, and for the first time—albeit guardedly—allowed her eyes to meet his. "We have nothing to do with each other. We lost touch a long time ago."

"Bud and Gail don't see him either?"

"Not anymore. He never encouraged them in the first place." This was reported matter-of-factly and followed by silence. Matt took two long swallows of his drink and looked at her over the rim of his glass. Her still-youthful beauty was flawed only by the faintly bluish circles under the eyes and by a tendency to hunch her shoulders; these detractions, he presumed, might be related to the arthritis. There were certainly no other indicators of her illness. Below the hem of her pleated skirt were the most beautiful legs he had ever seen.

"Is the arthritis giving you much trouble?" "Trouble," he realized immediately, was an idiotic choice. The disease had forced her to quit working.

"There are good days and bad. You can't predict. Except when it's damp," she added with a stiff smile. She sat back a little farther into the sofa and smoothed down her skirt, rather primly, to cover her knees.

"You have a beautiful home. I assume Bud did a lot of the work."

"He did all of it."

"Well, then, I'll be more than pleased if my apartment turns out half as nice."

The doorbell rang, and she briskly left the room. Her fleeting but undisguised look of relief at the sound of the chimes mirrored his own feelings. The past ten minutes had been work. He hoped that Claudia would prove more adept at conversing with this woman than he was.

There was the rustle of greetings and of coats being shed before the three of them entered the living room. Joanne kissed her father, sat with her mother on the sofa, and Lucille went directly to the makeshift bar.

"Claudia, I forgot to buy white wine today. Bud's getting it now. Will you have something else while we wait? Club soda?"

"No thanks."

Lucille looked at her watch. "He should've been back by now, I can't imagine what's keeping him. Joanne, gin and tonic?"

"Please."

After Joanne's drink was made, Claudia launched a short discussion about the weather, inquired after Lucille's health, complimented her on her skirt and blouse, and then bowed out of the lead by lighting a cigarette. Lucille, now in the other chair which faced the sofa, seemed to relax a bit when she spoke to Joanne. "When are you and Bud going to make up your minds about the wedding date?"

Joanne chuckled. "One of these days. But it'll definitely be in September, October, or November."

"I guess," said Lucille, "June weddings aren't as popular as they used to be."

"No, they're not," Claudia agreed, then turned to her daughter. "I do wish you'd make it September. The weather in October can be tricky and November is always dreary."

"We're getting married *in*doors."

"Yes, but some of the guests will be traveling long distances to get here."

"That's something to consider," said Lucille.

Matt found it amusing, this eagerness on the part of the

mothers to get the bond sealed. Smiling to himself and feeling inexplicably uplifted he held out his glass and asked Lucille for a refill.

"Was that one all right?" she said.

"Perfect."

For the next minute the rattling of ice and the pourings from the bottles were the only sounds in the room. Then, as if summoned to rescue them from silence, Bud's car hummed into the driveway on the other side of the shuttered windows. The four of them waited without a word during the interval that the car door slammed and the back door of the house opened.

"Hello, everyone," he called out from the kitchen, two rooms away. "Be in in a minute."

Matt eyed the glass of ginger ale in Lucille's hand. "You don't drink?"

"No." Her face colored. "I could never develop a taste for it," she said, as if this were a fault.

Bud's voice approached them before he actually appeared. "Hang on, Claudia, we're on our way!"

She laughed and called back: "For heaven's sake, I'm not exactly perishing."

"Oh, no?" He rounded the corner from the hallway, a wineglass in one hand, a beer in the other. "I thought I heard you gasping when I came in."

"Yes, my withdrawal symptoms," she said with a smirk and took the glass. "Oooh, it's chilled. How nice."

"Sorry it took so long. I had to go to the party store. Bonner's doesn't have a cooler."

"You shouldn't have bothered. Really."

As soon as Bud sat down Matt said: "You've done a terrific job in this room."

"This isn't all," said Joanne. "He wallpapered the hallway and dining room himself and put down a new floor in the kitchen and completely relandscaped the back yard—wait until you see it in the spring."

"He put new plumbing in the bathroom too," said Claudia.

Matt turned to Lucille. "If I were you I'd think twice about letting him go."

She smiled weakly, excused herself, and went into the kitchen.

The dining room they ate in was as airy and inviting as the living room. After Matt complimented Bud on the wallpaper and the wainscoting Claudia told him that Bud had built the sideboard and the table they were eating at.

"When you finish with my apartment," said Matt, "I'll expect photographers from *Better Homes and Gardens*."

"I plan to be completely finished by Sunday."

"I think we're ready for dessert," announced Lucille. But as she started from her chair Bud's words halted her.

"Stay. I'll take care of it."

Matt watched her settle back uncertainly. With the way she kept wanting to return to the kitchen he wondered if this were an acquired instinct from her waitressing days.

"The lamb was delicious," Claudia told her. "You're the only person who's ever made it for us."

"Bud said it was your favorite." Then, as an afterthought: "And I do like it myself."

After dessert they had coffee in the living room, and Matt asked if he could see what Bud had done to the upstairs. Lucille turned to her son, opened her mouth to speak, then closed it.

"Sure," said Bud, "but all I've finished is my room and the bathroom."

"Yes," his mother said quickly. "Don't show him my room. It's such a mess right now."

To Matt, the bathroom was an imaginative gem, the walls covered with light gray barnsiding, the plumbing fixtures impeccable antiques: the toilet had an overhead tank and pull chain. "Had a hell of a time putting that in," said Bud. "The hardest work is being patient."

"My God, you really are a craftsman."

His bedroom was pale yellow with a large multicolored Moroccan rug in the center of it. The desk and drawing board faced the window and the chest of drawers was angled against the far corner. The narrow bed ran along one wall, and therefore the middle of the room appeared hollow and austere. When Matt did not immediately offer comment Bud spoke up. "This is my cell," he said with a grin. "I've purposely kept it as empty as possible so I have room to pace. When I hit a snag in something I have to start moving around."

Matt thought of that last afternoon in Terry's room, the boy lying indolent on the bed with a cigarette hanging from his lips and looking as if he were never going to move again, as if he would go to seed among his nude centerfolds and cheap music. Matt imagined the only thing that would make his son pace the room was a failure to make a drug connection. Although he told himself comparisons were unfair—unnecessary—he could not pull back from drawing them.

"This is my sister's room," said Bud, switching on the light. "Just as she left it." Plainly appointed in brown and beige, its only feminine distinction was the frilly bedspread.

Bud led him to the stairs. "We'll honor her wishes and skip her room," he said, nodding in the direction of the far end of the hall.

They all had a second cup of coffee, and during it Matt thought Lucille looked stiff and agitated. The arthritis, he assumed, and he admired the way she camouflaged the discomfort and went on with her duties as hostess. He admired, too, Bud's helpfulness and made another comparison to Terry.

As they walked to their cars he accepted Claudia's invitation for a nightcap. When they were settled into her living room she asked him if he had enjoyed himself.

"Yes, as a matter of fact. But I wonder if Lucille did. Toward the end there she looked like she was in pain."

"Maybe. Aside from that, though, she never seems to really relax. She's so eager to please, like we were rich relations or something. But she's very fond of Joanne and that's what counts."

"It took me a long time to get even this close to her," said Joanne. "She's so shy. Now with the illness she's even more withdrawn."

"Before you got there I had to really work up conversation with her," said Matt. He paused, then added: "She told me Bud's father won't be coming to the wedding. She said Bud and Gail don't see or hear from him anymore."

"Bud's never seen him at all," said Joanne.

"What do you mean, 'never'?"

"He left before Bud was born."

"But he must have come back to see them."

"No. He lives somewhere near Detroit. For a few years Gail would go to vist him, like once every summer, but Bud never did."

"Why not?"

"His father never wanted to see him. Apparently, he left because he didn't want Lucille to have another baby. When she wouldn't get an abortion he walked out and never came back."

"Did she ever divorce him?"

"Finally. When Bud was three or four."

Claudia sighed. "Lucille hasn't had it easy. Being deserted that way and for that reason. She never did remarry and, God knows, she must have had a few chances."

"But don't you think it's strange she'd let her daughter visit the man when he wouldn't see his own son?"

The look Claudia gave him said Let's drop it—who are we to question her? Their eyes locked for only a second, just long enough to acknowledge their one mutual failure.

She picked up the two bowls of cocktail nuts and the cups and saucers, using her left arm as a shelf as she had done for years, delivering lunch and dinner orders at the restaurant. When she reached the kitchen Bud was filling the sink with water.

"Leave those," she said. "The new dishwasher's being delivered tomorrow."

"These glasses should be done by hand."

"I can do them in the morning."

He did not answer but continued the washing. She took her armload to the side counter, dumped the nuts into a large can, and snapped on the plastic lid. "Well, I think everything went smoothly."

"Except for getting the wine," he said pointedly.

"I said I was sorry about that," she murmured.

"It was on the list I gave you. Third item from the bottom."

"I must have passed over it."

His head did not move but his eyes slid sideways to find the next dirty glass. "You must have had other things on your mind."

She breathed deeply but did not reply. She put the nuts in the cupboard and the carton of cream in the refrigerator, then said: "Don't bother with the cups. I have to go to bed now. I'm exhausted."

She left him there, switched off the lights in the dining room and front hall, and started up the stairs, chiding herself. It was so stupid to have forgotten the wine, far stupider to have left the list at home—idiotically careless not to have checked it when she came back with the groceries. For months he had been waiting for one tiny confirmation of his suspicions, and today she had given it to him, dropped it right into his lap. Now, he would be watching her even more closely.

She washed her face and brushed her teeth and thought about the evening. She had been unprepared for encountering Matt Sessions alone, and she did not like his curiosity about her and Bud's father. He had appeared satisfied with what she said, but he could still be trouble. And the single announcement she hoped and waited for daily had not come: a definite wedding date.

Oh, God, she said silently, let it *at least* be September.

She took four aspirins to combat the pain in her hips and knees.

At her bedroom door she unfastened the top button of her blouse, slipped her thumb and forefinger between her breasts and withdrew a key which she inserted into the cylinder lock. She swung the door open and paused for a moment with her hand on the knob, debating whether or not to get a glass of water for her bedside. She decided she was too tired even to be awakened by thirst.

Then she closed the door quietly and locked it again from the inside.

On Sunday morning, Bud arrived at Matt's apartment an hour before dawn, determined to work as long as was necessary to finish every last detail. Matt had promised to stay away—at Adele's, no doubt—so there would be no interruptions.

His energy was boundless, for this was truly a labor of love.

He had already painted every wall, supervised the laying of the new carpeting, installed the track lighting with a dimmer switch, and put up the five free-hanging bookshelves on the wall opposite the sofa. Now, he began to nail in the decorative molding around the ceilings, an easy task and a finishing touch that the builder should have provided in the first place. By midafternoon the wallpapering of the bathroom was done. He went down to the parking lot to his car and brought up the bleached-cypress boards that had been precut for quick assembly: within an hour they became a large rectangular coffee table.

At four-thirty he walked around the living room, down the hallway, into the bathroom and lavatory, and back again, all the time willing himself to be as critical as possible. Convinced at last that he had judged everything with the eyes of others, he allowed himself a broad smile of satisfaction. Pleasure and fatigue settled upon him simultaneously, but there was one last detail to accomplish before leaving.

From a large cardboard box he withdrew seven pictures, all in frames that matched but were smaller than the frame of the picture he and Joanne had recently given to Matt. These seven were enlargements of photographs he had borrowed from Claudia's collection. She appeared in five, Matt in five, he himself in four, Terry in one, and Joanne in all of them. He did not want to clutter the walls of the living room which, of course, would have been the obvious place to hang them. He chose instead Matt's bedroom, on the wall above the dresser and opposite the bed. The large one of him and Joanne was centered with the others flanking it like satellites. He stood back, walked here and there, assessed the arrangement from every conceivable angle, and as he did, his eyes kept returning to his two favorites. In one, he was seated on the sofa with his arms around Joanne and Claudia while Matt stood behind leaning over him. In the second and more candid one, taken at the engagement party, his and Joanne's faces were in profile, her thumb at the corner of his mouth wiping away cake icing.

The glow he felt was so intense it could not be diminished even by a glimpse of Terry whose surly, unsmiling face he hated. He had known the boy only seven months before his death, but that had been long enough to fathom what he was: a spoiled, self-indulgent, ungrateful weakling who appreciated neither the parents nor the home he had. The early death was not in itself unjust, for the boy had courted it with his addiction. No, the tragedy lay in the consequences for Joanne, Claudia, and Matt. Matt would not have turned to another woman if Claudia had not turned him out—and behind all of it was Terry.

The longer he looked at that face, the more he realized that this boy should have been *his* mother's son. They were certainly made of the same selfish stuff.

He turned away and made a final tour of the apartment. He knew he had done a better job than anyone Matt could have hired. Matt would offer him money again, and again he would refuse it. This was his gift, an unspoken repayment for being admitted into the family—the kind of family he had always deserved.

As he drove home, his thoughts shifted reluctantly to his mother. After six years of good behavior—false behavior—she was up to her old tricks again, not caring in the least that she might ruin his happiness and good fortune. But then, she had never cared about that. Still, he was not going to allow her to shame him before Joanne, Claudia, and Matt.

There was still time before the wedding to get to the bottom of what she was up to. And to put a stop to it.

6

The following afternoon Matt lied to Adele for the first time since he had known her. He called her from work and said the day had been horrible, everything had gone wrong, and that he felt he was coming down with a virus. All he wanted to do was to get to his apartment, soak in the tub, and climb into bed. Her voice grew distant when he refused her offer to make him soup at her place and then tuck him in early.

"All right," she said, "but call me before you go to bed and let me know how you're feeling."

He wanted to see and relax alone in the final results of Bud's work. And he needed to regain his composure which, of late, was riddled with apprehension. There was the impending separation from Adele and still the lack of will and words to initiate it. There was Judy's open resentment over having agreed to Adele's counteroffer to the prospective buyers that had sent them running to buy another house; now reduced to the asking price Judy originally wanted, there were still no takers. And there was the upcoming lunch date with Ted Brainard, two weeks away, that would require the almost impossible balancing of "understanding" and noninvolvement.

He opened the door of the apartment, found the dimmer switch, and stood still in amazement. At first sight, and then the realization deepening the longer he looked, it was apparent that

Bud had read his need more clearly than he himself had. The light gray-and-beige motif—accented with brown, cream, and dark red in the pillows, lamps, and vases—managed to be both softly inviting and as practical as a corporate conference room. He turned the dimmer up full and watched the whole room flood, then adjusted it to low and saw how the lights were angled to illuminate the vertical blinds at the sliding glass door, the stereo console, the vase of silk flowers near the hallway, and the teacart in the corner that served as a bar. Silk flowers, they looked real and fresh and required no care. The cypress coffee table, elegant yet rugged, was the kind of thing you could put your feet on without having to kick your shoes off.

Matt had expected quality but he had not expected this: the kind of apartment you hated to leave in the morning and that you raced to at night.

He turned on the radio, sat down with a drink and the evening paper, and discovered that on the coffee table Bud had left him four copies of *Architectural Digest*. He put aside the paper and began to thumb through one of the magazines. By ten o'clock he had had three drinks and read nine articles. He had never been interested in houses although until three years ago he had always lived in them, and despite the fact they were Adele's passion and she always talked about them. But now he read with a new curiosity and fascination, thinking all the while that perhaps he should take up a hobby in which he would have to use his hands.

The telephone rang on the kitchen wall.

"You're still up?" said Adele. "I thought you were going to bed early."

"Just about to."

"We sound very mellow," she teased.

"I'm having a nightcap with my aspirin." God, he thought, I haven't eaten yet. With the receiver tucked between his ear and shoulder he set about to make himself a sandwich.

"I wanted to let you know that Judy might start calming down now. The people who looked at it today are putting a binder on it tomorrow morning."

"Good, good."

There was a pause. Did she suspect his deceptions, his plan to leave her?

"Call me in the morning," she said, "and let me know how you feel."

He ate the sandwich hurriedly, without tasting, without caring to taste. He should have called her earlier to say he was on his way to bed. And then another lapse in duty occurred to him: he had not called Bud to thank him, to tell him how pleased he was. He dialed while he swallowed the last corner of his meal.

He started off with the excuse that he was so overwhelmed with the beauty and comfort of the place he had simply sat admiring it and, in the dimmed light, gone to sleep on the sofa.

"I really don't have the words to tell you how pleased I am. But if you're free tomorrow night I'd like you and Joanne to come by and then I'll take you to dinner."

"Sure, we'll come. But let's eat there." Bud chuckled. "The whole point, Matt, was to make it comfortable for everything. Just broil a steak and bake some potatoes."

"You're right. Good idea. Seven o'clock?"

"Okay. Uh—shall I ask Claudia to come too?"

"Oh . . . sure." Shame flushed through him. Claudia had never been invited here because he was ashamed of it. But now—why hadn't he thought of it himself, considering how many times she had had him for dinner? Remiss for the third time tonight. Was he becoming so self-centered?

"See you at seven."

After hanging up, Bud stood still and basked in the echo of Matt's praise. Overwhelmed—yes, he knew Matt would be, that that was the natural initial reaction. Gradually, he would arrive at a greater appreciation when he found the practicality and comfort matched the visuals.

He left the kitchen, entered the dining room where his mother sat with a cup of tea and a magazine next to it. His gaze pushed on past her to the sideboard where one of the drawer handles was coming loose. He went to the basement and returned with the screwdriver.

As he worked at tightening all the handles he kept her at the edge of his vision. She appeared to be wholly absorbed in what she was reading; the absorption, he knew, might be real or feigned. He gave the magazine a brief contemptuous look of recognition. It was one of those inane women's publications with recipes, diets, fashions, and pedestrian flower arrangements. It would never occur to her to read a news magazine or to own a library card, as Claudia did. But then, it would never occur to her to behave as Claudia did either. She had had the chance to, or at least the opportunity to learn, when Claudia on several occasions invited her to join her circle of friends and offered to teach her golf and bridge. She had refused with her most convenient excuse—she had to work. She had never had to work. She had chosen to. And what she chose was to be a waitress.

She flipped the page, glanced up, and casually asked how many handles had loosened.

"Just one."

She flipped a few more pages and began to read. He had lived with her long enough to know that casualness was her ground-cover for guilt; now it was being used to hide her guilty whereabouts this afternoon. With disgust, pity, even bitter amusement, he evaluated how limited she was, how incapable of discarding this old act for a new one.

Upstairs, he sat at his desk with an open textbook before him. Occasionally his concentration would waver and give way to the evidence of the afternoon. He had called the house at two o'clock. There was no answer, just as there had been no answer the seven previous times—erratically spaced—that he had calied at the same hour. He would not confront her and let her lie, not because her lying insulted him but because it only disgraced her further. He knew why she was not home at two. She was with a man, the one she had been seeing secretly for at least the past four months.

Be patient, be careful, he cautioned himself silently. She'll show her hand soon, and if not you'll find a way to make her do it.

At eleven o'clock he heard her go into the bathroom, come out again, then close the door to her room. He listened for the turn of the cylinder lock, and when it came he closed his eyes and shook his head. It was so pathetic, her assuming that there was anything in that room he wanted to see or get his hands on—more pathetic for her to believe that a lock could stop him.

A little before midnight he closed the book and got up to brush his teeth.

Wiping his mouth on a towel he glanced at her shower cap hanging on a wall hook. He stared at it for nearly a minute: it had a floral pattern similar to the one in the bathing suit she wore on that August day ten years ago, the day she fully revealed herself by letting him know that she wanted him dead.

Claudia could not come because of the meeting she and Margaret Brainard had to attend at Mrs. Richardson's. When the couple arrived, Joanne told Matt how deeply involved her mother was getting.

"She and Margaret do public relations. They make the rounds to stores in all the shopping malls trying to convince the managers to put up the group's warning posters. They're not having much luck but they're out there pitching."

"Why no luck?" asked Matt.

"They think the posters will distract the customers from the merchandise. Anyway, the important thing is she's keeping busy and enjoying it."

Bud was not listening to this at all. He was looking up at the corners of the ceiling. "You know, Matt, I'm not sure now if those moldings are quite right. They could really be larger and a little more elaborate. Maybe concave instead of convex. And with a groove or two."

"Bud, they're fine just the way they are. Really. I'm more than pleased with everything you've done."

"I don't know," he murmured, his eyes still investigating.

"The perfectionist," Joanne said with a smirk. "He worries every detail to death."

By the time he was ready to broil the steak Matt found he had overbaked the potatoes. They sounded like rocks when he dropped them onto the countertop. "Damn, damn!" he hissed, furious at himself.

"Take is easy," said Bud, squeezing his shoulder. "Plenty of butter and sour cream will moisten them up."

"Hell, you do a first-rate job on this place and I can't even fix you a decent meal."

"It'll be fine." He grinned. "Stop stewing over it or you'll burn the steak."

After the meal Bud had another beer and asked Matt what he planned to do with the small bedroom. "You know, that furniture's way too big for it."

"Yes. Maybe just a twin bed and a small chest of drawers. Now that this room is so comfortable I don't really need a den."

He and Bud took Joanne into the large bedroom to show her the picture arrangement on the wall. She advanced up close to it, looked at each one, and when she lingered at the frame that housed Terry, Matt's heart began to sink. But he was instantly revived when she turned around with a smile.

"Very, very nice." Then she said they really must go; there was studying she had to do for tomorrow night's quiz.

"Why on earth did you take a night class?" asked Matt.

"Because the morning section interfered with the Age of Pope." She saw his lingering concern and pressed his arm. "Don't worry. Bud takes me and picks me up."

"That's pretty inconvenient."

"No, it's not. I study at the library while she's in class."

Matt wanted fresh air and offered to walk out with them.

Bud had had to park in the far corner of the lot. It was the darkest area, and for the past two weeks it had been even darker due to a burned-out light attached to one of the carports. When the three of them arrived at the car they found one of the rear tires flat.

"Hell," said Matt, "it couldn't have happened on a colder night."

"Better here than on the road," replied Bud.

Matt thought: What if this happened on his way to pick up Joanne from class? He pushed Judy out of his mind and turned his attention to the business at hand. "Go back inside, Joanne." He handed her his keys. "I'll stay and help."

She went across the lot to the building while Bud opened the trunk and pulled out the jack and the spare.

"What can I do?"

"Would you get the flashlight out of the glove compartment."

It was not in the glove compartment. Bud was busy prying at the hubcap, so Matt searched under the passenger seat. Nothing. But when he slid his hand under the driver seat one of his fingers was poked by a sharp corner of a small square object. He withdrew it and saw that it was a flat packet containing a prophylactic. With a curious mingling of amusement and distaste he felt the ringed formation under the foil.

"Find it?" The hubcap clanged onto the pavement.

"It's not in here." He replaced the packet where he had found it.

"Look on the floor of the back seat."

There, among a scattering of tools, was the flashlight.

His body trembled in the frigid wind but he held the beam steady for Bud until the last bolt was tightened.

After they were gone he took a hot shower and sat in the living room with the lights dimmed and the radio on. He could not get the foil packet out of his head; he supposed it was because he had never thought of them having sex, not in any graphic terms. He wondered if they could be so naive as to believe that those outdated things provided real safety. Hadn't Claudia ever discussed "protection" with Joanne? Hadn't Bud been told—no, there was no father to tell him and Lucille did not look the type a son could approach with this matter. Still, there was sex education these days and surely Bud had friends he talked with . . . .

Well, he decided, it was *their* business and if anything did happen they were getting married anyway. There was no point in adding another worry to his roster.

The dead-white glare from the sunless January sky was barred from the motel room by a thick drapery, but it pushed through the frosted glass of the bathroom in which Ted Brainard was showering. When he got out and dried off he dabbed lightly at the scars where the cancerous lymph nodes had been removed. They were, of course, not at all fragile but he pampered them out of respect and awe. They were proof that God or fate or mere chance had sentenced him to death and then spared him. That was his first reprieve. The woman in the adjoining room was his second.

He slung the damp towel over the rack and placed a fresh one and a washcloth on the edge of the basin for her. He then opened the door and softly approached his clothes that lay on the bed they hadn't used. She was sound asleep in the other one. As he dressed he checked his watch and calculated that he could let her sleep another fifteen minutes. And, he knew, she definitely needed it. Her health was more of a concern to him than his own.

Fully clothed, he sat on the undisturbed bed and stared at her. His body was sated, he was assured of her love, and still he tingled with desperation—the kind that comes from having stumbled upon unlooked-for good fortune and then being afraid it will disappear.

He got up, knelt beside her, gently pressed her hand. "Time to wake up," he whispered. She stirred, nodded without opening her eyes, and began to drift off again. "It's twenty to three, Lucille."

A direct statement of time always roused her. She got out of bed on the other side and walked swiftly to the bathroom. He listened to the shower run, passed his hand over her skirt and sweater, and thought of how his desperation would subside if he had half the hold on her that her son did. Repeatedly, she made it clear that they could not consider marriage until Bud was married. He kept wishing that Bud and Joanne would elope, although he knew that people didn't do that anymore.

She came out, smiled at him as she dressed hurriedly, then returned to the bathroom to comb her hair.

"Can I see you Thursday?" he called.

"I think so. I'll call you in the morning. Ten-thirty."

As usual. Never, under any circumstances, was he to phone her.

Ready to leave, they kissed at the door and he felt the rigidity return to her body. She hated motels, particularly the entering and the exiting—even now, being twelve miles outside the city. But soon he hoped to have an arrangement that would eliminate the need for motels.

Her hands stopped sweating, her grip on the steering wheel slackened to normal when she realized she was running ten minutes ahead of schedule. It was only three-ten and Bud would not be home until five to four. Plenty of time to relax and shed the "just-got-in" look.

But her heart sank and her breathing stopped when she turned into the driveway and she saw his Nova at the end of it. As soon as she switched off the ignition she looked again at her watch, raised it to her ear, and heard it ticking.

How could he be home? He would never cut a class! Slow down, she told herself, don't panic: it's the panic he always looks for.

She managed to walk slowly to the back door although her legs felt no more substantial than paper.

He was not on the first floor. She opened the door to the basement, descended to the fourth step from which she could see his workbench in the far corner. He must be up in his room. If only he would stay there until dinner.

She was peeling potatoes when he appeared in the doorway. Her voice even, she said: "You were home early. You didn't cut a class, did you?"

"It was cancelled."

He stood there, volunteering no explanation for the cancellation, and she would not ask for one either. "Dinner will be ready at six."

He took a stalk of celery from the refrigerator and went back upstairs. Her hands stopped working the paring knife on the potato skin. Through the window she watched a small flock of sparrows investigate the breadcrumbs she had thrown onto the hardened snow just before she went off to meet Ted. One bird went directly to a crumb larger than its head and tried to fly off with it. When the crumb fell, it made a second and third attempt. "Don't bite off more than you can chew," she muttered almost sardonically. As though it had heard her, the sparrow abandoned the prize for a smaller, more manageable one.

Upstairs, Bud braced himself against his desk and breathed deeply for control so as not to confront her. The heat of his emotion was fired by the tug-of-war in his blood, the struggle between satisfaction and outrage: satisfaction that she was confirming everything and proving him right, outrage that she carelessly overlooked details that he did not. In the kitchen he had seen the damp and matted half-moon curl of her hair sticking out incorrigibly in the back. Somewhere this afternoon she had taken a shower or a bath and in her haste not bothered to use her fingers to check the extremities of her hair. It was just like her to expect a few strokes of a comb to return her to respectability. . . .

She had cheated him out of a father, a normal childhood; he was not about to let her cheat him out of Matt and Claudia's respect and have that respect dissolve into pity when they discovered what she really was. The thought that in a few years she would be a grandmother and still the *same* filled him with revulsion.

The damp curl leered at him, coaxing him to imagine exactly what went on this afternoon. He paced, then dropped to the floor and did pushups until his arms were numb. But his fury was not vented in the least. It merely left his chest to become a hardened knot in the pit of his stomach.

Adele looked across the table at Matt. "I wish you'd say it."

"Say what?"

"Whatever's going on in that head of yours. First, we plan to eat at home and then at the last minute you press for Pierre's. Second, you've said about six words since we got here. Third, you haven't looked me in the eye once. Need I go on?"

He had decided not to make the announcement at her house where he could easily be undermined by tears, argument, and his own temptation. Meeting in public was the coward's way out and gave him an unfair advantage, but it was also the only way to let his reason prevail. He pushed aside his half-eaten pâté. "Let's wait until after dinner."

"Let's not. Suspense has never been good for my digestion."

"Adele, I . . . want us to separate."

She put down her fork. "That's a cute way of putting it. Better than saying 'I want to leave you.'"

"Not want to—*have* to." He fisted one hand and cupped it with the other. He was stranded in the silence; she at least had a cigarette to retreat to.

After three drags she asked: "May I assume this is not a sudden decision?"

"It's not."

"Are you going back to Claudia?"

"Don't be silly. You know what my reasons are."

She said nothing, only stared and smoked, waiting.

"I made certain things clear to you soon after we met. I also told you not to expect me to change my mind."

"Self-fulfilling prophecy," she muttered.

"You're sadly mistaken if you think this is easy for me."

"I would hope it's not easy for you to be this foolish. But on second thought, maybe it's easier than you're letting on. I think probably the rest of your life will be devoted to finding the easiest way out of—or into—any situation. It's such a waste, Matt. You're too good for the easy way."

His temper flared. "Is wanting some *peace* so terrible? You're young, Adele, you haven't—"

"—been through a lot of things. Yes, yes, yes, we know that song. Now I'll tell *you* something. A lot of people lose their children and some of them in worse ways than you lost Terry. And plenty of them manage to still have a life and not crawl into a shell to hide."

"I lost more than Terry—in a space of twenty-four hours I lost my family! Everything I worked for and believed in went up in smoke and suddenly I had two judges telling me I'd been wrong, *always* been wrong. I don't need any more judges, especially one in the cradle."

"So, what's it going to be? Going to look for a woman who doesn't want a family? There's enough of them around."

"I'm not going to look for anyone."

"Don't kid yourself. Some people are happy living alone, but you're not one of them. Besides, with the kind of life you're planning, there will have to be someone to bring you your hot milk and rub in the Ben-Gay."

The waiter brought the entrées, but neither of them reached for the silverware.

"Your mind's made up completely?"

Her tone of defeat made him cringe: he had never seen her defeated by anything. "Yes, completely." He looked at the rack of lamb. "I *told* you I wanted to wait until after dinner."

"Go ahead and eat," she said stonily. "Look at it as the Last Supper. You be Judas."

"Don't turn the knife, Adele."

"I won't cry, I won't make a scene, but I'll turn the knife all I want."

They drove to her house in total silence. When they turned into the driveway he said, "What I've decided is only fair."

"Strange, isn't it, how this 'fairness' cheats us both. Do you want your razor and toothbrush?"

He would not be lured inside. "No."

"I'll keep them then. As a reminder to stay away from the shell-shocked. Goodbye, Matt."

Next to the beam of the headlights she walked toward the house, rummaging through her purse for her keys. He saw her fumble at the door, watched one hand lift to wipe her eyes. Keeping her head turned from him she raised her other arm and with two sharp jerks of it motioned for him to get going.

Back in his apartment he sat down with a drink and put his feet up on the cypress coffee table. "Cheats us both": but she would be cheated only temporarily, until the right man appeared with every capability of giving her what she wanted. For himself, there would be . . .

Well, for starters, there was this new "home." One thing at a time.

He looked about him and then at his feet resting on the table. Comfort. Peace. He lifted his glass and toasted the room, gratified that *someone* understood his needs.

When Bud's car backed out of the driveway and the sound of it faded down the street, Lucille put aside her magazine and rubbed her aching knees. The pain always had two variations. Sometimes she felt as if dry ice had been injected in her bones, burning and freezing them; at other times, it seemed that an electric buzzer were going off in her joints. Today she was feeling the buzzer.

Bud had awakened early that morning, at seven, and stayed in the house until now, four-thirty, working on a lamp down at his workbench before coming up here to the living room to read—and watch her. Her pain had started at midmorning and she clenched her body against it so as not to give him any hint. Whenever he saw her pain there was a struggle in his eyes between satisfaction and sympathy. That struggle sickened her because it lay bare her own shame: if she were ever to come upon him broken and bleeding, her own emotions might be solidly divided.

She looked at the enormous poinsettia at the window and recalled the four-day respite at Christmas when she had gone to visit her daughter in Orion, sixty miles away. Gail, already an officer in a bank and preoccupied with a new romance, had not thought it in the least strange that Bud should want to stay home and near Joanne. Bud and Gail got along quite well, like many brothers and sisters whose lives take different paths and who respect but do not love each other. During her stay Lucille had said nothing about Ted, or Bud's watchfulness. This matter was strictly between her and Bud, just as in the past the matter of Fred, of Hugh, of Walter had been. Bud had used different methods for getting rid of each one—different methods, but she herself was always his instrument. She was determined not to become his instrument again.

If it were any other man but Ted she could, at this last chance in her life, stand up to Bud and say "I want him, I mean to have him, I don't care what you think." But Bud would never accept the absolute coincidence of the man being Ted. He would suspect her of having gone after him when in fact the pursuit had been the opposite. And the irony of their initial meeting would only infuriate Bud: she and Ted laid eyes on each other for the first time at the engagement party Claudia had given.

She continued to rub her knees and remembered the day she had told Bud the doctor's diagnosis and warning. She needn't have said anything but perhaps the reason she had was to balance the scale, to affirm that she was paying—in terms he might consider appropriate—for that day ten years ago. Instead he had given her a look that said "Do you expect this to make any difference?" Nothing *would* make a difference except his marriage to Joanne. It would be her own release from him. Her gratitude to the girl, however, was for a good deal more than that. She herself had lived with her son's hatred for so long that she had come to doubt his capacity for any other emotion. Then, almost miraculously, Joanne appeared in their lives and tapped some hidden root in the boy and made it flower. Claudia, to some degree, had done the same. His tenderness, his devotion to both of them made his hatred of *her* totally bearable, and the past three-and-a-half years had been the most tranquil since his birth. She guarded her pleasure and concealed the magnitude of it, for fear that Bud, to spite her, might spite himself and leave Joanne. She hoped that his love was stronger than his hate, but she had no intention of gambling.

Only now she *was* gambling, with Ted. Perhaps the calm of the past three years had lulled her into believing that Bud was preoccupied and no longer watching her. And when she had stopped resisting Ted and began to see him regularly she made every attempt to carry on as usual. But Bud's perceptions were not in the least dimmed by his involvement with Joanne. It was as if she gave off a scent, mingling joy and fear, that he detected at once. Within two weeks of her first meeting with Ted she was aware of Bud's probing gaze across the dinner table, his calculated silences, his waiting for her inability to meet his challenging eyes.

The furnace clicked on and the heat crackled softly in the register. She looked at the room around her. A beautiful room, a beautiful house—everyone said so. And how could she refute them? Who would believe that everything in it had been meticulously planned as a punishment, imprisonment? There wasn't a stick of furniture or a lamp or even an ashtray that *she* had chosen. After Bud got rid of Walter he spent a year on the "facelift," painting and reconstructing during those hours she worked at the restaurant. It was, she knew, meant as a reward to her for having dropped Walter so readily and without a fight.

Only now, she *would* fight. Fight the impulse to drop Ted and return to a safe but empty tranquillity.

After Bud was married, the break with her old life would be complete. She and Ted would not live in this house or in this city. He wanted to take her to Florida or Arizona to get her away from the winters; he had no idea that she had something much more debilitating to get away from. He wanted to take care of her and she was ready to be taken care of.

Whenever she dared to think their escape possible, she felt capable of enduring anything. Even when the specter of Ted's wife threatened to halt her, she could still go forward with the plan by telling herself if she let guilt rule her now Ted might very well find another woman to leave Margaret for. Having seen her only once, at the engagement party, she knew that her best protection was never to see her again.

She could even push herself past the certainty of Claudia and Matt's hard disapproval of her: she and her prize would be thousands of miles away.

It *was* possible. During the months she would have to wait, patience and extreme caution would be strenuous. But in the long run they would prove to have been a very low price for the future they bought.

7

Four days after the breakup Judy came into Matt's office to ask if what Adele had told her was true. He confirmed it, and she stood rooted and wide-eyed. Pained by her reaction and flustered by her silence, he asked how the proceedings were going on the sale of her house. She only nodded, making that answer enough, then turned and left.

During the empty nights since the one at Pierre's, Judy and Jane Richardson had been on his mind when Adele wasn't. And each morning as he drove to the station he singled out one statement from Judy's "confession": "If I hadn't done that program with her it might not have happened." He wanted to tell Jane but knew he could not. He broke into a sweat each time he deduced that if harmless Judy could become a victim then Jane, the diligent activist, would be a prime target for the rapist.

He did not want to call her "hotline," but her private number was not listed in the directory or with information. But after rummaging through his desk he found the number she had given him while they were working on her program.

"Hello, Jane, it's Matt Sessions . . . thank you, and a belated Happy New Year to you too. I wanted to speak to you about something—I don't know why it didn't occur to me before. For the past few weeks I've been thinking— "He went on to say that her television appearance and the article the local newspaper did on her might antagonize this rapist into a retaliation against her. He was surprised when she chuckled.

"Well, I appreciate your concern, Matt. But surely you must realize I've gotten plenty of hate mail since I started the group. And a million crank calls."

"But that's—so dangerous."

"I wouldn't say *so* dangerous. I'd be a little worried if anyone sent me a letter here at home, but so far they've all come to the post office box I keep for the group's business. And the crank calls come on the hotline number, never on my personal one. I'm unlisted."

"I know. Don't you report all this to the police?"

"I give them the letters. They offered to put a tap on the hotline but I can't allow that. It would violate the privacy of those women who want to remain anonymous."

"You've got more guts than I would have."

Again she chuckled. "I'll tell Hippolyta you said so. A statement like that from any man pleases her to no end. By the way, I'm very happy to have Claudia and Margaret in the group. They're going to be real assets."

"I'm sure they will be. And if there's anything *I* can do to help you out, don't hesitate to let me know."

"All right, do you happen to play bridge?"

"Well, yes . . . "

"Are you free Sunday night?"

"I think so."

"Good. I've been playing for years with these friends of mine, a couple, and *he* always likes another man at the table. Our regular fourth has left us."

"I'm not an expert, but I'd enjoy it."

"We play for fun, not blood," she said.

"I'll look forward to it."

A gift, this invitation. If the evening proved successful maybe he could become the permanent fourth.

Since the split with Adele he had mailed off four magazine subscription forms and had read three paperbacks. It was time he got out of his apartment in the evening, and he did not want to wait until Sunday. Singles bars had depressed him before he had met Adele; he knew he would be able to tolerate them even less now. He decided to go to a movie.

The one he chose was playing a block from the university campus. He had dinner in a restaurant nearby and was bolstered by the fact that half the patrons were eating alone, appearing perfectly content to do so.

The movie laid little claim to his attention. He counted the half-dozen times he and Adele had gone to the movies, then tried to remember the names of them. He thought about Judy and her avoidance of him. He looked forward to Sunday night at Jane Richardson's.

He came out of the theater and departed from the crowd at the first corner. Waiting for the walk light he glanced aimlessly up the street. His recognition of the color and the grill of the approaching car barely registered before he saw the driver go past. It was Bud, heading for the entrance to campus. Matt remembered: this was Wednesday. Joanne's class got out at ten. He glanced at his watch. It was almost ten after.

Driving home, he was annoyed first with Bud, then with himself. Why would Bud, so meticulous at everything and so devoted to Joanne, allow himself to be late picking her up? Well, he reasoned, this is probably the first time it's happened and why are *you* laboring over it? He recalled how, for a long time, he had fantasized Adele's death in her overturned convertible—most likely a lingering fear from Terry's accident.

Nonetheless, he called Claudia's at ten-forty-five, on the pretext of asking who her cleaning woman was. She provided the name and an overlong hymn about the woman's thoroughness and efficiency, but what Matt listened to and was reassured by were the voices in the background, Joanne's and Bud's. He chided himself for this foolishness, poured a nightcap, and set his thoughts to how he was going to handle Ted at lunch tomorrow.

Ted was halfway through a club soda—with three olives in it—when Matt slid into the booth. He ordered a white wine, and after the waitress brought it he glanced about the handsome room that was humming with conversation. "Nice place," he said. "This is where Bud's mother used to work."

"Is it?" Ted took a long swallow and shifted in his seat. He looked uncertainly at Matt. "Claudia told us you and Adele have split up."

"That's right."

"Was it an argument?"

"No. And it's not a temporary separation."

"Do you want to talk about it?"

"No." He realized from Ted's face that he was being overly cool and abrupt. "I mean I'd rather not, for the time being."

"Has, uh, Joanne decided on a wedding date yet?"

"Nothing definite. Sometime in the fall."

A pause.

"What do you think of Claudia and Margaret being in this women's group?" said Ted.

"It's certainly a worthwhile activity."

"It's all Margaret talks about lately. She's the last person I'd have expected to become community-minded."

"People change."

Ted looked hard into Matt's eyes. When he spoke, his voice was lowered to a more intimate register. "I'd like to drop the charade and level with each other."

"About what?"

"About the fact I've wanted to talk to you for some time now and you don't want me to."

"What makes you think that?"

"I'm a lawyer, Matt. Maybe not the greatest one in the world but I can read unwillingness a mile away. Since you met Adele our friendship has changed. Been altered, really. I regret it but I guess it's to be expected. Obviously, you didn't need anyone else but her. Now, *I* know the feeling."

Matt took a long swallow of wine and ached for a cigarette.

"The difference is I'll never separate from her." Ted lowered his voice further. "It must be a strain for you to be without Adele, even if it's no more than the change of routine. I don't want to add to your troubles, but I need to tell you something. And I need a favor. I've met a woman I want to marry."

"Marry—!"

"She wants to marry me too, but she has complications that require us to wait."

"You mean like a husband?"

"No. Relatives."

"Does Margaret know?"

"She suspects *something*, but I've been very careful. I don't want to go into it with her until my plans are definite."

And leave her dangling until *you're* ready, thought Matt. But before this censure could harden he realized that dangling was precisely what he had done to Adele. "What's the favor?" he asked.

"It's not easy for me to ask. And I want you to know I'll repay you in any way I can. You're absolutely the only one I can trust and I—"

"What's the favor, Ted?"

"I'd like you to let me use your apartment a few afternoons a week. Until we're able to work something else out."

"What arrangement have you had up to this point?" His own voice surprised him; the tone was one Margaret might use if she knew.

"We've gone to motels. But she's . . . well, delicate. For her, motels seem to taint the situation."

How quaint, thought Matt, the old-fashioned type even while she's after another woman's husband. He wondered if Ted would dare ask this favor if he had a house instead of an apartment. "And what explanation do I give Margaret if she finds out?"

"She won't find out, I promise you. This favor is just between you and me. Even this woman won't know it's your place. We won't go beyond that little second bedroom."

"My name is on the bell downstairs."

"Not at the rear entrance."

What thoroughness—a legal mind in every respect. "Why don't you just rent a small place for yourself. You can well afford it."

"Several reasons. It would mean a separate checking account. Landlords are suspicious of cash and money orders. And there's the chance a landlord or someone in the building would find out who I am—a successful lawyer with a wife, a big house, sizable assets, all of which could add up to petty blackmail."

"How could you be blackmailed if you're planning to marry this woman?"

"Because we have to wait a while, until she can work out some family complications."

"How long will that take?"

"We don't know yet. I'd just want the arrangement long enough to figure out something else. As I said, you're the only person I can trust."

"Lucky me."

Ted closed his eyes and when he opened them they were all supplication. "Matt, ever since the illness and the operation I've been treading water, grateful to be alive but with no real reason to be—clichéd as that may sound. Margaret and I used to be a lot alike, and because of that we had a good marriage for a long time. But I've changed and I can't help it, just as she can't help being the same."

The same? Matt questioned silently. She never used to drink the way she does now.

"She wants parties, she wants to travel, she wants to be surrounded by people and activity. I'm just the opposite and this woman wants what I want. Naturally there are differences, but under the surface there's—a kinship. We can be together and not say a single word for the longest time. Margaret can't live through a full minute of silence. And, well, it's embarrassing, but I feel we're like brother and sister and I don't want to spend the rest of my life with a sister."

"And how will Margaret spend *her* life?"

"I don't know, Matt. She doesn't want to lose me but she can't really be happy with me, either. Don't you think when one of the two has a chance at happiness he ought to take it?"

"And it just so happens you're the one."

"That's exactly it: it just so happens. I didn't plan to meet this woman, I didn't go out looking for her."

"You had to have made some overture."

"Yes, after great consideration." He smiled wryly. "Matt, you're in the wrong job. You should have been a prosecuting attorney."

"I'll get a key to you. Just one thing: I don't want to know any more about your situation. The less I know, the less I have to hide from Margaret and Claudia. I don't even want to know this woman's name."

At this last request, a warm relief passed through Ted, for he had been saved from having to tell Matt the one necessary lie.

On Friday Ted came by the station to pick up the key. Matt handed it to him, then pretended to be busy so as not to have any renewal of the luncheon conversation. Apologetically, Ted said: "I'm very grateful to you. You don't know how much this means to me." Matt supposed that he didn't.

At seven o'clock he arrived at Claudia's for dinner and was heartened by Joanne's presence. Bud had been invited but had too much studying to do.

As soon as Claudia fixed the drinks and sat down she looked at Matt coyly and said, "So you're going to Jane's on Sunday."

He attempted nonchalance. "Yes. But I'm afraid I'll be too rusty for them. I haven't played in so long."

With a knowing smile she answered, "It will all come back to you after a few hands. Besides, I'm sure she and her friends will be as interested in your conversation as they are in your card playing."

Joanne's embarrassed and averted eyes told Matt she knew what he knew: Claudia was more than a little jealous and, despite all her customary dignity, could scarcely conceal it. He had wondered how she would act once she learned of his breakup with Adele; now, with the added complication of Jane Richardson, she was exceeding his expectations. His mind raced in search of a change of subject but his tongue remained dead weight. He saw Claudia glance at Joanne, saw how the girl's embarrassment sparked her own. She blushed and struggled to bring her gaze back to Matt. "You know, it might turn into a weekly thing. I think it would be good for you."

"We'll see." Because Jane, more than Adele, was at the center of this exchange, it was not too obvious a shift when he asked how she and Margaret liked the group.

"It's been a real education. I had no idea what a common occurrence rape is. We've got three women, besides Hippolyta, who were raped in their early teens and this is the first time in their whole lives they've told anybody. Can you believe it?"

Yes, he could, as he thought of Judy's daily regret at having confided in him and Adele.

"Some of the women have adjusted quite well, but the others . . ." She shook her head. "At our first meeting with her, Jane warned us both. Be understanding and compassionate, she said, but don't let it depress you—after the meetings, go home and do some light reading or watch television. I'll tell you, the group is successful because she's organized and works damned hard, but the most important thing is that she's level-headed. Some of the women aren't likable in the least—in spite of their misfortunes—but Jane handles them like a pro. Do you know, she never had a single course in counseling or sociology or anything like that."

"I don't think they teach you that much anyway," said Joanne. "Either you've got compassion and understanding or you don't."

Matt was pleased to hear her speak her own mind, and so firmly too. The moment served to remind him that here was no longer a girl but a young woman.

The dinner conversation went smoothly. They discussed the newscaster he had had to fire because of a growing drug habit. Not once did Matt see any sign in the two of them that they were thinking of Terry. Perhaps at last the wounds were closing to form less painful scars.

They were just sitting down to coffee in the living room when the telephone rang. It was Margaret, and after a minute of conversation, Claudia turned to Joanne. "I'll talk upstairs. Hang up for me, will you?"

Claudia started up, and Joanne spoke into the phone. "Hello, Margaret, how are you?"

Matt watched her blink twice and look at the ceiling.

"Oh, the usual," said Joanne. "Never enough time but they keep shoving the reading at you . . . yes, I know . . . all right, goodbye." She sat down and looked glumly at her father. "She's had a few."

"Oh?" Sweat prickled under his collar and he saw the key passing from his fingers to Ted's.

"I feel so sorry for her and yet I like them both. I wish they could work out whatever problem they're having."

"It's probably more than just one problem."

"Mmm." She sipped her coffee. "How are *you* doing?" Her eyes completed the question: . . . now that you're alone.

"All right. For one thing, I'm really enjoying the apartment. It's wonderful to come home to. I cozy in and the evening goes like that." He snapped his fingers.

"Well, it's good to get out once in a while."

"I do. But sometimes it's nice to sit and daydream. About my grandchildren." In the midst of this most pleasant prospect, the key still lingered like a burr stuck to his brain. To absolve himself, he added: "Later on, Bud can fix up that little bedroom. I'll put in bunk beds so I can have two at a time overnight. Between your mother and me you'll never have to worry about a babysitter."

She smiled. "Now don't get carried away. There'll be a little bit of a wait. We're not starting a family until we've built our house."

Until. Until meant prevention. "Joanne, did your mother . . . ever discuss sex with you?"

"Of course. When I was about eleven."

When she was eleven he was living in the same house. Had Claudia told him she had talked to her? Had he forgotton, being too wrapped up in his job to deem this important enough to remember? "I assume," he said with considerable uneasiness, "you and Bud take precautions."

"Yes."

"Something you can trust?"

"I have a diaphragm."

"You use it—each time?"

Her brow creased. "Yes."

"I don't mean to pry into something that should remain private. But you wouldn't want to get caught in a mess you're not ready for."

"We're aware of that."

"You don't use prophylactics, do you?"

She laughed. "God, no! I didn't think *anyone* used those anymore."

"Bud's never used one? Not even once?"

"Dad, we're a little smarter than that." After a few seconds, she laughed again, shaking her head.

Matt's smile was a weak one. "Dumb question. Sorry." He heard Claudia starting down the stairs. "Don't give me away to your mother. Or to Bud."

"I won't. I've got to go study now."

She brushed her hand over his hair as she passed by him, and for the moment he was uplifted: it was a more natural and affectionate gesture than a peck on the cheek.

"What are you giggling about?" asked Claudia.

"Nothing. Dad told a joke." She disappeared up the stairs.

"What's the joke?" She sat, winced at the taste of her cold coffee.

"No joke. I just said something dumb. What's with Margaret?"

"A merchant in the Kingston Mall called her tonight and agreed to putting up one of our posters."

"Well, that's good." Pause. "Joanne said she sounded like she had had a few."

"A few," she answered, sounding very protective.

He refused a second cup of coffee and left. During the drive home Joanne's laughter stayed with him. Under any other circumstances he would have welcomed it.

He tried to comfort himself with a nightcap and dimmed lights, tried to reassure himself with the beautiful room he sat in. And he grasped at likely explanations. Maybe Bud had lent his car to a friend who left the prophylactic in it. Maybe Bud had bought it as a joke and then forgot about or misplaced it. Maybe he and Joanne had used one once or twice for experimentation, diversion. But these possibilities were contested by others. Maybe Bud, like Ted, had another woman on the side. Maybe he had several—and of the type that made a cautious man want to use such protection. Maybe there was an aspect of Bud's nature that required—would always require—an occasional roll in the mud.

There was two nights ago when Bud had not been at the library, his car heading *toward* campus and Joanne ten minutes late.

Matt got up, walked down the hallway, and stood at the door to the little bedroom. There was no way in the world he could tell Joanne anything and risk hurting her, then losing her. He could not tell Claudia or Margaret about Ted; quite the opposite, he had to hope and pray they never found out. And while Judy ducked away from him at every opportunity he still had to hide the reason why and honor his promise.

Anger and self-pity ballooned inside him. He had given up the woman he loved in exchange for peace and tranquillity. Now, these people were robbing him of both. Why should he be included in their misfortunes, their indiscretions? Why did he have to be exposed to their hidden selves?

He watched television for an hour and nearly succeeded in clearing his mind of all the unwanted baggage. But when he turned out the lights and lay on the pillow with his eyes open, the weight of it all returned and pressed even harder. His lips pulled back tight against his teeth as he hissed: "Why me? Jesus Christ, why me!"

The following Wednesday night Bud dropped Joanne off at her class and went to the library. He slipped into one of the study booths, opened a book but did not read it. He was preoccupied with the memory of Saturday night when he sat up with Claudia long after Joanne went to bed. He knew that her evenings out with Dr. Zimmerman had come to an end, and he told her how much he wished she and Matt could get back together again. She smiled embarrassedly but, pouring her third glass of wine, she admitted to the same wish and to the unlikelihood of it ever coming true. Then she told him of her attempt at sleeping with the doctor: she would never be able to sleep with any man but Matt. He reached across the table, took her hands in his, and said he felt the same way about Joanne. Later, in his room, he sat up until nearly dawn, engaged in a rigid comparison of his mother with Claudia. Claudia deserved a man, his mother did not, and what hardened the comparison was the fact that Claudia would never accept the kind of relationship his mother would. In the beginning, with Fred, she at least had had the decency to drop him on her own but by the time she got to

Hugh and Walter her decency was gone, and the responsibility for getting rid of them fell into his own hands.

Unseeingly, he stared at the book before him and remained oblivious to the footsteps passing by the booth, going to and from the stacks. In his head he lined up Fred, Hugh, and Walter shoulder to shoulder, the way an executioner lines up three of the enemy before the firing squad. . . .

Fred had owned a string of laundromats, and exactly where his mother met him was never clear. She was not working then so it could not have been at the restaurant. It could have been anywhere: wherever she went, men looked at her *that* way—lingeringly. He himself was seven at the time, young enough to judge on instinct alone, and the first time he and the man met, his instinct told him that Fred did not and never would like him. In a single glance Fred's ice-blue eyes assessed and then dismissed him, as if they were viewing a stray animal that had been brought into the house but would promptly be put out again. "Hi, junior" were the first words to come through his loose grin. "Don't call him junior," his mother said "he's not his father's son, he's not going to be like *him*. Call him by his name." And he did. On the rare occasions they were in a room alone together Fred would whistle softly and say, "Here-Bud-here-Bud-here-mutt" and, eyes glittering, would beam satisfaction as the boy backed away in fear and confusion. He ran to his mother and reported tearfully. "He didn't hear me right," Fred answered when confronted. "Seems to me he's awful sensitive, Lucille. You better be careful with him." She said, "Never mind, just speak clearly when you talk to him." Fred did *not* call Gail by her name. He called her Princess and bought her a hair dryer, a record player, and a goose-down parka. He bought the boy a baseball bat and glove that he refused to touch or even keep in his room. The boy told his mother he didn't want Fred to come to their house anymore, and she replied that both of them should try to get along. For a period of months he mutely accepted the man as an inevitability and would remove himself to his room or to a friend's whenever Fred was due to arrive. But then one winter night he was confronted with the realization that Fred might become a permanent fixture. The night before, he had awakened to the sound of retching and crying in the bathroom.

He got up to find his mother holding on to Gail who was bent over the toilet bowl. She told him to go back to bed, but he remained to watch her apply a cold washcloth to his sister's forehead and pour mouthwash into a paper cup. The girl asked to sleep with her mother, and after Lucille got her tucked in she came out to put her son back to bed. The next evening Fred was still sitting in the living room when the boy went to bed. The boy propped himself up against his pillows and strained to stay awake for his upcoming mission. He did fall asleep but woke up a few hours later, ungroggy and clear-headed as though he had slept the entire night. When he reached his mother's door he heard a soft moaning within. For a few seconds he was angered by the possibility that Gail had got there ahead of him. Then he remembered that Gail was not home but sleeping at a girl friend's. It was his mother who was moaning. He turned the knob, pushed the door, and although he could see nothing in the darkness he heard a terrific rustling of the sheets followed by a furious "Jee-zuz Chirst!" He stood frozen at the recognition of Fred's voice and then his mother's: "Close the door, Bud, I'll be right out." It was the first time he had heard fear in her; Fred was making her moan, hurting her—she was *letting* Fred hurt her—but she was afraid of *him*. "Bud, *please* close the door, I'm coming out." He did as he was told, and when she came to him the fear was in her eyes and he could not say the words he had practiced all day: "I'm sick, I want to sleep with you." She put him back to bed, scarcely looking at him as she did so, and after a few minutes he heard their voices on the staircase. "You gotta be firm with him or you're gonna have a mama's boy on your hands." "Keep your voice down." "Why don't you send him to live with his father for a while?"

He lay awake long after Fred's car pulled away from the house. *Send him to live with his father.* He had never seen his father, but Gail went now and then for a weekend at a time. Before the divorce, his mother would take his sister into another room when she returned from a visit and ask her questions about their father. The answer to his own questions was always: "Your father isn't *well*, he doesn't know what he says sometimes, and he can be mean. I only let Gail go because she's older and he won't be mean to a girl."

One night, he stood unnoticed at the kitchen door and saw Fred give his mother some money for a coat she wanted. She refused it at first, but he kept insisting she take it, and then he laughed loudly and said after they were married she would probably be demanding it like any other wife. She replied she hadn't made up her mind yet about getting married. He said he'd help her make up her mind and kissed her long and hard on the mouth, lifting her right off the floor. When she asked his sister and him, Gail was pleased but he could not even protest because his throat was swollen with panic. Gail left the room and his mother assured him that she wouldn't marry Fred right away, she would wait until the two of them got better acquainted.

He ran away. With a bag of sweet rolls and a carton of milk he lived for two days under the back porch of an abandoned house three miles from his own. At night, the memory of his mother moaning and her allowing herself to be lifted off the floor would squelch his fear of the darkness and the rats that occupied the other end of the crawl space. When his stomach was as empty as the bakery bag he emerged and made for a nearby grocery store; while he picked out potato chips and candy bars the clerk telephoned the police.

He was escorted by the officer up the front walk, and without a word he passed his mother who stood at the door and whose face looked as if it would never regain its color. After she finished with the police she came up and sat on the edge of his bed. For a time they only stared at each other, and her eyes zigzagged over his face as if searching for an entry into his head. "Send me to my father's," he said at last. Her eyes closed, her chest heaved and fell. "Why do you hate Fred?" "Send me to my father's," he repeated. Fred never came to the house again, and after two weeks' time she stopped seeing him outside too.

Between Fred and Hugh she only had "dates" with men. But he knew there was something wrong with all of them, that her going out with them was wrong because whenever she introduced them, the familiar fear of *him* would be there in her eyes and voice, as it had been the night she was in the bedroom with Fred.

He was eleven when she began seeing Hugh—a year after his

father remarried and Gail stopped going to see him. Hugh was a soft-spoken widower with a son a year older than the boy, and he was determined that the two should be friends. However, neither was enthusiastic about the other's parent; on every occasion they were together the son reminded Bud that he and Gail would "be supported" by Hugh because their own father wouldn't support them. His mother assured him this was not the case, that she had enough money of her own and Hugh would never have to support him and his sister. But when Hugh made the engagement official with a ring, Bud said he didn't want to be supported by anyone, not even her, and took on two paper routes, morning and afternoon. His questions about his father increased and became constant: Why didn't Gail go to see him anymore? Why couldn't *he* go to see him? Why didn't his father ever come here? When he learned from Gail that their father had a baby son by this new wife, he asked his mother how this could be possible since his reason for leaving them was that he wanted no other children after Gail. His mother answered all his questions with the same reply: his father was a strange and frequently cruel man and they were better off not seeing or hearing from him.

On a Sunday afternoon in July, in the back yard, Hugh's son told him he and Gail would soon be coming to live in *his* house. Bud said he was staying right where he was, and the boy answered that was impossible because this house was going to be sold. "You're coming to live in my house and you'll go to my school." Bud broke two of the boy's teeth and opened up three of his own knuckles doing it. Hugh was briefly outraged; Bud's contempt for him swelled when Hugh still strained to be friendly and was still determined to marry his mother. The afternoon he broke the teeth his mother took him to her room and lashed out at him: "There's no reason for what you've done!" He told her she was not going to sell this house, he would live in it alone. She said that was impossible and if he could not behave himself she would send him off to boarding school. "Just send me to my father's." Her anger bowed to fear and he was relieved to see that he still had a handle on it.

However, for a month, she barely spoke to him, and her face took on a new stony expression of strength and resistance.

When he mentioned his father he got no response. The panic that seized him went to the bone: beyond his fear of having to live in Hugh's house lay the possibility that he had gone too far, pressed too hard, lost her love for good. But the panic quickly turned to anger. She expected him to give up his house, his school so *she* could be comfortable. While he delivered his newspapers he often imagined her laughing with Hugh's son while he watched at a distance outside an invisible circle. The image would not leave him and enlarged to a definite probability. He came to realize he was in a trap from which there was only one escape.

On a Saturday in late August Hugh employed another tactic in his campaign to win him over. Leaving his own son at home, he took the boy and his mother to Lake Michigan. With a picnic lunch they arrived at a secluded dune. Hugh gradually but cleverly got the coversation around to his house and told him he would have his own room—the largest. He replied that he didn't like large rooms. "Then your mother and I will trade with you." He glanced at his mother's face and saw its newly acquired determination. She was impenetrable. He stood up and told her, "I'll never live there," then walked over the lip of the dune and crossed the narrow strip of beach to the water. He turned and waited but she did not follow. She had made her choice.

A jagged chain of dead fish lay on the shore and trailed off into the distance on either side of him. He stared at one whose skin appeared ready to burst from bloat. A sudden horror filled him, not because of the bloat or the flies or death itself but because the creature, in life, had never been able to close its eyes. It seemed to him the worst imaginable punishment—like living in Hugh's house.

As they had driven out of the city Hugh had laughed and admitted he did not know how to swim, and the boy remembered this as he stepped over the fish and waded into the water. His mother swam but he would be too quick for her. She would try to reach him and fail.

He continued on until the water covered his shoulders. He would wait until she arrived at the chain of fish, then submerge himself and swim out farther and take the final gulp.

He yelled as loudly as he could. Keeping up his artificial

struggle he let his mouth and nose go under but not his eyes. She came running from the dune, across the strip of beach.

Then she stopped.

His arms flailing, he went under and came up again. She was standing bent forward, ready for movement but not moving. Hugh appeared, calling her name. This seemed to release her and she shot into the water and started swimming toward him. Clearly, dying would be no victory at all; the searing hurt and rage that her hesitation unleashed in him now fed his will and determination to live. Taking a deep breath, he disappeared under the surface where he opened his eyes and charted the approach of her floral bathing suit. When she was almost overhead he shot upward to meet her face to face. There was no more than two feet between them and he saw his triumph at once. Her face seemed to crumple toward its center and as her red eyes grew redder from tears she whispered his name in supplication. He swam past her and straight to shore.

On the way home Hugh was the only one who spoke, commenting on speeding drivers. At the house Bud went to his room and stayed there until his mother came in. She told him that shock and panic had made her hesitate at the water's edge, but it sounded as if she were trying to explain this to herself. When she broke off in midsentence he said: "I won't live in *his* house. Send me to my father's. He can't be any worse than you."

Two weeks later, he was lying on his bed again when Hugh fought his way past his mother and bounded up the stairs. His face was the shade of red that borders purple. "I won't—let you—rule your mother," he said between ragged breaths. "I don't know all the tricks you use but I'm on to you, mister!" If the boy had learned anything it was that calmness and self-possession were the best weapons, no matter what feelings raged inside. "Get out of my room. No one *she* picks is going to support me." The man took a single step toward him, then stopped and clenched his fists. He left, and downstairs he argued, telling her it was insane to let the boy have his way; she answered but her voice was inaudible. Back and forth it went until the front door slammed. He had gone through it for the last time. The boy switched off his lamp, rolled over, and immediately went to sleep.

117

A year after Hugh's departure they were left alone to circle around each other in their private bubbles. Gail went off to college but not before she admonished him to be kinder to their mother.

Three months after his sister left, his mother went to work as a waitress; she took the late shift so that she did not arrive home until after nine-thirty. And during that year after Hugh left, his grandmother began to withdraw from him. Occasionally, he would come downstairs and creep through the dining room and listen to their hushed voices at the kitchen table. His grandmother was forever on the topic of her daughter being a waitress. "When I bought this house for you and Myron it wasn't with the idea you'd someday go to work as a waitress. Good God, I can send you back to college if you want to go."—"I like waitressing, it keeps me moving. Besides, I should have gone to work a long time ago. Living off the money Grandpa and Dad left me has made me soft. I'd like to harden up a little."—"You're working to get away from that boy is what you're doing. He's becoming a regular tyrant, not a bit like Gail."—"He's had it harder than Gail. At least she's had a token father."—"She'd have a full-time father if you'd had that abortion."—"Well, I didn't and that's that. You live with your decisions."

Three years later, his grandmother died and his mother met Walter at the funeral. He was a second cousin to her—twelve years older, divorced, and a recent grandfather. His first few visits to the house were missions of consolation, but soon he was picking her up from work and taking her out for coffee and coming for dinner every Sunday. Tall, gangly, bland-faced, and reserved, he had about him the kind of neuter quality some clergymen evince. The boy liked him the way he might like an untroublesome cat that lies in the sun all day: the two of them had practically nothing to talk about but the silences between them were more comfortable and never strained. Their only common interest was watching tennis on television. The boy's other interests now included woodworking and furniture refinishing and daily physical exercise. Still committed to supporting himself, he worked in a grocery store after school every day and then came home to jog and exercise on the parallel bars and with the weights he kept in the basement. Except for one corner where his mother had her washer and dryer the basement was his, with the workbench and tools at one end and the gym at the other. After his workout he would eat and go to to his room to study. Consequently, he and his mother saw each other no more than half an hour a day, a few minutes in the morning and even fewer minutes between the time she arrived home from work and he went to bed. On weekends, he went out with friends or built cabinets, lamps, knickknacks and repaired furniture for money. But during this particular year, the year of Walter, he had a private preoccupation, an anticipated adventure. When his driver's training class ended he would have only a week and a half to wait until a friend's uncle sold him his car. He had big plans for initiating the license and the car.

He drove down to Dearborn with Myron Hanes's address and telephone number in his pocket. These he had obtained from the city library, in the section that provided telephone directories of the state's major cities. At midafternoon on a Saturday he found the house, a plain brick-and-wood box set among others like it on a maple-lined street. He circled the block several times, then decided he should have some lunch first. By nightfall he still had not mustered the courage to pull up at the curb and get out. And a little before midnight he saw the light behind the draperies go out. A few miles out of town he found a country road that had a number of tractor-tire turn-offs, and he chose one that wound into a wooded area. There he spent the night in the back seat, sleeping fitfully until dawn. In the men's room of a gas station he washed his face and combed his hair and debated whether or not he should phone first. A man's voice answered; his own voice locked and would not work. He hung up and felt the temptation to get back on the expressway and head for home. Breakfast, however, renewed his courage. At ten-forty-five he rang the doorbell and stared at the decorative *H* in the aluminum grillwork on the lower half of the screen door. When the inside door was opened he found before him a husky man, blond and balding, whose face in no way resembled his own but whose body did. "Yes?" he said in a guarded tone, neither friendly nor hostile. "Are you My–Myron Hanes?"—"Yes, I am."—"I'm Bud, your son." For a second or two there was nothing, and he wondered if he had actually spoken. A woman and a small boy appeared behind the man; when the boy started toward the door she snatched him back and held him by the shoulder. "You are not my son," the man replied at last in a low but firm voice. "Yes, I am. Lucille is my mother, Gail is my sister."—"I know that, but you're not *my* son." He closed the door. Bud stood where he was, unable to think or feel anything, unable to move except to ring the bell again. This time the woman answered, and the man and the boy were nowhere in sight. Her plain face was pinched and anxious. "Did your mother send you here?"—"No."— "Please go away and don't come again."—"He said I . . . I'm not his son." She bit her lip and nodded. "But he was married to her when I was born." Again she nodded and her eyes, filled with tears, implored him to arrive at the answer on his own without her having to give it. The answer must have registered in his face, for she turned her head and said in an agonized voice: "Now please go. I'm very sorry. But this hurts him as much as it does you. Your mother should have . . . " Just before she closed the door he saw the tears start down her face.

All the way home his body was gripped by a wincing that would not let go. And his mind was gripped by the remark his mother had made to Fred years ago: "He's not his father's son, he's not going to be like *him*." Once again he heard the moaning behind her bedroom door, saw his sister packing her suitcase to go visit her father. Her father. So, he had left them because he didn't want another child—well, he had another one now, and a boy too. And his wife was plain, plain—but good and decent and unable to hold back tears when she had to hurt someone she didn't even know.

By the time he reached the house he had regained his composure although it was not needed because she was napping, purring contentedly on the sofa. Quietly, he sat and watched her. There was an insistent, strangely thrilling pressure in his throat and in his loins while his rage suckled at her tranquillity.

She had driven his—no, *Gail's*—father away from them. She had not bothered to marry his own father, whoever it might be. Or maybe he hadn't wanted to marry her. Maybe there had been nothing more between them than a few moans in the night.

And the story she gave and stuck to, the one he had believed. Or tried to. All those years she had played him for a fool!

Deprived him of a father and later, with Hugh, tried to deprive him of his home and all the while playing him for—

She stirred, and he froze. When she turned over, with her back to him, he had decided that she would never know of today's visit.

For a fool.

After he crept from the room he looked back into it, then at the hallway he stood in. Once, she had almost taken this house away from him. Now, he was going to claim it totally as his own, he would do it over completely, the way he wanted it. She would merely live in it, but it would be his until he was ready to leave it.

He had no idea if she was planning to marry Walter, but that hardly mattered. She deserved no man, in or out of marriage, and he began searching for a way to get rid of this one. He now watched Walter carefully, looking and waiting for some kind of inspiration. It came, like a gift, one afternoon when the three of them went to a city tennis tournament. He noticed that Walter's eyes occasionally left the court and settled on a long-haired shirtless teenaged boy who was sitting down a few rows to the left. He looked at Walter's pale neuter skin, the long delicate fingers, and a stratagem began to form in his brain.

In the middle of the following week he made sure that Walter was coming on Saturday to watch a tournament on television, and on Saturday morning he made sure his mother was going grocery shopping while the tournament was on, as she often did; he ensured her long absence by giving her a list of things he needed from the hardware store. She left soon after Walter arrived. He and Walter took their usual positions in front of the television but this time he sat with his shirt off. He waited for a single furtive glance from the man but it never came. When he got up and brought back a bowl of pretzels he made sure his arm grazed Walter's as he set the bowl in front of him. There was no response. Convinced that he had not misread what he had seen the previous week, he was furious that Walter would not give himself away now.

Then it occurred to him that Walter didn't have to *do* anything at all.

Before his mother returned he went to his room and stayed

there; he refused dinner and did not come down until Walter left at ten-thirty. She asked if he wasn't feeling well. Effecting a stammer he told her how Walter had made an advance while she was out. Fully prepared for the doubt in her face, he challenged it by looking at her unflinchingly and saying that although he was repulsed by Walter he did feel sorry for him. She said she was going to call him right away and tell him to come over so the three of them could have it out. He countered by affirming that Walter would only deny it, and he advised her not to say anything: "He's your second cousin. You wouldn't want it to get around the family." Her eyes, then her shoulders drooped. "You want him out of the house, don't you?" she murmured. "Yes, after what he's done." Her head tipped back, her eyes closed completely. "Don't lie about him, don't lower yourself that way."—"Lower *my*self? Once you wanted me to drown. Now you want to let a fairy come after me?"—"Just tell me the truth."—"I am telling you the truth."

By some method she never revealed, she unloaded Walter. And then a letter from him arrived. The boy brought it in from the mailbox and was tempted to steam it open. He reconsidered: if he did it and she found out she might turn on him and take Walter back. So, he left it for her on the dining-room table, and she took it to her room. The next afternoon he went in looking for it. He searched the drawers of her nightstand and then those in the dresser. Finding nothing, he decided to look in the closet and under the mattress. As he turned around from the dresser toward the closet his hand collided with a small decanter of perfume that spilled onto the rug. Even after the mess was cleaned up there was no way to conceal his intrusion. He continued his search but never found the letter.

"What were you doing in my room?"—"I know I knocked over your perfume. I was looking at your dresser and nightstand. I'm thinking of refinishing them."—"I don't want them refinished. Stay out of my room." The very next afternoon he came home to find the lock installed on her door.

He was surprised at and even vaguely sorry over the way she gave up Walter without a fight. She went about the house and off to work like a sleepwalker who always takes the same course; she lived on the path of habit with no emotions to divert her.

When he proceeded to redecorate the house his way she offered no objections. She walked around stacks of lumber, stepped over paint cans without seeming to notice them. "Leave *my* room alone," was all she said about his project. His regret over her zombielike existence was soon reasoned away: if she would not make herself come alive without having to have a man, then her misery was her own doing. He would not be swayed from his determination to make her live as she should. . . .

Somebody clamored into the study booth in front of him, sneezed twice, and broke his thoughts. He pulled his open book closer to him but after reading a single paragraph he was drifting away to mull over his failures. On Monday he had cut a class—his first cut ever—and borrowed a friend's car on the pretext that his own wouldn't start. He drove from campus to home and parked at the end of the block to watch and wait; he figured that it being Monday she would definitely meet the man after a weekend of separation. She emerged from the house at one-fifteen but went only to the dry cleaners and her hairdresser. He could not keep cutting classes and he was furious that she had given him no results.

His other failure was last Wednesday night. The cheap red-head who ran the cash register at the discount drugstore in Eastbrook Mall had not left when she was supposed to, at eight-fifteen. She had kept him waiting, waiting while he watched her—through his windshield and the store window—as she did some kind of inventory work on a stepladder. He had encountered her plenty of times. From behind the cash register she always had a big smile for him, as she did for every good-looking man; with women she was abrupt and with the attractive ones, rude.

He slipped out the side entrance of the library and walked to his car in the metered lot. Within minutes he blended with the traffic on the avenue which bordered the west campus and which would deliver him to Eastbrook.

The third traffic light was red, and while he waited at it he glanced to his right where the cross street ran down to meet the one Judy Kent had lived on. "So nice to have met you, *Bob*"— and telling him what a gem he was getting in Joanne, as if he didn't know it better than she did. "So treat her well," as though he were getting something greater than he deserved. *Bob.* Her attitude toward him had been a summary of what she was on television and what she was in life. Stupidly insensitive, empty and, to those with any brains, a self-inflated laughingstock.

But she wasn't those things anymore. He could see the change in her right on television, and he knew how deep it went when he heard Matt say she had put her house up for sale. She would never be silly and unfeeling and false again.

He now felt something for her which he could not begin to explain. It was a sentiment very close to affection.

8

Ted Brainard stood at the bedroom window and looked down anxiously at the parking area. She was already five minutes late. The tea, in a pot on the desk, would be getting cold. The living room had been inspected to make sure there were no telltale signs of identity; the door to Matt's bedroom was closed so as to avoid the chance of her glimpsing the display of family pictures on the wall. Their first meeting here had not been a smooth one. He had to keep assuring her that his friend had no idea who she was and could not be less interested. His friend, he said, was another lawyer who could be trusted not to make a surprise appearance.

He watched her car pull into the lot, saw her get out and look up apprehensively at the window. He left the apartment and went down the stairs to the locked rear entrance which was not hooked up to the buzzer and intercom system. She gave him a brief smile of apology. "I didn't realize I was on empty. I had to stop and get gas."

She climbed the steps ahead of him, stiffly, cautiously, as if eggs were placed before her. It might have been her propriety and fear: Don't Alert the Neighbors. But it could also be that her pain was holding out against the medication. He knew that her body had rejected the gold shots to the same degree that *his* had responded to the chemotherapy.

He closed and locked the front door and led her back to the bedroom. Gesturing at the desk, he bowed and said, "Madam is just in time for tea."

"I'll pour it."

"No. You sit. You don't wait on anybody anymore."

The tea was orange and spice, her favorite, and he had brought along corn muffins to have with it. He watched her and noted how gracefully she ate, as gracefully as she had carried plates at the restaurant. He was certain that it was her gracefulness as much as her beauty that attracted the attention of men. It had been, in fact, one of those long and longing glances from a customer—a man much younger and better-looking than himself—that touched his jealousy and gave him the courage to ask her to lunch.

At Joanne's engagement party he had been unable to keep his eyes off her, fascinated but frightened too: after only an hour he realized that inside him there was more than just the ashes of desire, there were embers and this woman ignited them. He spoke no more than two sentences to her when they were introduced and then kept his distance, like a child at a zoo who wants to reach through the bars to pet the pretty panther but knows better. For days afterward he could think of nothing else, and her face loomed before him even as he delivered a summary to a jury. After two weeks of resistance he submitted to the danger one evening; before going home he stopped at Graff's and watched her wait on the early diners.

The first week and a half he would have his two club sodas at the far end of the bar, away from the service area, and she would nod and smile only once at him in silent greeting. His next step was bolder. He would come in and take the stool next to the service area and talk to her whenever she came to fill drink orders. She was timid and cautious, yet he knew instinctively that she liked him and even looked forward to his presence although nothing more than superficial chatter passed between them. Up close, he now saw her stiffness, watched her subtly brace herself against the bar to hunch and then relax her shoulders, to straighten and slacken her legs. He noticed too the hint of circles under her eyes and one evening told her she looked a little out of sorts. She smiled guardedly and said she was; he knew then that she was a sick woman and persevering to hide the fact, perhaps to keep her job. It was the first thing he loved about her.

One night he saw a handsome and younger man, a "regular," staring at her with what appeared to be much more than simple lust, and this made him feel there was no time to be lost, that he had been thrust into a race. When he asked her to lunch she eyed his wedding band and said she didn't think it was a good idea. His defense was that it was "only lunch" and that he had not in a long time enjoyed talking to anyone as he did to her. After three lunches he learned the full measure of her disease and saw the fear that its acceleration would soon cost her her work. The second thing he loved about her was that she didn't have to work but wanted to; she preferred her job to social activities.

He got her to talk more readily about her illness by telling her of his own and how it had redefined his values and outlook and had changed his marriage. She listened with quiet fascination, asked him to elaborate here and there. And in her eyes he could see they were turning a corner and heading in the direction he wanted.

After the seventh lunch he was burning, like some repressed adolescent, to kiss her deeply and lingeringly. He was not afraid to gamble and to make the move but the question was *where*. He was dropping her off at work and she would be certain to rebuff an advance while parked at the curb. Halfway to Graff's he saw his opportunity. He turned into a carwash, and as soon as they were out of sight from everything but brushes and suds he leaned over, took her chin in his hand, and kissed her until the rinse cycle was over.

Their next meeting was not for lunch but at a motel. Before they left it, she warned him that their situation would have to end if it were ever discovered, but the warning was so vehement as to sound like a threat. Bud's relationship with the Sessions family could not be compromised in any way. He admired her devotion to her son, understood her firm insistence upon discretion but at the same time he sensed a disproportionate fear behind her caution. Once, recklessly, he told her if anyone did find out about them he could file for divorce immediately, after which they could go away. Her eyes turned wild and she said that the greatest proof of his love would be to make sure their secret was well kept. That was precisely why he had asked Matt for access to the apartment. If Matt ever discovered the woman was Lucille, he could be trusted to say nothing, even to her. . . .

He poured her a second cup of tea, sat down, and stroked her hair. "Is it bad today, the pain?"

"Yes, but not terrible."

"We don't have to go to bed."

"I want to." She set the cup aside and rested her head on his chest. "I forget about the pain when you're making love to me."

He forgot about *everything* when he made love to her—even the hurt and resentment in Margaret's eyes, for which he was more than just partly responsible. Lucille's physical need of him was like an enormous white-crested wave seeking a wall or a bank to contain it, beautiful within itself but also revealing the vast emotional need beneath it. He sensed she was looking to come to rest somewhere, and he wanted that somewhere to be him. Yet she continued to test him by explaining graphically what her disease might eventually do to her body. He replied that only the future would allow him to prove himself.

After the final quiver and their return to normal breathing, he pulled the blanket up over their shoulders and huddled next to her. For a while there was no sound but their breathing and the ticking of the clock on the desk.

"They've set the wedding date," she whispered. "October twenty-third."

"It seems so far away."

"I know. But we have to be patient. We can't afford to be careless now."

He stood at the front door of the apartment and watched her descend the steps less stiffly than she had climbed them two hours ago. She had made the bed while he dressed; now, he washed, dried, and put away the teapot and cups.

October twenty-third was eight months away. She was right: they had to remain patient. At the wedding she would sit on the groom's side, he on the bride's. He grinned at the idea that no one, not even Bud and Joanne, would rival him in joy the moment those rings were exchanged.

*   *   *

Matt's evening at Jane Richardson's had been a success insofar as it was just the first of many to come. Her friends, the Harleys, were outgoing, humorous, and refreshingly uncomplicated people. The four of them had played cards nonstop until midnight. The only black mark on the occasion was Mrs. Harley's observation about the change in Judy; she commented on how tense Judy seemed, how frequently off-putting she was with guests on "Personality Parade." Matt saw the questioning concern in Jane's face although she asked nothing. He replied that Judy was having a family problem—with an aunt, he thought—and that she had just made a big decision to give up the house she had lived in for twenty-two years and go into an apartment. He was relieved when both women nodded in understanding.

And so, the Sunday night ritual began and he knew he looked forward to it, depended upon it, more than he should. During the week, from Monday to Friday, his "drifting" was more of a task than a luxury: relaxed and aimless movement was always hindered by thoughts of Adele. Seeing her agency's sign in front of houses did not help his efforts to forget her. Occasionally, he would go to Pierre's after work, for a drink but never dinner, and take a place at the bar from which he could view "their" table, the one where they had had their very last conversation. This was pure and simple masochism, he told himself, and still he would go each time he felt the pull. And each time he returned to the apartment, it took longer and longer to be reassured and fortified by his beautiful and comfortable surroundings. He would map out the future; the boundaries of this territory were, of course, defined by Joanne and Bud. October twenty-third. His walk down the aisle with her would be the second stage in his own new beginning and would perhaps lessen the pain of the present stage. Whenever he thought of that distant day, his chest would crowd and flutter with impatient anticipation. He hoped that by then he would have a firmer grip on himself, that he would have learned how to gainfully employ all his free time. He looked at Bud's craftsmanship which surrounded him and decided he must start seriously thinking of a hobby.

On his way to bed he paused at the door of the little room and wondered if Ted and the woman were in it that day. There was never a hint that it had been used: the draperies were always open in the same position, the decorative throw pillows exactly placed at one corner of the pull-out sofa. Surely, the woman would have her family complications ironed out by October, and the apartment would be entirely his again.

As always, when he thought of Ted—and what was being done to Margaret—the memory of the prophylactic wormed its way back into his head. But now he was able to dismiss it more readily, as a mystery that did not require solving. During the past two months he had been around Joanne and Bud enough to witness the foundation of Claudia's ecstatic testaments. No woman was ever more loved, respected, cherished than his daughter. What made all this more valuable was that Bud was clearly her equal and no drooling inferior amazed at his luck.

In his own bedroom, he undressed and looked at the pictures on the wall. His gaze came to rest on the only one of Terry. Still, after all this time, his blood accelerated at the sight of the boy. Usually, he turned away after a few seconds, but now he lingered, confronting the surly face, and silently instructed Joanne and Bud: Don't ever have a child who's *that* difficult to love—have children like yourselves.

Bud picked her up at six-thirty and read her mood at once. However, he said nothing until they were a third of the way to the campus.

"Will you relax. It's only a quiz."

"I hate them, with those picayune questions. I'd rather have a big test or an essay."

"Don't worry about it."

"You can afford to talk, Mr. Four-Point-Average."

"Three-point-nine-six."

"Heavens, we're slipping! I'd be happy to graduate with a paltry three-point-four."

"Look, we both know your record for that first year and a half had nothing to do with your ability. You had bigger problems to face than anything in a syllabus. You've got to consider how well you've done *since* then."

"I know. You're right. But I still wish I had your confidence about school. You never get rattled by a test or a project or anything."

"That's the secret," he said, gently squeezing her knee. "Don't get rattled. There are more important things."

They drove on in silence, until the headlights glimpsed and passed over a familiar sign to both of them. "For Sale. Densmore Realty."

"I have the feeling Dad misses Adele more than he lets on. Mom's worried that he's becoming a hermit. And drinking too much."

"He just needs time to adjust."

"I don't know. I think he really loves her." She paused. "Maybe I should have discouraged him when he told me he was planning to leave her."

This last statement made his stomach sink, as though he had swallowed a stone. "He told you beforehand?"

"Christmas Day. When we took a walk."

"You didn't tell me."

"He asked me not to say anything until he had definitely decided."

"I thought you'd have told *me*."

"Bud, I didn't even tell Mom. Apparently, Adele wants a family and he doesn't."

"Well, he already has one," he answered evenly, hiding his real concern.

He dropped her off and continued along the one-way street. But a block before the library he made a turn. There was something he wanted to see before he settled into a long session of studying.

He had not been told; his exclusion from their confidence rankled inside him. However, there was no time to belabor the resentment now.

Excitement charged through his stomach, up his spine, and down his legs as he pulled into the Eastbrook Mall. He had come to check on her twice since the night he abducted her, but she had not been in. He hoped she had not quit her job.

She hadn't. Through the large plate-glass window he saw her behind the cash register. He entered, and with a tube of shampoo in his hand, joined the line. His advance was slow—she ran out of dimes and had to wait for the manager to bring her a roll—and he appreciated the ample opportunity for looking her over carefully. Her shoulders were slightly rounded now, the arrogant squaring of them gone; she kept her eyes on the purchases instead of the customers; when she called out for the dimes he could hear how the harsh bray had been whittled down to a nasal whine. He stared at her boldly while she rang up his shampoo and bagged it. The hair and make-up were the same but *she* clearly was not.

His gratification waned and his thoughts returned to Joanne and Matt's secret. In the library he climbed to the second floor, taking the steps two at a time, and slipped into a study booth. He opened a book but his mind was too restless to concentrate.

He should have been told—after all he had done for both of them. *Claudia* told him everything.

All right, he reasoned at last, it's not so important. Joanne might have said something if they had got around to the subject. But she was always preoccupied with school, and now with the wedding plans, too. It's not so important. It will take time for Matt to come around to depending on you the way Claudia does. And he will, once he learns that he *can*. Time. There will be plenty of it.

And time enough to find out who this mystery man is that *she's* hiding. The question is how.

He did not linger over the question. The solution would come to him eventually. The solution always came. He was lucky that way.

Matt woke up on Saturday morning with an evil hangover, the kind that aspirin cannot touch and that inspires a terrible remorse. The night before, he was not depressed—or thought he wasn't—but had read and sipped on scotch until nearly midnight. Afraid that a full meal would kill the buzz and ruin his sleepiness, he ate only a container of yogurt before climbing into bed. Now, his head was a swamp, his muscles jelly, and the brilliant morning sun stood as a judge to condemn all indulgence of the night.

He punished himself with a cold shower and sorted out what

must be done during the day. There was, of course, nothing he *had* to do—except to stay busy. Despite the hangover, he was capable of arithmetic and he calculated thirty-six hours to fill before bridge at Jane Richardson's.

He went first to the dry cleaners and then to the supermarket where women raced through the aisles to save time while he squandered it. Next came the bank (blessedly, a long line at the drive-up window) and the shoe repair shop. Then, it was on to the bookstore for a new paperback, a stop for a very late lunch, a trip to the carwash. It was three-thirty when he arrived back at the apartment complex, and he figured that doing his laundry in the single washer and dryer in the basement would take him up to five o'clock.

He unlocked his letterbox and found a solitary white business-size envelope. The return address on it was Adele's. He carried it upstairs and made himself a cup of coffee before sitting down to read the contents.

Dear Matt,

I hope this finds you well but not so well that you'll dismiss what I have to say. First, I don't intend to make this a fountain of regret. At this point I'm much more interested in hope. I've been lonely, far lonelier than I ever expected to be, and so I've had plenty of time to think. What I believe I've sorted out is this: you're deeply concerned with what you think you can't do, whereas I'm concerned with what you can do. Believe me, I do understand the heartache and horrors you've been through. After all, didn't those things partly shape you into the man I love? Your fear is only natural, it would be abnormal for you not to have it. But you don't have to carry it alone. You can lean on me without being afraid or ashamed to. Don't forget that you give me plenty—more than I could ever hope for from another man.

Please consider carefully and at length everything I've said. I'm in much less of a hurry than I thought I was. And I hope you're in less of a hurry to escape me.

Yours,
Adele

He read it six times. What he realized was that her desperation was accompanied by courage. His was not. He would never have written such a letter. He knew now that what he had as a

133

young man was not courage at all, merely ambition and an inflated faith in himself—faith in his talent for doing his job, for handling Sloane, for giving his family everything *he* thought they wanted. But for the lack of courage he could now substitute fairness, his one remaining major virtue, although Adele would never understand it.

He awakened twice during the night, picked up the letter and put it down again. By midafternoon the next day his regret shifted into anger that he had yet to inure himself to the temptation she presented.

As he drove to the bridge game he told himself he should be following Jane's example in how to live alone with dignity and purpose. It had been eight years since her husband's death and still she kept and maintained their large four-bedroom house on the outskirts of the city—in addition to heading the women's group, in addition to having a social life and enough time for her two small grandchildren.

She was running behind in her preparations. After taking his coat she rushed back off to the kitchen, asking him over her shoulder if he would build the fire. He was glad of the chance to contribute something and by the time he lit the kindling he had, for the first time in twenty-four hours, pushed Adele's letter out of his thoughts.

She returned to mix the drinks. "John and Barbara called to say they'd be a little late. Just as well. I need to relax a few minutes." She handed him his glass and sat down with a sigh.

"You look like you've been chasing a train."

"No, it's been chasing me. Our most recent victim." She took a long swallow, reached for one of her self-rationed cigarettes and held it between her fingers without lighting it. Matt knew she would keep it there for five or ten minutes before succumbing to the temptation. "She came over this afternoon and stayed and stayed until I shooed her out a few minutes ago." She grinned and raised one eyebrow. "She's gotten past mistrusting me so now I get to hear *everything*. And now the fear and hurt have given way to raw fury. Today she was ranting about the insult added to injury."

"Insult?"

"What the attacker said to her and what he wore." She offered him the plate of cheese puffs. "He called her a 'cosmetic pig' and, as with all the others, he performed the act with a rubber."

"What?"

"He always wears one. It's part of his trademark."

"You didn't say anything about that on the program."

"I had to spare the viewers a few details. The purpose was to create enough awareness to inspire caution. I thought some people might find the rubber business amusing and I didn't want to chance any levity."

"But why would he wear it?"

"To keep himself distanced from the act. Or maybe to keep himself from being sullied. He can violate the woman without having to touch her, so to speak. Pauline is right—the act itself is terrible enough but his words and the use of the 'protection' is the crowning insult and denigration."

"Christ, what kind of man would do that?" The question rang ridiculous to him as soon as he asked it.

However, she answered seriously. "Several possibilities. He might simply hate women or he might desire them and something—religion or a wife—prevents him from pursuing them in a normal way. And—"

"A wife! How could any woman live with a man like that?"

"She can when she doesn't know the other side of him."

"It would be impossible for her *not* to know it."

"Oh ho, you'd be surprised at the case histories I've read where rapists have been married men, long-time married men, with families. Right now there's one in prison in Arizona who has five children and sixteen grandchildren. His wife never suspected a thing. They got him with fingerprints and an eye witness and yet two of his *daughters* are leading the fight for an appeal. These men are really Jekyll-and-Hyde types and very clever at it."

"But how could a man live normally with one woman when he actually hates women?"

"Some don't hate *all* women. You can subdivide rapists into categories, but each man has his own individual story that will defy a strict categorization. For instance, I know of one case where a man was tormented all through childhood and adolescence, tormented by boys, not girls. He proceeded through his twenties with what looked like a normal life—the wife, the children. When he was thirty-two he was fired from his job but he didn't confront the man who gave him the ax. Instead he raped the man's wife. Then he went on to rape three other women before he was caught. When you're dealing with any aberration you'll find that each person had his own means of arriving at it. That's why psychiatry in the courtroom complicates the law, often hopelessly. Is all this boring you?"

"Not at all."

"The old cliché is true: violence breeds violence. If you'd been here this afternoon you'd have seen it in Pauline. Over and over she kept saying how she'd like to mutilate this man. And," she added, rolling her eyes, "she did not spare me the graphics of her revenge. Now, she's fighting with her boyfriend all the time. By some magic, she wants him to understand her feelings when she won't even tell him what's happened."

"Why won't she?"

"The reason a lot of women don't. Fear of loss, fear of being accused of having invited the attack. And as irrational as it is, some women begin to believe they did invite it. That, of course, can be more crushing than the violation itself."

The memory of the addendum to Judy's confession came rushing in on him: "You have to promise me you won't tell anyone. Not even Lyle. *Especially* Lyle." Certainly, this was irrational: for all of Sloane's faults, he would never turn his back on Judy even if she were accused of murder.

A vague, ragged shadow circled his thoughts, stalking the center, and he fought to keep it from moving in closer: he wanted it to disappear before assuming definite form.

The Harleys arrived and he was glad of the escape to the bridge table. Yet his concentration remained splintered. At one point, Mr. Harley had to remind him that hearts, not diamonds, were trump.

He drove home with the window cracked to get some air, regretting the earlier conversation with Jane. The shadow he had kept at bay all evening now stood before him as Bud. Bud with another woman, deceiving Joanne—the way Ted was deceiving Margaret. He imagined Joanne living with a husband for thirty years and never suspecting the presence of a mistress—or mistresses. Joanne the dutiful, caring for her children and tending to Bud's comforts while—

No, you must stop this. A foil packet has you off and running with the craziest, the most negative fantasy. There could be a dozen reasons for its having been under the seat of his car but you *choose* to assume the very worst.

Living alone: you're letting it make you drink too much and now your imagination is going wild. You had better shape up before you turn peculiar. You've got to start doing something with your time.

He arrived at the complex and parked in his assigned spot under the carport. Crossing the pavement to the sidewalk he looked up at the window of the little bedroom and told himself it was more than surplus time and solitude that distended his imagination. Under his breath he muttered: "Damn you, Ted Brainard, why couldn't you keep your affair out of *my* life!"

She knew better than to proffer soup and sympathy whenever he was ill, for his eyes would only mock her, silently accusing her of trying to use the situation to buy him back. And so, during his bout of flu, there were no trays taken to and from his room, no fresh pajamas laid out for him while he bathed. Their routine continued as usual with him coming downstairs for his meals and changing his own linen when it got stale. No references to his health passed between them.

She lay on her bed and heard him go twice to the bathroom and once downstairs. The shades were pulled against the afternoon sun. Concentrating on a patch of peeling paint at one corner of the ceiling, she felt the pain in her knees begin to subside. She had done her prescribed exercises, climbed the stairs six times since the morning, and taken a dose of buffered aspirin. But more than these, it was the patch on the ceiling that drove the aching out of her bones. This was the one room Bud was not allowed to touch, to make over. She would let the patch grow until she put the house up for sale after the wedding. It, like the lock on the door, reassured her whenever she doubted her courage and strength to fight him until October. Silence, caution were her weapons and in this room she sharpened them.

She wanted to limit the afternoons with Ted to only three or four a month, thereby lowering the risk of discovery. This, however, would arouse Ted's suspicions as to just how much was at stake: if he found that out there would be other layers she would have to reveal. The complete circumstances of her situation could not be understood without an account of that day at the water's edge. She did not want to have to look into his eyes and explain. It had taken years to explain it to herself. And still it was unforgiven.

What did he know of subterranean ties? From everything he told her, his relationships with his three sons were extraordinarily normal. The oldest was an oceanographer in California and Ted's face was always awash with pride whenever he spoke of the boy and his "wonderful wife"; the second caused disappointment and concern because he had little enthusiasm for anything but daydreaming and drifting; the youngest had been an honor student and a star athlete in high school whose too easily won self-assurance was now abandoning him as he faced the more rigorous demands of college. She sensed that everything between Ted and his sons, from love to hostility, transpired on the surface within view. How could he be expected to absorb the fact that while she hated everything Bud did to her she still understood *why*? Something irreversible had happened to both of them that day at the beach, and their shared willfulness had been the catalyst. How could she explain—and make it sound sensible—that the loveless void between her and Bud was a far greater bond than the bond of uncomplicated love between her and Gail? She had marked him and he in turn left his mark on her: inside, they carried identical scars. Her husband had betrayed her, murdering trust and love, and twelve years later she did the same to her son. The difference was that she had had no means of revenge for the crime against her, but Bud did have means for the crime against him.

Through the wall she heard the water running in the bathtub. He whistled a few moments and then stopped. She was grateful for the fact that he was still capable of whistling.

She returned her eyes to the patch on the ceiling. In October, everything would be untangled. Thousands of miles apart, they would not of course ever forget each other. But they would not have to remember so often.

9

Had he not had the flu he might never have arrived at the solution. It was so incredibly simple and logical that he nearly laughed out loud when it was handed to him.

Except for tennis matches, Olympic events, and an occasional late movie he rarely watched television, but on the second night of his confinement he was too weak and tired to read. He settled for a made-for-television movie about a man who hires a detective to go to Chicago in search of his missing daughter. The story was dull, poorly plotted with too many loose ends, but there were sprinklings of comedy here and there as the detective was constantly duped. While Bud watched this bungler he became aware of the possibility that he himself might have to interview more than one man for the job.

Pleased that he could actually turn the difficult task over to someone else, he took the stairs slowly, his mind already working out the scenario he would present to whomever he hired. When he reached the hall at the top he paused and looked at her door. She was behind it with her own television on. He smiled at the irony that she might have watched the same program.

Yesterday and today she had been at her most serene—which meant she was working doubly hard to hide her anxiety over how long his virus would last, how long she would be restricted from seeing the man. After lunch today she had gone out to the store and very likely to call him and explain why she wasn't free.

The next morning she slept late and he, eating breakfast alone, flipped through the Yellow Pages until he found "Detective Services—See Investigators, Private." He was astonished at the number of them in the city—sixteen. He eliminated the large agencies at once, figuring they would have waiting rooms where he could be exposed to other clients and to receptionists and secretaries; besides, they were likely to charge more, and the job he wanted done was relatively uncomplicated. The list of possibilities was narrowed down to four, then to three when he discarded Adam Strong, a name he found pretentious and quite possibly an alias. By the time he finished his bacon and the bowl of wheat germ he had decided he would first try Dwight Percy. The name conjured up the picture of a competent and discreet bank officer.

But he was in no hurry. He wanted to savor the plan before executing it, to work out all the details in the case he would present. Now that he knew where he was going he had to make certain that the path was clean and clear.

For a week and a half he entertained himself by silently constructing one fabrication after another. In the end, however, each had to be discarded because of overelaboration. He must keep it simple. The fewer holes for this detective to see through, the better.

With this new way open to him, the guarantee of a leap into discovery, his rage was expiring. But to his surprise and confusion, the temptation returned—on Wednesday, just an hour before he was to pick up Joanne and drive her to her night class. His mind could not speak what his body knew: that the rage and the temptation had been, for the past six months, always intertwined one with the other. Now, the temptation existed by itself, strong and firm without the need of support. A dull, even chill settled on him as he braced himself for restraint.

"You're awfully quiet tonight," she said after they had driven several blocks without a word.

"Just thinking," he answered.

"About what?"

"Our house."

"Oh, God. You've already built it twenty times in your head. What is it now—cedar or redwood? Stone or stucco? Two stories or one?"

"No. Basement or no basement." He grinned and reached across the seat to stroke the back of her neck. As always, the touch of her smooth, innocent, unselfish skin comforted him.

When he stopped to let her out, there was no quick kiss and brief goodbye. He shoved the stick into park and pulled her to him. His mouth pressed urgently upon hers, his jaw working like that of a famished, suckling babe.

"Well," she said when he pulled away, "what's the occasion?"

"Nothing. Except I love you like crazy."

"Glad to hear it. I've got to go. I'll be late."

"Listen. When the weather warms up why don't we take your father and show him where we want to build the house. We could have a picnic there."

"Sure." She opened the door.

He kept hold of her arm, gently. "You and he aren't still keeping secrets, are you?"

She looked confused, then recognized the reference. "Oh, Bud, come on! That was *one* little thing. You're being silly now."

"Not silly. Jealous, maybe."

"You know better than that. Now I have to go."

He waited until she was safely inside the building before he drove off.

In the study booth with a book open before him he told himself he was under control. And he had every reason to be, for in a matter of weeks he would have his mother back under control. But his eyes betrayed him each time they drifted to his watch.

The municipal library downtown closed at eight o'clock—an hour earlier than it used to because of the city's fiscal troubles—and that tight-lipped, self-satisfied, dictatorial crone, Miss Stanton, would leave between ten and twenty after. He had already followed her once and discovered that she lived alone in a small frame house a mile out of town on a main highway. The garage sat behind the house, a good twenty yards from the back door. There was an outside light which she left on but this would be no obstacle since her entire yard was closed off from her neighbors' by tall hedges. Easily, he could hide behind the garage, silently follow her as she approached the house.

He knew her kind, an absolute stereotype. Frustrated by her own inadequacies, she had built a brittle wall around them and from the top of it imperiously trumpeted the faults of others. The two librarians who worked under her—one of them a man—darted about like small-footed animals dodging bullets, performing their tasks with bowed heads but exaggeratedly alert eyes. Miss Stanton's surveillance of them was calculated to be erratic; whenever she approached one she made sure she did it silently and from behind. Tonight, she would get a taste of her own medicine.

By eight-twenty-five he had parked his car on the less-traveled street behind hers and casually walked around the block to her driveway. With all the traffic on this main highway it would not do to try to sneak into the yard, so he simply ambled down the drive as though he lived there. Only when he reached the garage did he look quickly to the right and left. Then he slipped into the narrow space between the back of the garage and the hedge.

A slice of the beam from her headlights struck the hedge just inches from his shoulder. In a moment he heard the engine quit on the other side of the wall. Waiting, he expected her to close the garage door but she did not.

He sprang from his niche, saw her already halfway to the door, heard the arrogant spank of her sensible shoes on the concrete.

Approaching with long, silent strides over the damp and cushioning grass, he felt the beautiful rush of clean night air through the holes of his mask.

She held up her key ring for a quick search, found the right one and inserted it, then swung the door open and reached for the light switch inside. But before her fingers could locate it, he was upon her.

At the next Sunday bridge game the Harleys were already there when Matt arrived. Jane appeared distant the entire evening and proved it by playing passively and by smoking four cigarettes—a doubling of her usual ration. When she left the table for a few minutes Mrs. Harley told the men that there was a problem with a new victim but offered no explanation as to what it was.

"Was it the ski-mask rapist this time?" asked her husband. She nodded.

"We didn't have any report of it at the station," said Matt, "and there's been nothing in the paper."

"That's part of the problem. Shhh, here she comes."

Matt left before the Harleys did, and at the front door Jane asked him if he would like to come to dinner the following Thursday.

He looked forward to it but then suddenly became nervous as he drove out to her house. It would be the first time in over two years that he had had dinner alone with any woman but Claudia and Adele. And the fact that he *was* seeing a woman alone brought back the unwanted feelings of loss.

His distraction was only mild and he thought he was hiding it well. But as soon as the meal was over Jane settled back in her chair with an unmistakably sympathetic smile and lit a cigarette. "It's not quite the same as being with Adele, is it?"

He was almost too struck to speak. "I—wasn't thinking that."

"No, just feeling it. I'm a pretty bold person, Matt, and I find that speaking my mind usually profits me more than not speaking it. First, I want to assure you that I have no designs on you—"

"Jane, I—"

"Please let me finish. No designs except as a friend. I'm around women all the time and I do need male companionship now and again, for rejuvenation. There's a wonderfully gentle side to you that I like very much."

"There's another side too."

"I'm sure. And another and another." She took a deep drag from the cigarette. "How I love these things. I think they give me the courage to ask impertinent questions. Why did you and Adele split up?" She put up a hand to postpone the answer. "Let me tell you first that I am not working for Claudia. I had to reassure *her* that my intentions in inviting you to dinner were strictly honorable."

"You don't have to treat Claudia with kid gloves."

"Only when it comes to you. I think you know that. Back to my impertinent question. If you like, you may tell me to mind my own business. But I *am* curious."

"She wants a family."

"I see. And you've had enough of that exciting experience?"

"Yes."

"So it's a situation that doesn't allow for compromise."

"That's it."

"And of course you miss her terribly."

"Some days aren't as bad as others." At that second he recalled that Lucille Hanes had said something similar about her arthritis. Would his loss of Adele develop into an ongoing disease?

"You'll have to keep busy," warned Jane.

"I know. I'm starting . . ."

"Claudia said that joining the group is the first really active thing she's done since your son's death. Activity is the only antidote for grief. And loneliness." She told him about the year she stayed in the house and lived in her robe after her husband died. "Then I had the heart attack and realized how much I wanted to live. I had a friend who'd been raped so she and I started the group. She moved to Colorado and I kept on with it. Although I didn't know it at the time, that heart attack was the best thing that could have happened to me. I might still be—" The "hotline" telephone rang. "Excuse me. Why don't you go into the living room, we'll have our coffee and brandy in there."

She disappeared into her office off the kitchen—a converted sunporch—and he moved on to the living room. In the fireplace two logs were glowing and he took the liberty of throwing a fresh one on top of them. The light snow that had been falling when he arrived was now a torrential sleet. He watched the new log ignite, listened to the icy pelting on the windows. He decided he liked—very much—Jane's boldness and borderline audacity. Maybe they *could* become good friends. Maybe, too, some of her energy and optimism would rub off on him.

She returned carrying a tray with coffee and brandy on it. "Well, I don't think our rapist will be out in this weather. That call was from our latest victim." She sat down and poured. "She's not easy to talk to, not at all easy to like. That's her third

144

call this week to make sure I haven't gone to the police."

"When did it happen?"

"A week ago last night. He was waiting for her, hiding in the yard when she came home from work. She fought him tooth and nail—half of that phrase literally. She broke off a fingernail digging at his neck. At first I thought that would be a good clue for the police so I've been prodding her to go to Lieutenant Whelan but her stand is adamant, to say the least."

"You don't think it's a good clue now?"

"Whatever the wound, it's already beginning to heal. And after the release of such information Whelan would be swamped with calls and most likely not one of them worth a lead. Most of the calls are anonymous and from cranks—people who are paranoid or who have a grudge. 'John Doe is the ski-mask rapist, he lives at such and such,' click. In any case, I can't give Whelan the clue without handing over the victim, so there you are. And is she going to be a real treat to try to help. A bitter old maid with a disposition that makes Hippolyta look like Shirley Temple."

"I'm surprised you can still joke, being surrounded by it all the time."

"I *have* to joke. If I didn't I'd be in the dumps right along with them."

They talked on, about their marriages, their children, that ogre called "middle-aged boredom" that was always rearing its head. She seemed to understand perfectly his inability to meet Adele's conditions. And yet when he looked around the room he found that it reminded him precisely of Adele. Far from exuding the rigid order that his apartment did, it was arranged—or disarranged—by a person who had weightier concerns to attend to.

They talked until it was too late for him to leave. The sleet had not abated in the least and when Jane turned on the radio the excited voice reported the already numerous accidents and cautioned everyone to stay off the roads.

"Well," she said, "I've got three spare bedrooms for you to choose from."

"If you wouldn't mind, I'd like to sleep right here on the sofa and watch the fire go out."

"You're in luck. It's a convertible."

She brought him a pillow and two quilts, and a pair of her late husband's pajamas.

He lay with his head propped in one hand, sipping the last of the brandy, and allowed himself a few moments of reverie in which he and Adele lay in front of the fire as they used to. But when he became misty-eyed he upbraided himself; he wasn't going to let liquor and a glowing log make him sloppy.

His mind switched to everything Jane had said about herself. Definitely, a heart attack was a more traumatic episode to get through than a terminated love affair. Or was it? Anyway, she had used it to her advantage, as an inspiration to start moving again. He aligned her with Claudia and Lucille Hanes, then grinned at how chauvinistic his resolution would sound to her: if these women could make it through life without a mate, then surely *he* was capable of the same.

The phone was ringing when he entered his office the next morning. The salt trucks did not come out Jane's way until eight o'clock and so the two of them had had a leisurely breakfast until the job was done.

"Where *were* you all night?" Claudia said wildly. "I've been calling and calling and calling."

"Is something wrong?"

"Nothing except I didn't sleep a wink."

"The roads were impassable. I had to stay over at Jane's."

"Oh?" The single syllable was sufficiently weighted to make him respond.

"On her sofa, for God's sake. What was it you were calling about?"

"I just wanted to tell you that Bud's going to stop by your place tonight. If you'll be there. He said something about replacing the broken stopper in your washbowl, he's got a new one for it. I thought the management took care of those things."

"The manager's on vacation in Florida and his son knows nothing about nothing. Bud insisted on fixing it."

"There's not a thing that boy can't do." She paused, and he fidgeted with his ballpoint pen, clicking the top of it up and down. "Well, I'm relieved to know where you were and that you're all right."

When he hung up he was resentfully embarrassed for her. That her jealousy and newly sparked possessiveness, since he had left Adele, should propel her to the point of sitting up and worrying all night made him wince. Lately, she had begun to assume an almost maternal manner with him, a façade perhaps that concealed her real hopes. *His* hope was to see more of Joanne and Bud outside her house.

Bud came after dinner and brought with him a small case of tools and the new fixture for the washbowl. He said he could not stay long but Matt insisted they sit a few minutes and have a drink. No sooner did he hand Bud a beer than he saw the dark eyes wandering the room until they paused at the molding. Matt smiled and gave him a mock warning. "Don't you say a word about that molding. I like it the way it is."

"The trouble is it doesn't have enough texture to it, the lines are *too* smooth."

"I'm the one who lives with it, and I happen to like it." He saw the merest shadow of hurt in the young face and wished he had chosen other words: the memory of his last minutes with Terry rose up before him. "I'm sorry. What I mean is you've done a beautiful job down to every detail. And if you'll let me give you some advice, you're going to be facing ulcers and maybe an early grave if you don't stop worrying so much."

Bud's lips parted in a wide smile and he put up his hands. "All right. If you like it the way it is, it'll stay the way it is. You can't argue with the customer." He took his beer and his tool case into the bathroom.

Matt opened the evening paper to the program listings to see if there was anything better than the tepid novel he was halfway through and didn't care to finish. Nothing, until the eleven o'clock sit-com reruns. Reading it would be.

He had read two pages when he heard a clattering of metal against wood. Arriving at the bathroom door he found Bud on his knees, his head and torso buried in the cabinet under the washbowl.

"Anything wrong?"

"Dropped the wrench. This wood's so warped there must have been some big leaks over the years. This is really lousy plumbing." He withdrew from the cabinet, reached into the bowl, and jiggled the stopper. Keeping his fingers on it he lowered his head to the cabinet opening and craned his neck to see what the jiggling was doing to the other section of the fixture. At the rim of his turtleneck appeared one border of a large Band-Aid patch.

"What's that on your neck?" said Matt.

"What?"

"On the back of your neck."

"A boil."

"Have you been to a doctor?"

Bud looked amused. "I've had them before. You just let them come to a head. I don't have to pay a doctor to tell me that."

"Sometimes they have to be lanced. You don't want to get an infection."

"It'll be all right."

Matt returned to the living room. Minutes later, Bud called him back in to try the new stopper. He did, and it worked perfectly.

"Have you got a new lady friend?" asked Bud.

"What?"

Smiling, he nodded at his own fingers which held several long strands of dark hair. For a moment Matt could not figure it; then it rushed in on him. "I had some people in from work," he lied. "You never know what guests are going to leave behind."

"Well, keep the drains as clean as you can," Bud answered, scraping the hair from his fingers with a tissue. "The plumbing is bad enough as it is."

He offered to pay Bud for his labor and got the refusal he expected. Bud put his jacket on, zipped it up, and hesitated. "Matt, now that you're not with Adele anymore, I don't suppose you and Claudia . . . you know."

He shook his head. "I'm afraid not. Too many—complications."

"She's a wonderful woman."

He smiled. "You don't have to sell me on that point. But what you suggest just isn't possible."

Bud picked up his tool case. "Well, I'm glad you're at least friends. And I'm glad things are going well between you and Joanne."

"So am I."

"I'd like us—you and me—to be just as close. Anything you want to confide in her you can confide in me too."

"I'm happy to know that."

Bud opened the front door. "We're going to take you on a picnic as soon as this weather clears. We want to show you the spot where we'd like to build our house. Remember to keep those drains clear. Goodnight."

"Goodnight, Bud. And thanks."

Matt went into the bathroom and worked the new stopper again. He cringed with a shame that ran so deep as to be nameless—the same shame he felt whenever he remembered the sound of his foot puncturing Terry's drums. At the sight of the Band-Aid he had allowed himself to imagine, during a fleeting few seconds, that it and the prophylactic were the exact evidence the police and Jane sought.

A boil.

He pulled the knob of the stopper back and forth, back and forth. Bud was busy enough with school, with Joanne, and probably doing repairs for his mother, but he had found time to come and take care of this. Innocently, touchingly, he wanted to play matchmaker. And the last, "You can confide in me too."

Oh, Jesus, a boil, a *boil*. But before he had the chance to tell you what it was you allowed yourself to—

He turned away, went to his bedroom, and stood staring at the only picture of Terry. Even in the creation of this wall display Bud had been sensitively, exceptionally considerate: to have omitted the boy entirely would have served to create a *greater* presence of him. One picture was enough and just right.

Terry's surly face looked back and said: "I know you. Now you're going to start in on *him*. I know you."

No, I won't, he answered silently. You're wrong. I'll *prove* you wrong. And with that, he turned away from the eyes that continued the challenge.

Nearly a month had passed since that morning he consulted the Yellow Pages for a detective, and he had yet to make his move. The idea of having the job done for him was satisfying, but the reality of having to deal with and trust an outsider kept holding him back. Even Joanne—and, of course, *especially* Joanne—had never been allowed a glimpse at the true state of affairs between himself and his mother. Naturally, his mother cooperated because she wanted him gone. Gone, so she could spring her trick on him later.

But now, to enlist the help of a stranger—it made him uneasy. Again, he reminded himself that his lies to the man must be simple ones, nothing too complicated and overexplained (as his mother's lies always had been) and therefore transparent.

For the first time in his life he went beyond simple self-chastisement and plumbed deeper to arrive at the murky and nearly suffocating depths of self-doubt. He had the key to the solution, so why hesitate to use it? Don't you, he asked himself, want to get yourself back under control? Of course he did, had every reason to—he was getting the girl and the family he had always wanted. He had not yet lost count of the number of women he had "changed," but he sometimes confused the sequence they came in. Losing count would be next if he did not get a hold on himself. The temptation would have absolutely no foundation once he discovered the identity of his mother's lover and put an end to their sordid mess. The temptation must be beaten down, destroyed immediately . . . well, at least after he got the results of the investigation. But the timetable for getting those results was entirely up to him.

It could not be this week or the next. Final exams for the winter term were at hand and he did not want to be distracted as he knew he would be if he were involved in his plan. In fact, the week after next was no good either because of his spring vacation: his mother would never take the chance of keeping to her trysting schedule when he was not in school. Oh, no, she would sit at home in the afternoons, wearing her mask of innocence and serenity.

He decided he would go to see this Dwight Percy on the Friday before he returned to classes. It would be the perfect time, for after a full week of separation from her lover his mother would most likely run to him on Monday. There was a distinct possibility that the detective's job would take only one day.

He whistled to himself as he got into the shower. Over the ridge of the glass door and on the opposite wall he saw his mother's shower cap. As always, it brought back the memory of that day at the lake, and he used that memory to squelch the tiny and unaccountable twinge of pity he felt for her. Selfish she was but, oh, God, what an amateur at deceit. As much as he despised her selfish and whorish nature he regretted the fact that in any battle, open or silent, she was never a match for him. He touched the nickel-size scab on the back of his neck. Even that dried-up reed of a woman, Miss Stanton, had fought like a hellcat, twice escaping his grasp to kick, slap, and scream before he could get the bandanna around her eyes, the dishrag into her mouth, and get the rubber on. During their struggle in the living room they knocked over two lamps and a tier table, and when he thought he had her arms sufficiently pinned under her he felt her hand whiz past his ear and quickly, expertly dig under the rim of his mask. He had had to bind her to her brass bed and then cut the receiver from the telephone before he left. Three days later, he went to the library and there she was, her face more hardened than before. But the hardness was no longer reserved solely for the two who worked under her; she would stare into space, sometimes squinting as if she expected her new-found enemy to materialize before her. And when he checked out a book she squinted at him but not with any specific recognition. Now *every* man was the enemy, and this reality, he could see, secretly claimed the bulk of her attention. Her surveillance of the two employees was so diminished that they now dared openly to exchange glances of wonder and judgment.

He turned his eyes away from the shower cap and reached for the soap. Yes, in three weeks he would go to Dwight Percy. Until then he must think only of his resistance and restraint. He must not lose himself to a habit. Since he was seven, he had been battling her to *gain* himself. Once again, with her, he would be the victor, but now there was another victory he must work toward.

To celebrate the end of final exams Matt invited Joanne and Bud to dinner at Pierre's. He supposed that Claudia was miffed, hurt, at not being included but she, after all, had the two of them to herself much more often than he did. To assuage his guilt, he decided to wait a week and then ask her out to dinner alone.

He made the reservation for seven o'clock and requested a table far from the one he and Adele had always occupied. Arriving at six-forty-five he treated himself to a martini at the bar. Pierre himself came over to give an unctuous welcome and to report mischievously that Adele had been in just the night before. "With another young lady," he added in a reassuring tone whose presumptuousness irritated Matt. But he managed a half smile and retreated to his drink.

They came through the door at exactly seven and the maître d' led the three of them to the table. When Matt ordered their drinks the waiter politely reminded him that although "the young gentleman" was wearing a sports jacket, ties were also required at dinner. Turtlenecks were acceptable only at the bar. But of course they would make an exception this evening.

After he left, Matt spoke up. "Have you still got that boil on your neck?"

"No. It broke finally and now it's healing."

"*Please*," said Joanne, "not before dinner."

For an appetizer Matt recommended the escargots which neither of the two had ever had but were willing to try. When they were brought Matt looked at the green bottle and the glass in front of Bud and said, "Doesn't beer dull your appetite?"

"No. I don't drink much of it. But since we're celebrating"—he grinned—"I *will* have another."

The heavy garlic in the escargots delighted them. Joanne, at first apprehensive about biting into a "snail," now ate with gusto. They decided to split another order before the entrée.

Soon after the waiter brought it and left, there was a commotion at the bar. "We said seven-fifteen and it's seven-thirty now!" a woman shrilled.

All other conversations expired.

"Madame, we are doing our best," said Pierre whose voice stretched thin like a rubber band. Joanne and Bud had a full view of the scene from the banquette but Matt had to twist around in his chair. "The girl who took your reservation says you told her eight-fifteen."

"I said seven-thirty!" For emphasis, she pulled open her heavy fur coat and attached her hand to her hip, then teetered and caught herself against the edge of the bar.

"You just finished saying seven-fifteen," noted Pierre.

There was a soft tittering among the tables. Matt glanced at the woman's male companion, middle-aged and flashily dressed like her, and dead drunk on a bar stool behind her.

"It's seven-fifteen," she slurred now in confusion. "We got reservations for seven-thirty."

"By that calculation," said Pierre, "you still have a fifteen-minute wait, don't you?"

"Ya keep saying, fifteen, fifteen, stop saying fifteen!"

Laughter erupted at the nearby tables.

"Whatcha bastards laughing at!" She teetered again with the effort to turn and address the room.

"I'm afraid you'll have to leave." Pierre signaled the bartender and waiter.

"I'm afraid *you'll* have to go to hell. We're staying."

Her companion looked as if he were going to slide from the stool and become a pile on the floor; the chin under his open mouth was now lodged against his chest. Together, the bartender and waiter converged on the scene. The bartender gripped the man under the shoulders and brought him to his feet. "Leggo of him!" the woman bellowed just before she herself was seized by Pierre and the waiter. She struggled as they began pulling her toward the door, but the heavy coat seemed to entrap her as much as the men did.

"You can't do this, I have American Express!" Purposely, she went totally limp in their arms so that they had to lug dead weight; the toes of her shoes scraped across the carpeting. "Wait'll my husband hears about this—he'll let you have it between the teeth!"

Pierre did not answer but with the waiter increased his step. Unlike the woman, the companion was thoroughly manageable, willing to be led wherever the supporting bartender took him. The woman now yelled at him.

"Ivan, stand up and slug that bastard!"

But he and the bartender disappeared out the door.

"Fuck the French! We'll go to Graff's, they're *American*. And I'll report you to the police! And my husband'll—"

Well aware of his audience, Pierre quipped: "When you report me to the police, be sure to mention how good our service is."

The room roared with laughter. Matt himself was still tittering as he turned back around in his chair, his head slightly lowered. The first thing his eyes caught sight of was Bud's hand wrapped around the beer bottle. The knuckles were bloodless and white and for a second he thought the glass would shatter. He looked up into Bud's face but saw nothing in it to match the grip—it, like Joanne's, was still pointed at the door but expressionless. The disturbing contrast walled Matt into silence. Pretending to read-just the napkin in his lap, he maintained his gaze on the hand and held his breath for the shattering of glass, the slicing of flesh, and the spurting of blood. But gradually the fingers slackened and withdrew from the bottle, and for the remainder of the meal Bud was untalkative; when Joanne commented on this, he replied that he was exhausted from his two exams that day.

"That's a new one," she said. "You always breeze through them and leave before the time's up. And," she added to Matt, "still gets his A."

She and her father ordered the chocolate mousse but Bud refused dessert. Instead, he drank a fourth beer.

He dropped her off but did not go inside, using his earlier excuse of being tired. They kissed goodnight, teased each other about the garlic, and he waited until she switched off the porch light before he drove away.

There was no light at his mother's window, and when he got upstairs and found that she was locked in her room he assumed she must be asleep. Quickly and quietly he changed his clothes, pulled the mask out from under a pile of sweaters, and left.

His excitement had grown feverishly and yet he was aware of the strong possibility that he would not find her.

The parking lot behind Graff's adjoined another belonging to a pharmacy that was now closed for the night. He pulled into the pharmacy's lot and slunk down in the seat; should anyone approach him he would pretend to be sleeping.

If only he had got a glimpse of the car they were driving. He made a bet with himself that it was the baby-blue Lincoln with the white vinyl top nonconformingly angled across the yellow parallel parking lines.

He watched and waited and thought of those years his mother

had worked in the restaurant. There were a dozen other jobs she could have looked for. She could have gone back to college. At first, he had been puzzled by her choice, then angered and shamed when he learned the reason for it. Once, he had had to pick her up because her car was in the shop. He arrived early and had a beer at the end of the bar and he watched the men's heads turn in her direction, watched her nod at some and return their smiles. It was the first and last time he entered the place. On principle, he would never take Joanne there, and he found an excuse by saying that he had seen the kitchen and it was filthy.

His resentment over his mother's waitressing was kept in check until he realized there was a new man in her life. He was probably a customer, one of the smilers, one of a group that wouldn't give a damn if they were told why he didn't have a father and a real home. He could hear any one of them saying "Tough luck for the kid" while they eyed her body in anticipation.

During the next twenty minutes three groups of patrons emerged. He counted the cars that were left. Five.

While he planned the words he would say to her, another part of his mind paralleled this situation with the very first one eight months ago. The first woman had been with a man when he saw her but he himself had not been prepared. But he had been wise enough to wait, to plan and ponder how to become prepared before he struck. He had been in the Eastbrook Mall walking along the row of stores and wondering where and how often his mother met her new man. Then, as if the thought had conjured her, she materialized before him: not ten feet away the door of the Green Parrot Lounge opened and she came out with a man, her head thrown back and her neck arched in laughter. He was so startled that he pressed himself against a store window and sidestepped his way to the small arcade. He squinted the sun out of his vision and realized when she lit a cigarette that it was not his mother. Nonetheless, the resemblance was strong enough to arrest him, and so was her behavior; as she and the man walked out into the parking lot his hand descended in stages from her shoulder to her buttocks. They paused at one car but only she got in. The man moved on to another. Hers followed his to the exit and directly across the highway to the motel. They stayed in the room less than an hour, but time enough to undress and moan. He sat in the parking lot, his stomach and legs prickling in response to a new and alien emotion, one that combined disgust and arousal. Several times he asked himself why he remained, but he did not leave. Until she came out.

He followed her across the city. She led him past Graff's and, farther on, past the school he would have attended if his mother had married Hugh; a few minutes later, from the expressway, he saw the spot where he had hidden under the house the time he ran away. The house was gone now, replaced by a cement company. She seemed to be a thread that was connecting the events of his life, defining his losses and the things he had never had. Although he was looking at the back of her head as she drove, it was her curved throat he saw and her laughter he heard.

She arrived at a house near the downtown business district, a section that was being renovated and reclaimed by whites. He did not dare stop and so continued on around the block. When he passed by again she was standing on the porch talking to two teenaged girls who were slumped on the steps drinking sodas. The woman's casualness made him bristle: she looked as if she had returned from shopping or lunch with friends.

When one of the girls looked up, almost in his direction, he sped away. But he returned that evening and saw the woman sitting on the porch reading the paper. And wearing glasses. A voice spiraled through him and it said: "She's not that."

He stayed away a week but could not get her out of his mind, could not connect the images of her laughing on her way to a motel and then, a few hours later, sitting on her porch wearing glasses. She had to be one or the other.

One night he dreamed of her. She held him in her arms and stroked his hair and then asked him to light her cigarette. He had no matches—and her smile said she knew it—but a faceless man suddenly appeared, struck a match, and everything became a glare so that he saw nothing but white. He heard the man invite her inside where, he said, they would be able to see and they went off to leave him alone and sightless. He awakened with a brutal start, kicking the wall next to the bed. Poisoned with

156

anger, he was, however, aroused, and it took less than a minute to relieve himself.

When he knew and fully accepted what he would do he bought the mask and prophylactic. In no way could the anticipated act resemble the one with Joanne. The woman would be touched but his own body would not.

Within a week he learned her schedule and one night waited for her in her open garage. His groin swelled and knotted when her headlights swung into the driveway, and he pulled on the mask. She let go a muffled yelp when his hand covered her mouth, but she turned rigid at the sight of the knife. He gave her the warning and the instructions: if she honked the horn or tried to signal anyone on the road he would use the knife.

When they reached the boarded-up country school ten miles outside the city he told her to lie on the ground. It was a hot and humid night but he could see her shivering while he opened the foil packet.

Her cries and gasps were interspersed but stopped altogether when he growled the words. "Remember this with the next man." She braced her body as if for a collision, then turned and vomited in the grass.

He left her there, drove her car back to the city, and picked up his own. He waited two weeks and then passed her house every chance he got. At last, he saw her on the porch with a man who had blond hair. They were playing cards and he saw her laugh once. That she was capable of laughing so soon afterward infuriated him. He glimpsed the name printed in decals on the porch post, then called her on the telephone. "Remember me," he growled, "when you're with your blond-haired man." The sharp involuntary cry she gave before hanging up satisfied him. . . .

He watched two couples come out of Graff's. Now, three cars remained, one of them the baby-blue Lincoln. The kitchen, he knew, had closed half an hour ago but patrons could drink at the bar until eleven. He was willing to wait. If she *was* in there all he might be able to do—because of the man—was follow to see where she lived.

At five after eleven they staggered out, she ahead of her companion. She stumbled, dropped her keys, and when she stood up from retrieving them she turned to find the man standing and swaying with his back to her.

"Whaddayuh *doing*?"

"Peeing."

"Why dincha do it in there?"

"Didn't have to."

It was the Lincoln. She took the driver's seat and the man fell into the passenger's side. It took three attempts before he got the door closed.

The faulty muffler gargled as she shot toward the street. She signaled left and turned right.

He followed them out of the city, his heart pounding with the fear that her speeding and weaving would attract the police.

She turned onto a road he had been down many times. It was an area that was developed before World War II; the houses were large, individually styled with first-rate materials and craftsmanship, and each one sat on no less than three acres. The one the Lincoln arrived at appeared to sit on five or six.

The garage she pulled into was situated close to the road, attached to the house that sprawled out on the other side. Cautiously, he continued on, turned around in the next driveway, and came back. Seeing no other cars he took the chance of switching off his lights. He cruised up slowly until he arrived at a clump of trees at the side of the road; through them and the open garage door he could see the woman trying to pull the man from the seat. In exasperation she stuffed him back in and went into the house.

He looked around again for cars, then backed up and pulled off the road into the trees. With the mask on he approached the garage.

The man was sound asleep, his mouth hanging open, his legs curled up under the steering wheel.

On the wall he found the light switch and turned it off. He assumed he would have to enter through a window but first, on the off chance that it might be open, he checked the door from the garage to the house.

She had not locked it, had not even closed it tightly. He crossed the enormous slate-floored kitchen, his ears searching for her whereabouts. When he reached the dining room he heard her overhead. He moved on to the formal entrance hall which gave access to the living room on one side and the staircase on the other. He paused at the edge of the living room, looked down the expanse of it to the bay window through which he could see the swimming pool and cabana. It was, he decided, absolutely the wrong place for a pool.

At the foot of the stairs he stopped dead still in amazement. Both the banister and the steps were done in marble.

Somewhere above him there was a crash and he heard her hiss "Goddamn it." After a pause, water began to run. He started up, stepping lightly on the Oriental runner.

He told himself she would be his last—and, oh, what a magnificent place for it, the finale. He wanted desperately to stroke the marble but could not afford to leave fingerprints. But after a few seconds, the opportunity occurred to him. So simple, like most things.

He slipped off one glove and continued up, letting the *back* of his hand trail along the smooth cool banister while he determined how unworthy she was of owning it.

10

Matt filled the next day with the customary Saturday errands and looked forward to the following night's bridge game. He was not looking forward to this evening's dinner engagement at the Brainards'. He had refused them so often that there were no excuses left.

Margaret had already had her "few" when she opened the front door. The glazed but widened eyes and the overzealous hello announced her condition; the panic and depression underneath reached out to touch and define Matt's own. Greeting her, his smile was so false that the pressing of a button might have produced it.

She pulled him toward the bar where Ted was waiting and said, "Will the dead please make a drink for the living." The humor was forced, and Ted offered no rejoinder.

"Hello, Matt," he said. "The usual?"

"Yes."

There was a long silence. Then Margaret said: "The weather's really done a turnabout, hasn't it? Today you'd have sworn it was summer."

"Just a lure to take down the storm windows," Ted answered. "And next week it'll snow."

Another silence. My God, thought Matt, are we going to have to fish around like this all evening?

"Why don't you tell Matt the good news?" Her question was edged with innuendo.

"Oh, yes. Kyle called us on Thursday to announce that Linda's four months along."

"That's wonderful!" Matt's congratulation simply hung in the air, intercepted by neither of the Brainards.

"I thought we could fly out and see them before the baby's born. It looks like I might have to go alone—Ted has such a full agenda." Now, the innuendo carried no disguise whatever, and obviously realizing she had gone too far in front of Matt she excused herself from the room. "I have to put on the rice."

"It's impossible lately," Ted confided. "I don't know how much longer I can wait it out."

"How much does she know?"

"Absolutely nothing for sure. But the other night I caught her at the clothes hamper checking my underwear."

"Your—friend, she hasn't settled those family matters of hers?"

"Not yet. But I promise you, I'm trying to work out another arrangement. Although I do love that little room of yours."

"If you're going to pull out, why do you have to wait until this woman is ready? Why can't you leave now?"

"I just can't. I have to wait."

"And let Margaret squirm?"

"Matt, not all marriages end the way yours did, with a loud dramatic bang. Some just dissolve. If I left Margaret now it wouldn't be any easier for her than it will be in a few months."

"The point is she doesn't want you to leave at all."

"Yes, and Claudia wants *you* back. Be fair." He poured himself another club soda. "Is anything serious developing between you and Jane Richardson?"

"No. What makes you ask?"

"Margaret had some of the women's group over last night but Claudia and Jane were absent."

"That doesn't mean anything. Claudia's still in the group. There's no tension between them," he said firmly and hoped there wasn't.

"Well, I should have holed myself up and stayed away from

them last night. It was supposed to be a social gathering but it turned into a rally. With me caught in the middle."

"The defender of his sex," Margaret said from the doorway. "Men will always stick together, no matter what." She advanced to the bar and stood next to Matt.

"I was not defending the man," replied Ted. "I just think— well, it's natural to want punishment, but too many of those women are obsessed with it. And they're not interested in any opinion that differs from their own. Most of them were simply looking for a fight. With a man."

"Just because they're willing to argue for what they believe in—"

"What they believe in is public hangings and—"

"You're damned right, in some cases!"

"In *which* case, that Bewick woman should be the first to grace the scaffold."

"Don't try that tactic! Hippolyta's an exception—there's a misfit in every group."

"I still say," he answered quietly, "that too many of them approach the issue totally in terms of black and white."

"Black and white, huh?" Her eyes glittered triumphantly above a small, crooked smile. "Let me *show* you something in black and white." She walked over to the chair in the corner and returned with the evening paper. Slapping it onto the bar she pointed to the headline: MASKED RAPIST ATTACKS AGAIN. "At least he didn't take this one out into the wilderness and dump her. I suppose," she said to her husband, "you regard him as quite the gentleman since he was considerate enough to rape her in the comfort of her home."

"We're not going any further with this subject." Ted reached over to whisk the paper from Matt.

"No," said Matt. "I want to finish reading."

"The perfect hostess," Ted told her. "Handing out newspapers to a dinner guest."

"We could," she said icily, "go into those things *you're* perfect at."

During the meal, an unspoken truce was established between the couple. Margaret asked Matt how he liked Jane's friends, the Harleys, and how work was going. He answered perfunctorily, extending nothing into conversation. Excellent as the food was, he had to work it down his suddenly swollen throat.

Black and white. He wished she hadn't shown him.

After coffee he escaped with the lame excuse of being tired. Ted and Margaret said goodnight in tones of apology; most likely, they believed that the evening's poor start was the reason for his early departure, but there was no way to tell them otherwise.

The black-and-white newsprint pursued him as he drove home. *Took place at approximately eleven-thirty . . . had left Graff's restaurant at closing time . . . victim admitted to being intoxicated . . . masked attacker "reeked" of beer and garlic . . . a family friend had been asleep in the car in the garage . . . no forced entry . . .*

He saw before him the white-knuckled grip on the beer bottle, in contrast to the expressionless face that took in the woman. *Fuck the French, we'll go to Graff's. Turtlenecks are acceptable only at the bar. It's healing now.*

The foil packet under the —.

"No," he whispered, then repeated it loudly.

The car picked up speed and his eyes kept darting down every cross street he passed, as if searching the night for an alternative answer.

After five hours of fitful sleep he sat in his living room trying to arrive at a pretext for calling on Lucille Hanes. Taking something—flowers, a plant, candy—would look like conspicuous charity for a sick woman: the idea of using her disease to gain entrance chafed his conscience. But go he must. When he had got back from the Brainards last night he called Claudia to discuss the rape and then in a roundabout manner learned that Bud had dropped Joanne off at nine-thirty on Friday and gone directly home.

"Directly home" was what he urgently wanted to believe.

At 2:00 P.M. Lucille answered the door and was unquestionably startled at the sight of him. "Bud's not here," she said immediately.

"I know," said Matt. "They told me Friday they were going to a flea market today. I was just out for a drive and when I found myself over this way I thought I'd drop in for a few minutes. If it's not inconvenient for you."

163

"No. Come in." Her hands trembled when she took his coat and as she led him into the living room she moved stiffly; he was guiltily aware of the likelihood that he had caught her on a bad day.

"I don't make a habit of doing this," he explained. "I just thought since I happened to be in the neighborhood . . ." His voice trailed off uncertainly.

He was left alone while she prepared coffee. Again he appraised the room as he had the first time he saw it, only now he was perplexed by an unanswerable question: how could *anyone* so bright and talented, so generous and disciplined, possibly be so obsessively brutal? Jane's generalized and matter-of-fact statement gnawed at him: "These men are real Jekyll-and-Hyde types."

"I have saccharine if you don't take sugar," said Lucille, returning with the tray.

"Thanks, I don't take either."

She slid a plate of cookies in his direction, poured cream into her own coffee—all without once looking him in the face. Already, he felt another suspicion being born—how could a boy as outgoing and affable as Bud be the son of a woman so shy and socially awkward? And had she always been this way or had the hardship of illness changed her?

It was his responsibility to break the silence which she seemed to want to maintain. He watched her hand tremble as she set her spoon aside. "Well," he said, "Claudia's going full speed ahead with the wedding plans."

"Yes. We talked about the guest list just the other day."

"Will there be a lot of your family coming?"

"My sister from Minnesota, her husband and children. My brother in Maine will probably consider it too big a trip. His wife's an invalid."

"There won't be any of Bud's father's family?"

Her eyes touched his for only a second, then dropped to the spoon on the tray. "No. Both grandparents are dead and there's just an uncle."

"What about Bud's father himself? It's possible that something as important as a wedding could cause a change of heart. And he might have mellowed a bit with age."

"He's not the kind of person who mellows. He becomes more determined the longer he sticks to something."

"I was thinking if *I* could talk to him, as one father to another—"

"No." Her hands flew to her lap and gripped each other. "No, that would only antagonize him."

"Into doing what?"

"I don't know. It's been hard enough for Bud to adjust to the situation with his father. It would be unfair to *him* if we stirred everything up again."

"Again?"

"I mean—we just don't talk about it. Neither does Gail."

"Then it must still be a soft spot with Bud."

"Soft spots harden with time. I'm sure the same is true for you and Claudia in the case of losing Terry." There, she thought, I've dared to say it, now if he will only drop all this.

But on he went, more quietly, more gently, "I want to ask you—why did you let Gail go to her father when Bud couldn't?"

"Because I thought she could soften him and make him come back." She looked first at the floor and then her eyes moved from one spot to another, charting a map of the past. "For over three years I hoped and waited. Sometimes he would call me after she'd been there. He'd be drunk—he was not a drinker—and he'd say how much he loved me and Gail and how he wanted to come home if I'd get rid of Bud. Naturally, I couldn't accept those terms and he stuck to them."

"It's so irrational. There must hae been a more legitimate reason."

"He's an irrational man. And very jealous. I never knew how jealous until . . . A friend of his made passes at me several times. I said nothing about it but one night the man showed up when Myron wasn't here, a little drunk and very determined. I slapped him and he left, but I decided to tell Myron. He went wild, he confronted the friend, and instead of denying it or telling the truth he said that we had actually—you know." She pulled the hem of her skirt farther down over her knee. "I was pregnant with Bud, about three months along, and Myron demanded I get an abortion. It became a contest as to which one he was going to believe—me or the friend. He chose the friend, with absolutely no good reason. Then he said I could "prove my love" by agreeing to the abortion. I wouldn't and he left. He got this fixation that he was not the father of the baby and made all kinds of wild accusations. But he didn't want to give me up. An abortion was supposed to wipe the slate clean. Well, there was nothing dirty on it. I wanted my baby and even after I'd seen this wild side of my husband I still wanted *him*. I was young and so I waited, waited for him to come to his senses. It took me three years to see it was pointless."

"Then you divorced him?"

"Yes."

"But Gail still continued to see him?"

The color rose in her cheeks. "He was her father. He treated her well, and one of Myron's conditions for a smooth divorce was visiting rights—if I tried to fight them he threatened to accuse me and the friend in court. So, to make everything look normal as possible he got visiting rights for both children."

"Bud must be very bitter about it."

"I think he's learned to live with it."

"Maybe."

"Maybe?" Only now did she look him squarely in the eye. Go ahead, go on and say it. "I want to ask you something. When you came to dinner that night I had the feeling you were looking us over. Is that what you're doing now? Do you have any doubts that Bud is worthy of Joanne?"

Cornered by the appallingness of her account and the ill-disguised hurt in these questions, he answered: "Not at all, Lucille. He's been a godsend to Joanne. After her brother died he helped her and Claudia in a way I couldn't."

"He does love Joanne, deeply. And he has the most complete respect for you and Claudia. He'll be a good father too. Not like his own."

He swallowed the last of his coffee and was tempted to leave without fulfilling his purpose for having come. However, as he slipped into his coat at the front door he smoothly approached his original intention. "I hope Bud enjoyed dinner on Friday." Now, the nugget of deception. "You know, he looked a little pale to me. Did he look that way to you when he came home?"

"I didn't see him. I was asleep. He looked fine in the morning, though."

"Asleep? He must have been home by nine-thirty."

"I went to bed long before that."

For cover, he concluded: "I hope he's not letting himself get run down. He does so much and at such a fast pace."

"I know. But he's always been strong."

The atmosphere between them had relaxed somewhat, and he could have departed comfortably with nothing more spoken. But he felt the need to pay for this stealth by reassuring her. "He's an exceptional young man, Lucille, a son you can be proud of. I'm truly sorry about the hardships his father put the two of you through."

"That's why there's no reason to tell him about the wedding. It should be a happy event. Let sleeping dogs lie."

She watched him descend the porch steps, and when he was halfway down the walk she closed the door and sagged against it, her heart thumping in relief. Gone was the fear that he suspected her involvement with Ted. But he *had* come to look them over, despite his denial. She was confident she had told him enough to quell his curiosity, to prevent him from seeking out and talking to her ex-husband. Thank God he had come to her first. . . .

That Matt Sessions was fully satisfied with her account and would pry no further was now one more factor she had to leave to chance until October.

Dwight Percy's office was above an insurance agency on a downtown side street and Bud drove to it on the appointed Friday afternoon. He had called the day before and arranged the time with the secretary whose nonsolicitous, discreet voice reassured him.

He parked his car at a meter and eyed the surroundings. Visible across the river was a multi-angled rat-colored complex of senior-citizen housing, depressing enough to make its occupants perhaps wonder if the graveyard could be any worse. During its construction all the mature trees had been pulled down and now scrawny saplings were sprinkled here and there, struggling for life. It was the epitome of the type of architecture he hated, the kind a builder put up and then ran away from so he would never have to look at it again.

He himself looked away from it, turning to face the two-story brick buildings across the street from his car. All of them had been recently painted, some rewindowed, and the one Percy and the insurance company occupied was the most appealing, with café-au-lait walls and new walnut-stained trim around the windows and doors. He found something valiant in this holdout against decay and against the temptation to flee to a newer, more sterile building, scores of which dotted the perimeter of the city. Still, as he crossed the street he was overwhelmingly glad that Joanne was as eager as he to build their house in the country—in the spot they were taking Matt to tomorrow for the picnic.

The insurance company occupied the entire first floor. Access to Percy's office was provided by a private, enclosed staircase right off the sidewalk. He climbed the green-linoleumed steps and was impressed with their cleanliness.

He was greeted by Percy's secretary, a gaunt gray woman whose officious smile lasted just long enough to convey welcome and which said there was no obsequiousness here. Bud saw that they were the only two in the office and hoped this had actually been planned through a careful staggering of appointments. Formally, but unnecessarily, the secretary led him across the four-foot space to Percy's open door.

"Mr. Hanes is here."

Percy stood up behind his desk, and the woman backed out and closed the door. He was average height, lean, with healthy coloring in his face. About fifty, he had the nondescript appearance of a businessman and gave no observable clue as to what that business was. This, along with the firm handshake and direct blue eyes, increased Bud's confidence in the choice. He sat in the chair Percy gestured at.

"Now, Mr. Hanes, first things first. Are you twenty-one?"

"Twenty-two."

"May I see your driver's license, please."

He handed it over.

"Sorry for the inconvenience," explained Percy, "but consider it assurance that we protect our clients as carefully as we do ourselves. Thank you." He returned it after a single glance. "My fee is a hundred twenty-five a day plus expenses if the assignment requires travel. There's a hundred-dollar bonus if I get results—"

"You'll get results. The assignment is simple."

Percy merely nodded. "If you require any information from confidential records the fee varies according to the difficulty in obtaining that information."

"I won't be needing that. And I'd like to pay in cash."

"That's always welcome. Now what exactly is the nature of the problem?"

"I want you to follow my aunt and find out where she goes in the afternoons. She's my mother's sister and she's emotionally unstable, not violent or anything like that, just forgetful and subject to extreme depression. She's always been pretty much of a hermit, but lately she's been leaving the house in the afternoons and staying away hours at a time. When she comes home she can't remember where she's been. Or that's what she says. My mother thinks she might be meeting someone who could be taking advantage of her in some way. Maybe a man. I would like you to find out if there *is* a man." He gave Percy his address, a description of his "aunt" and her car, and the approximate time of her afternoon departures.

"Is there a strong resemblance between your mother and aunt?"

"No, why?"

"A photograph would help. I wouldn't want to waste your money by following the wrong woman."

"Oh, that won't be a problem. My mother's an invalid and confined to the house."

"Shall I phone you as I acquire information or do you prefer to contact me?"

"I'll contact you."

"Is your mother aware of this assignment—I mean, will she call for information too?"

"She's aware of it but she won't call. She wants me to handle everything."

"There's an initial deposit of two hundred and fifty upon signing our standard form."

"I would just as soon skip the form. I'll give you a deposit of five hundred instead—for four days work, although I don't think it will take that long."

Percy bit his upper lip and said, "You're very trusting, Mr. Hanes. The form protects you as well as myself."

"I have to trust someone," he said softly. "My mother is a sick woman and worrying over my aunt only makes her sicker."

"If I do discover she's meeting someone, do you wish to know who it is?"

"Yes, I do."

"That could take additional time. When did you want me to begin?"

"Monday, if you could. I have enough with me now for the deposit."

"I'll give you a receipt, then." He did, and they stood to shake hands again.

He drove home in the fading light, his blood speeding with both excitement and relief. Percy would get results, all right, and after that *he* would get his own results.

On Saturday Matt woke up so early that he had five hours to fill before Joanne and Bud would pick him up for the picnic. While he sipped coffee and stared out the window at the light gray, undecided sky his preoccupation was back on the fulcrum where it had been all week. His thoughts would dip to the side of the clues that were nearly impossible to dismiss as coincidences, and then the weight would shift to the other side where Lucille's information prevailed. There was no *reason* for Bud to have a generalized vendetta against women. If anything, the boy should hate his father.

As if to mock and minimize his anxious state of mind, the weather suddenly transformed itself from dreary to glorious. The overcast evaporated and there appeared large clouds, driven by a mild wind, which looked like white sponges come to wipe away the last sludge of winter. He wondered if a vacation would help him to think more clearly, rationally—or better yet, not to think at all.

They buzzed him from downstairs at noon but did not come

up. When he reached the parking lot they were waiting with the engine running.

"Wait until you see this place, Matt," said Bud as soon as they started off. "The perfect spot for a house. A clearing in a woods next to a stream."

"Bud's got to find out who owns it and see if they're willing to sell. We could buy it now and hang on to it until we're ready to build."

"How did you find this spot?" said Matt, who could not take his eyes off the area under the front seat where he had felt the packet that winter's night. He longed to lean forward and feel the floor again.

"Just driving around," Joanne answered. "We take rides in the country all the time. One day we got on this old road and then another one and there it was, out of nowhere."

They exited from the expressway and drove a few minutes on a paved road before turning off onto a gravel one. The next turn-off was nothing more than a pair of tire tracks through a woods, an elongated scar which the branches of the trees seemed to want to conceal; in several spots they had grown to meet one another so that brittle fingers of wood scratched along the sides of the car. Matt closed his eyes and imagined what it would be like for a woman to drive this path in the dark, at knifepoint. When he opened them he saw the clearing, a large oval through which the stream ran diagonally.

He walked to the edge of the water while Joanne and Bud hauled the picnic basket and blankets from the car. Although few birds could be seen, a noisy chorus of chirps and squawks echoed in the woods, echoed in counterpoint to the gentle, sluggish pattering of the water over rocks. Tranquil now, he thought, but at night it could be more terrifying than a dim dead-end alley.

Damnit! his reason hissed at him. *Drop it, shake it off!*

"Isn't it something!" Joanne said reverently, behind him. "And not a can or a bottle or a scrap of paper anywhere. It's hard to imagine someone hasn't found it and ruined it already."

He still could not help himself: his gaze drilled into the trees which, when fully leafed, could easily conceal more than birds.

171

"Well?" she asked.

"Yes, it's hard to imagine."

"But isn't it beautiful?"

"Very."

They invited him to go scouting with them and were disappointed when he declined. "I didn't sleep so well last night. You go. I'll have a little lie-down on the blanket."

He watched them walk into the trees and when they disappeared over a small ridge he ran for the car. Not knowing which he hoped—to find another or to find nothing—he thrust his hand under the front seat on both sides, then opened the glove compartment.

Nothing. Nothing.

He glanced at the keys in the ignition. Maybe the trunk . . . no, Joanne had helped Bud take the picnic things from it.

He walked to the blanket they had spread out on the grass and sank down onto it. He had only half dared to question Lucille about her son; now he must fully dare to question his own daughter. But first he needed to rid himself of the hangover. He closed his eyes and let the chirping birds lull him to sleep.

The couple climbed and then sat on the wooded hill that Bud was seriously considering as a building site for their future home.

"Do you think he likes it here?" Bud asked.

"Of course. Who wouldn't?"

"I like the idea of him being the first one we've shown it to."

She did not answer but was touched by his childlike eagerness to please and honor her father. She leaned over, kissed his ear, and nestled against his shoulder. Within a minute he had eased her onto her back and slid his tongue into her mouth. "Let's claim this spot right now," he said.

"Claim it how?" And then she understood his sly smile as she felt the insistent erection against her leg. "Bud, we can't. Dad's down there waiting for us."

"He knows we've gone for a walk. We'll just make it a *longer* walk."

"No, I'd never be able to relax."

"You're with me. You'll relax."

"Not without my diaphragm."

172

"We'll be all right. Come on—for me. I want to make this spot ours right now."

She acquiesced, partly out of guilt. Long ago she had accepted the fact that he was stronger, more stable, and more talented than she, but it was painful to admit that he was also more romantic. *She* should be the one to think of "claiming" this hill and making love where their house would one day stand—even though her father was waiting for them less than a quarter of a mile away.

After kissing and stroking her he entered her, but only halfway. "Who's here?" he whispered. She moaned, and when her hips moved to bring him farther in he withdrew a bit, tauntingly. "Who's here?"

"My husband," she murmured.

The wet tip of his tongue lightly circled her lips. "Who else?"

She did not answer but tried to capture the tongue that darted away to feather her cheek and ear. "Who else is here?"

"My—king."

"What does your king live for?"

"To take care of me."

"Yes?"

"And protect me and keep me loved."

"Oh, *yes!*" he rasped and plunged until her muffled cry acknowledged the full penetration.

When they finished he lay still and watched her dress. He was flooded with satisfaction; for what they had just done, in secret, canceled out the slight he had felt about her and Matt not confiding in him about Adele last Christmas.

"You go on back," he told her. "I'm going to lie here a few minutes."

"Not too long. I'm starving."

He grasped her ankle and kissed it. "I'm going to build you a house as beautiful as you are."

"All in good time."

The clinking of silverware woke Matt and he found Joanne setting the places on the other blanket. "How long did I nap?"

"About twenty minutes since I got back."

"Where's Bud?"

"Surveying." When she said it he noted the smile, so small as to go unnoticed if not looked for, one which said "Surveying, just what I would expect him to do, a habit of his I love." That smile almost destroyed his resolve.

"Do you two come here often?"

"No, we just found it a few weeks ago, but now that spring's on the way I suppose we'll come a lot."

"Are you sure you really want to build here? It's so isolated."

"That's what we want. But Angus is only three miles away." Angus was a village with a population of two thousand.

He waited a moment. "Joanne, I want to ask you something personal, just between us."

"Yes?"

"We talked once before about you and Bud—sleeping together."

A sharp bird screech from the woods censured the statement, as did her hesitation. "Yes."

"Well, you know, you young people are exposed to so much violence and brutal sex in the news and in movies I sometimes wonder if the influence doesn't rub off on the men of your generation, even the best of them." He took a breath and leapt. "Is Bud always a gentle lover with you?"

The question speared her with embarrassment. Did her father possess some intuition, some telepathy that allowed him to guess what she and Bud had just done? Or more simply, did the aftermath of lovemaking show in her face? She cringed first and then laughed. "He's no Little Lord Fauntleroy but he's not Jack the Ripper, either. I'm very happy with . . . his lovemaking." The look on her father's face—the look of *relief*—erased her humor and replaced it with annoyance. "I don't understand how you could ask such a thing about *Bud*."

"Maybe it's this business of that rapist running loose, and Jane Richardson has told me about so many women who are secretly brutalized by their husbands—I don't know, I guess I've let it get to me, that's all."

She picked up the thermos and wiped the cap where it had leaked. "Don't you two talk about other things?"

"Meaning?"

"You know. Are you getting interested in each other?"

"Will I be answering this question for your mother too?"

"I wouldn't say anything to Mom one way or the other."

"I'm very interested in Jane, but only as a friend."

"And Adele—no chance at all of getting back together?"

"No chance."

"I wish you'd find *someone.*" Her smile and voice turned maternal. "And stop worrying about things you don't have to. Like Bud and me."

He heard a distant crunch of wood under foot and twisted around to find Bud emerging from the trees. "I was just being foolish and overprotective again. Let's forget it, and please don't say anything to Bud."

"I won't."

Bud was chewing contentedly on a small twig. "What I wouldn't give to own this property." When he knelt on the blanket to help Joanne dish up the food Matt positioned himself behind him and looked at the back of his neck, exposed now by the loose collar of a flannel shirt. The flesh was smooth and unblemished.

Bud settled back with his plate and announced happily, "I scoured the woods and there's no sign of intruders there, either."

"Since the two of you don't own this yet," said Matt, "*we're* the intruders."

Bud grinned and replied in a stage whisper, "You're right. But we won't leave a clue that we were here."

By the following Wednesday Bud's patience was beginning to fray: nothing had happened. Dwight Percy provided a detailed account of every trip she took in her car, but not one of them led to the man. It was true that she had a cold but since it did not keep her in her bed he figured it would not keep her out of the man's. On Thursday, there was still nothing; he now suspected either that Percy was lying, stalling to get more money, or that he was a bungler who had made himself obvious and thereby alerted her.

Over dinner he looked at her sitting so placidly with the magazine next to her plate. He told himself he could not have been wrong all these months, he *knew* there had to be a man. Maybe the affair had dissolved by itself. He hoped it hadn't, for he wanted to have a hand in ending it, wanted to teach her a lesson once and for all. When she became a grandmother he was not going to have her shaming his children the way she shamed him, and of course she would never be let near enough to them to hurt them as she had hurt him.

Maybe the man was out of town, or *from* out of town, and their schedules simply had not meshed that week. He decided to give Percy another three days—tomorrow, skip the weekend, then Monday and Tuesday.

With this settled, he went up to his room to study. But his restlessness grew more intense and after half an hour he closed the book and left the house.

In the Kingston Mall he wandered from store to store, but he was not looking at the merchandise. The reason he was here he did not fully admit to himself until he picked her out. She was trying on watches in a jewelry shop, making the clerk pull out this one and that one until the top of the glass case was littered with plastic boxes. With her was a man roughly twice her age, and he had The Drool stamped on his face. He hovered next to her as if he expected her to flee, but Bud could tell she would never flee the opportunity for gold and silver. He stood at the other end of the display case, told the solitary salesman he was "just looking" so that the salesman continued with the couple.

The only time her jaw would stop working her gum was when she held out her wrist to inspect a watch; as soon as the watch was dismissed, the rapid chewing resumed. Under her blond wig was a plain face that even false eyelashes and a rainbow of make-up could not improve. Not once did she look at the man with her. Her appraisals and dismissals were addressed to the salesman or to the watches themselves.

They left without buying and Bud followed them out into and down the arcade. It was sufficiently crowded so that he dared to walk just paces behind them.

"I don't know why you can't give me the charge card and let me go by myself," she said irritably.

"Lynette, you can do that with charge *accounts* but not with credit cards," he answered as one would to a child.

"How can I pick something out when you're breathing down my neck?"

"I didn't say a word about any of them. I always let you pick out what you want."

"But you're always standing there—I can't concentrate."

"At the next store I'll wait outside for you."

"That's still being there. I like shopping alone."

While they talked she kept her face turned away from him, aimed at the store windows they were passing.

"Let's go home then," said the man. "In the morning I'll go to the bank, then you can meet me for lunch and I can give you cash so you can shop in the afternoon."

"I can't meet you for lunch, I get my hair done on Fridays, you *know* that, why do you think I'm wearing this damn wig."

"It looks nice."

"It looks like hell. You go to the bank and I'll stop at your office before my appointment."

"All right," the man muttered disappointedly.

"Listen, if you're going to sulk you can just take me home right now."

"I'm not sulking, I'm tired."

"You're always tired," she said to the pair of shoes she had paused to look at.

Bud followed them out and watched them walk in the opposite direction from where his car was parked in the lot. If he ran, he might have ample time to spot them before they got to the highway.

But he stood still. Although excited, he was in control. No need, he told himself, no need—and the longer you control, the easier it will be.

Something will happen. There will be results. She can't hold out forever.

Driving home, he resolved that if Percy produced nothing by Tuesday he would wait a week or two and then hire someone else.

She glanced up at the bedroom window and saw Ted looking down, smiling. As usual, he reached the rear entrance of the building by the time she did and followed her up the stairs to the apartment. He ushered her past the living room—so quickly that it might have been a Victorian parlor full of stiff-backed, condemning old ladies—and down the hall to the small bedroom. The tea was prepared and waiting. He helped her out of her raincoat, flung it over the chair, and immediately drew her to him.

"Can I squeeze you or are you fragile today?"

She laughed lightly. "Squeeze away. These past few days my bones have felt like steel."

They brushed their lips over each other's neck, jaw, cheek before their mouths met for a lingering kiss. With a shudder she rested her head on his shoulder and stroked his hair. "Two weeks," she whispered. "How they dragged by ."

"Didn't they though. I'll never take a case as big as this one again. Those lunches with the clients—I hated listening to them. Talk about a futile exercise in concentration. No, never again."

Her relief at seeing him and her momentary abandonment now subsided. "We still have to be careful."

"Darling, we *are* careful, so let's not talk about it."

He undressed her, a ritual which in the beginning had embarrassed her but which she gradually accepted and now enjoyed. Within minutes, their lovemaking became intense, frantic, almost violent with their need to reclaim each other. Afterward, he lay in the crook of her arm and passed his fingertips over her face the way a blind man would. Then he got up and filled one cup with tea and brought it back to the bed where they took turns sipping from it. He looked into the cup and his thoughts drifted.

"What are you thinking?" she asked.

"About the summer. Bud *will* get a job, won't he?"

"Yes, he always does."

"Do you think he'll take a vacation and go away?"

"I doubt it."

There were two things on his mind but one of them he dared not mention: the reason for the trip he and Margaret would take to see their son and daughter-in-law. From the beginning, and now at every turn, he had to assuage Lucille's guilt over his being married, albeit the marriage had long been defunct for him. Any mention of the anticipated arrival of a grandchild would only inspire sentimentality in her and refuel the guilt.

The second thing on his mind, however, he did venture to tell her.

"Sometime during the summer I'd like you and me to go away. Just for a few days. We could pick out a place and meet there."

She knew why *she* could not but covered by saying: "No, Ted. Margaret would suspect for sure and she could find out so easily. She tells Matt and Claudia you're gone, Bud tells them I'm gone—it's too risky."

"Suppose I left her, moved out before then?"

Her eyes turned wild. "No, you promised! We don't make a move, we don't do anything until after the wedding."

"But my moving out wouldn't link us in any way."

"It might, it might," she said, adding silently: *He's* watching and his mind is always working.

"Would it be *so* terrible if Bud knew about us? Couldn't we sit down and simply explain the situation to him? I'm a lawyer, Lucille, and I can be pretty convincing, especially when I'm telling the truth."

"He still wouldn't believe—understand it."

"If you don't mind my saying so, he sounds awfully puritanical."

"He is," she murmured. "Like his father."

They lay still for several minutes. With two fingers she lightly caressed a scar on his neck where a node had been removed. "Are you sure you know what you're in for with me? In a few years you might be wheeling me around."

"I wouldn't want another man to be doing it."

"Not many would."

He huddled closer. "Listen to me. For years I've been afraid the cancer might come back. Now all I care about is getting you and keeping you until my time runs out, and no matter what physical condition you're in—"

"Shhh." She pressed a finger to his lips, then smiled. "We sound like we're in a hospital."

He arched one eyebrow lewdly. "Mmm, torrid meetings in the terminal ward."

She laughed and sat up. "It's time to go."

After they dressed he pulled her to him. "You're sure you

wouldn't like to slip away and spend three days in the sun with me?"

"I'd love it. But not the risk."

When she had gone he whistled to himself while he made the bed, washed the teapot and cups, and gave the place a general inspection before locking up.

As he drove back to the office, his disappointment at her refusal subsided. A three-day holiday with her on pins and needles would really be no holiday at all. Perhaps he was acting too desperately; with her nervousness and illness she did not need additional pressure from him. Never again would he suggest altering her terms with his own impatience. Soon, they would be talking about and planning where to move to.

For the rest of the drive he was preoccupied with weighing the virtues of Florida against those of Arizona—so preoccupied that he could not have noticed the brown sedan following him from the apartment all the way downtown.

11

"Matt, I think you're interested enough in rape to join our group." Jane Richardson winked playfully and handed him his drink.

"Do I seem *too* interested?"

She eyed him quizzically and waited.

Purposely, he had come half an hour before the Harleys would arrive. "I want to tell you something in the strictest confidence."

"All right," she answered seriously.

"Judy Kent was raped last October."

"Oh, no!"

"Adele and I got it out of her but she made us promise to tell no one. That's why I was concerned about you and called with my veiled warning—since you and she had done the program together." He told her of Adele's suspicions when she had first gone through Judy's house. "Judy resents having told us anything—she avoids me like the plague now. But in her story there was one detail that hasn't appeared in any of the accounts you've told me about other women. Instead of speaking at first, he instructed her with a note. Are you sure none of the other women were approached this way?"

"None who have come to me. Are you thinking he was afraid she would recognize his voice?"

"At first, although he growled words during the attack."

"Do you have anyone in mind?"

"No."

"Well, a note is certainly a break in the pattern. But then the clever ones often establish a pattern just to break it. He started out abducting them in their cars but the last two were attacked at home. There were two consecutive rapes on Wednesday nights between eight-thirty and nine-thirty, then he switched to a Friday night at eleven-thirty."

A dull chill went through his bowels. "What time on Wednesdays?"

"Between eight-thirty and nine-thirty."

The night he had come out of the movie and saw Bud heading toward campus to pick up Joanne. At the library, he was supposed to be at the library.

"Was Judy raped in that time slot?"

"She—didn't say."

"You don't think she could be convinced to come into the group?"

"Never. Do you think the business of the note would be a clue for the police?"

"Not if she's unwilling to talk to them. Matt, you can level with me. All this interest of yours: do you suspect someone at the station?"

"Not at all." He thought quickly to find an excuse. "It's just this thing with Judy has me wound up."

"I can imagine. But as time goes on maybe you can convince her to come to me." She looked at her watch and stood. "Let me get the snacks ready and then I'll tell you about the little vacation I'm planning for myself."

She left him alone with his solidifying suspicions and labored breathing.

After an overnight deliberation he resolved to press Judy, gently and reassuringly. At lunchtime, he followed her into the dining room, approached her at the steam table, and said he would like to sit alone with her. The fear flared in her eyes and warned him to harden his caution.

They sat down and he commented on the weather while she

started her salad. The tremulousness in her movements was now overcome, but the former gracefulness and vigor had not returned. The gesturing of her hands looked calculated—a studied counterfeit of the lost original. The turquoise eyes held no trace of the innocence that once defined them, that had defined her entire face. He realized now that her attractiveness had always been dependent upon a girlish quality which, of course, was gone forever.

"Have you got your apartment completely furnished?" he asked.

"Not quite. I'm taking my time."

"Is the building well maintained?"

"Yes. It should be, for what I'm paying."

"You're not sorry you sold the house?"

"No."

He paused. "You know, there was another incident—"

"Yes, I read the paper and listen to the news," she answered, cutting him with a look that said this was precisely what she had expected from him.

"This woman remembered his breath. And one of them before her dug his neck. Every little clue the police acquire may help."

"What are you getting at? Why are you talking about this?" She looked about the room, beginning to panic.

"Judy, no one can hear us. I've brought it up because you might remember something you hadn't thought of before. Do you know you're the only one he confronted with a note? If you could remem—"

"How do you know I'm the only one! You've been talking about this to Jane Richardson, haven't you?"

"If you could remember what the handwriting was like," he whispered, "anything at all the police could use."

"Haven't you?" she insisted.

"Jane and I have talked about the rapist, I haven't and never will mention you."

"Really! And what guarantee do I have? How do I know what you've told her? Or what Adele's told someone else?"

"That's not fair to Adele."

"I don't care, I care about what's fair to *me!* I don't want to talk about it, I don't want you to bring it up ever again."

"I thought you would want to see this man caught."

"I do, but I can't help."

"You saw him in the light for a minute. If you could describe his height and build—"

"All I remember is the mask and the knife. The note was printed in block letters. That's it. Now will you *leave me alone?*"

She picked up the tray and carried her lunch to another table.

His heart was so enlarged with excitement that it, rather than his legs, seemed to propel him up the green-linoleumed steps to Percy's office. Once again, the gaunt secretary greeted him, and this time he thought he saw satisfaction and pride in her smile, a blend that said: "I'm sure you doubted us, how silly of you." Percy's face, however, remained impassive as he motioned him to the client-chair. Bud sat and, watching the man shuffle together some papers, beat down his quick impatience. At last, Percy had the papers arranged. Next to them, Bud laid out the crisp new bills that totaled the amount due.

"Yesterday, your aunt met a man at twelve-fifty and was with him until two-twenty. His name is Theodore Brainard, he's a lawyer with the firm Belding, Brainard, and Stockman."

"Theodo—" His lips remained rounded on the last syllable as he reminded himself to betray nothing to this man. Oh, she had really outdone herself this time!

"They met at an apartment on Crescent Drive. From the parking lot I had a view of them in a bedroom until Mr. Brainard lowered the shade." He produced a photograph that marked the window and the two figures in it. They were slightly blurred but recognizable. As much as her choice of lover, her brazenness in meeting him in the same complex Matt lived in magnified the transgression.

"Mr. Brainard's name is not on the bell or the mailbox for the apartment. I checked the possibility of the name being an alias but it's not. The apartment is rented to a Matt Sessions."

His stomach dropped, taking his breath with it. He waited a few seconds to make sure he could speak without quivering. "Was this Matt Sessions in the apartment with them?"

"I doubt it, but I can't be sure. Your aunt left, as I said, at two-twenty. Mr. Brainard left at two-thirty-five and I followed him. Now, if you'd like me to get some more information on Mr. Sessions—"

"No, I . . . this is enough," he said, glancing at the photograph.

There was nothing more to say. Percy offered his hand and Bud shook it. "I hope this information will in some way ease your mother's mind about your aunt."

"Oh, it will."

He passed through the outer office and before he reached the bottom of the stairs he was crying. Not until he crossed the street and slid behind the wheel of his car did he realize that his uncontrollable sobbing was mostly over Matt. How could he have lowered himself and allowed this thing to go on in his own apartment? How could he have betrayed *him* after all he had done to smooth the way back to Joanne? *Letting them meet in the very place he had decorated and worked on so hard!*

And then he remembered the strands of long dark hair he had found in the sink when he repaired the stopper. He looked down at the fingertips that had held the hair. . . .

He sat there, immobile, moaning "Ahhh" over and over and sounding like a man being beaten with fists. Then, the noise became a word and the word became a chant: pig, pig, pig.

It took fifteen minutes to gain enough possession of himself to drive. Finally, it was acceptance that calmed him—acceptance of the fact that he now had *double* business to take care of.

It would mean cutting a class, perhaps two, but he could do what he had to and still be back on campus by four o'clock to pick up Joanne.

His mother had met Brainard on Tuesday and he figured she would meet him again on Friday before the weekend separated them. So, at one-fifteen Friday afternoon he called the house. There was no answer. At one-forty he turned onto the drive which wound through the apartment complex and delivered him to the parking lot behind Matt's building. He saw her car at once: the impact was equivalent to finding her in bed with Brainard.

He parked in the empty spot next to hers and looked up at the shaded window of the small bedroom. For half an hour he stared

at it as though it were a movie screen showing all his disappoint-
ments and deprivations. The life she had provided for him was a
complete reversal of the kind of life he wanted, and up there in
that room she was carrying out her commitment to that reversal.
And now Matt had shown himself to be the same breed as she.

Tears stung his eyes and the window wrinkled as he recalled
the work he had done on the apartment. Planning it, preparing
sketches had made this past Christmas and New Year's the
happiest of his life, now dished back to him as delusion. Joanne
and Claudia were the only ones left to trust. Soon, he would
begin the task of separating them from Matt.

The rear door of the building swung open and she came out.
His fingers gripped the bottom of the steering wheel in an effort
to steady the rest of him: it was important that she see nothing
but deadly calm in his face.

When his car disappeared around the corner of the carport she
was still standing, rigid as stone, where she had stopped the
moment she saw him. Over the years he had taught her fear, but
it was more than that which held her now. Like that day at the
lake when he shot like a bullet to the surface of the water to
confront her, the meeting of their eyes defined his strength, her
weakness—his will and her lack of it. She was rendered a void,
incapable of movement and stripped of every motivation to
move.

Finally, she did move, propelled by the need to look up at the
bedroom window. The shade was still drawn. She would have
time to get away before Ted saw her and questioned her delay.

She stopped at a luncheonette and ordered coffee. The bitterness of it only advanced her nausea. She pushed it aside and ran
for the restroom. When the retching subsided she pressed her
cheek against the cool metal of the stall. Thinking now of Ted,
she wished she had just vomited her cowardice; if anything,
however, she had spent her stomach to make room for it. Bud's
eyes carried unfairness and malice, but they carried certain
truths as well.

Two women entered. She remained in the stall, waiting for
them to leave so she could rinse her mouth in private.

They went to the sink. "No, no," protested one, "you use *cold* water to keep it from staining. Here, let me do it. So, I says to him, 'Who the hell do you think you are, barging in on me at this hour?' 'I'm your boyfriend,' he says, like he's the lord and master. 'You *were*,' I says, and then I told him to get out." A rustling of paper towel. "Jesus, you would have to spill tea. Why couldn't you knock over the water instead?"

"So then what happened?"

"So he says he's not going anywhere, he wants to spend the night. Nothing doing, I says, I gotta get up early. So he starts taking off his shirt. Well, I told him if he took off one more thing I'd call the cops. What does he do? Takes off his shoes."

"And then?"

"I called the cops. Boy, was he mad. So were the cops when they got there and found him gone. Listen, this is the best I can do. You'll just have to wait and see what happens when you wash it."

"Has he called you?"

" 'Course. I told him to get lost. He's the real clinging type, ya know what I mean? Always breathing down your neck. I don't let anybody cramp my style. Besides, he's been outta work for five months and I—"

They swept out and there was the sound of suction as the door closed after them.

She began to laugh and could not stop. *Call the cops, tell him to get lost.* Oh, God, so simple, so easy. . . .

After she washed out her mouth and dampened her cheeks she looked into the mirror to see if her decision registered in her face. It did not: it was the same face she had had for fifteen years. But no matter. To be defeated without having fought would be the greatest betrayal of the quality of love she shared with Ted. And in this fight she knew she must give her all.

He looked at her as if she had just announced she was going to the moon. But when her eyes held firm, his own hardened with his face.

"There's no limit to you," he said. "With all the men in this city you had to go after him."

"I did not 'go after' him," she answered coolly. "It just happened. I realize it's awkward but—"

"Awkward! That's what you call it?"

"What do *you* call it?"

"By its name," he jeered.

Not wincing in the least she replied, "I love him and he loves me. His marriage was finished long before we met."

"The oldest story in the world, the oldest excuse. Do you love him like you loved my father?"

"I loved him blindly, that was my mistake. And we've all paid for it, even Gail."

"I'm not talking about Gail's father. I'm talking about mine—if you can remember who he was."

"What are you saying?"

But he only stared at her, his eyes advancing like two silent drills.

"He *is* your father and he wanted me to abort *you*. I'm going to tell you . . . going to tell you something that I've never told anyone but your father and your grandmother." She put one hand over the other on the kitchen table, looked at them for a moment, then looked up at him. He was leaning against the sink with his arms folded. "When I was three months pregnant with you one of his friends—raped me. With Gail asleep upstairs. I told your father and he confronted the friend. He said I led him on and that I didn't put up a fight. I did fight—not as hard as I could have because I was afraid he would hurt you in some way, I was afraid Gail would wake up and come down and see . . . she was just four, I'd had a birthday party for her the day before. Your father wanted me to get an abortion, he couldn't stand the idea of another man being that close to his child. And if I got the abortion, then he said he'd believe me instead of the friend. I wouldn't and that's why he left."

"Are you telling me that's why he'd never see me?"

"Yes."

She saw the disbelief in his face but continued in spite of it. "He became deluded, started accusing me wildly but he still wanted to come back—if I'd get rid of you. When it was too late for an abortion he wanted me to give you up for adoption. So I waited for him to change his mind and he waited for me to change mine. Then I divorced him. He forced me to let him have visiting rights with Gail. If I contested him he would bring the friend to court to testify against me."

"Why didn't you press charges against the man?"

"I was afraid."

"Of what?"

"The odds."

No, the truth, he said silently. He could hear her with the man, the way he had heard her with Fred that night he opened her door.

There was a long pause, and during it he watched her face go stony, the look of determination identical to the one she had that day at the lake when Hugh told him what bedroom he could have in his house. She was always determined when she had a man there to back her up.

"Now you know," she said. "And suddenly it doesn't matter whether you believe me or not. But believe this: I love Ted and I'm going to marry him. We're willing to wait and say nothing to anyone until after you and Joanne are married. It's all up to you. Don't entertain any hopes of stopping me because you can't." She looked down at her hands again. "You were raised without a father and that's unfortunate. But I've lived all these years without a husband and I'm not going to live the rest of my life without one. Ted and I will be going far away, so you and I won't have to cross each other's path anymore."

Going away, into the sunset, without a fiber of guilt in her whole corrupted body. And threatening him with powerlessness too. "Have you told Brainard about our trip to the lake? Not that I suppose he'd care."

"If you want to tell him, I can't stop you," she said dully. "I'm done paying for that day. Do you honestly believe—I've never loved you?"

"You love yourself. And it's not your love I want," he added, grimacing. "All I want from you is to act like a decent—"

"Don't tell me about decency! I won't have you *or* your father pointing fingers at me anymore! I'm sorry it had to be Ted but it is."

"And it had to be Matt's apartment you used."

"What are you talking about?"

189

He shook his head, sadly, exhaustedly. "Don't pretend. At least spare me that."

"I don't know what you're saying." But the realization came flooding in on her.

"Snakes, the three of you. Everything you've ever done is to go against me but this is really your crowning touch. And now I find I'll have a father-in-law to match you. Maybe you should drop Ted and move on to Matt." He crossed to the table and leaned on it opposite her. "You want to ruin our wedding, go ahead. Why should you change your colors now? It was stupid of me to hope Joanne and I could start out in a normal way. But you'll make sure we don't." He headed for the dining room, then paused in the doorway. "You should have had that abortion. You'd have saved us both a lot of trouble."

She listened to his footsteps recede and climb the stairs. She had no tears for what he had just said, no anger for Ted's deception about the apartment. There was only the searing regret that she understood why Bud felt as he did, that she could not blind herself to it. And the deeper regret that their lovelessness had never grown firm enough to establish a total absence of feeling.

Always determined when she had a man there to back her up. The solution was to eliminate the man, but Brainard could not be chased off, he was willing to leave his wife for her. No, the way to end it was through *her*—to strike the right chord, find the right key. There was only one possibility open to him and it must be exhausted at once.

The next morning, between classes, he stopped at a phone booth. The information from the first call would determine whether he could make the second one.

"Belding, Brainard, and Stockman, good morning."

"Is Mr. Brainard in?"

"He's with a client. May I ask who's—"

He hung up and dialed another number.

"Hello, Mrs. Brainard? This is Bud Hanes calling."

"Bud—? Oh, hello."

"Mrs. Brainard, I have a problem, a situation, you can help me with. I'd like to talk to you about it as soon as possible. In private."

"A problem *I* can help you with?" She sounded incredulous and amused.

"Yes, you'll see why when I explain it to you."

"Well, if you say so."

"Could we make it this afternoon?"

She agreed to meet him in the student union at a time while Joanne was in class.

"Please keep this confidential. Don't tell anyone, not your husband or Claudia."

She laughed. "All right. Mum's the word."

At ten to three, he held up his arm and motioned to her as she entered the grill. It was a large L-shaped room and he had taken a booth near the entrance. She approached, and he stood up and said, "I'll get you some coffee. Would you like something to eat too?"

"No thanks. Just coffee. Black."

When he returned with it he settled in and observed her carefully while she took the first few sips and lit a cigarette. She was not a beautiful woman like his mother, but she was an attractive one despite the creped skin—no doubt the result of liquor. Once or twice Claudia had mentioned to him how much her friend drank; now, he assumed that Brainard was the reason. The genuine pity he felt for her justified his task even more.

"Well, now," she said, smiling broadly, "I expected you to be wearing your cloak and dagger."

"Mrs. Brainard, what I have to tell you isn't easy for me. And before I do tell you I have to ask something personal. Do you love your husband?"

"Do I—?" She stiffened. "I don't understand."

"It has everything to do with what I have to say."

Her tone became arch. "Yes, I love him."

"Then you'd like to keep him?"

She blinked, squinted, but did not reply.

"I'd like to help you keep him," he said softly. "I'd like to help in any way I can. He's having an affair and he's planning to leave you."

"I don't know what you're talking about. You're making the most impertinent statements." She reached for her purse in preparation for flight.

"Mrs. Brainard," he said, purposely letting his voice quiver, "he's having an affair with my mother."

Her hand remained on the purse for almost a minute.

"I'm sorry," he said. "I've known about it for some time, but I didn't know the man was your husband until a few days ago. A friend of mine saw them together."

"How does your friend know it was my husband?"

"He said he'd seen my mother with a red-haired man in a yellow Mercedes. The other afternoon I followed my mother and I saw where they meet."

Her composure worried him. But a few seconds later he was heartened when the coffee cup shook in her hand. "You're absolutely sure it was Ted?"

"I would never say anything to you if I wasn't sure." He look down into his lap. "I can't tell you how ashamed I am about all this."

It worked. Her voice softened when she asked, "Bud, why should *you* be ashamed?"

"You're Claudia's best friend and I'm going to be part of the family and now my mother and your husband are planning to get married after Joanne and I do. To get married and go away."

The color left her face.

"Of course, there's nothing that can be done if you want to let him go."

"I *don't* want to."

"There's something else I have to tell you, but I need your promise that you won't say a word to Claudia. You and I can't be spared but she and Joanne can be."

"But what do they—"

"Mrs. Brainard, what's almost as bad is *where* your husband and my mother meet. They've been using Matt's apartment."

"What!"

Eyes closed, he nodded gravely. "I wouldn't have believed it if I hadn't followed her and seen for myself. Do you see why we can't tell anyone? Imagine what it would do to Claudia. I know what it would do to Joanne." It would all be exposed in good time, when it could be more effective and suited to his purpose.

Her mouth hung open and her head swayed to the left. "I see what you mean. Oh, but I'd love to tell Jane Richardson," she said, her voice deep and livid. " 'A jewel of a man, a man who's *genuinely* sensitive to women'—for weeks, she's been going on like that to Claudia and me."

"I think it's better not to say anything for the time being. You know, he was very vague and secretive about his breakup with Adele Densmore. It might be she saw his other side."

"Yes."

"Is this Jane Richardson getting involved with him?"

"I think so, without realizing how deeply. She's been very susceptible to that quiet charm of his." Now the tears rose in her eyes. "Oh, God, *him* too. I should've known."

"Known what?"

"That he'd side with Ted and even help him out."

"Well, *I'm* going to help *you*."

She lit another cigarette to steady herself. "You must think I'm a fool for wanting to keep him."

He reached across the table and held her hand in his. "I don't think you're a fool at all. I think you're a fighter."

"We're expecting our first grandchild—I thought it might be a new beginning. And now this . . ."

"Then, together, we'll do our best to see that it is."

She squeezed his hand. "I wish I'd met a man like you thirty years ago."

He turned the conversation to proposals of what the two of them could possibly do to change the existing situation. Within twenty minutes, they had a solid and detailed plan—one he came up with but which she, upon leaving, was thoroughly convinced she had contributed to.

12

"Hello, Matt. It's Adele."

"Hi." The reply was barely audible. The hand holding the receiver tightened in reaction against the weakness moving up his legs.

"I was wondering if you ever got my letter."

He was tempted to lie but reconsidered: sending the letter could not have been easy for her, and she should not be made to speak what she had already written. "Yes, I did. I . . . appreciated it."

Pause. "Enough to think seriously about what I said?"

"I always think seriously where you're concerned."

"And?"

"Adele, we'd be right back on the same old merry-go-round. You *know* that."

"Do you like living alone?"

"There are easier things. But I'm getting used to it. Other people do."

"But many of them don't have the chance you do." Another pause. "Is there anything between you and Jane Richardson?"

"Good God, we're just friends. Where do you get your information?"

"A lot of married couples started out as 'friends.'"

"That won't be the case here."

"Would you come to dinner tomorrow night so we could talk face to face?"

The lure, the temptation. But he answered: "I can't."

"Then you name a night."

"You know what I mean. I can't any night."

" 'Can't.' You always confuse that word with 'won't.'"

"All right, won't."

"I might be around and available for a while, Matt, but not forever. And I won't call again. Goodbye."

Along with the words, the definiteness in her voice signed his release. Yet it sounded like a judgment too—the harshest sentence for an odious offender.

He spent the rest of the evening in the living room, not attempting to read or watch television or listen to the radio, only staring at the contents of these quarters Bud had designed for him. After three drinks, the self-pity that was usually kept in check began to leak out, then ran in a torrent. He did not deserve his suspicions about Bud, and if they touched the truth he did not deserve to know it. What he deserved was ignorance and peace of mind.

The next night, he went to Claudia's, uninvited and unannounced. Depressed by Adele's call and determined to get over it, too restless to remain in the apartment, he knew he could not tolerate a movie or any other diversion that required he be alone.

Claudia was surprised and altogether pleased to see him.

"I thought I'd pop in for a few minutes. I won't stay long."

"You don't have to make conditions."

He refused a drink but accepted wine. She brought in two stemmed glasses filled to the rim and said, "This is a pleasant surprise. You ought to do it more often."

"Is Joanne around?"

"No," she answered, smiling wryly. "You're stuck with me alone. She and Bud are at the library." She sighed. "That girl is going to drive herself nuts competing with him. She's running a C in the Russian Revolution. She can't seem to get a handle on what the instructor wants, so every spare minute she's got her nose in that book. You should see it—it's as thick as Webster's."

He waited, then said: "I dropped in on Lucille a couple weeks ago."

"Oh?" The smile returned. "Are you going to start playing the field between her and Jane?"

"That's not funny," he said impatiently. "These innuendoes are tiresome and you should know better."

"Should I? I remember you as quite red-blooded. And Lucille's more than available and very beautiful. Jane's not exactly hard on the eyes, either."

"I have no attraction to either of them."

"After two years with Adele, cold turkey can be tough."

Pointedly, he replied, "I found out about cold turkey before I met Adele." This was sufficient to make her drop her eyes and the topic. "Lucille told me some pretty horrible things about Bud's father."

"Yes. But in a way I think they were lucky he deserted them. He sounds awful, it's better that Bud *didn't* have him around as an example."

"Maybe. But he must hate him deeply."

"I don't think so. Bud doesn't bear grudges."

"He's only human."

She tipped her head back. "Is this the beginning of criticism: I hope you're not going to start finding fault with him the way you did with Terry."

"Claudia!" If not squarely, she had nonetheless struck the nail on the head.

"I'm sorry." She looked into her wine. "But I couldn't stand it if you started criticizing him. I know he must have faults, but you'd have to look hard and deep to find them. What he's done for Joanne—and for me—is way beyond *any* call of duty." She glanced back up at him. "Now that the wedding date is set, are you sure you're not having a case of 'No one's quite good enough for my little girl'?"

"Don't be ridiculous. All I said was he's only human."

"He's far better than most humans I know." She stood, raised one hand to her hair—ash blond now, no longer that artificial beige both he and Bud had disliked—and asked if he would like to see the new dress she had just bought. Clearly, the offer was intended to lighten the air between them.

While she was upstairs he heard voices approaching the front porch.

"I've read this stuff a hundred times. If I don't get an A on the next test I'll scream."

"Honey, don't get so worked up over it."

"She's a lousy instructor and neurotic besides. If I pull a C in this course it's going to ruin my grade-point. I won't graduate with honors."

The front door opened and they entered, Joanne frowning, Bud placid—until he saw Matt. For scarcely more than three seconds, there passed over his face a dark resentful look, and the smile that followed, Matt could tell, was forced and false. It disappeared when Joanne stopped where her father was sitting and rested her hand on his shoulder.

"Were you here for dinner?" she asked.

"No, I just dropped in. Hello, Bud."

"Hello, Matt." Another smile but this time something smoky and smoldering behind it.

"Where's Mom?"

"Upstairs. She'll be down in a minute."

He watched the two of them move on to the kitchen, listened to the clinking of jars and bottles in the refrigerator. Suddenly, he was panicked by Bud's smile, the timbre of his voice: it was as if the boy had read his mind and knew his suspicions. But that was impossible.

They returned, she with her soda, he with his beer, as Claudia reappeared, wearing the new dress. "Let's see what the men think," she said to Joanne who had obviously seen the purchase beforehand. It was a black and olive-green hound's-tooth, black belted at the waist. "It has to be shortened a little. On sale, forty percent off."

Matt thought it made her look pale and rendered the tint of her hair almost pink. "Very nice," he said. "The print seems to add a little weight to you, which you need."

Bud looked the dress up and down and said nothing until Claudia pressed him. "I'm not crazy about it, but if *you* like it . . ."

"What don't you like?"

"It does add weight but those aren't your colors. They wash you out."

"You know, I wondered about that when I was trying it on, but you can never tell with the lighting they have in those stores. There was another in the same print in maroon and gray."

"That would look good on you," said Bud.

"But I already have so much gray." She shrugged. "Well, I'll decide tomorrow." She went back upstairs.

Matt asked Joanne what in particular was wrong with this history instructor. She told him the woman was vague in her assignments and expectations; she had been in her office twice to ask what she was "doing wrong" on the quizzes and the instructor seemed annoyed that her time should be intruded upon. During all this, Matt kept Bud in the circle of his vision. Bud stared at the floor and appeared to be lost in his own thoughts.

After Matt left he realized that something else was wrong, something missing. When Bud said he had to be going he walked out without giving Matt's shoulder the customary affectionate squeeze.

It was *impossible* that Bud knew his suspicions. But there was no mistaking the change of attitude, the absence of the squeeze—

Yes, now he understood! Lucille had told her son about his surprise visit, his coming "to look them over." Of course, Bud would resent it.

Jesus, he thought, are you going to make a new mess of things? "I hope you're not going to start finding fault with him the way you did with Terry."

He did not want to find fault. But how could there be *so many* coincidental clues pointing to Bud? He had not gone looking for them, they simply presented themselves; and now, like unwanted little animals, they had built a nest in his brain that he could not get rid of. . . .

The next afternoon, Claudia called him at the station. She was going over the guest list for the wedding and wanted to know if he thought the Greens, friends of theirs who had moved to Kentucky years ago, should be invited. After telling her not to bother, he asked about her dress.

"Oh, I took it back this morning and got the other."

*   *   *

The chimes rang, and when she peered through the fantail window of the door she saw only the back of a woman's head. Not until she opened the barrier between them did she recognize, through the storm-door glass, Margaret Brainard. Their eyes locked and held each other's; she stood inanimate until Margaret spoke.

"May I talk to you?"

She unlocked the storm door, opened it a crack to show that permission was granted, then stepped back and aside—as she might for an oncoming vehicle. Margaret's eyes scanned the entry hall, moved on to the dining room ahead, then landed on the staircase. "Are we alone?"

Lucille nodded.

"Can we sit down somewhere?"

"Yes. I'm sorry. Yes." She reached out to take the woman's coat, then drew back her hands. She did not want to, could not, touch her. Instead, she went to the closet and withdrew a hanger while Margaret removed the coat herself.

"Don't bother with that," said Margaret, dropping the coat onto the straight-back chair. "This will be all right."

"Would you like some coffee or tea?"

"No, thank you, I won't stay long."

She led the woman into the living room, offered her a chair, then sat on the sofa. Already the dry-ice pain was climbing upward from her knees as Ted's wife let her eyes trail over her, from her face to her ankles.

"Do you mind if I smoke?"

"Not at all." Lucille got up and brought her a tiny, shallow ashtray, the kind that is usually found in a house where no one smokes.

Margaret dropped the match into it, turned her head to exhale the smoke away from the woman. "You must have guessed that I'm here to talk about you and Ted." No reply, just the overlarge black eyes looking back at her—a dog's eyes before it is whipped. "This won't be comfortable for either of us. I haven't come to berate you or . . . I just want to know, are you planning to marry Ted?"

"What—has he told you?"

"Nothing. He doesn't know I'm here and I'd prefer he never knows. But that will be up to you."

"I think you should talk this over with him instead of me."

"No. I have a hunch *you're* the one holding the cards. And I want you to know my side of things. You haven't answered my question."

In her lap she meshed and squeezed her fingers until they burned. "If he didn't tell you, how did you find out?"

"This city is a lot smaller than you think. Someone I know has seen you together."

"That's impossible, we . . . "

"Were discreet? Not discreet enough, I'm afraid. Now, will you answer my question: Do you plan to marry him?"

"I've considered it," she said weakly.

"Then he's *asked* you to?"

"Yes," came out in a rush, the final gasp of confession.

Margaret waited. Then, quietly: "You know we have children."

She nodded, eyes closed.

"And that we're about to have our first grandchild."

The eyes opened, looked at her, then looked away.

"You know that Claudia Sessions is my best friend. And that Matt—well, he's still *Ted's* best friend. And your son is marrying their daughter." She squashed out the cigarette. "Besides all that, I'd like you to know that I still love Ted and would like to keep him. You're a very beautiful woman, Mrs. Hanes. Certainly, there are other men out there who wouldn't present all these complications."

No reply.

"Our marriage is far from ideal. I don't mean this as a threat, just a fact—I'll fight to keep him. And naturally any fight like that can't be kept private."

At this announcement, terror climbed her spine. She saw before her the condemning eyes of Matt and Claudia and, worse, Joanne.

"I'm not a saint, Mrs. Hanes, and as a matter of fact sometimes I'm not a very good wife. I drink too much, I've lost interest in the house and in cooking now that our sons are gone. But along the way I *have* made some sacrifices to keep our marriage going. I wanted to stay in college but Ted's education came first and then there was law school and I had babies to look after. I always wanted a daughter but Ted didn't want a fourth child. And when I was pregnant with the third he had a little fling with a law clerk but I said nothing because I knew a lot of men do this when their wives are expecting. Then there was the cancer that changed him, in more ways than one. I'm not a particularly uncommon case but I have had a lot to take in stride—as I imagine you have. That's why I was hoping you might be able to put yourself in my position before . . . you continue on."

"What about *my* position?" she said, just above a whisper.

"Is there anything you would like to tell me?"

"I love Ted."

"I assumed that. And so do I."

What should she say next?—tell the woman she was no longer loved by her husband? Explain how she herself had come to live for nothing but October when she could make her escape? Try to justify how marriage with Ted would be a "coming to rest"? She could utter none of these. Had Margaret Brainard given even the slightest hint of being a pampered and spoiled mercenary she could have refuted her. The marriage might be far from satisfactory for Ted, but it far from finished for this woman. Lucille now knew the full measure of why she had never wanted to see Ted's wife again.

"I guess there's nothing more to say." Margaret stood. "Except . . . Claudia once told me your husband deserted you and your children but, if I remember right, you waited four years to divorce him. Was it because you wanted to keep him?"

"Yes," she murmured.

"Then you know the feeling. Whichever way you decide, I'd be grateful if you said nothing to Ted about my coming here. Please don't get up, I can let myself out." She reached the archway of the entry hall, heard the "Wait," and when she turned around she saw that Lucille had shifted herself on the sofa so that her back was to her.

"Yes?"

"If I gave him up it would cost me more than you know."

"I'm sure of that. None of us ever fully knows what someone else pays."

"If I . . . "

Margaret watched the woman's back heave for breath.

"If I give him up it's going to cost *you* too. It'll cost you the truth."

"About what?"

"About your source—how you found out about Ted and me."

"I've suspected for months and then, I told you, a friend of mine saw you."

"Saw me where?"

"At Crescent Drive."

"Go on."

"Well, she recognized Ted's car and she must have seen the two of you and then from her description I remembered you from the engagement party."

"You're lying," she said, keeping her back to her. "And you're not good at it. If you want Ted as badly as you claim you do, you'll have to tell me the truth."

"I'm not lying, why should I?"

"This 'friend' who saw me—bring this friend to me."

"I—I couldn't possibly. I made a promise not to involve her."

"Her? Well, break it. Break it and you'll get *my* promise. You'll get Ted."

She stood there, unable to speak the name, yearning to flee. She recalled her promise to Bud, his softness, his touching shame over the situation, his concern for *her*. But she knew, too, that this woman was willing to sit there forever with her back to her, withholding all assurance until she got what she wanted.

"If I tell you, will you promise not to—"

Lucille let go a ragged, mirthless laugh. "Oh, no, Mrs. Brainard, you want all the guarantees. Isn't Ted enough for you? Now, tell me who this person is. I won't ask again."

She blurted it out. "Bud. Bud told me." When there was no reaction at all she realized that Lucille Hanes had known the source all along. "I'm sorry you made me say it. I didn't want to cause any more trouble than was necessary."

"You've got my promise. Goodbye."

"Truly, I didn't mean—"

"Goodbye, Mrs. Brainard."

As she walked to her car, she tried to figure exactly how the tables had turned: the hollowness, the defeat in Lucille's voice made *her* feel like the other woman, made *her* body feel gritty with shame.

Driving home, she could think of nothing but the promise she had broken and what she was taking away from this woman. And when she turned into the driveway she thought of the long shower she was going to take. Never before had she needed so desperately to be cleansed.

The blurting out of the name did not produce any shock or horror. On the contrary, the very predictability of Margaret Brainard's source snapped some invisible, taut wire inside and left her . . . relieved.

She was still sitting on the sofa and staring out the window when he arrived home from class. She would concede, but in her own good time, on her terms. She listened to him enter the house and come through the kitchen, then pause at the opening to this room just a few feet behind her. He waited several seconds before he spoke.

"What are you looking at?" he asked.

She did not answer. She was staring at a group of small children playing in the yard across the street and she wondered what future surprises awaited their parents. At the same time, she could hear the uncertainty in Bud's lingering. Finally, he left and went upstairs.

At dinner, neither of them spoke for the first five minutes. Then he said, "What's wrong with you?"

She met his eyes and saw the anxiousness that was always there before he claimed a victory. "Your new friend Mrs. Brainard was here today. Don't pretend you don't know."

He did not pretend. He simply waited to hear the rest.

"She did your work for you."

"You're not going to see him anymore?"

She shook her head. "I want you to move out of here. You should have done it when you started college. You can get an apartment."

"So you can start back up with him and carry on here? I'm not moving anywhere."

"I told you it's finished. But I want to be alone now, I want you to go."

"I'll go in October." He finished his meal without another word and went upstairs.

She knew very well she would not make him leave, would not jeopardize that distant event in the autumn. She thought of Ted's deceits—lying about the apartment, concealing the expected arrival of a grandchild. These were deceits that did not even measure up to her own, but she might have to use them to her advantage when she announced her decision.

She sat at the table for an hour, using her fork to make crisscrossing trails in the laminated place mat. She had not been able to fight Ted's wife for the same reason she had never been able to fight Bud successfully: too easily, she could stand in their places and look back at herself, at what she had done to them. But after October twenty-third she would not put herself in someone else's place ever again.

In his room he lay on the bed staring at the ceiling, savoring the first portion of victory and anticipating the next. Closing his eyes, he visualized Matt's apartment and felt the festering of his new hate for the man: behind that façade of decency hid a traitor and a pimp. He knew he must proceed slowly, subtly, in wrenching Joanne and Claudia away from Matt, and yet his stomach turned whenever he pictured Joanne touching or kissing her father.

Although he resolved to go carefully, his blood called for an immediate and temporary revenge. His thoughts touched upon Adele but promptly left her; her separation from Matt had now been long enough to prove itself permanent. Claudia's hints and Mrs. Brainard's outright affirmation were leading him now in another direction.

He sat at his desk and studied for three hours with unhampered concentration. His wrath and the scheme for venting it were pushed to the back of his brain where they huddled and plotted, seemingly independent of *him*. By the time he closed the textbook and got to the bathroom he knew exactly what he would growl into Jane Richardson's ear.

"You don't mean that, you don't know what you're saying." Ted gave the telephone receiver a brutal squeeze—as though it, not she, were responsible for the message.

"I know what I'm saying," Lucille replied quietly. "I realize now I can't go through with it. I can't pretend I will, so there's no point in continuing."

"Meet me for lunch, we've got to talk."

"No, Ted. It won't get us anywhere. My mind's made up and I—I'm sorry."

"*Sorry!*" He drew breath and wiped the corners of his mouth. "Something's happened, hasn't it? Something's happened to upset you. Did you hear something from the doctor?"

She hadn't thought of *that*. Yes, she decided, use it and simplify everything. And so, she answered his question by remaining silent.

"You heard something from the doctor, didn't you? Didn't you?"

"Yes. But nothing you can say will change my mind. I don't want—" Her voice broke. "I haven't got the strength to argue. It's got to be this way."

"Lucille, listen to me." He lowered his voice. "You know I'll take care of you, you know I love you."

"Please don't make it any harder. I've made up my mind. Please." She hung up and waited. Just as she expected, the phone rang within seconds, twelve times. When it stopped she went up to her room.

She lay on the bed and consoled herself with the absolute stillness of the house, a stillness she would own all to herself come autumn. It would be enough. She would *make* it be enough.

The telephone rang off and on all day. A little before four o'clock the chimes sounded, and through the door's fantail window she saw Ted. She shook her head emphatically, then heard him shout, "I have to talk to you." She shook her head again and withdrew from view but the chimes resounded furiously, sputteringly, until she thought the mechanism would burst. The doorknob twisted and then he began to ram the barricade with his shoulder. When she realized he was going to continue until he injured himself she shot forward and opened the door. His face was dark pink, his breathing loud and labored, and his eyes—which appeared wide and squinted at the same time—took her in as though she were the most awesome, dangerous creature on earth. He closed the door, leaned against it, and held her with his unblinking stare. Her trembling hands had nowhere to go except behind her back: there she stood in the pose of the defendant before a judge, the pose she had first assumed in the fifth year of her marriage.

"Do you—" He stopped for breath. "—know what you're *doing* to me?"

Inwardly, she withered but she allowed no sign of it. "I know," she murmured. "I wish I couldn't hurt you."

"Three days ago there was no sign of this, no sign at all. What exactly did the doctor tell you?"

"It's accelerating rapidly and it won't be long before . . . I don't want to talk about it. Ted, I've already decided."

"*You've* decided! I've done everything you've asked, I've been willing to wait according to your timetable. And I've told you a hundred times I will take care of you even if this disease does its worst."

"I know. You've been more considerate than I deserve."

"No, not more than you deserve. But *I* don't deserve this, having the rug pulled out from under me." He cupped her face in his hands. "Do I?"

"No," she whispered, "you don't deserve it. But it has—" She stopped cold and stepped back from him at the sound of Bud's car pulling into the driveway. "You've got to go now, I told you my mind's made up, nothing we say will make any difference!" Outside, the car door slammed and she watched Ted cock his head to listen; from the look on his face she knew he intended to hold his position. "Pleeease!" she rasped. Now, she felt like some circus freak, normal to the eye while clothed but about to be disrobed.

As soon as the back door opened and closed, he trained his gaze down the short hallway toward the dining room.

She heard the footsteps behind her. They advanced, halted, advanced again, but she could just as easily have charted her son's approach by the growing hardness in her lover's eyes. She stood still, watched the contempt ripen in Ted's face, and she knew—without having to see it—that Bud's expression matched his. Fred, Hugh, Walter, they all passed before her as if this were her dying second. What kept her on her feet was the knowledge that she would never go through this again.

Ted's eyes slid from Bud to her and back to Bud again, making the connection. Still, nothing was said. Then Bud strode past them and climbed the stairs without a backward glance.

"I had a feeling it wasn't the doctor. It's *him*, isn't it? He found out."

She flinched but did not answer.

"He found out. And you're letting him—I saw it in his face. You're letting him decide for you. How can you?"

"It's more than that." It's your wife, too, she could have said but would not. "Now will you go?"

He looked up the empty stairs and then back at her. "My God, you *are* a coward."

The truth struck every nerve in her, and it was the complexity of it that brought the tears to her eyes. She moved backward, nodding.

It took him just three steps to reach the door; he grappled with the knob as if he could not get away fast enough.

From the living-room window she watched his Mercedes lurch from the curb and race down the block. Then there was only the ticking of the clock and the muffled sound of the shower running upstairs. She sank onto the sofa, wondering if the resignation she already felt was only temporary or the blessed beginning of something permanent.

When the shower stopped she could hear his soft whistling. Between the bathroom and his bedroom he paused at the top of the stairs and called down to her matter-of-factly: "I won't be here for dinner. I'm eating at Claudia's."

Only at work could Matt succeed in wrenching himself from the preoccupation with Bud. However, one glimpse of Judy would crumble his willed forgetfulness: seeing that altered face always provoked the question of Why *her*? which then led to the more general question Why *any* of them?

He had nothing concrete to give the police; Claudia would say he had lost his mind; Joanne might banish him forever from her life; and he lacked both the courage and the ingenuity for confronting Bud. Yet there was one possibility for unloading his burden of suspicion. Jane Richardson wanted badly enough to see the rapist caught and would listen seriously to what he had to say. She was due to leave on Friday, and by Wednesday night he was debating heavily whether or not to mention anything to her just before the trip. She needed this vacation and she deserved a total severing from her work while she was away. Still, during the week she was gone another woman could be attacked.

He was mulling this over when the buzzer sounded. At the other end of the intercom Ted's voice was slurred. "Can I come up?"

Matt buzzed, then opened the door and waited. Ted weaved up the stairs, ricocheting off the wall once and the railing twice. Matt got a whiff of gin when Ted passed by him and into the apartment.

"Want some coffee?"

"Hell, no, not unless you've got arsenic to go with it." He collapsed into a chair and stared dumbly ahead. It was the first time Matt had seen him drunk since before the illness, and then never this drunk.

"Did you drive over here?"

Ted nodded.

"You could've killed someone. And yourself. I'll drive you home and take a taxi back. And I'll get you some coffee right now."

"No. Aspirin and ice water. Please."

He drank down a full glass and Matt brought him another.

"I came to return your key."

"Oh?"

"She's ditched me. One week she's going to marry me and the next week it's goodbye, good luck, I'm sorry." He attempted a laugh which neither his throat nor his face could carry off.

"Cold feet?"

"And a heart to match." He flung his head back. "No, that's not true. A warm heart. Warm and quivering with fright. I wanted to take her away and take care of her . . . " His voice went nasal and Matt hoped he wasn't going to cry.

"I take it she couldn't settle those family matters."

"What?"

"You told me she had some problem with relatives."

"There's a problem all right. Now it's *my* problem. He's got her in the palm of his hand, his cold smug hand. I don't know how he's managed it but she's afraid of him. He's behind it all, I know that—some way he found out about us, and now he's ended it."

"Who has?"

"Her son. Your son-in-law-to-be."

"*What?*"

"We were being so careful. She insisted we wait until after his wedding, she was worried about him and Joanne and you and Claudia finding out. She promised me just as soon as it was over . . . we'd go away."

"*That's* who you were bringing here?" Involuntarily, his anger shot through the question.

"She'd meet me here. She always came in the back way. She never knew the apartment was yours. It was the only safe place for us, or at least I thought it was."

"Jesus! Does Margaret know?"

"She knows something but she doesn't know it's Lucille."

"But suppose she ever finds out you were bringing a woman here? Suppose some night you get drunk and confess? Do you realize I'll be involved in it?"

"Oh, I know how you hate to get involved. In anything." He hoisted himself to the front of the chair. "Thanks for the water."

"Wait a minute. I didn't mean that the way it sounded. Now tell me exactly what happened."

He did, and with much extraneous detail. When he got to the part about their last meeting at her house, his face darkened and the recollection seemed to sober him completely. "You should've seen the way he looked at me. Like I was an insect, something he could just flick away or step on if he felt like it. He didn't bother to say a word to me, he *knew* I had no influence over her." He turned his head. Matt could see only half his face and he watched him swallow hard, twice, for control. "I don't know what I'm going to do without her. In the movies they find someone else or go to a shrink or just get over it. I won't get over it."

"You will."

"Are you over Adele?"

Not by a long shot, was the truth but he said, "I'm getting there."

"Well, I'm not that strong, not anymore. I tell you, these past six years I've been afraid. Not a day—literally, not a single day went by that I didn't think about the cancer coming back. Every little ache or pain was a sign. But I'm not afraid anymore. Now I don't give a damn."

"Give yourself time."

Ted removed the key from his pocket and tossed it onto the endtable. "You don't know how much your favor meant to me. I'll always love that little room back there."

"Let me drive you home."

"Thanks, but I can make it all right. Drinking coffee to sober up is a myth. It's water that does the trick."

Matt's sympathy abruptly turned to pity as he stood at the hallway stairs and watched Ted, stoop-shouldered, go down them, stroking the banister familiarly, lovingly.

Back inside, he walked to the little bedroom and switched on the light. As he stood there in the doorway he considered how appropriate it was that this was the one space Bud had done no work on.

The next evening he phoned Jane Richardson and got her answering machine. Wishing her a good trip, he instructed her to relax completely and then said he and the Harleys would miss her on Sunday. He sat down with the newspaper and when he separated it the large picture on the front page of the second section jumped out at him. It was a photograph of Adele standing at a lectern. The title of the article was "Those Who 'Do,' Teach—The Growing Trend in Practical Education." Below the picture the caption read: "Adele Densmore imparts her knowledge and experience in real estate." She was one of four instructors who were profiled but the only one photographed. It was no mystery why. Her beauty was all the more enhanced by the look of intelligence and purposeful vitality.

The wound was reopened like stitching under a knife. But he

had no right to self-pity, as Ted did. *He* had left the letter unanswered and refused her offer to meet.

By midnight he had looked at the photo a dozen times, and each glance made clearer the fact that she really was going her own way without him.

Liquor, he knew, would not drug him sufficiently. He poured out his drink and took a sleeping pill.

The following morning he wasn't in his office five minutes before Judy appeared at the door. "Wasn't that a wonderful article about Adele?" she said.

"Yes."

"She photographs just beautifully!"

"I know."

"I'm going to drop her a note and mention I saw it. Maybe you should too. I'm sure she'd appreciate it."

You would appreciate it, he thought sourly, so you would feel your confession was safe again. "I might do that," he lied.

At eleven o'clock he was in the production wing of the Colonial House talking with the program director when one of the new young employees ran up to him, melodramatically out of breath.

"Mr. Sessions," the boy panted, "your wife—I mean *Mrs.* Sessions is on the phone. She says it's urgent."

He walked quickly across the flagstone lobby and wondered, with grim amusement, if this "urgency" was a joke, prompted by Claudia's having seen last night's paper.

In his office, he picked up the receiver and punched the lighted button.

"Matt?" Her voice was so markedly raw that he knew instantly she had been crying.

"What is it, what's the matter?" Oh, God, please, nothing about Joanne!

"It's Jane. She was attacked last night."

The announcement went straight for his windpipe. "You mean raped?"

"Yes."

"Where—how is she?"

She let it out with a sob. "Oh, Matt, she's dead!"

13

His car seemed to drive itself across town while his head reeled with a single conviction: this was not Bud, Bud could never kill.

The moment he was inside the door, Claudia collapsed against him and wept. "Shh, easy," he whispered. It was the first time he had held her since before Terry's death. He sat her down on the sofa, then poured each of them a brandy.

"I don't know all the details," she said, shivering from the jolt of the liquor. "Hippolyta found her. She was going to drive her to the airport." She wept again, this time turning her face away from him. "She was tied to the bed and her nightgown was torn."

This last was graphic enough to make him light-headed, and his legs would not support him. Sitting, he asked, "Was she strangled or what?"

"I don't know." She wiped her eyes but her breathing remained ragged. "He must have gotten in while she was packing. Her suitcase was open and only half full. Oh, if she had only left *yesterday!*"

They said nothing for a while and finished the brandy. Then she mumbled, "I'm going over to Margaret's. Do you want to come?"

"I can't. I have to go back to work."

He did not go back to work. He went to his apartment where he called the station and told the receptionist he would be home the rest of the day. All afternoon he lay on his bed and stared at the collection of photographs on the wall. His attention kept focusing on the large one at the center: in it Bud still appeared as soft and gentle as Joanne.

Alternately, his nerves and spine would stiffen with rage, then sag in grief. He had to move, he had to do something, and yet he could not get off the bed.

It made the front page of the evening paper and was the leading feature on WGRS's six o'clock report. The intruder had entered the house through a French door from the patio. The cause of death was still unknown, pending the autopsy, but the initial examination of the body disclosed that she had indeed been raped.

He called Claudia to see if she had calmed down since the morning. She had, she said, thanks to the Valium Margaret gave her. "You keep those doors locked," he admonished her. "I've been there and seen Joanne come in without using her key."

"Yes."

He had to be careful now and make the questions appear to be in the same vein of concern. "Were the two of you home last night?"

"Yes."

"And was Bud with you?"

"Yes, till about ten. But, Matt, he can't be here *every* night. And what about Lucille being alone? We can't let ourselves become so preoccupied that we're afraid to move. Jane used to warn us against that all the time."

The silence between them said: And where is she now?

After he hung up he began to undress. It was only nine-thirty, but he was exhausted and ready to sleep. A solitary prayer began to take shape, and in it he asked for the police to find that Jane died before ten o'clock.

The next morning he felt more controlled, but this proved to be a deception. When he entered his office the first thing he looked at was the chair Jane had sat in the day they met. He clenched his jaw but could not prevent the crying jag that over-took him.

He ate lunch with the chief engineer to whom he was privately grateful for rattling on about solar heating. At one point Matt glanced up to find Judy at the steam table. He watched her move down the line and when she turned in to the seating area there was no mistaking that she saw him and pretended not to. She chose a table that allowed her to sit with her back to him.

Later, he entered her office, closed the door, and leaned against it. Sitting behind her desk she squared her shoulders to make her body a rigid T; one hand slid into a drawer as if going for a gun.

"I don't want to talk about it," she warned him.

This time he was not gentle but firm. "She's dead, Judy. *Dead.*"

Hysteria, always at the ready, now filled her eyes. "I know, but there's nothing I can *do!*"

"Nothing you can remember, nothing that would help?"

"I've *told* you. Nothing. How many times are you going to ask me?" Her voice rose to a shrill. "When will you stop tormenting me? Don't you realize what happened to her could have happened to me? There's nothing I can do!"

"I'm sorry, I won't mention it again. I promise."

That night, the paper and WGRS dutifully reported the result of the autopsy. The cause of death was a massive heart attack, suffered during or after the assault.

There was no mention of the exact time of death, but the police disclosed that fibers of wool yarn had been found under her fingernails.

Bud was pensive as he drove along the rain-slicked streets toward Joanne's. Spring was here but it was not bringing for him the new beginning he had expected. There were too many unalterable reversals that would take time adjusting to. His mother was trying to punish him by playing the zombie; he had watched her do the same after Walter left but now the attitude ran deeper and with an air of permanence about it. Matt had already punished him, cruelly and for no reason, and two nights ago mere chance punished him when Jane Richardson started that strange breathing.

He braked as he turned the last corner and the tires held the pavement. It was his insides that were skidding. For control and balance—and to lift the heavy weight of depression—he knew what he needed.

"Where are your books?" Joanne asked when she answered the door.

"I didn't bring them. I thought I'd help you study for that test."

"I don't see how you can. You never took the Russian Revolution."

"I can ask you questions, we'll work something out. But first . . ." He gripped her shoulders and drew her to him. Claudia, he knew, was at the Brainards' for the evening. "Why don't you take a little break now." He nuzzled her ear.

"Bud, I've *got* to study—"

"You have all weekend. Even generals take breaks during a long battle. Helps them to think better." He picked her up and carried her toward the stairs.

"Bud, put me down!" But her protest ended in laughter. "You're going to break your back. Who do you think you are— Rhett Butler?"

"I could carry you across a desert if I had to," he said, looking earnestly into her face. "Or through a snowstorm."

"Well, I hope you never have to." At the top of the stairs now, she asked: "Is something wrong? You seem so intense."

"I just need you."

In her room he helped her undress, kissing the back of her shoulders and her spine as he did so. Her shudders of pleasure told him he had fully wrenched her from all preoccupation with studying.

When she returned from the bathroom ritual of the diaphragm she lay on the bed to watch him finish undressing. "You're so beautiful," she murmured. "Some men are just handsome, but you're beautiful."

He basked in her admiration of him. It had been there from the very beginning, from the night he had taken her virginity. He was reasonably well-practiced in sexual techniques and they had helped him when his instinct told him this was the girl for him, the one he wanted to keep. He had had the luxury of time and comfort that first night and was able to proceed so slowly, so gently and according to *her* need, that he knew when it was over he had every chance of hanging on to her forever.

He shed his socks and as he did he looked at her maimed foot without appearing to. The sight of it always added immeasurably to his tenderness and arousal. A body as lovely, soft, perfect as hers could, in passion and in the dark, conceal an inner hardness, emotional stupidity, deceit. But such deficiencies would never be hers. The foot, the loss of her brother had *improved* her virtues. The fact that she had suffered loss made him love her all the more, in a way he could never explain to her.

He lay down next to her and put one leg over both of hers. "My sweet beautiful girl," he whispered against her breast. "I'll always take care of you, I'll never let you go." Between his lips her nipple hardened and rose as his penis did the same next to her thigh. "Your king will never leave . . . never leave," he murmured and entered her.

She was satisfied twice, and her cries and gasps told him just how completely. But something was wrong, something that had never happened before—this delay. He always had perfect control, the ability to time himself so that they reached the same pitch within seconds of each other. But now his erection drove on and he felt miles away from spending himself.

And then another cry escaped her, far from ecstatic. It was a cry he knew, one he savored when it came from other women. Now, coming from Joanne, it froze everything except the driving hips which seemed to work independently of his brain.

"Bud, please don't! It hurts!"

Instantly, he withdrew and rolled away from her—still hard. He crooked his arm over his eyes. "I'm sorry. I just can't come."

Lightly, her fingertips stroked his ribs. "Is there . . . something you'd like me to do?"

"No, I just can't—" He groaned.

"Bud, it's no big deal. I just don't want you to be uncomfortable."

Keeping his eyes covered he used his other hand to pinch her chin. "I'm all right. Go do what you have to."

She hesitated, then kissed his shoulder and went off to the bathroom.

He lay still with both hands fisted and tried unsuccessfully to will away the sexless erection. Without warning, *she* had risen up in his mind to make him useless. He recalled how she had fought him, her petite middle-aged body belying the enormity of her strength. When he had dared to growl the two words— Sessions's whore—she let go a gasp and her lips bubbled with saliva. Her back arched in such a way that he had thought, with horror, she was going to *cooperate*. Then, all at once, everything in her collapsed and became inert. Below the bandanna covering her eyes her mouth hung open, the uncertain breath whistling inside it like wind through a cave. Scrambling with revulsion from the bed he had waited until he got to the patio door to adjust his clothing . . . .

He was fully dressed when Joanne returned. He embraced her and rubbed a lock of her hair across his face; for the moment, the fragrance of it erased Jane Richardson from his mind. And, at last, he felt the slackening inside his trousers.

"Okay, sweet worrywart," he whispered, "let's go downstairs and get you through the Russian Revolution."

Matt went to the funeral with Claudia. Part of him was apprehensive about Margaret's refusal to ride with them; she arrived in a car with three other women from Jane's group.

During the eulogy he stared at the floral carpeting while women wept on all sides of him. He stared with purposeful determination, to keep his eyes off Hippolyta Bewick. A ten-second glance at her had been sufficient to register the metamorphosis. Her ever-ferreting eyes were now listless, un-focusing to the point of appearing gelatinous; the shoulders hunched forward as if they wanted to meet and hide some erosion in her chest. While the minister droned on and on, Matt found himself wishing that Bewick would leap up and deliver a scalding invective. Instead, she sat perfectly still, bent at the waist in such a way that her lap might have been a net prepared to catch her head and torso when they toppled.

On the sidewalk, after the service and before the trip to the cemetery, Claudia introduced Matt to a short bulldoggish man whose belly pushed defiantly against the vest of his polyester suit. "This is Lieutenant Whelan," she said. "He and Jane knew each other quite well."

Whelan self-consciously tapped his cigarette twice although there was not enough ash on it to flick off. Matt saw at once that the man was uncomfortable in this highly charged emotional atmosphere. As they shook hands, two women from the group appeared and Claudia turned away to talk to them.

"Jane told me how you worked to get her on that program with Judy Kent," said Whelan. "She was grateful to get the exposure."

"We were glad to help her. She was . . . genuinely dedicated."

"Yes, she was." Whelan dropped the cigarette and, with the toe of his shoe, squashed it much longer than was necessary. "She had earned that vacation," he said with the kind of offhandedness that is used to disguise something deeper. "We heard your last message on her answering machine."

"The news said you found yarn under her nails. Was it from a mask?"

"Could be. But it's the same kind used for sweaters."

"Were there any fingerprints?"

Whelan's eyes let him know this was a ridiculous question, but his answer was not glib. "No," he said quietly, "we didn't expect any."

"Aren't there any suspects?"

"Plenty of them. Like always."

The two of them watched the casket being slid into the hearse. This finality—and the fleeting look of defeat in Whelan's face—snapped Matt's restraint. "How is it *possible* this man can go on and on with being caught!"

"Because he's as smart as he is sick."

"Don't people report suspicious characters? Don't you get leads?"

"Sure we get leads," he said, openly cynical now. "As soon as Jane's death hit the news we got fifty-one calls, every one of them convinced they know who the man is—their husband, their brother, the next-door neighbor, the plumber who made a pass at them. And every one without a shred of evidence. The simple fact remains that if you don't catch a rapist in the act you usually don't catch him at all." He lit another cigarette and said goodbye but Matt walked on with him to his car.

"But when these people report their suspicions you have to check them out, don't you?"

"Sometimes."

"And then you follow the suspect?"

Whelan sighed. "Yeah, we follow each one twenty-four hours a day, seven days a week. We just ignore the murder and drug cases and the burglaries, auto thefts, arson, etcetera."

"But doesn't Jane's case fall into the category of murder?"

"Manslaughter, maybe." He dug into his pocket and withdrew the car keys. "We can proceed only with evidence, Mr. Sessions, and that's something that even Jane took a long time to accept." With his forefinger he gently stroked the teeth on the key. "I liked her—I didn't realize how much until the report came in. My wife was always bugging me to ask her over to dinner, but I never got around to it." He rolled down the window, got in, and closed the door.

"Lieutenant, did they establish the time of death?"

"Around midnight. Why—you got a suspect?"

"No."

"Thank God," he said and started the engine. "You might be able to do me a favor. You might persuade Mrs. Sessions or Mrs. Brainard to take over the group. I wouldn't want it to fall into the hands of that Bewick woman. Things are tough enough as it is."

As Matt walked back in search of Claudia, he saw Hippolyta Bewick standing in the dappled shade of a tree, staring into space like an amnesiac. Sadly, he thought that Whelan had no need to worry.

At work the next day Matt's distraction was obvious enough to elicit questions of concern from a number of the employees. Twice he picked up his telephone to call Whelan. The first time he dialed five numerals, the second time three.

The simple fact remains that if you don't catch a rapist in the act you usually don't catch him at all. And with no concrete evidence you don't point your finger at the man your daughter loves.

He hid in his office all afternoon and halfway through it he phoned Claudia. "Are you feeling better today?"

"Yes, quite a bit, thanks to Bud."

"Oh?"

"He was here last night and after Joanne went to bed he sat up with me until almost two."

"What did you talk about?"

"Everything. How these things—these tragedies—are meant to test us. He's so wise, so clear-headed. He said how we have to keep everything in proportion, you know—balanced. We've got a wonderful daughter and someday we'll have wonderful grandchildren, and we can't linger over misfortunes."

"That's all very nice, but it doesn't help Jane."

"He was helping *me*—he didn't know Jane." Then, with annoyance: "You sound awfully testy."

"I'm tired."

"You've been looking tired. I think you should get away a while, take a vacation."

"It'll take more than a vacation or an evening of pep talk from Bud for me to forget about Jane."

"No one's forgetting!" Her voice was burning. "And as for 'pep talk,' if you'd ever once sat down with Terry the way Bud does with me he'd probably still be here!"

There was a long stretch of nothing but the sound of their breathing. Then: "I'm sorry, Matt, I didn't mean to say that. We're upset over Jane and I know you were becoming good friends, but that's no reason to take a swipe at Bud and me."

"You're right," he muttered, "you're right."

That night he got drunk but only his body felt blurred. His mind refused. Sitting on the balcony of his apartment with the scotch bottle on one side of him and the ice bucket on the other, he stared at the newly sprouting flowers in the courtyard below. One of the other tenants, a retired teacher, maintained the garden and was now pulling up weeds. In what used to be called a "housedress," a white-and-green gingham, and in cream-colored oxfords she stooped and yanked, stood and scouted. This went on for half an hour and not once did she look up at him, so absorbed was she in her work. Watching her, he felt the old fear come creeping back: that he was so bored, so unre-sourceful at filling the emptiness in his life without Adele that he had overblown the "clues" against Bud, had bent and twisted them until they produced a pattern. What refuted that pattern were two unanswerable questions: Why Judy? Why Jane?

Impulsively, he leaned forward to the balcony railing and called down. "It's a lot of work, isn't it?"

She looked up, her old leathery face stretching into a smile. "I'll say. When you think you've got them all there's a slew of them just waiting to pop up."

"Mother Nature's a real cynic," he said, hoping the words did not sound slurred.

The woman tittered. "Maybe you're right. I know she makes about a hundred weeds for every flower."

In his living room he continued to drink, with the lights off. He tried to plan a vacation but this only recalled the fact that Jane died the night before she was to leave for hers. And then a flood of details, her attractive mannerisms rushed to memory: the moist, mischievous, life-loving chuckle; her remarks of exasperation over Hippolyta Bewick that failed to disguise her real sympathy and affection for the woman; her surprising Las Vegas-style shuffling and dealing of the cards at the bridge table, with her two rationed cigarettes lying next to the score pad. . . .

As the evening dragged on he mulled over all she had told him about the personalities of rapists. "Jekyll and Hyde" kept echoing in his mind while he brushed his teeth and got into bed.

A little after midnight he was lingering in that halfway territory between dozing and real sleep when the jolt came: his legs scissored open the way they do when one dreams of falling.

Bud's failure to squeeze his shoulder as a way of welcome, his change of attitude into avoidance; Ted's implication that Bud had made Lucille end the affair, which meant that Bud had to know some of the details, perhaps *where* the two of them had been meeting; the case Jane told him about where the man took his revenge on his boss by raping the wife.

Matt sat upright with sweat prickling all over him. There was the answer to one of the two questions. It was possible, entirely possible, that the attack on Jane had been intended as a punishment of *him*.

*　　*　　*

221

He watched her face appear in the fantail window, then disappear again as she stepped aside to open the door. His purpose for coming almost expired when he got a full view of the circles under her eyes, the deadness in her face.

"Are you just out driving around again?" she said, alluding to his last surprise drop-in. Then it had been a Sunday, but this was a Tuesday and at an hour he was supposed to be working.

"No, Lucille. This time I've come for a specific reason."

"I wish you'd called first," she said flatly.

They went into the living room but she made no overture at offering him anything. They both sat and her eyes, dulled now, did not try to avoid him.

"Lucille, I know about you and Ted," he said softly.

"I assumed that's why you came."

"Partly. I'm sorry it had to turn out the way it did for you."

"I wouldn't have expected you to feel that way, considering you're a friend of Margaret's too."

"Yes, but now I know how much you mean to Ted."

At this, she closed her eyes wearily and reopened them away from him.

"Ted is convinced that Bud is the reason you broke it off with him."

"I know how Ted feels. But Ted is not in my place."

"*Is* Bud the reason?"

Now, she appeared alert. "Bud and Joanne."

"They're adults—or on their way to becoming adults. They'll have to learn to accept things they don't like."

"Are you here to make a pitch for Ted?"

"No." In preparation, his hands squeezed the arms of the chair. "Ted is also convinced you're afraid of Bud. Overly afraid."

"I'm concerned for his happiness."

"And your own happiness?"

"It was foolish of Ted and me to get involved. But it's over now."

"Not for Ted. And frankly, Lucille, you don't strike me as the type to lead a man on, promising to marry him, and then out of the blue tell him it's over. Unless something or someone forced you to."

"I wasn't forced. I make my own decisions. I don't want to go on talking about it. I'm tired, I was just about to take a nap."

"All right. But I want to tell you something. *I'm* afraid of Bud."

Her face all but collapsed. "You? Why should you be afraid?"

"He knows where you and Ted used to meet, and now he's changed his whole attitude toward me."

"I'm sorry you had to get involved, Ted never told me the apartment was yours, he said—"

"That's not my point, Lucille. The point is this change in Bud. Disappointment in me would be one thing, but I feel more than that coming from him. I feel something a lot closer to hate."

The last word went to the bone but she concealed it with casualness. "Aren't you exaggerating? He's probably angry . . . "

"You and Ted were being very careful, I know. How could Bud have found out unless he *wanted* to find out—and knowing he'd be able to get you to change your mind?"

All at once, she was in motion: she uncrossed her legs and recrossed them in the other direction; she arched her neck and rubbed the back of it.

But he drove on, mercilessly. "Has it ever occurred to you he might be . . . a little disturbed?"

Now her eyes flashed, with the rancor of an animal cornered. "You mean disturbed enough to run a car into a tree with his sister in it?" She paused to let the question strike its mark. "Just because suddenly he's angry at you—which from his point of view he has a right to be—that means he's disturbed? My God, he worships Joanne, and Claudia too—you don't have to be a genius to see that. Can't you put up with a little anger from him for a while?"

It was a plea—forged, he knew, from maternal blindness— and he had no choice but to honor it. "You're right. I guess I should think of *his* feelings. I'm sorry, I was overreacting."

He watched her rise with effort, and his heart crowded his throat. Whatever her son had done to her and for whatever reasons, it was apparent that she clutched the belief he was good for *someone*.

And as he walked to his car he knew that all hope of finding allies was gone. If Bud was what he suspected, then the task of exposing him rested solely upon his own shoulders.

But the question of where and how to begin left him in limbo. Conspicuous to him—but seemingly not to Claudia or Joanne—was Bud's absence whenever he himself was invited to Claudia's. Joanne looked happy although preoccupied with some class of hers, and her face never failed to light up whenever the wedding was discussed. Often, he would catch himself staring at her, wondering if one day Bud would make her into the same lifeless, defeated woman that Lucille was. He did not allow himself to think what else Bud might do to her. . . .

The days crept by but the weeks, in reflection, seemed to have flown. The few times Bud left his mind, Adele moved in to fill it, and he would taunt himself with the likelihood that she was already being pursued by someone else.

At the university, spring-term classes ended and final exams began: between Jane's death in early May and this second week of June there were no reported attacks by the ski-mask rapist. During that week of Joanne's exams he learned from Claudia that the Women's Self-Protection Group was almost at the point of dissolving.

"There's really no one who can take Jane's place," she told him one night over dinner. "With her it was a full-time job. And everyone's afraid that what happened to her might happen to them if they did take over. Even Lieutenant Whelan thinks it's possible."

"How did you come to talk to him?"

"He addressed the group."

"Did he say anything about the rapist's current inactivity?"

"Just that the man is probably not homicidal and Jane's death scared him. He said there are cases where rapists have stopped for months—sometimes years—before they start up again. And there's always the chance he could die or move away."

"*Fat* chance. Why don't you take over the group?"

"Well, thanks for suggesting I put my life on the line. Besides, October will be here before you know it and there's all the arrangements."

He did not like to consider October being here before he knew it. "Then what about Margaret?"

"I imagine she's busy enough keeping her eye on Ted."

"Has she mentioned anything to you about Ted's supposed affair?"

"No, and I don't ask, following *your* example."

"Wouldn't Bewick take over the group?"

She shook her head. "She's gone into complete seclusion and won't even come to the meetings."

In complete seclusion. It was where he wished he could be.

The woman was leaning on both arms against the car door, talking to the man inside, her body bent in a way that advertised her round and ready rump. It was packed into a pair of hotpants which, Bud thought, no woman her age should be wearing. He watched her smile, giggle, playfully slap the man's arm, then shift her weight from one leg to the other so that the rear cheeks traded levels. But it was more than the outfit and the vulgar, pathetic attempt to counterfeit a long-lost youthfulness that attracted his attention. Occasionally, his gaze would leave her and fix upon the battered, rusted-out station wagon where the children waited. There were four of them. For the second time, the smallest—a boy of six or seven and shirtless—hung half his body out the open window and bellowed, "Ma! Let's go-o-o!" The woman twisted around and yelled over the five parked cars between them. "You shut your mouth! Sharikay, sit him down and keep him quiet. What do you think I pay you for?" The child was yanked back into the car by a sullen-faced teenaged girl; the woman's smile was fully returned by the time she swung her head around to the man again. There followed a general commotion in the station wagon as the girl attempted to subdue the boy. Minutes ago, he and she and the two others had finished their pizza and had thrown the napkins and paper plates out the window. Bud took in the litter flanking the car and then returned his attention to the woman.

The temptation was there in full force and keen on being satisfied—but for new reasons. With Joanne he had faked too many orgasms, and too often she would return from the bathroom afterward with that cloudy expression of puzzlement. Whenever he was inside her he could not control the appearance of the Richardson woman in his head, and once she did appear

225

Matt inevitably followed, and then came images of Matt and Joanne laughing affectionately, enjoying each other while he himself was tormented by a corpse. Twice in the past month the images were so vivid they overtook him, and both times Joanne's body stiffened under his as she cried out "Bud, *please*, you're hurting me!" He did not want to hurt her, not in any way. It was Matt he wanted to hurt. Because of Matt he had chosen Richardson; because of Matt he had been touched by Death.

But hurting Matt would have to wait. More immediate was the need to make right again his lovemaking with Joanne. And it seemed that the only clear way was to strike again, to record to memory every second of the encounter with another woman and thereby banish the ghost that haunted him.

Joanne came out of the bookstore and made straight for the car. About twenty feet from it, something made her halt: it was the peculiar look on Bud's face, one she had never seen before and one she could not define. He was squinting and she followed the line of his gaze to the woman. She waited for what seemed like minutes but his concentration did not waver; then she advanced stealthily. Through the open window on the passenger's side she said: "Getting an eyeful?"

His head jerked around so quickly that it looked as if it would fly off his body. When she opened the door and got in, his face was red with guilt. Yet he said: "What do you mean?"

"You know what I mean. Hotpants over there."

"Well, she *is* putting on quite a display."

"Yes, and you were glued to it. What were you thinking while you were watching her?"

"Nothing . . . nothing at all."

"You had the strangest look on your face—like a bomb could go off under you and you'd never notice it." She looked out at the woman as he started the engine. "She's a little old for you."

"For God's sake, come off it. I wasn't thinking anything like that."

She was neither appeased nor fully convinced. Outside of bed his love and interest in her were apparent and firm as ever, but in bed, recently, he gave her cause for doubt. Impotence was one thing, but *his* problem she had no understanding of. Maybe what he had told her was true: maybe it was just a phase.

Suddenly ashamed of her accusation, she said: "I'm sorry. I was just being jealous and petty."

He smiled. "I'm always glad to have you jealous even though there's no reason for you to be."

His smile vanished by degrees as did his shock at having been discovered by her. One thing he must never lose was caution.

When he reached the expressway his thoughts had returned to those concerns in the parking lot, although for the time being—especially with Joanne beside him—he wanted to leave them behind. He hit the accelerator but could not speed away from the picture of Jane Richardson's gaping mouth, her jaw cranking in a furious yet futile fight for life.

Commencement was not the happy occasion which, ten weeks earlier, Joanne had looked forward to. She received a C in her history course and was consequently deprived, by a slim margin, of the necessary grade-point average for graduation with honors.

"She's livid one minute, heartbroken the next," Claudia told Matt. "She blames the unfairness of the instructor, then blames herself for not having dropped the course when she could have."

"Can't she accept that she came damned close?"

"'Damned close' isn't close enough." She looked at him with a smirk. "Her perfectionism reminds me of someone else I know."

Bud graduated with high honors and so had a double asterisk next to his name in the commencement program. At the party Claudia gave after the ceremony he took Joanne aside, opened a program, and showed her where he had inked in a single asterisk before her name, so carefully with a fine-point pen that it looked entirely legitimate. "This will be *our* official program," he told her. Her eyes welled with tears and then she laughed and threw her arms around his neck. Matt was standing a few feet away and, as the couple hugged, he and Bud caught each other's eye. It was only for a few seconds but long enough to be uncomfortable—and then terrifying. For Bud's eyes were as cold as knifepoints, trained on him in such a way that he knew at once what Ted meant by "You should have seen the way he looked at me, like I was an insect, something he could just flick away or step on if he felt like it." Then, with a smile so subtle that it did not part his lips, he ran his hand up Joanne's back, up her neck and into her hair, and moved her head to rest on his shoulder. For Matt it was more than a gesture of affection; it was a statement of conquest. Bud's eyes stayed on him until he himself was forced to turn away.

Oh, God, he *does* know how to love, Lucille said silently as she watched them from a lawn chair at the edge of the yard. She then looked to her right at the border of the patio, the exact spot where she was first introduced to Ted. He and Margaret were not present today, and she wondered what excuse they had given Claudia. After a minute she pulled her gaze away from the patio: there was no profit in reminiscing and regretting. She saw Bud and Joanne now talking with Claudia and one of the women from that group Claudia belonged to. Bud said something and the three laughed heartily. Pride was not a familiar feeling to her but something very close to it filled the moment. He was liked, he could make others laugh, he could love. No one would ever have to know what he had done to her—and by the same token what *she* had done to *him*.

Claudia saw Matt talking to a couple and seized her opportunity when he broke away from them and went to the makeshift bar by himself.

"Have you spoken to Lucille?" she said almost in a whisper.

Matt glanced across the yard where Lucille sat alone with a glass of untouched champagne in her hand. "No, not yet," he answered.

"She doesn't look well at all. And she's more remote than ever. The only time she perked up was when we chatted about the wedding."

Yes, he thought, I'll bet she did.

14

Joanne got a full-time summer job in a department store and would not start graduate school until the autumn. Bud, however, enrolled in one night class which met on Mondays; during the day he worked for the county road department, performing the same labor he had done the past three summers. He easily could have found employment with an architect or contractor but he wanted more strenuous work, work that would leave him and the temptation exhausted at the end of the day.

In any extended conversation Matt had with Claudia she never failed to comment on Bud's ambition, stamina, drive. And in this day and age, she said, it was a miracle for any woman to find a man she could really lean on when she had to, a man who was solid as a rock yet gentle and undomineering. To everything she said about Bud, Matt responded in agreement, for self-protection. The image of walking Joanne down the aisle took him from frustration to outright fear. If Bud were discovered and captured after they were married—worse, once they had children—the trauma would border on the unbearable. And if *she* discovered Bud's secret before anyone else, what might he do to her in order to protect himself? This latter consideration made him tremble and hate his helplessness because he lacked admissible evidence.

But he was now a stalker, learning and exercising stealth like a criminal who works at becoming a master. Bud's Monday-night class got out at eight-thirty, and at eight-fifteen Matt would pull into the parking lot some forty yards to the side of Guilfoyle Hall and set up watch on Bud's Nova in the other lot across the street. Each time he started the engine and followed the trail Bud led him on, he thought about his own hopes. He *should* be hoping that the boy was not guilty, that the clues against him were all coincidental and merely food for a monstrous delusion. But he had glimpsed too much: the look Bud had given him over Joanne's shoulder at the commencement party, the destructive hold Bud had on Lucille which, in the end, crushed Ted. No, what he hoped was that Bud would strike again, and soon, with himself as a witness. He would pull off the mask so that the woman could identify her attacker. To preserve this hope of exposing Bud he had to keep pushing from his mind the nightmare that would *begin* for Joanne, Claudia, and Lucille.

All through July, Bud led him nowhere except to Claudia's or Lucille's. Following cautiously and almost always with another car or two between them, Matt often had the sinking feeling that the world was ordered for Bud's protection, that Bud would live out his life hiding that other side of him from everyone but those who were powerless to expose it. By the end of July this feeling became conviction: on the trail Bud took was a house that now had Adele's real-estate sign on the lawn, and whenever Matt passed it he was reminded of what his own life might have been and what it was now—spying and slinking through the city.

And yet he would have spied every night had Bud provided the opportunity. Sometimes he would drive past Lucille's, and if Bud's car was not there he would proceed on and pass Claudia's. If Bud's car were at neither house he would wait the next day for news about last night's rape.

But there was no news, and he learned from Claudia that no new women had joined the group since Jane's death. Quite the opposite, the group was shrinking every week.

The fruitless Monday-night ritual was almost a joke to him now, and he yearned for a vacation. But going away, even for a few days, would accomplish nothing; he would never relax, and without the distraction of work there would be just more time to think about Bud.

But the first Monday night in August the trail took a detour when, at the third turn, Bud made a left instead of his customary right and slowed down in front of a cluster of two-story brick buildings on the south end of campus. He slowed to a crawl and then stopped. In panic, afraid to advance and risk being seen, Matt turned sharply onto the road that ran behind the stadium. He had no time to signal and the car behind him nearly clipped his fender; the driver protested with his horn.

Instinctively, he switched off his lights and stopped. Through a row of trees he could see the Nova pausing at the complex. His chest tightened: Did Bud suspect he was being followed?

The Nova started up again, slowly, and did not resume normal speed until it cleared the buildings. Matt now had no courage to follow. He waited until his breathing became regular before turning back onto the main road. Then he, too, slowed down at the complex. It was well-lighted but his squinting eyes searched the few shadows between the structures. He saw nothing that he could imagine would arrest Bud's attention.

As he proceeded on he saw, in the ray of his headlights, the arrow sign of identification on the grass between the sidewalk and the street. The sign said FACULTY HOUSING.

All week he searched for meaning in the detour and found none. Worse than this was the possibility that Bud had seen him and slowed down simply to trap him. But then, he reasoned, Bud could have tried to trap him on the usual route.

On Saturday, he rented a compact car. He would drive his own Cadillac by day, the other by night. Should anyone happen to see him in the compact he would say he was testing it for a while because he was thinking of making a trade-in. God, he was getting clever!—clever enough, he hoped, to continue tailing Bud without notice.

Sunday, he went to Claudia's for dinner. Hurriedly, she fixed his drink and then, with the bursting enthusiasm of a child, said she had something to show him, raced upstairs, and returned with a large white box. "We picked up the material for Joanne's dress yesterday." Beaming, she set the box on his lap and lifted the lid. "Isn't it beautiful?"

It was thick white lace done in a pattern that looked like large teardrops. As he lightly passed his fingertips over it his breath came short. What had once been a general vision was now a specific one: with her arm looped through his he would deliver her up to the enemy.

Claudia did not notice how little he ate. She was too busy telling him about the dressmaker they had found, an eighty-year-old woman who really knew her craft and paid meticulous attention to details. The veil was to be "slightly Spanish," whatever that meant. When this topic was finished she moved on to Joanne's summer job. "It's been the perfect tonic. She really needed to get away from books and all that studying. And she's pretty much over the disappointment about not graduating with honors. Besides, she's had a little taste of revenge. Someone told her that instructor is being let go after summer term. Apparently, there are a lot of other students who have been complaining about her."

Revenge. Jane. Something clicked as he recalled Bud presenting Joanne with the altered commencement program. "Yes, I'm sure she does feel better knowing she wasn't the only one. What was that instructor's name? I've forgotten."

"Well, *I* haven't." She chuckled. "Dolores Mueller. They were household words around here for two months."

After a quick cup of coffee, he said he had to leave. He drove ten miles over the limit and almost knicked the support pole of the carport when he pulled in. He sprinted past the rented black compact he had parked in the open lot area.

In the kitchen he yanked open the drawer under the wall phone and grabbed the directory. He flipped to the *M*'s and ran his finger down one column.

Mueller DL 14 Kane Vill 555-7742

Dread rivaled his satisfaction. 555 was the campus exchange, and he knew without being told that Kane Village was faculty housing.

This woman was the perfect choice. The trouble she had given Joanne made her deserving of what was coming to her; and afterward, he would be able to use her to cancel out Jane Richardson. Richardson had become a wall between him and Joanne, but this new woman would be a bond. In a way, the act would be an early and unspoken wedding present to Joanne.

In the university's booklet of summer course schedules he found that she was not teaching a full-term class but rather an intensified half-term one that had begun two weeks ago: the Russian Revolution, Tuesdays and Thursdays, 7:00 to 10:00 P.M. He had just three weeks in which to plan and execute. The history department was letting her go, and once she left the university she would undoubtedly leave town.

He had already followed her twice, seen the difficulties involved, and realized he was going to have to trust a little more to chance than he had ever done before. The first difficulty was that the building in which the class met had a very small parking lot, and at ten o'clock she came out to her car with the unrealized protection of a dozen or more students who also parked there. In addition, she had a rider, a girl whom she dropped off at a dormitory on the circle drive. The second problem was the faculty housing setup. There were six four-story units that formed a hexagon around a well-lighted courtyard; the parking area behind two of these buildings was even brighter than that in the courtyard, with high-intensity lamps at the tops of tall metal poles. Even if he managed to get his hand over her mouth before she could scream he might easily be seen from a window. He knew now her assigned parking place but around it were no shadows for him to come out of.

Of course, he could follow her on another night, a weekend night, but that would involve hit-and-miss waiting and require too much of his time. Then, too, there was the distinct possibility she went nowhere on the weekends: she was a homely, thin-haired, bespectacled thing whose skin was almost the same institutional light gray of the building she taught in.

The Kane Village parking lot, he decided, provided his only opportunity. But those lights—something must be done about them. Well, he would not concentrate too hard and exhaust his mind with overtime. As had happened so often in the past, a solution might present itself when he least expected it.

Matt drove the black rented car Monday night when he followed Bud, and again on Tuesday and Thursday nights when he followed Dolores Mueller. He had considered warning her, through an anonymous call or letter, but then realized how cruel it would be to inject fear in her when she might never need it for protection. And that was now *his* biggest fear: that Bud would not strike in this arena but in another where he himself had no opportunity for surveillance.

Joanne came to his apartment for dinner on Friday. Bud had been invited too but, to Matt's relief, he backed out at the last minute and told Joanne he was too tired and had too much studying to do. Matt knew the real reason; Bud had not been inside the apartment since he learned that Lucille had used it.

Anxiously, and with a peculiar kind of dread that bordered on panic, he stood at the window of the little bedroom and looked down at the parking area where Joanne's taxi would arrive. Six months ago, he would have been thrilled, overjoyed to spend an evening alone with his daughter, but now he had to guard himself and hide his suspicions and fear. With her as with practically everyone else, each encounter required forethought that erased all spontaneity. Even the glass in his hand, a double shot of scotch on the rocks, was a requirement for facing her without trembling hands and stammered sentences. He was haunted now by the teardrop lace Claudia had shown him and he thought of the wedding that would be and the two that would never be—his and Adele's, Ted and Lucille's. And whenever he thought of Adele he considered what his life had become, a sour routine of working, drinking, stalking.

Joanne did not come in a taxi. Matt watched her park and get out of Claudia's car. At first, he was alarmed and then confused. So far as he knew, she had not driven since the accident.

He buzzed her in, went out into the hall to watch her climb the stairs. "You drove?" he asked before she reached the top.

"Yes." She blushed.

"I thought. . . . Do you still have a license?"

"Sure. You don't have to take a test or anything to get it renewed. I've been practicing lately, just driving around the block. So tonight I thought I'd go all the way and, well, I made it."

He wanted to hug her and crush her to him but he kissed her lightly on the temple. They went inside.

"I took the streets," she said in a tone that minimized the accomplishment. "I'm not quite ready for that expressway madness."

He fixed her a gin and tonic. Reaching for the lime, he caught her eying his drink which was still dark enough to suggest that the liquor was not diluted with mix. Censure would have been hurtful but tolerable; however, her face showed, for a second or two, a sadness that cut him to the quick.

"It's only my first," he said, attempting levity.

Again she blushed. "I'm not here to count."

"It, uh, sometimes makes the evening go faster. Although I don't want to rush *this* evening." Making excuses, muttering inanities—he must get hold of himself. He asked her about her job in the department store and was relieved by the way she picked up the subject and carried it, from the "regulars" who resented the summer help to the alarming number of shoplifters she saw every day. After this, they discussed the guest list for the wedding and then Claudia.

"Mom's really thrown herself into the preparations. It's going to be quite a letdown for her when it's over. And of course she'll be living alone then."

"Yes." Alone. *I with my scotch, she with her wine—the long winter's nap.* "I'm sorry Bud couldn't come tonight."

"Are you?" Before he could answer she added: "It seems that all summer you've been avoiding each other."

"Bad timing on both our parts, I guess."

"You're sure that's all?"

"Yes." His heart was pounding loudly enough to expose the lie as she appeared to be weighing his answer.

"I just wanted to be sure because I have to talk to you about something. Something that Mom and probably most women don't understand." With her finger she began to bob the lime wedge in her drink. "I wonder if men have as much 'intuition' as women are supposed to have. Do you remember that day we went on the picnic, you asked me if Bud was gentle with me? Did you know we had made love in the woods—I mean, could you tell when I came back?"

"No."

"Then what made you ask that question at that particular moment?"

"I told you. Jane and I had talked a lot about the increase of violence toward women and I see what kind of programs we run at the station, the movies that are popular. I don't think it's unusual to wonder how they influence all young men."

"Bud isn't *all* young men."

"No. No, he's not. I told you then it was a foolish question."

She hesitated, still playing with the lime wedge. "What's so crazy is that a few weeks after you asked me that, he began to have this problem. At first I thought it might be me, something I'd done, but now I know it's not. And I can't get him to talk about it."

His mouth went dry as his hands turned wet. "What kind of problem?"

"Half the time—more than half the time—we're together he can't have an orgasm."

"You mean he becomes impotent?"

"Just the opposite." Flinchingly she looked at him. "He stays erect even after it's over because he hasn't . . . you know. I realize how frustrating it is for him. And sometimes he tries so hard for so long that he forgets himself and hurts me. It ends up being something that *has* to be done and when that happens all the naturalness goes. I've heard plenty about impotence but I've never heard anything about this. Have you? Or did you ever experience it yourself?"

"This started after the picnic?"

"Yes."

"Can you remember exactly when?"

She looked bewildered by his urgency. "I don't know. It was before commencement. I guess in May."

For him, the boy was no longer a mysterious puzzle; he was a *familiar* one that could be taken apart and reassembled in a flash. "Early May?" he asked.

"What difference does it—"

"Please try to remember!"

"Yes, I guess it was."

236

Now he must be cautious, casual. "About the time Jane Richardson died."

"About that time. But that's not the point."

He looked at her young and lovely face, at the light gray eyes as soft as cashmere, and he thought of Claudia who once had a similar face that aged drastically and overnight right after Terry's death. He did not want this face to age the same way.

But Bud was hurting her. Since May. And how long before he might cross the line to another kind of hurt? How long before he might decide to make *her* pay for his own frustrations? He was now convinced that, years before Ted, Lucille Hanes had begun to pay an unfair price for being Bud's mother.

"Joanne, I have some things to tell you. You must listen carefully and not interrupt me. And for your own good you must promise that what I say goes no farther than this room."

Her bewilderment was now apprehension. She nodded.

He took a long swallow of scotch for the task. Despite fear and regret his mind was functioning rationally. He could not open with "Bud is—." No, the shock and the insult of it would only fortify her resistance to the deductions. His tactic must be *inductive*.

"That night last winter when you and Bud had the flat tire here, I had to get him the flashlight, and when I looked under the front seat I found —."

Each of her father's spoken discoveries opened in her head like poisonous seeds, and she began at once to fight their effect before it overtook her.

Yes, Bud had been late picking her up from class one Wednesday night, but that was because his watch had stopped.

No, she had not actually seen the boil on the back of his neck. And why should she? It was natural to keep it covered with a bandage.

Yes, Bud had been eager to get home after dinner that night at Pierre's, but it was the end of exam week and they were both mentally exhausted.

No, he hadn't mentioned what he found out about his mother and Ted Brainard but—

237

Here the poison nearly overwhelmed her. He hadn't said a word about Lucille and Ted.

But she would not, could not succumb. She could not allow one fault, a single deceit, to throw her into her father's corner with his preposterous assumption.

"All this time you've been thinking *that?*" she said in a raw whisper. "And now you're *following* him?"

"Yes. I've had no choice."

"No choice! No choice but to let these coincidences work into some crazy scheme? All these months you must have been watching and waiting, *wanting*—"

"No, Joanne, never wanting. Not for a minute. But I haven't imagined these things. I know what Ted told me about that day he went to Lucille's house, and I know what Jane told me— without my asking—about the attacks that took place on Wednesday nights while you were in class. And I *saw* Bud slow down and stop in front of Kane Village. He's stayed clear of me ever since he found out Ted and Lucille were using this place. No, I haven't imagined these things."

She now looked like Lucille the day he had cornered her with the suggestion that her son might be "disturbed." Her eyes moved to the drink in front of him and she said stonily: "Too much of that can make people see things that aren't there."

"I've considered it, even wished it were true, and you can think it if you want. But that won't help Dolores Mueller."

This prediction, said with such quiet certainty, struck deeper than all his wild "evidence." She began to shake in her attempt to hold back the anger and hurt.

"I know how you must feel," he said.

"Do you?" She turned in the chair to hide her tears and she struck out blindly with the last available weapon. "The same way you knew how Terry felt?"

He waited more than a minute, wondering if he should delay the rest or continue now while he had her here. He chose to continue, to risk her jumping up and leaving. "Joanne, if Bud is having this problem with you now, imagine what might be in store after you're married. And once you have children. . . . Even though he hates my guts now I'd still give anything for him not to be this man. But I'm convinced there's only the slimmest chance he's not." He watched her huddle her shoulders the way Hippolyta Bewick had done at Jane's funeral. "For the time being we have to assume the worst, because there's a woman out there who needs to be protected."

"Who you *think* needs to be protected."

"And if something does happen to her, how blameless are we?"

We. At this moment it was the ugliest word imaginable. *We* against Bud.

"What do you want me to do?" she said thickly.

"Let me know in advance any night you won't be seeing Bud. Tuesdays and Thursdays are especially important. It's only three weeks until the end of the term—she'll have to get out of faculty housing then. I feel if anything's going to happen it'll be. . . . Just let me know when you're not seeing him."

"And if nothing happens?"

"Then I don't know."

"When she leaves, how long are you going to keep spying on him? How many other women are you going to find that you think need protection? How long can it go on before he proves himself innocent!"

"I don't know. It'll have to be one step at a time."

She would not stay for dinner and he fully understood. But, ever cautious, he said, "Your mother will wonder what you're doing home so early."

"I'll stop and get a sandwich on the way," she mumbled. "I just want to be alone now."

"Are you sure you can drive?"

She nodded. Trancelike, she crossed to the door where she paused with her back to him. "If you're wrong about him—and I think you are in spite of all your clues—it's going to be very hard to forgive you. And you must realize how much I *want* you to be wrong."

"I know. But just keep the Mueller woman in mind."

Halfway home, the trembling returned and she had to pull into the parking lot of a supermarket. She leaned forward and rested her forehead against the steering wheel.

For over two years she had walked a painfully narrow line between her father and her brother, never taking one side against the other. And in the end, her neutrality had betrayed Terry: if he had felt he had an ally he might have been strong enough to overcome that last confrontation in his room. For all of the boy's selfishness and cruelty, her father had proven himself capable of even greater cruelty when he let his son storm out of the house. Now, once again, her father was forcing her to walk the line.

Her left hand opened and closed on the edge of the car seat and with each squeeze she damned her father's suspicion, Dolores Mueller's existence. Yet, this defiance brought no relief and failed to release her from the line so she could cross wholeheartedly to Bud's side. The story about Lucille and Ted had left just enough uncertainty inside her. If only Bud had told her. . . .

Early Sunday afternoon, Bud picked her up and drove out of the city to the place where they had had their picnic in the spring. The tire path off the road had been widened and most of the trees removed: the terrain was bulldozed flat and on it stood rows of buildings in various stages of completion.

"Condominiums." Bud spit the word out contemptuously. "Fifty-five units of third-rate construction. The developers didn't buy the property over there because of the hill. We could still build on it, but when the leaves fall we'd be looking out on this junk."

He got out of the car, opened the trunk, and withdrew a blanket and a large thermos of lemonade. While the trunk was open, hiding her from view, she slipped her hand under the front seat and searched both sides. She found nothing and when Bud called out, asking what was keeping her, she was already brimming with shame.

Using rocks for a bridge, they crossed the little stream and climbed the untouched wooded hill. A few feet from the top was a narrow shelf, a niche in the grade, on which Bud spread out the blanket. They sat, and from the corner of her eye she watched him take in the landscape—appraising, calculating. "A beautiful spot," he said reverently. "What a place we could have had here."

"We'll find another spot."

"Not like this one."

She poured lemonade into the thermos cap, took a sip, and passed it to him. "The last time we were here was with Dad. You haven't seen him much since then."

"I guess not," he said flatly, his attention still commanded by the stream below.

"Have your feelings about him changed?"

"What do you mean?"

"You seem so . . . cold around him lately."

"Did *he* say that?"

"No, but I've noticed it."

"Then you've noticed how much he drinks these days. People who drink a lot make me nervous, I can't help it."

"He's lonely. And"—she watched his face closely—"I think he's still very upset over what happened to Jane Richardson."

"Maybe. But drinking isn't a solution."

For the next few minutes they watched two squirrels chase each other around in the branches of a huge oak. "Your mother's been looking awful," she said. "I mean depressed."

"It's just the illness." Now, he turned to her. "What's with you today? All these grim observations."

"I don't know. I'd like them to be happy, that's all. Or at least happ*ier*."

"That's up to them, not us."

"But maybe we could help." The guilt she had felt in the front seat of the car returned at the threshold of her next search. "Why don't you and I take the two of them to dinner?"

"Take who?" The color rose in his face.

"Your mother and my father. They're both alone and, you never know, they might hit it off."

For a second he looked as if he had been slapped; his jaw tightened until the muscles under his ears became two granite disks. Everything inside her sank at his reaction. "That's crazy," he said. "What would make you say a thing like that?"

"What's so crazy about it?" She gripped the thermos to steady the quaking in her arms.

"It just is. I'd have thought you'd have more feeling for your mother."

"What has she got to do with it?"

"You know how she feels about him."

"But there's no chance of them ever getting back together. Your mother's gone most of her life without a husband, she's still very attractive—"

"She's got a disease."

"Well, that doesn't disqualify her from a little romance, does it? Or marriage."

His face turned totally expressionless, but the voice remained hard-edged. "I don't know why you're talking like this. Is it your idea of a joke?"

"I don't see any joke in bringing two people together and seeing what happens."

He stood, snatched up the thermos, and ground the cap into place. "Let's go. There are too many bugs out today."

All the way back to town he did not speak, and she kept her face turned to the window. Her thoughts could not focus on anything except two hopes. The first was that Bud had spoken the truth when he explained that the lock on his mother's bedroom door was installed because that was where she kept her jewelry and silver. The second hope was that Dolores Mueller would leave the city without incident.

15

On Monday night, he was just picking up his keys from the dresser top, ready to leave for campus in the rented car, when the telephone rang. His first instinct was to let it go unanswered but his caution—so fully developed now that it approached paranoia—warned him that it might be Claudia; later, she might mention her failure to reach him to Bud, and Bud might put two and two together.

"Hello?"

"Hello, Matt. It's Adele."

He was too disoriented to speak. She sounded so close, as if she were standing right next to him.

"Matt, are you there?"

"Yes, I . . . How are you?"

"Right now, very rested. I just got back from vacation."

"Oh?"

"San Diego. My old college friend Valerie lives there. I stayed three weeks and it was just what I needed." Pause. "We took a day trip to Tijuana and I found a little something there I thought you'd like. I was wondering if we could meet for a drink so I could give it to you."

"I—I'm awfully busy lately." She would be tanned, ripely brown, emanating more than ever vitality and undaunted optimism—and untapped fertility.

"Matt, I took this vacation to do some thinking. Serious thinking. And I've come to some conclusions that would make a difference between us. I'd like you to give me the chance to tell you what they are."

They were concessions, he knew. A sacrifice of what, next to him, she wanted most out of life. The flag of unconditional surrender was flapping in her voice. A peculiar kind of shame filled him, as if he were being offered a prize he had cheated to get. Scrambling for an excuse he said: "As a matter of fact, I'm planning a vacation for myself—I really won't be free until I get back."

"When will that be?"

"A few weeks, maybe a month."

"Will you call me when you get back?"

"Yes."

"I mean as *soon* as you get back."

"Yes, I will."

Pause.

"Well, have a good time." Then the good cheer was dropped. "I'm very sorry about Mrs. Richardson. I'm praying every night this man will be caught."

"So am I."

He hung up and pressed his forehead against the wall. He fought the feeling of persecution, the swell of self-pity rising up in him, but it seemed he had no will or defense left. Everything from Judy and Jane, Ted and Lucille, Joanne and Bud, was a cheat, and now here was Adele offering up, for *his* sake, the one thing she wanted from life. . . .

He might have lingered long enough to cry if not for the ticking of the clock. It reminded him he was running late and in danger of shirking his new-found, hateful responsibility.

In the rented compact he arrived just in time to see Bud's Nova pull away from its usual spot across from Guilfoyle Hall. His anticipation, a perversely hopeful one, withered when he was not led past Kane Village a second time. The final, familiar turn told him the boy was headed for Claudia's.

At work the next day he waited for the telephone to ring, waited for Joanne's message that Bud was not seeing her that night. He left early, before the five o'clock snarl of traffic, and raced to his apartment to wait. By twenty to ten, there was still no call. Well, he thought, if Bud is with Joanne, then there is no reason to go out and follow the Mueller woman from her class to faculty housing.

But at quarter to ten he turned the key in the ignition. For what he realized, sadly, was that he did not fully trust his daughter to call him as she had promised.

The solution lay in his closet, inside a large box that contained the artifacts of his childhood. The pistol was wrapped in a soft cloth that had kept it free of dust, and there was a container half filled with BBs.

Wednesday night, he came home from Joanne's, went directly to his room, undressed, set his alarm for quarter to five, and climbed into bed. He had to be at work at eight, but the first step in the new plan must be executed in the early morning when there would be less of a chance of anyone coming or going at the housing complex.

Still, even with the plan laid out before him like a perfect blueprint, he had trouble falling asleep. Since Sunday, Joanne's suggestion about Matt and his mother rankled inside him, and he felt a growing certainty that if she continued to see Matt regularly he would taint her with his filth. Here *he* was, about to use the Mueller woman to eliminate Jane Richardson, to knock down the wall between him and Joanne, but what good would it do if Joanne herself changed, *allowed* herself to be changed by her father? All right, he told himself, you'll take care of that after tomorrow night: you can't crowd things together—one step at a time.

He awakened to WGRS-FM on the clock radio. He dressed quickly and with his shoes in his hand stepped into the hallway and paused, listening for any stirring in his mother's room. There was none, and he proceeded on his way.

Traffic was sparse, as he knew it would be. At the fourth stoplight he reached under the seat and withdrew the pistol and the BBs. He was wearing large mirrored sunglasses and a sailor cap with the brim pulled down. This, he felt, was sufficient disguise should anyone look out from the apartment windows. Nothing, however, could be done about the car, but there were plenty of beige Novas in the city. At least no one was able to write down the license number; two days ago, when it rained, he had smeared thick mud on the plates and bumpers, and the next day's intense heat had baked it firmly into place.

He approached the lot slowly. There was no one in it. Next, he scanned the windows of the two buildings which faced the lot diagonally. Every single one had its blinds drawn. Still, he would have to be quick.

He pulled into an empty space and left the engine running. He reached into the back seat for the whisk broom, dust pan, and paper bag, then seized the pistol and BBs and got out. The pistol had no storage chamber and each BB had to be inserted individually. This was annoyingly, dangerously time-consuming, but he knew that worrying about it would only mar his aim. The secret was to proceed as if the task were already completed.

The first shot missed the mark; there was a *ping* on the metal hood that covered the fluorescent tubing. The second shot brought a shower of white shards, and so did the next. He tossed the pistol onto the front seat, then quickly swept the debris into the dustpan and dumped it into the bag. He scanned the windows again, glanced at the road, and got into the car. As he backed out of the space he rechecked the pavement: not a trace of glass anywhere. The damage would go unnoticed until the lights were turned on at dusk. Campus Maintenance would not get around to repairing it until tomorrow or perhaps the day after.

On his way to the exit he passed the rear end of Dolores Mueller's car. Tonight, she would drive it according to his instructions—and to the site of his most recent disappointment.

In less than two minutes the campus was behind him, and his mind was fully occupied with what he was going to order for breakfast.

"I thought I told you," he said over the telephone.

"No, you didn't," Joanne replied. Her anxiety was gathering in her throat and she struggled to keep it from becoming audible.

"The prof is having a little get-together at his house to talk about revamping the curriculum. He only invited five of us so it's kind of a small honor. I have to go."

"Will I see you afterward?"

"I doubt it. I have no idea how late it will run."

"Oh." Pause. "Where does he live?"

"I don't know," he said impatiently. "The directions are in the car. What difference does it make?"

"No difference. I just thought . . . if he lived nearby, you could stop over on your way home."

"Not if it's late. You know how early I go to work. Besides, I'm tired."

"All right."

"I'll see you tomorrow night. We'll go to the movies."

"I work until nine," she murmured.

"Then I'll pick you up at the store and we'll go to a late one."

"Yes."

"Is something wrong? You sound funny."

"Funny?"

"*That's* what I mean—you sound a million miles away."

"Maybe I'm tired too."

"Go to bed early."

After she hung up, she sat rigid in the chair. If only he had told her where the professor lived, she could drive by on her own to see if his car was there.

All week he had been cold and watchful around her, and no matter how much she tried she could not deny the exact time it started, the exact thing that inspired it: her suggestion, last Sunday, about her father and his mother. Since that afternoon he had not touched her, and his only kisses were for hello and goodbye.

All right, she thought, so what if he and his mother have some hidden bitter feelings about each other. Lots of people do. Maybe the reason he hadn't told her about Lucille and Ted was to spare her feelings and to make sure she didn't tell her mother, who might in turn tell Margaret.

But she had always told him *everything*. He knew all of her emotions regarding her mother and father and Terry; he had, in fact, always sought them out with questions of concern. And why should he now be so repulsed by the idea of an evening out with her father and Lucille?

Of course, he knew all her emotions but only now did the obvious occur to her: her emotions were the only ones they talked about. Since the accident she had taken him for granted, like a pillar that held up the roof over her life. He was never depressed; he could solve any problem coolly and rationally; he had a fine talent and took joy from it; he was a perfect student... yet, she could not recall ever having asked anything about Lucille beyond the perfunctory inquiries into her health. They had discussed her mother often and at length, everything from her loss of Terry to her failed romance with Dr. Zimmerman. What about Lucille? Why had she never remarried? Why had she thrown herself into a life of menial work when apparently her finances did not demand it? What reason was there for a woman so beautiful to slink around as though she were one of the most insignificant creatures on earth?

She had not thought about these things. Because she had thought too much about herself. But then, Bud never volunteered to . . .

Still, none of these considerations substantiated her father's wild suspicions. He was drinking too much, way too much. And he was lonely—without realizing it, he was looking for a little drama in his life. But to assemble haphazard occurrences into such an accusation—

She stood up and went to the staircase. There she paused and looked at the spot where her father had destroyed Terry's drums with his foot. She remembered her plea that he had ignored, a plea that would have saved the boy.

With a feeling of utter abandonment she climbed the stairs. Would she ever really know her father—or Bud? Were they both the same kind of man, the kind that hoards a whole section of themselves to themselves? Terry was what he was, up front. So, she believed, was she. So was her mother.

She would not call her father. It would be insane to indulge this fantasy of his—more to the point, it would be a betrayal of Bud.

Suddenly, she was exhausted. She switched on her air conditioner and lay down on the bed with her arm over her eyes, like a shield positioned to ward off all thought. Concentrating only on the hum of the machine, she was soon asleep.

He parked his car at a meter in the commercial district across from the west side of campus and, with a small gym bag in one hand, walked leisurely the half mile to Kane Village, approaching it through a field that bordered the rear of the parking lot. With a triumphant smile, he greeted the one non-functioning pole light. He had his hiding place picked out—behind the three-foot retaining wall that separated the lot from a sloping embankment of small evergreens. He was early because he wanted to get the feel of the place and chart the precise path to her car when she arrived. And he wanted to savor the anticipation.

As soon as he was crouched behind the wall, out of danger from any headlights that might appear, he withdrew the mask, knife, and bandanna from the bag. The night was insufferably hot and airless but, as he waited, the sweat on his skin turned cool and felt like refreshment. Joanne could never know what tonight would do for them, but that did not matter. For more than half his life he had been a practitioner of secrecy; rather than resenting that which could not be shared, he had come to cherish it.

He checked his watch. Nine-thirty-five. Another half hour or so. But already he was murmuring the words he would soon be growling: "Ugly, jealous bookworm . . ."

With a jolt, she awakened to the noisy rattling of the air conditioner. It was that damned removable front panel that had never fit right in the first place and had to be taped to keep from working itself loose. She switched on the light and discovered that one strip of the heavy electrical tape had pulled away. She readjusted it, then turned to look at the clock. Nine-twenty.

Keep the Mueller woman in mind, her father had said. She realized now that was what she had done all week. Off and on, the ugly little face with its two eyes permanently squinted in pugnacious defensiveness would appear before her, and she could hear that uncommanding voice which, to project authority, relied solely upon volume.

Her mind was made up, and yet she paced the room the way people do in the most banal melodramas. The accusation was crazy, actually demented. The drinking, the loneliness, his own guilt for letting Ted and Lucille use the apartment—these had unhinged some part of him.

But Dolores Mueller stayed in her head and so did the picture of her mother, weeping and fluttering about the house like a mad bird the day she learned of Jane Richardson's death.

Early May.

That day in the parking lot—the woman in the hotpants and that indefinable look on Bud's face as he stared at her. Stared and stared at her.

She picked up the telephone and dialed. She would indulge him tonight and perhaps one more night to prove him wrong. It was a betrayal of Bud, but he would never know it: she could and would have to live with it.

"It's me," she said when he answered. "I'm not seeing him tonight." The sentence was laughable and made her feel ridiculous to say it.

"All right." He spoke in a near whisper. "Thank you for calling me."

"Wait a minute. I want you to come pick me up. I want to go with you."

"No, I can't do that."

"I'm going with you," she insisted. She wanted to be there when nothing happened.

"Joanne, suppose—"

"Suppose what! You can't tell me the things you did and then expect me to sit still while you go out to play detective. You'd better hurry if you want us to get there by ten o'clock."

"But what will you tell your mother?"

"I'll think of something. You just pull up and honk. I'll be waiting."

At quarter to ten he pulled up but did not have to honk; waiting on the front-porch steps she started down the walk the second his car rounded the corner.

"I told Mom you rented this car to give me driving lessons. I said I needed to practice night driving on the expressways." This was revealed without her looking at him, and he was surprised

250

at how clever she was. He considered how Bud was making them both clever.

"Where did Bud say he'd be?"

"He's at his professor's house," she answered affirmatively, "with some other students. They're going to suggest changes in the curriculum."

"Maybe we should just drive by the professor's house."

"We would if I knew where he lived," she said sharply and in a way that asked to be spared any further conversation.

They arrived just as the Mueller woman was turning out of the parking lot. And so began the six-minute journey. He hoped to be returning Joanne home and then unlocking the door to his apartment within the hour.

She dropped off her rider in front of a dormitory and proceeded on. But at Kane Village she did not turn in. To himself he said, "Oh, Christ, don't tell me she's going out for the night!"

He moved into the left lane when she did and made the turn onto a street with a concrete median. Then, abruptly and without signaling, she swung into the parking area of an all-night grocery. But he could not take the turn and present himself so obviously. From the very first night he had seen that she was a terrible driver, and right now he would have liked to lecture her on the use of turn signals. He had to continue on and find a place to turn around.

He took a right, then another, figuring on making a complete circle back to her. His annoyance was heightened when he saw the sign in his headlights: DEAD END. He used a driveway to get himself pointed back to the main street but arriving at it discovered he could not cross the median to reassume the correct direction. Only after he had gone half a mile did he come upon the opportunity for a U-turn.

Approaching the grocery he was of course on the wrong side of the road. But it did not matter: her car was gone. For a minute, at the stoplight, he did not know what to do. Then he decided to go on to Kane Village and, if necessary, cruise through the lot to see if her car was there. If it wasn't, there was nothing for them to do but go home.

The next stoplight was also red when he got to it. Joanne remained silent, but he began to drum his fingers on the steering wheel, in time to the clicking of his turn signal. He adjusted the control on the air conditioning, pushing it up to full. Finished, he looked up and squinted in disbelief. Her car was approaching on the cross street which had the green light; in the intersection it went left. For an instant he could see her—and the change in her posture. Her shoulders were hunched, her head thrust forward over the wheel, like someone driving through blinding rain: she looked as if she were preparing to vomit. His skin prickled. She had obviously returned to Kane Village but was now driving away from it—and within a time span which could not have allowed her to take her grocery purchase into her apartment.

"That's her!"

Joanne's head snapped to the side to look where he was looking, but still she kept silent. When the light changed he made a U-turn and at the next intersection caught sight of her blue Pontiac speeding off at his left. He hit his turn signal as he glided over, and a horn blasted him from behind. Now back on the road with the median he drove in the left lane until he was on the tail of a dawdler whose pace was the same as a car at the right. He honked in three spurts, flashed his bright lights, and the dawdler sped up and moved to the right to let him pass.

He saw the Pontiac again just before it disappeared over the top of a hill. It was in the right lane and he himself had a clear way in the left. His foot jammed down on the pedal, and from the corner of his eye he watched Joanne brace herself.

They sailed over the hill. Only yards ahead was the right-hand entrance to the expressway and the woman was already on it. He swung his head around to find several cars in the right lane. He signaled, hit the brake, and tried to move over. The first approaching car, however, would not yield and answered with its horn; the car behind it would not yield either and he damned them both to hell. By the time he was able to shift lanes he was right on top of the entrance; another two or three yards and he would have missed it.

At the expressway he merged with the traffic and worked his way over to the left. No one was obeying the speed limit and so he had no fear about going up to seventy-five. A blue car came into view but it turned out to be Japanese.

Where the hell *is* she? he hissed to himself. An oil truck signaled and shimmied over in front of him like a giant caterpillar. He continued on behind it, his exasperation mounting. When the middle lane looked clear for a good distance he switched to that and took the spedometer to eighty.

A camping van in the right lane slid over to the widening apron that would become an exit ramp. He passed it, and in doing so was able to discern two cars in front of the van. One of them was blue.

He signaled, braked, and squealed onto the shoulder from which he could chart the courses of the vehicles when they reached the road below where the exit ramp terminated. The blue car made a left while the other car and the van went right.

Her one hand clutching the armrest on the door, staring unseeingly through the windshield, Joanne appeared frozen in place. And he knew why. His speeding and lane-shifting, this sudden pulling off to the shoulder—she was undoubtedly reliving her last ride with Terry. Now, her wide and glassy eyes were perhaps waiting for the tree that would stop the car.

But he spared only seconds for this thought. Something more immediate made his stomach shrink to cold rock as recognition filled him. Joanne turned to look down the ramp and at the road it fed, and when she turned back and their eyes met, the dreadful recognition was shared. It was the road that led to the stream and the clearing.

With his hazard lights blinking, he backed up along the shoulder until the rear end of the car was at the exit. He had to wait while two cars veered onto it. Then he shot backward, shifted into drive, and proceeded. Both drivers in front of him turned right at the foot of the ramp. When he turned left, his hands almost went numb at the realization that he and Joanne and the blue Pontiac were taking this route alone.

But he could not find its taillights as he sped along. What he did see was the white full moon suspended directly over the spot where the populated expressway angled off sharply and disappeared. On this darkened road there was no place to drop off Joanne—no house or gas station or country store. Still rigid and staring straight ahead, she looked like a mannequin propped up in the seat.

His shoulders jumped when she spoke. "You just missed it," she said. "We were out here last Sunday—they've bulldozed some of the trees away." The announcement sounded like a recording, like Judy Kent's voice.

He turned the car around and went back. When they reached the tire path he switched off the headlights, peered through the darkness, and saw nothing. Then slowly he nosed the car off the road and into the gouged-out area. He cut the engine and reached for her hand. "Stay here and keep the doors locked. Open the door only for me or for her." She nodded but turned her face away from him as she did so.

He got out, pressing down the lock and closing the door noiselessly. He cocked his head in an attempt to hear something. But unlike that day when the birds had screeched and the stream had pattered, there was no sound, not even a breeze to rustle the branches on those few trees that did remain. There was only the moon, his sweating hands, his held breath.

He started walking.

The dirt was hard and unyielding under his feet. He continued to move his head from left to right, his ears now functioning like a second pair of eyes in the absence of daylight.

But the light improved as he approached what looked to be the clearing where they had had their picnic. He then saw that most of the woods was gone, the area now filled with skeletons of houses, most of which had yet to be fleshed with wallboard.

A second after he heard the distant cry he saw the front end of the Pontiac protruding from a stack of lumber piled next to one of the two-story skeletons. In the entire surroundings, the chrome of the bumper was the only thing that gleamed, the only substance capable of attracting and holding the light of the moon. He crept toward the structure and then around it, in the direction that would lead to the rear of her car.

There was another cry. "Please, oh, please don't—" The words were cut off by the sound of a slap.

Matt moved on and looked through the support beams of the half-built house. The car door on the driver's side was open, but the light from inside was blocked by the two figures standing there. She wore a blindfold, he a ski mask.

254

"Lie down." The command was given in a guttural, mechanical voice.

"Please, I have money at home! Take me home and I'll give you—"

Both her wrists were gripped in one of his gloved hands. He used the other to pull her hair and yank her head backward.

"You can't!" she wailed. "I'm a virgin!"

Matt felt his own body blur and thought he would need new legs to remain standing. He drew breath and was about to call out the name when the woman suddenly raised her foot and jammed it into the attacker's knee. He yelped sharply, then rammed her against the car; her head struck the framing of the door. She slumped, chin on chest, but was caught under the arms by the gloved hands and lifted upward.

"Don't pull that fainting act," the voice growled. But the woman's head remained bent, her body dead weight in the hands that held her. "Come on!" He pulled the head back and slapped the face twice.

"Bud!" The single word emptied his lungs. The growl the boy had used was now spiraling through his own body; and as he thought of his daughter waiting in the car, sorrow and revulsion warred inside him with equal force. Next, he saw Lucille, the day she heatedly defended her son. And this was enough to allow sorrow to win, for what he knew was that this masked figure, now still as a statue, might have been his own son if chance had dealt the cards differently. He remembered the drums his temper had destroyed, heard Terry's last descent on the stairs and Joanne's unheeded plea.

"Don't hurt her, Bud," he said. "I'll—help you. I'll—" Do what, do *what*? "I'll take you to someone who can help you, so you won't do this anymore. I want to help you!"

He saw no movement from the boy although the woman's body was released and collapsed in a heap. The crickets chorused without interruption, trumpeting their safe invisibility. Matt waited, feeling that the air was thickening to the point of being unbreathable. The moon looked like a disk of ice but kept its coolness to itself.

For more than a minute each stood as motionless as the other.

255

Then, slowly, the boy turned until he completed an about-face and Matt stopped breathing altogether at the sight of the mask. He could see the holes but nothing in them; they were merely less black than the material surrounding them. But he did not have long to look at it. The figure bent to one side and dipped its hand into a bag on the ground. Matt could not see what the hand had secured, but his ears knew when they heard the click.

There was a brief pause before the mask and the blade began to advance.

The first few seconds, he had not believed the voice was real and thought he was hallucinating. Then when the plea came—"I want to help you"—he knew it to be a lie and recognized its giver. Glancing at the unconscious woman at his feet he felt suddenly like a child who has been caught doing something necessary and logical unto itself yet incomprehensible and repulsive to an adult. To the core his insides wrinkled with shame but only briefly: for *he* was the adult and always had been. He had always seen through his mother's lies. He possessed the ability to see what others failed to, entire lives that were lies. Like the life of this woman in front of him and that of Judy Kent who, by means of a talk show, pretended to be interested in other people but was concerned only with herself. And Jane Richardson, that self-promoting defender of "injured" women—she had chosen Matt, a whoremaker and supreme liar, for a constant companion.

Yes, he was the adult and yet behind him, just yards away, "help" was being offered by the worst liar, the one person he had looked up to, trusted implicitly, and whom at one time he had wanted to model himself after. Just once in his life he was blinded, duped; now, with the necessity was the opportunity to erase the mistake.

When he reached for the knife the weight of it in his hand unleashed a new and different kind of excitement in his loins, one which spread to every muscle in his body. More than any woman he had stalked, this man had courted his own fate. Within minutes, maybe less, that fate would be a deep and single slash across his lying throat.

Slowly, the figure approached, angling slightly to the left. Matt could not take his eyes off the mask, and so the body seemed to come toward him as though it were propelled by wheels instead of feet. His own feet were rooted, not in terror but in a paralyzing unbelief.

"Bud! Think! *Think!*" The words were shrill but made no impression on the figure or on the crickets that continued to chirp. The boy was advancing in a circular motion so that he himself had to make a gradual turn. Once, and only fleetingly, the blade of the knife caught and reflected the moon, then slipped back into shadow. Then came the noise from behind the mask. It began as a kind of asthmatic breathing, stopped off at a plateau of groans, and finally descended into a growling in which Matt could hear both disgust and ecstasy. The sound dried up his own mouth, numbed him from his throat to his knees, and part of his brain told him the knife was unnecessary, that the growling itself was enough to snuff out his life.

He dismissed the idea of running: he could never be as quick as the boy, and if he were going to die he did not want death to come from behind. And he did not want to lead him to the car and Joanne.

In his slow turning to keep the circling figure in view, his foot struck something hard and solid. He could not afford even the briefest glance at it and so worked his foot around and over it in an attempt at identification. A cinderblock, he deduced, or rather half of one. Swiftly, he stooped to secure it, and in the same second the figure rushed for him.

He came up with the block in his hand and thrust it forward, into the boy's chest. The sound of concrete against bone was followed by a long gasp as the boy reeled backward and struggled to regain his breath. With his free fist Matt rammed the arm that held the knife, and when the knife dropped he kicked it into the darkness. This action seemed to give his opponent the breath he needed. He lurched, his body following his fist, and Matt felt the shooting pain in his stomach which assisted the attacker in getting him to the ground. He fell on his side, one arm pinned under him. The boy straddled him securely and for several seconds did nothing but suck in air to feed his lungs.

Even this close, Matt could still see nothing in the holes of the mask, only the outline of the head and one ear where the black yarn trapped tiny slivers of moonlight. Then, the boy's breathing evened and he clamped both hands around Matt's throat.

Matt raised the arm that wasn't pinned and used the palm of his hand to push against the strangler's chin, but the neck rigidly held its place and the head did not yield. His last chance for struggle, for air, expired as the hands on his own neck tightened slowly—so slowly that they seemed to want to prolong their task. The moon, stationed behind the attacker's shoulder, began to assume an outline of green which then turned to violet, and as his hand left the chin and tried to claw the mask he knew he had already entered the approach toward death. Clutching at the yarn that kept escaping his fingers, he seemed to be pursuing something slippery and floating; indeed, he felt he was under-water, drowning instead of being choked.

Now, the entire moon was violet, bruising into purple. There was pain and strife in his throat which still fought for air but the rest of him was going limp. He knew it would be only a matter of seconds before his lungs gave up their defiance.

"Pig, whore-maker." The growl was a subdued, controlled roar, the words as tight and clenching as the grip of the fingers. "Turning my work into a whorehouse . . ."

Matt's lips rounded in a no, and another growl issued from the mask. But now there was something else, something so repulsive that it brought every nerve in Matt's body back to life, and he began to spasm as if a bolt of electricity were passing through him. For with the growl came the awareness of some-thing he had been feeling—along with the grip on his neck—but which only now he was able to define. Against his thigh, despite the barrier of his clothing and Bud's, was the stationary and insistent pressure of the boy's erection.

And the instant he defined that pressure he saw before him Jane's casket being slid into the hearse and he heard Judy's hollowed-out voice.

He began to struggle, bucking his hips to free his thigh from the weapon more odious than the hands on his neck and the lost knife. The diversity of emotions with which he had approached Bud just minutes ago were now melded into a solitary spearhead

258

of hate. The voltage inside him gathered itself in one arm and he shot his fist up and into the middle of the mask. There was a cracking noise, a snarl, a split-second weakening in the hands, just long enough for him to use his fist again. His neck was released and he rasped for air, unable now to buck his hips and breathe at the same time. He saw the moon-flecked mask move to the right, saw one arm reach out and paw the dirt. The arm found what it was seeking: Matt heard the scraping of the half cinderblock as it was pulled toward them. There was a groan of effort, and the block was raised to blot out the moon.

She had waited long enough. Having heard her father call out Bud's name she was afraid to breathe, afraid the sound of it would not allow her to hear what followed. She waited for the mistaken recognition, for her father or Dolores Mueller or both to come running, anxious to get to the police and tell them that the attacker—*who was not Bud*—had escaped.

But when she opened the door and got out and saw the clearing off to the left, the wooded hill in the distance behind it, she could no longer hide from the unlikelihood that any man but Bud would happen to choose this place tonight. Only five days ago they had sat on that hill, only five days . . .

She started forward in the direction she had seen her father take and soon a light appeared, dim and splintered by the support beams of a partial construction. Still, there was no sound except that of her own feet on the hard dirt.

When she reached the structure she saw the woman lying there, face down in the small pool of light by the open car door. Her hands flew to her mouth and she held her breath until she saw the regular movement of the woman's ribs, the proof that she was alive. Then she heard a scuffling that sounded like an animal rolling around on the ground. She moved on past the woman, past the rear of the car, and stopped cold. The two figures were far enough away so that, for a second or two, she could not tell which was which. But when one figure stretched out its arm she saw that the head was masked, and when he lifted the heavy object into the air she knew at once that it was being aimed for her father's head.

"Bud!"

259

Down it came, but its path went awry in mid-fall. It crashed next to Matt with enough force to make him think his eardrum had exploded and that he had imagined the scream. But the body straddling him was suddenly, momentarily paralyzed, confirming the scream.

And then it came again. "Bud! Don't hurt him!"

But *he* has hurt *me* was his first thought—and in ways you'll never know. Yet she must know, for she had come with her father to trap him. Yes, she knew and didn't care, like the men his mother had been involved with who were unconcerned with his feelings, his torments; men who wanted what they wanted without a single thought paid to *his* circumstances. Now, he realized the choice Joanne had made by coming here. Much more than being his wife she wanted to be her father's daughter. A deceitful pimp's daughter. And he himself was largely responsible, having championed Matt ever since the accident, and so intensely during the past year.

It was another betrayal in a life filled with betrayals, but the magnitude of this one did not fire his rage; just the opposite, it spawned a despair so complete as to slacken every muscle and bring on a fatigue he had never before known. He wished that Matt and Joanne and time would freeze in place so he could lie down and go to sleep on the dirt until his strength returned.

But her footsteps were advancing, running, and Matt began to buck again in an effort to throw him off. His own hand was still on the cinderblock and as he dragged it toward him and lifted it once again it felt as if it had increased five times in weight. When he got it as high into the air as he could she called his name again but this time it was no surprise and would not harm his aim.

Matt bucked and rolled his head to the side and once more heard the explosion inside his ear as the block smashed the ground. He heard Joanne's approach and screamed, "Stay back, for God's sake, don't come near him!"

But in an instant she was tugging on Bud's shoulders in an effort to pull him backward. In one swift and vicious swipe Bud's arm made an arc and his fist slammed into her stomach; she expelled a low *urrr*, stumbled to the side, and fell gasping.

The sound of her pain unleashed a new and alien venom

inside Matt, and this time his bucking threw the boy off. Quickly, he slung one leg over Bud's hip but the second he achieved a full straddle on the stomach those gloved hands shot up to resume their grip on his neck. Now, there was no savoring in the squeeze as before: like some expertly functioning machine that can't be turned off, the grip was going for the bone and at the same time even had the power to pull Matt's head forward and down toward the mask. He saw himself coming closer to the eyeholes which still revealed nothing but black depths. What *was* visible were the gritting teeth that seemed to match the effort of the hands.

There was just one possibility left for him while what little strength he had remained. Gripping the ears through the mask he rocked backward as far as he was able and aimed the head for the cinderblock. It struck the corner and although there was a cry of pain the hold on his neck did not weaken.

And then Joanne was up off the ground, behind him, and trying to pry the fingers loose as she wept Bud's name over and over.

The boy jerked his head, but Matt's hands held tight on his ears. The blow from the block, Joanne's traitorous struggle against him gave a clear view of the future. He would conquer and destroy both of them, he would be Claudia's comforter, they would adopt each other completely and it would be to her home—not his mother's—that he would bring a woman suitable to be his wife. Blood meant nothing. Claudia, not his mother, would be the grandparent to his children and they—

Matt reared back once more and brought the head down squarely on the block and although Joanne still worked at prying away the fingers, the grip held.

For strength, Bud closed his eyes and pictured his arm around Claudia, her head on his shoulder as they went forward to view the bodies. It would, of course, be a double funeral, and there would be those awful months he would help her get through. Maybe he would move in with her. Yes, he would move in and as soon as he had healed her he would bring home a suitable fiancée and the three of them would begin a new and decent family. . . .

It was Joanne's broken sobs that spurred Matt on even though he was now losing his sight to dizziness and panic. Again he reared back and pitched forward to ram the masked head against the block. And he continued the motion, rocking furiously but rhythmically—as if to still a wailing baby, until the hands began to slacken. Then, after the seventh or eighth thud the boys arms fell to his sides. From the mouth hole came a sharp hiss just before the chest collapsed and ceased to move.

Behind him, Joanne fell to her knees and held his shoulders as he rasped in the effort to breathe. The dizziness turned to nausea and he waited until it passed before attempting to stand. The two of them supported each other while they walked to the house frame; there, they sat on the plywood floor and he coughed until his spine ached. A long stretch of silence passed before she spoke in a voice that was nasal from weeping. "He tried to . . . he was going to . . ."

"Shhh." He took her sweating hand in his cold one, and they sat for another few minutes saying nothing while he waited for normal breathing. Now and then, she would shiver violently and their two hands would squeeze together like two pumps working life back into each other.

Finally, he pushed himself from the floor to the ground and told her to stay where she was. He went to look at the woman who lay in the light from the open door of the car. Mercifully, there was no blood and she was breathing, but the bandanna over her eyes made him wince. He knelt down and reached out to remove it, then drew back realizing he did not want to see her eyes.

"She's unconscious but alive," he told her when he returned.

"Yes," she whispered. He watched another shiver pass through her, and after a single ragged sob she screeched: "Oh God, what about Mom, what about Lucille! How could he—why did he make us do this, why didn't he *stop!*"

He gripped her shoulders. "Quiet, quiet." But his own head was not quiet; in it was the crying and wailing of Claudia and Lucille. "Be still now. We're not going to move, we're not going to do anything yet. Just be still."

Still shivering, she lay back on the plywood floor, but he began to pace. He walked back to the Mueller woman for reassurance that she was still breathing. This time the bandanna over her eyes made him think of another blindfolded woman: Justice with her scales. The newspapers, the WGRS reporting team would have their field day. "Rapist Killed by Future Father-in-Law." "Fiancée Present at Scene of Murder." They would hound Joanne, Claudia, and especially Lucille for interviews. He remembered the last time he saw Lucille, at the commencement party; if she was half dead then she would be a corpse by the time she went through a hearing and learned every grisly detail of Bud's activities and his murder. And he remembered her voice rising with pride and certainty when she said, "He worships Joanne, and Claudia too—you don't have to be a genius to see that."

Don't have to be a genius to see that. And what did most people see?—a handsome and smart, perhaps brilliant, young man who charmed everyone he wanted to charm, a young man thoroughly devoted to the woman he was going to marry, a mother-in-law's dream come true. . . .

The memory of Lucille's eyes gave off a spark in his imagination. It blazed into an idea that was wild, fantastic—but possible, if he moved quickly. And he must move quickly for Dolores Mueller's sake because there was no telling the extent of her injury. He gave her a final look of gratitude: the condition she was now in made his plan workable. Without knowing it she would be the prime instrument in sparing Lucille and Claudia. Three feet away from her he picked up Bud's small gym bag and went in search of the knife. In a few minutes he located it and shuddered. It had not been kicked as far as he thought, and during the entire struggle it had been within Bud's reach. He dropped it into the bag and then, bracing himself, stooped to remove the gloves and mask from the body. Although tempted, he did not look into the face. Remembering the detail of the yarn found under Jane's fingernails, he used the glove to brush any similar evidence from the boy's hair, neck, and face. In one front pocket of the trousers he located the car keys and in the other the prophylactic; he checked the rear pockets but found no wallet. These items joined the knife in the gym bag, and on his way back to Joanne he added the cinderblock for weight.

He grasped her hand and said, "We're going now."

They started for the car. "Are we going home? What about *her*?"

"I'm taking care of it. Joanne, I'm going to do something that'll involve you unless the police catch on. If they do catch on, then I want you to stay out of it. I can't explain now. I have to think, I have to be careful and think clearly."

He drove to Angus, the nearby village, and pulled up in front of a drugstore that was closed for the night.

"Crouch down out of sight," he instructed her. Without questioning, she slid into the space between the seat and glove compartment. There was always the chance he might be seen but she would not be. He walked to the phone booth near the door of the drugstore, looked in both directions up the empty street, then dialed the city police.

"Go see what happens to people who try to stop me," he growled, and then gave the location.

From the expressway he took the first exit, at the county line, and turned onto a road flanked by farmland. When the bridge appeared, he stopped, squinted into the distance ahead, and checked the rear-view mirror. Satisfied that they were alone, he got out and pitched the block-weighted bag into the river.

Twenty minutes later they arrived at his apartment complex and walked unseen from the parking area to the entrance. Upstairs, he made her take two gulps of brandy. He took four. He sat her down in the living room and went to the bathroom. After stripping off his clothes he inspected his body. While driving home he had envisioned a mass of bruises to match the ones he felt inside. But the only marks were two small dark patches on each side of his neck, blessedly below the collar line. He showered and put on fresh clothes.

She was still in the chair, staring at the ceiling. He sat on the sofa and quietly explained the phone call from the booth. "We tell your mother I took you out driving because I'm thinking of buying you a compact car. It makes sense."

Her voice was weak and quivering. "You think the police will think Bud wasn't . . . the one?"

"I'm hoping they'll think it. But this is important—if they ever do suspect me, if they ever find out, you weren't with me, you stayed here while I went out alone."

"No."

"Joanne—"

"No. If they ever find out then they have to be told everything. I saw. I saw him try to—" She gripped the arms of the chair and moved her eyes from the ceiling to him. "He would have killed you. And then . . . then he would have killed me."

Now, Matt had to look away. He picked up the glass and finished the brandy.

"It's so strange," she went on. "Right now, I don't feel anything, not a thing. I feel blank."

Tomorrow, he thought, it will all rush in tomorrow. "Do you think you're ready for me to take you home? I mean, ready to face your mother?"

She stood. "Yes. Take me home. I'll just tell her goodnight and go straight to bed."

He went into the kitchen and brought her back a sleeping pill. "You may need this tonight."

As he opened the door she turned and looked him in the eye. Her face was not sad but intense, more earnest than he had ever seen it. "I may not feel anything right now," she said, "but I *know* one thing. What you decided to do tonight for Mom and Lucil-le—" She reached out and ran her hand across his forehead and down his cheek. "I love you, I always will. More than anyone."

Before he could answer she was out the door and heading for the stairs.

16

In the morning he drank three cups of coffee and stared at the telephone which remained silent. Finally, he dressed and left for work.

Every time there was a knock on the door of his office he expected the police to enter. Then, at ten-twenty-five, the call came. From Claudia. The stillness in her voice indicated that hysteria was being delayed by shock.

When he arrived he found Ted Brainard waiting on the porch. Ted came down the sidewalk, gripped Matt's arm, and said, "Margaret's inside with her. Joanne's at work—no one's told her yet."

"Did the police tell Claudia?"

Ted shook his head and looked at the ground. "Lucille called her this morning to ask if Bud had spent the night because his boss called when he didn't show up at work. Lucille got in touch with the police to check the accident reports and they sent somebody around to take her to the morgue. She called Claudia right after she identified the body."

"They're sure it was murder?"

"The back of his skull was crushed."

Margaret was sitting on the sofa next to Claudia and she looked up tearfully as the two men entered. Claudia continued to stare at the opposite wall until Matt moved in to block her view. She lifted her face which appeared thinner than ever and said in a faraway voice: "It's a conspiracy, that's what it is. First Terry, now Bud. You'll be next, Matt, we'll lose you next."

He saw Margaret bite her lip and turn away. "No, you won't lose me," he answered.

"You can't promise that. It'll just happen. I knew something was wrong when Lucille called the first time. But I kept telling myself it would be all right, I kept saying there's nothing to worry about. And later I went to Joanne's room and took out the material for her dress and I thought . . . but then the telephone rang and I knew it was no good, I knew something was wrong."

Noiselessly, Margaret got up, one hand over her mouth, and walked to the kitchen. Ted followed, and Matt sat down next to Claudia.

"Lucille said they found him out in the country. *Found* him, like a lost dog or a stolen car, they just went out and found him!" Her eyes flared and then drooped. "Matt, I can't tell Joanne, I can't be the one . . . "

"I will," he whispered.

"I'm sorry, I just can't."

"It's all right, it's all right." He took her hand in his and squeezed it gently. She lay her head back against the sofa and closed her eyes. He stared at the sagging corners of her mouth and his thoughts drifted elsewhere. He was wondering who, if anyone, was sitting with Lucille Hanes.

Matt got to Joanne just before Lieutenant Whelan did. The three of them left the department store where she worked and went to the station. Whelan's questions were matter-of-fact but gentle and when he asked Joanne if she knew why Bud should have been at such a place at that time of night she told him of their original plan to build a house there and of Bud's contempt for the shoddy development that had usurped the spot. For a week, she said, it was all he had talked about.

"Was he angry enough to go there maybe with the intention of vandalizing?"

Through her tears Joanne expressed proper indignation. "Certainly not. We were out there last Sunday and he said then he wanted to come back when the partitions were up so he could see what the floor plans were." She went on to tell him that Bud had called her early in the evening; she had had no desire to go out to the site again and so called her father to arrange the driving lesson. Whelan looked puzzled by this but Matt motioned to him to ask her nothing more. When she was taken to the outer office he told Whelan about her fear of driving, especially at night, since the accident with her brother. Whelan nodded sympathetically and said Matt could go.

On the sidewalk the reporters were waiting, but those from WGRS cowered under Matt's withering glance.

The six o'clock report opened with the murder. The film crew had gone to the scene of the crime, and the on-the-spot reporter spoke into the camera while standing in front of the half-completed structure where Matt and Joanne had rested after the ordeal. Once, the camera panned the construction area and then zoomed in to the exact locations where the car and Bud's body had been discovered.

> Bud Hanes was a graduate student in architecture and this is where he and his fiancée, Joanne Sessions, wanted to build their dream house. That dream ended when Sachs-Stuart Corporation bought the property and began construction of condominiums. But there was no construction today as police searched for clues in the murder of Mr. Hanes and the assault on Dolores Mueller, an instructor of history who was abducted from the parking lot at Kane Village faculty housing last night. At knifepoint she was forced to drive to this lonely area—by a man wearing a ski mask. She was not raped because fate intervened, in the person of Bud Hanes. Miss Mueller was unavailable for comment but we were able to talk with Lieutenant Gerald Whelan. . . .

Whelan repeated what Joanne had told him, but without quoting her. The present theory was that Bud Hanes had surprised the attacker before he could rape Miss Mueller; a fight ensued, and after the murder, the killer returned to the city in Hanes's car instead of Miss Mueller's. The car was found abandoned near the campus. Everything seemed to fit the rapist's usual pattern—except, of course, the murder and the phone call afterward.

Last May, Jane Richardson, the founder of the Women's Self-Protection Group, died of a heart attack when she was raped in her home on Dial Drive. Police found fibers of yarn under her fingernails, the kind of yarn used for ski masks. Since that incident the police have received no reports of attacks by a man wearing a ski mask. But last night he surprised Dolores Mueller and tonight she's in Mercy Hospital being treated for a skull fracture. And Bud Hanes, who once dreamed of building a house for his bride-to-be, died where that house might have stood. I'm Donald Essex for WGRS.

Matt turned off his television and went to the kitchen. He unwrapped a pork chop, then wrapped it back up again: he could not eat alone, he had to go someplace where there would be voices, distractions.

He had just showered and dressed when the buzzer rang. The pit of his stomach told him it would be the police, with a new clue for a new theory. He pressed the intercom. "Who is it?"

"It's Adele, Matt. Can I come up?"

He hesitated, then buzzed her in. Standing at his front door he watched her climb the stairs. She was tanned, youthful as ever, but the hair was pulled back, uncharacteristically, into a bun and her face looked at once severe and haunted.

"Hello, Matt," she said softly.

As he closed the door he watched her take in the room. She kept her back to him as she spoke: "I saw the news. How is Joanne?"

"Numb, for the time being."

She nodded, lowered her head. He waited. Then: "I know I should have called first, but I didn't think you'd see me. Could I—have a drink?"

"Of course. Sorry. Martini?"

"Yes." She walked over to look at the bookshelves Bud had built. In the kitchen he knocked over a glass while reaching for the gin and had to steady himself against the counter before proceeding. He would not, he resolved, deliver her drink with a trembling hand.

She took it from him, sat down, and when she lit a cigarette, it was *her* hand that trembled. "You didn't take that vacation, did you?"

"No."

"Now you should." She looked into her glass. "If I had any sense of propriety I wouldn't have come . . . so soon after. But I thought this might be a weak moment for you. I *hope* it is." She raised her eyes. "I want you back. No children."

"Adele, don't—"

"Hear me out, please. I made the decision while I was on vacation but tonight, less than an hour ago, it became firm and I knew I could be totally committed to it. Because of Joanne."

"Joanne?"

"It will be a disappointment not having children, but it's one I can live with. I don't know if I could live through losing a brother and then the man I loved—and both dying so violently. I sat there watching the newscast and I had no choice but to measure my life against hers. And then against yours. It's one thing to sacrifice something willingly but it's quite another to have something—some*one*—snatched away from you, never to be returned. I don't want you snatched away, Matt, and the sacrifice is worth it because I'll have you."

"It's not that simple. Certain things have happened . . . "

She looked back to her glass. "Another woman?"

"No, not that."

"Then we could work it out, couldn't we?"

He did not answer but got up and went to the kitchen to pour a drink. Quietly, she came up behind him and locked her arms around his waist. Pressing her cheek against his spine, she whispered, "Don't turn me away now. There's no reason to. If you think my decision is charity, then just be big enough to accept it. Marry me, Matt."

He looked down at the whitened knuckles of her hand that gripped the other wrist, and he remembered the grip on his neck the night before, a grip of undiluted loathing. As he stared at her knuckles, the revelation was instant and complete. Without her, the remaining years of his life would continue to be held in Bud's hands, years that would be hate-haunted with no balance of love. To reject her now would be far beyond folly. It would be self-damnation.

She had no idea of who or what he was because of last night; and she would never know. He would hide it; her love would help him to hide it. "Yes," he said, "I'll marry you." And then the fluttering in his chest found release in deep but silent sobs.

She loosened her grip but held on. When he finished and the shaking stopped she said: "Come on, I'll take you home."

She helped him pack a suitcase, and when they got to her house he went directly to the fireplace. "I want to build a fire," he said.

"A fire! It's eighty-five degrees outside."

"I'll put on the air conditioning."

He brought in wood from the garage. When the flame was large and steady, his eyes left it, scanned the room, and stopped at the new acquisition on the oak chest. In a chipped wooden frame was a photograph of an ancient-looking Indian couple, both with toothless smiles.

"That's what I brought back for you from Tijuana. But I guess I really brought it back for myself. I bought it from a vendor who claims he knows them. The man's a hundred and two, she's a hundred and four. They've outlived all their children and grandchildren. The smiles look genuine and I thought . . . well, that it was kind of marvelous that they're still capable of smiling." She put her hand on the back of his neck and gave him a sly grin. "They still have each other. Get the point?"

She left him and went to fix dinner. He looked at the fire again, then closed his eyes and listened to its soothing crackle.

"Do you want beans or spinach?" she called from the kitchen.

"Doesn't matter."

What he wanted was the courage to face Lucille Hanes at the funeral.

Judy Kent, Lyle Sloane, Margaret Brainard, and a number of women from the Self-Protection Group were among the many who assembled in the funeral parlor which was on the other side of town from the one Jane Richardson had been in. There were reporters, too, but they remained outside.

With his jaw set, Matt accompanied Joanne and Claudia to the casket. Bud's "crushed" skull did not look it but the nose was now slightly crooked, and Matt recalled the cracking sound when his fist had connected with the face behind the mask. He and Joanne fortified one another by gripping hands, yet he had to look away when she bent to kiss Bud's forehead.

He got the two of them seated and proceeded to the rear of the room where Lucille stood accepting condolences. By the time he faced her, every phrase he had rehearsed was pruned away by her dark eyes: they looked tired but contained a strange, disconcerting glitter.

For the first time Matt met her daughter, and guilty sweat broke out all over him when they shook hands and he saw her tear-stained face. Then, gently and calmly, Lucille told her to go sit down.

"Ted thought it would be easier if he didn't come," said Matt. "He told Claudia he had to be in court. Margaret had to come or else Claudia would have been . . . hurt."

The look she gave him indicated that these complications were the farthest from her mind. She glanced in the direction of the casket and said, "You see that big wreath up there? The yellow one. Miss Mueller sent it. She wrote me a beautiful letter. Not a note, a letter. Sometimes, there *is* justice, in ways you never expect it. I've sent a copy of the letter to Bud's father."

Matt felt a wild pounding start up in his temples. "Is he coming today?"

She shook her head. "But today, all day, he might think about what he did. He owes Bud that much."

He stepped aside to let the people behind him have their turn with her.

The eulogy was a glowing one, delivered by a very young, recently ordained minister whose main message was that in the Christian's war against hatred and violence Bud Hanes had been a soldier whose commanding officer was his conscience and whose weapon was courage to come to the defense of a defenseless woman. The speech was as melodious as it was dynamic, but Matt's attention was on the listeners. Lucille sat as if in a trance and did not take her eyes off Miss Mueller's wreath. Lyle Sloane nodded here and there, most likely reaffirming to himself how rotten the world is; next to him, Judy kept a handkerchief wadded against her mouth and cast piteous glances at Joanne.

Margaret Brainard watched the minister, and Hippolyta Bewick stared at the casket.

Afterward, Matt's arms supported Joanne and Claudia as they left the parlor through a side door that opened on the lot where the limousines—and reporters—waited. The cameras were aimed at Joanne and clicked away.

He helped them into the back seat of a black Lincoln and was about to climb in himself when a hand clamped his shoulder. He turned to find Hippolyta Bewick. With a look of apology she stepped past him and leaned down at the open door.

"I want you to know," she said tremulously to Joanne, "that all of us in the group share your loss. It would be a better world for women if there were more men like him in it."

"Yes," Joanne answered. "Thank you."

Bewick stepped back and Matt got in and closed the door.

They were married the last week of September, in a civil ceremony witnessed by her parents. When they returned from a fifteen-day honeymoon in England they found that autumn had accelerated, the threat of winter already in the air. As early as mid-November the airport was shut down by snow and the Brainards had to stand by for twenty-eight hours awaiting the plane that would take them to see their new granddaughter. By December the Women's Self-Protection Group was fully reactivated with Hippolyta Bewick at the helm; each meeting opened with a minute of silent prayer for Jane Richardson and Bud Hanes. Joanne postponed her entrance into graduate school until winter term, and she and Claudia took a month's tour of the South which terminated in New Orleans.

The ski-mask rapist, it was presumed, had gone into temporary retirement since the murder of Bud Hanes.

The record-setting temperatures kept Matt and Adele at home most nights. Rituals were established: starting a fire after work and lying on the floor in front of it to sip drinks and play chess or Scrabble before dinner, then reading or talking before the eleven o'clock news. And, for Matt, there was ritual *during* the night— fragmented dreams peopled with Bud and Terry, Jane and Judy, but most often with Lucille.

Three days after Christmas he decided to call her. He had not spoken to her since the funeral, and with the New Year approaching he felt the need for some kind of conclusion although he had no idea what it could possibly be. She declined his offer to meet for lunch but invited him for tea.

Expecting to find a wizened recluse he stared in amazement when she answered the door. Gone were the dark circles under her eyes, the huddling of her shoulders. Her restored beauty was all the more intriguing for it now exuded an odd mixture of youthful radiance and the kind of serenity usually reserved for mystics or the contentedly insane.

They sat, and she poured out tea which was already prepared and waiting on a tray on the coffee table. He looked about the room and noted how nothing had changed since the last time he was in it. Even Joanne's picture remained.

"Congratulations on getting married," she said. "I'd have sent a gift but I didn't know about it until a few days ago. I ran into Claudia in the supermarket."

Joanne had told him how she and her mother had stopped seeing Lucille. There was only one thing for the three of them to talk about and that was just too painful.

"Have you heard from Ted?" he asked.

"Once. Certainly he must have told you."

Ted had, about her refusal to see him even for a cup of coffee. "I'm sure he thought that . . . Bud's being gone would make a difference in your decision."

"Margaret isn't gone. I wanted to keep *my* husband once," she said softly.

"Do you have any plans?"

"I'm going back to work at Graff's. As cashier and bookkeeper. The doctor says it's all right."

For more than a minute they only sipped tea. Then he said: "I think about him all the time."

"Do you?" It was plain that she was touched. "He would appreciate that. And his father . . . I want to show you something." She left the room and returned with a piece of paper. "I told you I sent Myron a copy of Miss Mueller's letter. I included some newspaper clippings too. For the first time in eighteen years I got a response from him."

Matt read the message:

Dear Lucille,

I received the letter and the clippings you sent. I sincerely regret your loss. I'm sorry I was wrong.

                                                      Regards,
                                                      Myron

"I know it doesn't seem like much," she said, "but coming from him it's quite a lot."

"He means wrong for leaving you?"

"Yes, and a lot of other things." She took the letter from him and sat down with it. "I didn't tell you the real circumstances for his leaving us. When I was pregnant with Bud one of Myron's friends raped me—" She went on with the same account she had once given her son, her disbelieving son. "The biggest mistake," she concluded, "was telling Myron. If I'd kept it to myself, all of our lives would have been different. I thought I could go it alone. I had enough money and I was careful with it, but money was not the battle."

He watched her glance at the pictures on the bookcase shelf.

"Bud was a lovely child for a time. Then I met a man and he changed. He began to look at me the way his father did just before he left us. That beautiful child's face—but his eyes could go right through me . . . Myron didn't want me to have my baby, and then Bud didn't want me to have a husband. It was like Myron had come home, only in Bud's body, to watch me, judge me. Sometimes I'd have these dreams where they would both be the same person. I know that's crazy but . . . " Her eyes left the pictures on the bookcase and returned to the letter in her lap. "Then one day I lived up to Bud's judgment—or *down* to it. I almost let him drown, almost killed him. He showed me what I was capable of thinking and almost doing. He proved me to myself."

"But he must have provoked you too," he offered.

"Yes, but I was the adult, I should have . . . Even now, I don't know if or how much I loved him. But I miss him. I wanted him to be happy with Joanne, and I know he would have been. He was one of those people who live by extremes. He could hate deeply but he could love deeply too."

Matt could not answer this. He leaned forward and said, "I'd like to do something for you. Isn't there anything you want? A trip you'd like to take?"

"No." She bent her head to one side. "You act like you owe me something. You don't."

"Is going back to work the only thing you have planned?"

"I'm grateful that I can. It's what I need."

Now, he saw there would be no conclusion, no final gesture of doing something for her. And he realized he had come not for her but for himself, come to offer charity in exchange for a secret exoneration.

"Sometimes," she said, looking at the staircase, "I have a sinking spell when I think how he died, the pain he must have gone through. But then I think about *why* he died and I tell myself if he fought that hard to help that woman, then somewhere along the line, maybe by accident, I did *something* right."

"I'm sure you did a lot of things right."

There was nothing more to say, but at the front door he hesitated. "Some night you'll have to come to dinner and meet my wife."

"Yes, some night," she said lightly, without conviction. And then her voice shifted to a note of finality. "Goodbye, Matt."

EPILOGUE

The sun and the morning breeze pushed at the draperies and coaxed—like children who have been up for hours—the lingerers to rise and join them. April had just bowed out to May and the air was still chilly, which made Adele's breath on his neck feel all the warmer. Her fingers nested in his chest hair, the bottom of her foot caressed the top of his.

"We have to get moving," she said. "The man at the nursery said he would hold those shrubs for me only till noon. And I want you to help me decide on some flowers too."

"Mmm." He did not stir.

"You have exactly fifteen minutes to put body and soul together." She rolled out of bed, arched her back, spread her arms out to the sides: she looked as if she would literally dive into the day.

While she showered he listened to the run of the water and tried to doze off. He wanted to fall back into the dream he had had: in it he was walking Joanne down the aisle, about to give her away to an unrecognizable but patently good man.

His yawn ended in a small self-deprecating smile. Just last night Joanne herself had lectured him, gently, about his propensity for wanting to "package and gift wrap" the lives of those he loved. "You're not God," she had said, "and it's a waste of energy and worry. Mom may meet another man and she may not, and I'll meet someone someday . . . when I'm ready to." Still, he had enjoyed his dream of her and the young man although he was aware of how Adele and Bud, in different ways, had prevented him from neatly packaging the remainder of his own life. . . .

She emerged from the bathroom in her robe, picked up the hairbrush from her vanity, and proceeded to the window. With a swoosh the draperies were drawn back, and he closed his eyes against the glare. Reopening them gradually he found her looking out at the backyard as she worked the brush over, under, through her hair. Her face angled off to the left, and he knew she was assigning locations to the new evergreens they would plant together.

The ages-old equation of spring and new beginnings was no longer an empty cliché or a fanciful notion expounded by poets. All his life he had regarded yard work as drudgery, a waste of valuable time, but now he looked forward to it, in the evenings and on weekends. Largely what appealed to him was the predictability, the certainty: blooms appeared exactly where their seeds had been planted and, given the prescribed care, they grew precisely the way they were promised to grow.

Lately, he had experienced other beginnings as well. The nightmares continued, but with decreasing severity and frequency; they no longer awakened him. At work, he was able to turn a deaf ear to Sloane's preoccupation with Bud's murder and to Judy's preoccupation with the grieving women Bud left behind. "The cops in this city couldn't round up a stray cat," Sloane affirmed constantly. "They'll never catch this pervert." At least once a week Judy made it her business to ask after Joanne and Lucille, and even after his report that they were "doing well," she would shake her head and mutter "That poor girl, that poor woman."

Now, more often than not, he could look at the full moon without regarding it as the witness to murder once stationed behind Bud's shoulder.

Adele kept brushing as she walked away from the window

and sat on the edge of the bed next to him. "Do I have to put dynamite under you?"

"One more minute." He stretched, then slipped his hand under the flap of her robe to find her belly. "It still seems awfully flat."

She grinned. "It won't be in another month."

Slowly, his hand rotated on the flesh which held the most important beginning—the most frightening but the most necessary too.

Recently, his initial ambivalence about the pregnancy has given way to cautious enthusiasm, this change owing in great measure to Joanne. Once a month she has dinner with him and Adele and once a month he has dinner with her and Claudia; twice a month they have dinner alone together. And on these latter occasions they talk about Bud and the murder. Talking about it, keeping it on the surface somehow renders it less haunting. Then Joanne invariably moves on to the subject of him and Adele and reassures him he is worthy of this second chance and capable of making the most of it. She does not tolerate from him any maudlin regret when he enumerates all the errors he made with both her and Terry. "We made *our* mistakes too," she has told him more than once. The night he gave her the news about Adele he expected to see a flickering of regret or resentment. But instead her face opened in a smile and she said, "Tell Adele I hope it's twins." He grimaced comically and thought how strange it was that there had never been much humor between them until after the horror of that August night. As with Adele, humor seems to be a major consummation of love—and the grounding wire for maintained optimism.

Yet, sometimes at night, in the dark, the optimism is undercut by his recollection of Claudia's face when he casually mentioned Adele's pregnancy. She managed a smile and a "Congratulations," but both were too weak to hide the disappointment. And bitterness. He knows she considers him as having come through two boys' funerals far less damaged than she, and that because of Adele she ponders life's random distribution of reprieves.

When her face lingers too long before him, determined to keep his thoughts mired in death, he turns in the bed to stare at

279

the profile of Adele's face or shoulder. He rests his hand gently on her belly and knows that she is, at once, the reminder of and his protection against the uncertainty in every tomorrow. When his eyes finally close it is the protection he thinks about, and he listens to her strong, sturdy breathing as it leads him into the safe and silent envelope of sleep.

———————————————